Must

BRICE AUSTIN

ISBN: **0692544143**
ISBN-13: **978-0692544143 (Cadifus Books)**

:

ACKNOWLEDGMENTS

Thanks to Barry Ratliff and Harriet Austin for considerable input on the cover design; to Lily Kailyn for technical support; and to Matt and Alex Austin for emotional and comedic support.

Prologue: East Africa

The elephant was close by, in the dark. Kip could smell him. Jomo, the strange one, could smell him, too; he was restless now, agitated. Simon Adongo raised a hand, demanding silence, and whispered for the others to stop. They crouched down, in the tall grass. There was a cool wind sweeping across the savannah, removing the memory of the hot day that had now ended. The elephant smell was strong, almost overpowering, the smell of a male in musth. This, then, was the one they had been hunting, the one the white woman at Tsavo, Doctor Jones, called Ajax. The one the Masaai warriors called Ikiye, Death. Kip felt a tightening in his stomach. This would not be easy, even though the men had guns. Kip had a gun, too, one that could shoot many bullets at once. Still, it would not be easy. Simon Adongo had told them they must not shoot the elephant until they were very close to him.

"Slowly," whispered Adongo and now they were moving again, stirring the grass like a gentle breeze.

They came up over a rise. Below them the savannah stretched out to the end of the world, to the *Oldoinyo Oibor*, the white mountain that lived far away, in Tanzania. Kilimanjaro, the white doctor called it. Out there, in the grass, there were enormous Baobabs, upside-down trees, their roots scratching at the moonlit sky. And now, among those trees, they finally saw him: Ikiye, the male elephant, an enormous shadow with gleaming white tusks.

Tusks the Colonel had said they could keep, if they would get the other thing he wanted. Tusks that would sell for many thousands of dollars. Even divided five ways, it was as much money as Kip could hope to make in one year, working for the white woman at Tsavo. He licked his lips. It would not be easy. He looked around him, expecting to see the park rangers in their painted jeeps. There was no one there. The rangers generally came out only in the daytime, and yet one never knew. Kip had heard rumors that they were making patrols by night now, trying to protect the elephants.

Simon Adongo said he had made "arrangements" with them, however, that they would not interfere. Kip wondered what sort of arrangements those were. Had Adongo promised them a share of the tusks as well, thereby reducing the shares of everyone else? Still, making such arrangements was necessary. Rangers would shoot a poacher on sight, without hesitation. Kip knew this; he had heard them say as much to Doctor Jones. He had heard them promise her this.

Simon Adongo led the way across the savannah, being careful to stay out of sight of Ikiye. Being careful to remain downwind of him. Kip followed, and then the others: Jamil, who would have come with them even had he not been paid, for the elephant had destroyed his crops and his village, and he wanted revenge. Hamisi, the scarred man, who had done this many times before, who had been gored by elephant tusks once and lived. And Jomo, the one with empty eyes, the one it was said was possessed by some evil spirit. Kip shuddered, sorry now that he had come, sorry that he had ever agreed to help Adongo find the elephant. He had not wanted to help him, but it was so much money . . .

Simon Adongo had come from Tanzania, where he worked for his mysterious Colonel, the one who of late had been on everyone's lips. What did this Colonel Muka want with the elephants? To kill them, of course, but Kip was surprised when Adongo had said he did not want the tusks. He wanted something else. When Simon told him what it was the Colonel wanted, Kip almost said no, that he would not help. But Jomo was with Adongo even then and Kip was afraid. There was no soul inside the man's eyes. And because the Colonel did not want the tusks, he would let Kip have them. A share of them, at least. It would mean a great deal of money. Far more money than Kip could earn by tracking the elephants at Tsavo, logging their numbers and whereabouts for Doctor Jones. Money he could use to help his family, his mother and father and two brothers. And most of all his sister, who was even whiter than Doctor Jones. It might even be enough money to help his sister, to send her far away from here, to some place where she would finally be safe.

Adongo led them through the tall grass. Up ahead was a grove of acacia trees. Kip could no longer see the elephant, though he could still smell its strong scent. That scent was everywhere now, all around them. Because of that, it seemed as though the elephant was everywhere now, too, all around them. This made Kip nervous. How could something that size disappear? And yet it seemed he had, at least for the moment. Kip knew that Ikiye must be on the other side of the acacias. And now he could hear him, tearing at the thorny branches with his trunk, eating. Ripping sounds filled the air. Kip swallowed hard. This would not be easy. Simon Adongo again raised his hand.

"Closer," he whispered, "we must get closer."

Why? Why not shoot Ikiye from here, through the trees? It would be so much safer. Kip knew why. It was because of what the Colonel wanted. There was no other way. Kip cradled his gun, hoping he would remember how to use it, when the time came. That time was coming soon. Where was the elephant now? He was no longer tearing at branches; he was silent. Incredibly, they seemed to have lost him in the acacia thicket. Kip froze, listening. The air was cold, as it frequently was at night on the Kenyan highlands. In the distance, he heard a lion's roar. Then Kip heard something else, something close by. There was something behind him. Kip turned.

There, in the moonlight, stood Death. The elephant, Ikiye. How had he managed to get behind them? Strangely silent, ghost-like, as if he had appeared out of a cloud. His white tusks were gleaming. One was long and straight, the other twisted, with a hook to the left at the end that looked deadly. Thick secretions were oozing from the glands on the sides of his head, a sign that he was indeed in musth, that he had succumbed to rage and desire. The smell was overpowering. It was as though time stood still for a moment. Kip could not move. He stared at the elephant's intelligent eye, glistening in the moonlight. Ikiye seemed to be studying them, trying to decide what to do. There was more of a soul inside of the elephant's eye than there was inside of Jomo's. And yet there were other things there, in that eye, things that frightened him. Rage, and pain. The elephant's trunk reached out towards Kip then as though it were some other creature, something quite separate from Ikiye himself.

A strange sound was coming from Jomo, the soulless one, a moan that swelled into a shriek that echoed across the savannah. Simon Adongo cried "Now!" And then guns on both sides of Kip were firing. The flashes from those guns lit up the grassy plains around him like lightning. They lit up Ikiye. The elephant trumpeted and came charging towards them. Kip lifted his gun but was unable to fire it. In the flashing light the elephant seemed to be in many places at once, just like Death for which he was named.

"Stand your ground!" cried Adongo.

The thicket of acacia trees was behind them and Kip wanted to slip away into it, to hide. But he knew that if he ran, the others would kill him. The elephant trumpeted. Bullets were biting into his hide like a cloud of stinging flies. There were streams of blood flowing down that hide now, striping it. There were streams of sweat on Kip's face. He was still unable to fire, unable to do anything but stand and watch. Jomo, the strange one, let out another cry, a shriek that hardly seemed human. He ran towards the elephant. Adongo was shouting for him to stop, to come back. The others kept *firingfiringfiring*. The sound of their guns, of the elephant's trumpeting, of Jomo's screams, seemed loud enough to wake the dead. Loud enough to bring the park rangers, if they were anywhere within several miles. For a moment Kip thought he saw the American woman, Doctor Jones, out on the savannah, but it was only the moonlight. Ikiye trumpeted, and charged. With his trunk he grabbed Jomo, and held him. Hamisi, the scarred man, and Jamil kept firing. The elephant lifted Jomo into the air as easily as if he were uprooting a small tree. Jomo was screaming. It was not a scream of fear, though, not the scream of someone who is afraid of dying. It was a scream of rage, and need. Kip fell back, into the acacia trees. The others kept *firingfiringfiring*. Ikiye slammed Jomo to the earth from up high and then lowered that evil-looking left tusk and gored him. Jomo barely seemed to notice. Free from the trunk, he charged at Ikiye again, screaming. Kip shuddered. Was it really true then, that the man had no soul? That he was a demon? The elephant grasped Jomo with his trunk once more, and this time hurled him off into the darkness, into the acacia trees where Kip now stood. The others kept *firingfiringfiring*. How many bullets had hit Ikiye? A great many. And yet still he came at them, trumpeting. The elephant would not die! The elephant truly was Death as the Masaai had named him; he was Death Itself and therefore could not die. The others were *firingfiringfiring*. Still, Kip was unable to lift his weapon. He had spent so much time watching these creatures for Doctor Jones, monitoring their whereabouts, that he could not bring himself to kill one of them now. If indeed, that could even be done.

The elephant was charging again. Kip backed up even further, into the trees. When he did he heard a moaning sound. It was Jomo. The strange one was lying there in the grass. Kip ran to him, bent over him. Jomo's back was broken. He was lying there in the grass, broken. His eyes were open. Those eyes still lacked a soul, thought Kip; they were eyes that were cold and empty. And yet Kip felt sorry for him. He was broken. Then Simon Adongo and Jamil and Hamisi the scarred man came fleeing back into the trees as well. Ikiye was right behind them. The flashes of light from their weapons were everywhere around Kip, showing him glimpses of the trees and the rampaging elephant. The elephant that would not die. That perhaps could not die. *Firingfiringfiring*. It was as though the stars had fallen out of the sky and were exploding all around him. The elephant, Ikiye, seemed to pause now, ever so slightly, at the edge of the trees. He seemed to stop in mid-step. Simon Adongo and Jamil and Hamisi had backed up until now they were standing right beside Kip again, in the darkness, in the trees. They were no longer firing their weapons. The elephant seemed frozen in front of them, in mid-step, so massive that his head rose above the short, scraggly acacia trees. Then, slowly, almost as slowly as the turn of the world, Ikiye began to fall. The elephant staggered and fell. He collapsed to his knees. In the moonlight, Kip could see streams of blood on his hide. The elephant fell. Death fell sideways and when his enormous body hit the savannah the earth itself trembled. The acacia trees around Kip trembled. The very moon and sky seemed to tremble. Wisps of white smoke, steam, rose from Ikiye's trunk and mouth, into the cold night air.

"Hurry!" cried Simon Adongo, "We do not have much time!"

Kip hesitated. "What of Jomo?" he asked.

Behind them, in the trees, the strange one was crying "Help me!" That voice did in fact have a soul. Unlike the man's eyes, that voice seemed human. "Help me!"

Kip turned, only to have Simon Adongo grab him roughly by the shoulder. "Go!" he said, "Leave him! We do not have much time!"

"But . . ."

Then Adongo fired his weapon again, many times. He fired his weapon at Jomo, the broken man. The strange, soulless one did not cry out again. Kip stared at Adongo in disbelief. Simon only laughed. "Be glad!" he said, "It seems your share has grown larger! Now go, we do not have much time!"

Jamil and Hamisi had already fallen upon the carcass of the dead elephant like a pack of wild dogs. They were making ready for what they had to do, what they had promised Simon Adongo they would do. Kip stood watching them for a moment, watching the elephant. *So,* he thought, *even Death Itself can die.*

"The blood!" Simon cried, "Hurry! He is losing blood!"

Hamisi, the scarred man, was standing beside the elephant's enormous head, holding a knife that gleamed in the moonlight. He was moving his hand along the elephant's neck, looking for something. Jamil was removing several large silver bags from the pack he had carried on his back ever since they had left the Land Rover on the dirt road in West Tsavo, to travel on foot. Again Adongo said: "Hurry!" There were streams of blood running down the elephant's enormous body, glistening in the moonlight. "Hurry!"

Kip awoke from his trance and ran to help. He took one of the silver bags from Jamil. He stood at the ready. Hamisi found what he was looking for, the precise spot on the elephant's neck that he had been looking for. He plunged his knife in. Blood came gushing out of the wound. Jamil filled his bag quickly and stepped aside. Kip took his place. Blood rushed out of the wound in a torrent. Kip could not hope to catch it all. The blood flowed over his hands and the lip of the bag. The silver bag filled up quickly but much blood was wasted. Kip stepped aside for Hamisi and Jamil to take their turns, and sealed up the bag as he had been shown. While he waited to take his turn again he looked at the body of the elephant. He felt very sad, thinking about Ikiye, this elephant the Masaai called Death. He *was* Death to any that stood in his way, but he was Life, too. He had been looking for a mate. The thick secretions oozing from the glands on the sides of his head, those secretions that confirmed the elephant was in musth, were proof of that. His smell was proof of that. What was it that the Colonel wanted with the elephant's blood? There was some magic at work here, no doubt, evil magic. The same sort of evil magic that led the witch doctors to desire his white sister's feet and hands. Perhaps with his larger share of the money from Ikiye's tusks, Kip could send her far away where she would be out of reach of such evil men?

It was his turn with the silver bags again. They must work quickly. Soon the jackals and lions and hyenas would come. And at dawn, the dark birds. And at dawn, too, something worse still than the dark birds. The park rangers. By then they must be far away. The blood was still flowing out of Ikiye's massive neck in a torrent. It spilled over Kip's hands. It spilled into the silver bag, and onto the rich, dark earth. It was a river of blood, a river that was destined to flow all the way to Mombasa.

Part One

City Full of Dead People

Chapter 1

It was just another day in Gulfport, Louisiana; then it wasn't. Detective John Briggs had dropped his son Hamilton off at Palmer High and was driving to the police station, listening to WRGU, when the DJ stopped tending to his morning zoo long enough to announce that something was going down at the Division Street Mall. The SWAT team was already there. Details were sketchy but it sounded like somebody with a gun had gone off again. Jesus Christ, what was the matter with people these days? He was glad it wasn't his deal.

Late-breaking news: a three-block area around the mall had been cordoned off. He wondered if Tom Etheridge was there. "Gone Off" cases were right up his alley. Best man on the Force, if you asked John, and for that matter his own Best Man, what seemed like a hundred years ago.

Late-breaking news: seems Gone Off had an assault rifle. Three people dead, and counting. How was the NRA going to justify this one? They'd find a way. He drove on through Palmer thinking about how much the neighborhood had changed since he was a kid, how it seemed even farther away now from Society Hill.

Late-breaking news: there were reports coming in now that Gone Off had really gone off, that on top of everything else he'd raped some girl in broad daylight. Jesus *Christ*, what was wrong with the world?

There was the station, up ahead at the corner: red bricks and dirty glass. John turned into the underground garage and parked his car and when the radio died the Division Street Massacre wasn't real anymore; it was just something going on across town. And there was always something going on across town. He was glad this one wasn't his deal.

#

"Morning, Detective."

"Morning, John."

"Morning, Briggs. Say, the Chief is looking for you already."

"He knows where to find me and what time I get in." John shut the door to his office and sat there at his desk for a minute. He could feel a headache coming on already. Through the mini-blinds on his side of the glass he could see the bee hive that was the rest of the station, stirred up like it always was, Monday mornings. The phone rang.

"Briggs."

"Is this John Briggs?"

Wasn't that what he just said? "Speaking."

"Mr. Briggs, this is Vice Principal Sleeper at Palmer High School and I . . ."

How the hell could Ham be in trouble already? It was eight thirty-five in the damned morning! "Uh-huh. I see. Wouldn't stand for the Pledge again? Well, you do know he has that right? Yes sir, I can appreciate the fact that some people want to beat the crap out of him, believe me. I've been there myself."

John listened to him rant for thirty seconds more, which was about all he could take. "Isn't that *your* job, Mr. Sleeper? Tell you what, you tell those two punks that Hamilton's daddy is a police officer with a real bad temper. No, I never said I was trying to intimidate anybody. Just tell them that the same way you just now told me that two hooligans are out to get my son. For their information, if you know what I mean? Look, I have to go. The Chief wants to see me. You have a good day now, Mr. Sleeper."

Ed Horsebreaker was standing in the doorway. Knocked but then came on in like he always did. He was a good egg, though, in spite of that one bad habit.

"Morning, Chief." John never had quite come to terms with that, with calling the Chief "Chief" when he was an honest-to-God Indian. No matter how you said it, it didn't come out right. It sounded like you were making fun of him when you weren't. Not that Horsebreaker ever took it the wrong way, as far as John could tell. He was a good man and a good cop, even if some of the guys did call him Heap Big Horsefucker behind his back. The way John looked at it, being the Chief was a lot like being a parent: if people didn't hate you every now and then you probably weren't doing your job. "What's on your mind?"

"You heard about Division Street already?"

"Yeah, just now, on the radio. Glad it's not my deal."

"Maybe it is." Ed's face looked like it had been chiseled out of the side of a mountain. He closed the door behind him. That was rarely a good sign.

"You want coffee?" The Chief shook his head. John poured himself a cup, black as the heart of the District Attorney. "You think maybe he was on something?"

Horsebreaker shrugged. "Maybe. Just a hunch. And then there's the video."

"There's a video?"

"Isn't there always, these days? If you hurry you can see it on YouTube before they take it down."

That was the kind of world it was now. You couldn't use a public toilet without worrying that your dick might show up on the Internet. Everybody was a reporter and yet nobody was. Cameras and people's brains both had gotten damned near microscopic. "I'll take a look."

"Hold on." Something was coming in over Horsebreaker's Bluetooth. It looked like a big cockroach stuck to the side of his head. "The SWAT team just took him down."

"What's the body count?"

"Eleven dead, eight injured. Could be twelve and seven by tomorrow morning."

"And you really think he was on something instead of just Columbine crazy?"

Ed grunted. "Have a look at the clip."

John fired up his PC and while it was booting he asked Horsebreaker: "Is there something you want me to do, Chief?"

"Yeah. After you see the footage, go down to Division and have a look around. See what you can find out. I guess we'll know more after they give us a tox report from the autopsy, but that could take a while. I've got a feeling about this one, though."

John lifted one eyebrow. Horsebreaker's "feelings" had gotten him in plenty deep, plenty of times before.

"Maybe I'm wrong about this one," the Chief said with a shrug. "Take a look at the clip, though, and see what you think."

He stepped out and closed the door. John took a sip of his forty-weight coffee and surfed the web for a video from the Division Street Mall. It came up in less than a second.

Sidewalk café, looked like DeAngelo's. Tipped over tables and chairs. Red and white outdoor umbrellas, some on their sides, getting dragged around by the wind. There was the perp, waving his gun around. From the back he looked normal enough, even with that long brown ponytail. Plenty of guys were growing their hair out these days, Hambone included.

On the other side of the shooter John could see people running, trying to save their hides. He wondered where the guy with the camera was filming this from? What was he using, a cell phone?

Gone Off let loose with a volley. He wasn't trying to pick anybody off, at least; he was just spraying bullets around like a dog marking his yard. The footage didn't have any sound with it and that was a little eerie; the gun jumping around in Gone Off's hands was the only way you could tell he was firing. That and the flash at the end of the barrel, whenever it swung back this way.

Now Gone Off had some girl by the hair. Where the hell had *she* come from? Must have been hiding under one of the tables. He had her by her black hair. She actually *was* screaming; John didn't need audio to tell him that. The camera zoomed in.

He had her by her black hair. He threw her onto the red brick pavers in front of DeAngelo's. The camera rolled on. Why wasn't the Joe who was taking the pictures doing anything to help her? Maybe he was too far away. Maybe he was just smart. Who in his right mind would rush a guy holding an assault rifle when all you had was your cell phone?

Gone Off had his back to the camera now. He was distracted, raping her. You couldn't see much through all those turned-over tables and umbrellas, but enough to know he was raping her. John wanted to look away but couldn't seem to. Maybe the same was true for the Joe with the camera. Maybe that was true for everybody. Maybe that was why this clip was up on the web already, why it was racking up hits faster than Alex Rodriguez. John just hoped for the girl's sake they'd shut it down before it went viral.

15

Gone Off was done doing his business. He came up out of all those umbrellas, zipping his pants. Then John saw his face. He clicked on the video to pause it. He saw what the Chief meant. There was something about his eyes. John wasn't sure what it was, but there was something about his eyes. Seems like there was this reddish tint to them. He was King-of-the-World. He was joyriding. But was he sky high on something or just Texas Clock Tower crazy?

Twenty years old, John was guessing. A kid, a man, a kid who wanted to be a man and thought something like this might get him there faster. Where the hell was his daddy to whip his ass and point him in the right direction? Gone off, maybe, like all the rest of them.

John clicked in again but there wasn't much more to see: the gun was pointing right at the camera now and the clip ended in a hurry. He took another sip of his coffee. It wasn't hot anymore. He wondered again what the world was coming to, then got up and put on his jacket and drove to the Division Street Mall.

Chapter 2

There was a reason why they called it Division Street: it drew a line—
was the line—between Palmer and Mayfair, between what used to be the
bad and good parts of town. That line wasn't as clean now as when John
was a kid; you couldn't always tell anymore what part of the city you were in
just by looking at the people and buildings. The open air mall had
something to do with that. It was the centerpiece of Mayor Crawford's
push to rescue downtown from what he called "forty years of urban blight,"
in that deep voice that made it sound like his renewal plan was written
down in the Bible.

Well, what happened on the mall that morning sure seemed Biblical
to John, and not in a good way. Just the latest indication, Grandma Briggs
would say, that the Second Coming was coming, any second. He didn't
really believe that himself, but when this kind of thing happened it did make
him wonder where the world was headed, and how fast it was getting there.
He had to show his badge three times before he got to the crime scene, and
when he finally did he wished he'd been turned away.

He went straight to DeAngelo's. Tom Etheridge was already there,
like John knew he would be. He seemed surprised when he looked up from
his clipboard.

"Hey, Briggs. Nobody told me they were bringing Narcotics & Vice
in on this one."

"Chief's got another one of his 'feelings.'"

"Son-of-a-bitch is usually right. I think it's because his mother was
on peyote while she was breastfeeding him."

Every town's got a Tom Etheridge: former basketball player who wasn't quite good enough to go pro, married to one of his cheerleaders. He was a guy that both men and women would agree was good-looking: tall, built like he worked out, black hair and a bushy mustache, a big smile and nice-guy eyes. John, who was five feet eleven himself, always felt short standing next to him. And just a bit chubby.

"How's Ham?" he asked.

John sighed and ran his fingers through his thick brown hair. Sweat was already building up there. "In trouble again, at school. Minor shit, at least."

Tom laughed. "He's a good kid."

Nice of him to say so. His boys were stand-up guys, both on the basketball team at Palmer. His daughter Julie was a future princess. John used to think maybe Ham might date her when the two of them got older. Sometimes it felt like Life let you come up with shit like that just so It could show you later on how much of a dumbass you really were. "What have you got so far?"

They were standing in front of the sidewalk café. It looked like a bomb had gone off inside. There was glass and blood everywhere. The window that used to separate the indoors from the outdoors was gone. Tables and chairs were tipped over, both places. John could see cups and saucers and forks and knives strewn all over the pavers. The wind had picked up and was scooting things around the crime scene: loose newspapers, empty cigarette packs, paper napkins. Behind him, in the square, he could hear the sounds of flags cracking.

"From what I can tell it started here, then moved west down Division."

John looked along the street past the daffodils and tulips blooming inside their raised beds, and you would have thought a tornado had been there. He saw parked cars with bullet holes in them, and more shattered storefront glass. Bloodstains. White chalk outlines of murdered people, looking like drawings on the wall of a cave.

"Where the hell do you suppose he got an assault rifle?"

Tom shrugged. "Gun show, pawn shop; the way things have been going lately, maybe a candy store."

"Anyone else involved?"

"Not as far as I can tell. Looks like a lone shooter." The wind kept blowing Tom's red tie around and finally sent it up over the shoulder of his starched white shirt.

"You think he was crazy," asked John, "or is the Chief onto something?"

Tom looked up and down the street, like maybe he thought there was some clue he'd missed in the first go-round. "I don't know, John. It sure looks like the guy went psycho, but there are a few things that don't fit the profile."

"Like him raping the girl?"

"That's one. Usually the perp is too busy shooting fish in a barrel to bother with much of anything else. He's going after people one at a time, too, with a purpose, even if he doesn't know who those people are. According to eye witnesses, this guy just sprayed a lot of bullets into the crowd. They say he didn't seem to be aiming at anybody."

"That's the way it looked in the video."

"You saw that, too, huh?"

"Who the hell hasn't?"

The wind was dragging one of DeAngelo's red-and-white striped outdoor umbrellas across the patio, making an ugly, scraping sound. March was coming in like a lion. "Do you know anything about the shooter yet?"

"A little. Tad Wellington, twenty-four. Kid from Society Hill who never quite found his way after college. He'd been bussing tables at Trudy's. Lived in an apartment two blocks from here, on Oak. Jerry's there now, talking to people."

"Let me guess," said John, "Such a nice boy, they can't believe he'd do something like this."

"Probably."

"Was he using?"

"Yeah, but from what I hear so far just stuff you don't even bother keeping track of anymore." Tom paused, then said: "You know of any drug that could make somebody go off like this?"

"Almost anything, if he'd had enough of it." But John was already running through a short list in his mind and nothing was matching up real well with what he was seeing. Crack? Crank? Angel? Maybe that new South American paste they called "Paco?" Violence flowed out of all of those pretty freely. And when somebody was addicted bad enough to anything, you didn't know what they might do to get their hands on more of it. But there didn't seem to be any intent to get more drugs here, or to steal money to buy more drugs; in the clip it sure looked like Gone Off—Tad Wellington, he guessed he ought to say—was just joyriding. "When do you think we'll have a tox report?"

"Tomorrow morning, if we're lucky. A week, if we're not."

John nodded. "To tell you the truth, I'll be surprised if they find anything."

"So you think Horsefucker's wrong about this one?" Tom grinned. "Wouldn't be the first time would it?"

That brought John up short. "On this kind of thing? Yeah, actually it would be."

#

By the time John left the scene it was close to noon. He decided to look in on Grandma Briggs before heading back to the station. He tried to do that two days a week, if he could, besides having lunch with her on Sundays. She was at the Center and he felt bad about that, but she was eighty-five years old and had diabetes. He wasn't home enough to look after her proper, and neither was Ham. He sometimes thought about hiring somebody to help out, but this way seemed like it might be better; at least she had other people to talk to.

"Well there you are, John. Am I glad to see *you*. They've been cutting in on my programs all morning with this awful business at the Mall downtown. You aren't mixed up in that are you, Honey?"

She was sitting on the pea-green couch in the common room, which was where he usually found her, parked in front of the TV set. They must have just done her hair because it looked real nice, like a swirl of white cake frosting. John admired her for that, how she always looked so sharp, even just for sitting around at the Center. When he was off duty he usually wore jeans and some ragged old t-shirt that he didn't want to throw away because he was fond of it, because it reminded him of some time in his life that he didn't want to let go of.

"Not much," he said, bending over to give her a kiss on the cheek. "Tom Etheridge gets all the crazies." He was still hoping Tom would get this one.

"Well, you tell Tom I said he did good work, shooting down that son-of-Satan. I don't know what the world is coming to, John, I honestly don't."

He didn't bother telling her that it wasn't actually Tom who'd shot the "son-of-Satan." He sat down on the couch beside her. Just then they cut in on her program again, this time to show a picture of the shooter, Tad Wellington.

"See what I mean?"

It was a photo of him when he was at the State University, dressed in his cap and gown. He didn't look like a son-of-Satan to John, just some kid with his whole life ahead of him. Suddenly, he felt worse than he had all morning.

"What on earth is the world coming to?" asked Grandma again

"I don't know," John answered softly.

Her program came back on and they talked about that for a while, until John had to go. "How's Hamilton Briggs these days?" she asked as he was getting up to leave.

"Oh, he's fine."

"When will you be bringing him out here to see me again?"

"One of these days." John wasn't about to tell her that Ham wouldn't stand for the Pledge, that he liked to dress all in black and sometimes wore eye makeup. She had heart trouble already.

"You know, I'd feel a whole lot better about him if he had a mother." John started edging towards the doorway. He didn't want the conversation going off in *that* direction again! "But then I guess he never really has had one, has he?"

Yeah he did, for a while. But Grandma never did think too much of Jenny. "I've got to get back to the station," John said. "You take care now, Grandma. I love you."

"I love you, too, Honey. I'm so glad you're not mixed up in this thing."

"You and me both." He was hoping it would stay that way.

Chapter 3

After he got back to the station, John kept thinking about what had happened that morning, wondering how a Society Hill kid like Tad Wellington could get to the point where he'd kill eleven people. Tom kept him posted throughout the afternoon; his unit wasn't finding any of the usual mass-murder markers. None of Wellington's friends would describe him as "angry." He hadn't written any rambling, hate-filled diaries or blogs. If some girl had recently dumped him, nobody had heard about it. Seems he was just your basic kid with your basic minor drug problem. Could that be the key? John kept coming back to it, not only because of Horsebreaker's "feeling," but because nothing else was making much sense. As far as anyone knew Tad was just a stoner, but what if he'd recently started using something else besides weed?

Rick, the little shithead the Chief had hired as an intern, knocked on John's office door and stuck his face in. "What's up?" John said in a tone of voice that was about two degrees below zero, hoping the kid would get the hint. No such duck-fucking luck.

"Detective Briggs, Chief Horsebreaker wanted me to tell you that the critically injured victim from Division Street just passed away."

"Thanks." Kid was polite; John had to give him that. Too damned polite. It was like he was in suck-up mode all the time. So the body count was up to twelve now. Worst mass-killing ever, in this state at least. The national news was all over it. Their camera crews were down on Division

22

already, interviewing everything that moved. No surprise there. People were thirsty for blood and if you wanted to keep your ratings up, you'd best give it to them.

What about the drug angle, though? He still couldn't think of one that would set somebody off like that, at least not without some gas-on-the-fire factor like hate or love or religion thrown in. Or money. That was what drug-related killings were usually about: the money. A hundred people were gunned down in Mexico just last week, because they got in the way of the flow of money. But that didn't seem to be the case here.

Any chance Wellington was using more than one drug at a time? Back when John and Tom were in college, they had this kick poster on the wall of their dorm room, some chart showing what would supposedly happen if you doubled up on your drugs. You'd pick LSD from the columns and peyote from the rows, and match them up to find something like this: *You see Jesus. You ask Him where to get the best tacos. You die.*

Tom's coach hated that poster, thought it reflected badly on the Athletic Department, and after a while made them take it down. They weren't using, though; they were just two kids pretending to be cool. Was there some combo out there that could turn you into what Grandma Briggs called a "son-of-Satan?" Maybe. John wanted that tox report but when he left the station at six it still wasn't there and it was looking like it wouldn't be until at least the next morning.

#

John still lived in Palmer, where he grew up, which he figured was either sweet or just plain stupid, depending on how you looked at it. He had a row house on Figueroa, three stories high if you counted the garage. The second floor was where he spent most of his time, at least while he was awake.

"Ham Sandwich, you home?"

"Yeah, Dad!"

John relaxed a little. He hated it when Ham took the bus, though that was most days. Made things easier on him at work, but he'd just as soon pick him up himself if he could. Ham's voice had come from the den. That was good. Sometimes he would hole up in his room on the top floor, when he was in one of his moods. John poked his head around the corner and saw that his son was watching TV, more news reports about what they were calling the Division Street Massacre. Christ, he was only fifteen. John wished there was some way he could protect him from this kind of crap. It couldn't be good for you. "How was your day?"

"Better than yours, I'm guessing. Are you mixed up in this at all?"

"A little." No mention of the Pledge-of-Allegiance thing. It probably wasn't worth talking about. Ham was dressed completely in black like he always was, these days. Goth or Sabbath or Midnight or something. John couldn't keep up with it. That didn't bother him nearly as much as the cross-gender stuff, the black nail polish and eyeliner, but maybe Ham would grow out of that, too. None of it would have worried him much if he hadn't found a couple of pairs of women's underwear in Ham's chest-of-drawers the week before, when he was doing one of his drug checks.

"This guy must have really gone over the edge."

Hard to argue with that. Question was: what pushed him? "I don't feel like cooking tonight," said John, "You up for Chinese?"

"Panda Li's?"

"Yeah."

"Sounds good. I'll take . . ."

"Let me guess: grilled tofu?"

"Yeah, and be sure to get . . ."

"Chopsticks?"

"Yeah."

"Show off. I'll give Li a call." John hung up his coat and took off his tie. He went to the kitchen. He turned on the little set on the counter so he could see what Hambone was seeing. The same pictures, over and over. Yellow police tape, flashing red and blue lights, bloodstains on the pavers out in front of DeAngelo's. Every little thing they could dig up about Tad Wellington's life. He picked up the phone.

"Delivery. One grilled tofu, brown rice. Chopsticks. One kung pao chicken, extra spicy." He'd have heartburn in the morning but what the hell? "Fried rice for me. No, no chopsticks. Stick a shovel in it." He gave the address. As soon as he'd hung up the phone, the doorbell rang. He was used to Li having their food ready fast, but this was ridiculous.

"I'll get it!" said John. Like anybody else was going to. The little TV in the kitchen and the big one in the den were both blabbering on. Wellington's mother still lived on Society Hill and reporters had staked out her place like she was the criminal. John didn't know her but felt sorry for her all the same; she hadn't done anything wrong but her life was pretty much over now, too. She'd been voted off the island.

He went down the steps to the entryway and looked through the peephole. Wasn't one of Li's runners yet. It was Mick. Friend of Ham's, gender unknown. He/she/it was a Visigoth, too, or whatever they called themselves, dressed in the same black clothes. Nice kid though, really, as far as John could tell. Had only been coming around for a week or two, and John was still holding out hope that maybe Ham had found himself a girlfriend.

"Hey, Mick," he said, "How'd you get way over here?"

"Rode the bus. Hope that's OK, Mr. Briggs. Is Ham home?"

"Yeah, sure, come on in. I just ordered Chinese. If I'd known you were coming, I'd have got something for you."

"Thanks, Mr. Briggs, but I already ate."

Mick went up the stairs ahead of him like It owned the place. That thing It was wearing almost looked like a skirt. Maybe, just maybe? John couldn't tell for sure. Nice kid, though, and seemed to like Hambone. The two of them were hanging out a lot lately.

"What do you think of the Division Street Psycho, Mr. Briggs?"

Was that what they were calling Wellington now? "I don't know what to think yet."

"I think his girlfriend must have dumped him."

"Is that right?" From what John had heard he didn't have one. That sounded like something a woman would say, though. Maybe Mick was short for Michelina, after all?

She was in the den now, with Ham. They were sitting on the couch together but at opposite ends, talking up some video game. Next thing John knew they were playing it. First person shooter, with zombies. He shook his head and went back to his real-life video game, the one that was still running on the box in the kitchen. No zombies there but the woman from Channel 4 looked like a vampire, with her white teeth and red lips and black hair.

She was talking about the clip that had been up on YouTube that morning. She couldn't show it because the images were too disturbing, but you could tell she wanted to so damned bad. You could tell she was thinking what a ratings boost it would be for her station. All she could show, though, was one still-frame of the shooter. Even that was a bit graphic, she said, so if you wanted to look the other way . . . Right. That was TV-talk for *Please turn your attention to the Center Ring*!

It was pretty much the same frame John had paused on in his office that morning. Wellington was still waving his gun around. There was still that same strange look on his face. What the hell *was* that? Now they had Tom Etheridge on, talking about how he didn't know much of anything yet, but was following up on all the leads. John thought: *Better you than me*. Tom was used to that kind of crap, talking to reporters. He'd been interviewed after every basketball game since he was fourteen.

The doorbell rang again and this time it really was the delivery boy from Panda Li's. John wondered if he'd remembered the fortune cookies.

#

John popped a Bilge Light and ate at the counter in the kitchen, so as not to disturb the Visigoths. Channel 4 was doing profiles of the victims now, and that got hard. It was one thing to say "twelve people dead" but something else once you found out that Mark Williams, 37, was the father of two young girls. John didn't know any of them and apparently neither did Wellington; the shooting was looking more and more like a random thing. Something must have set Tad off, though. What the hell *was* it?

The news looped on, 24/7, like it always does. Talking heads were all trying to put their own spin on it. Anybody who had ever said two words about mass murderers was popping out of the woodwork to pitch his latest book. Republicans and Democrats, the new Crips and Bloods, were each trying to hang this thing on something the other gang had got dead wrong. After a while, Mick came into the kitchen.

"Guess I'd better be going, Mr. Briggs."

"All right, Mick. Good to see you again. You got a ride home?"

"Same way I got here: the bus. I'll see you tomorrow, Hamilton!" she called back towards the den.

Had to be a girl. No guy would call Ham "Hamilton," unless he was riding him. His mother used to call him that, but then she was the one who named him. "Hamilton" never had seemed quite right to John; it wasn't the kind of name that went with a place like Palmer. But then Jenny was raised on Society Hill. Up there, they liked giving out names that sounded like

26

they came from the Revolutionary War. He wished Jenny was here now. He wished Ham had really known his mother. With that blonde mop of his he looked more like her than he did John, whose hair was what Grandma Briggs liked to call "chestnut brown." John wasn't even sure what the hell a chestnut was.

He smiled to himself, wondering what Jenny would think about all this Midnight stuff, the black clothes and makeup. He wondered what she would do about it. Nothing, probably. She'd just laugh it off, go along with it, remembering that she'd done the same kind of thing when she was that age. So that's what John tried to do, too, even though there were times when he just wanted to kick his son's ass sideways.

After Mick left, John went into the den to watch TV with him. They didn't say much, just a word now and then, but it felt good to stay connected even like that. There'd been times in the past when they'd been a lot further apart. A year ago Ham was calling him a "narc" and didn't want to have anything to do with him. If John even mentioned his job, Ham would say he had "narc-o-lepsy" and pretend to fall asleep on a dime. Did that at the breakfast table one morning and his face actually hit the cereal bowl, spraying milk and Cheerios all over the kitchen. It seemed funny now but at the time it was pretty bad because John had been under a lot of stress at work and he'd been worried, too, that Ham might be getting into drugs. He still worried about that sometimes, mostly because of what had happened to Jenny.

"Guess I'd better go up and do my homework, Dad."

"Good plan." He was a good kid. John wished he was more straight-up sometimes, like Tom Etheridge's boys, but then he wished for a lot of things. He wished Ham hadn't lost his mother. He wished kids like Tad Wellington didn't go off and kill twelve people in an outdoor mall with a machine gun.

After Ham went upstairs, John popped another Bilge Light. Sitting there in the dark with the news on he thought back to one night when Ham was nine years old and they were watching some old movie together. Ginger Rogers and Fred Astaire. Jenny hadn't been gone all that long at the time. After a while, Ham had asked him something.

"Dad, when did the world stop being just black-and-white?"

John had thought about that for a minute, watching the light and shadows dance across the TV screen. Then finally he'd said: "I'm not sure, Hambone. I'm not sure."

And he still wasn't sure, even now.

Chapter 4

When John got to the office the next morning, a copy of Tad Wellington's tox report was waiting on his desk. While he sipped at his coffee he gave it the once-over, working his way through the rows and columns. Then he tilted back in his chair and frowned. There wasn't anything there. The coroner had looked for everything from Coke to household cleaner and had come up empty. Not even any THC in the kid's bloodstream, for Christ's sake. So, it was Tom's case after all. John should have felt relieved by that, and did, but at the same time something kept nagging at him. Maybe it was that look on Wellington's face in the YouTube video, his red eyes. Maybe it was the rape. Maybe John was starting to have "feelings" about things like this, the way Chief Horsebreaker did?

Bullshit. He let out a puff of air. He wondered if the Chief had seen the report yet, and if he had what he thought about it. He didn't have to wait long to find out. A half-hour later Ed was there in his office, serving up one of his famous stony Indian looks.

"You saw the report?"

"Yeah." He was going to leave it at that but when Horsebreaker didn't say anything, felt like he had to. "Nothing."

Ed grunted. He looked like he didn't believe it.

"You look like you don't believe it," said John.

"I believe they didn't find anything. But I'm not convinced that Wellington wasn't using."

It was a little strange to hear the Chief put it that way, to hear him say that someone was "using." He'd worked in Narcotics for fifteen years, sure, but that was back in the day. Now he wore three-piece suits and spent most of his time talking to the Press, and the Mayor. His street cred was even lower than John's. "Well . . ."

"These reports don't always turn up everything, do they?"

"Umm . . . no." John had seen that a few times himself over the years: junkies that lived strung-out lifestyles coming back clean in the autopsy. It all depended on how long it had been since they'd taken anything and exactly what it was they were taking. Some shit cleared out of the bloodstream in a hurry.

"Etheridge isn't turning up anything that makes sense," the Chief said.

"It's early."

"Maybe, but when somebody shoots a lot of people, it usually doesn't take long before the investigation points *somewhere*. Kid wasn't mad at anybody. No mental health issues, as far as we know. Didn't have a girlfriend. He wasn't a loner, though; had some friends he liked to play basketball and get stoned with."

"At the same time?" The Chief wasn't amused. "You know," John said, "sometimes people just fall off the edge. They don't always have to have a reason—or a drug habit."

"Maybe." He didn't sound like he was buying it. "Anything else from the coroner?"

"Yeah. He determined the cause of death. Seems Wellington died from multiple gunshot wounds."

"No shit?"

Horsebreaker stood there silently for several long, uncomfortable moments, until finally John asked him: "What do you want me to do now, Chief?"

Ed was looking out through the window behind John at the street down below, like he was scanning the horizon. "I don't know. Keep your eyes open and one ear to the ground, I guess, like you always do. I think there's something out there."

Buffalo? John almost said that but then thought better of it. "Sure."

"You got any meetings coming up with your people in the field?"

"I see a couple of them this afternoon."

The Chief nodded. "Good. Ask them if there's any word on the street." Then he was gone, leaving John to look over—yet again—what might as well have been a blank report.

#

At lunch John drove out to Seaside, eating a cheeseburger on the way. Panda Li's last night, McBypass today; at this rate he'd be the next one on the coroner's table. And people worried that illegal drugs were bad for you!

Seaside was another one of the Mayor's pet projects. When John was a kid they called it "the wharf," and even he wasn't stupid enough to go down there alone. Back then it seemed like there were more murders on the docks than boats. It was different now. Shops, restaurants, condos; it was kind of upscale. There was a concrete path called The Ribbon that ran alongside the Gulf for miles. People walked there, and jogged, and paid to get pulled in pimped-out bicycle rickshaws. You could still get to actual docks along that path if you went far enough, and wanted to, if watching boats get loaded and unloaded took you to a happy place.

John parked in one of the public lots and then blended in with the stream of people headed west on The Ribbon. It was a nice spring day. The wind coming off the ocean was brisker than usual; you could see little whitecaps on the water all the way out to the horizon. He was standing at one of the overlooks, watching the sea gulls wheel and dive, when Marianne Harding came up to the railing beside him.

"Nice day."

"Yeah, it is," said John. "A little breezy." Marianne was twenty-nine but looked seventeen, which came in handy when you were trying to blend in with a younger crowd. She had long, wavy black hair. Green eyes. A face that was pretty but not too pretty. Tom Etheridge had asked him once why he didn't date her, but there was an easy answer to that. In fact, there were several. For one, he was her boss. For another, she was almost young enough to be his daughter. And for still another, after Jenny he'd promised himself that he'd never get mixed up with another junkie, even a used-to-be. "How's life been treating you?"

"Can't complain." She gave him her report in less than five minutes. Nothing out of the ordinary. It had been a quiet couple of weeks in the Underworld.

"Are they serving anything new at the cafeteria?"

She shook her head. "Just the same old tacos and enchiladas."

These days everything came from south of the border: all the worst stuff and all the worst news. Some people upstairs wanted to blame Mexico for that, but the way John looked at it the problem wasn't the people who were selling, it was the people who were buying. He never had understood why, in a country that had so much going for it, so many people were hell-bent on throwing their lives away. It made no sense to him, and never had, even going back to before he first met—and busted—Jenny.

"You think there might be something new on the street?" Marianne kept brushing the hair out of her eyes, kept on watching the horizon. There was a ship coming in.

"I don't know."

Neither one of them said anything for a minute. "Well . . ." she finally whispered, "You got any new orders for me?"

Her voice was a little flirty, like maybe she was hoping he'd ask her to dinner—or to strip for him. Or maybe, he thought, I'm just a widowed, middle-aged man with too lively an imagination. "Just let me know if you see or hear anything unusual, OK?"

"If I do, you want to know about it right away?"

She filed reports like this one every couple of weeks, though not always at the same time and place. If she needed to see John sooner the protocol was she would ring his cell once so he'd have the number she was dialing from, and then he'd get back in touch with her.

"Call me," he said.

She lit a cigarette. Make that four reasons he never would date her. He was allergic to tobacco. "Does this have anything to do with what happened yesterday on Division Street?"

"Call me," he said, pushing off from the railing. He started walking east down The Ribbon. He didn't look back at her.

#

A little later on John met Hotwire down at Kim's, where they sell the good oysters. Kim had come over from Korea about six years ago and started off pedaling one of those bicycle rickshaws for lazy tourists. Before you knew it he had an oyster stand and was living the American Dream—if your idea of the American Dream was working eighty hours a week shucking mollusks and driving a powder-blue Mercedes. Kim did both and from what John had heard took care of a big family back home in Busan.

32

Kim was a stand-up guy. Hotwire wasn't.

Hotwire—that was a name he'd given himself, by the way—could best be described as a lovesick weasel. Kid was skinny as a beanpole and white as a sheet; it looked like he hadn't been out in the sun since the turn of the century. His hair was almost as white as his skin; Christ, even his eyebrows looked like they'd been soaked in bleach! John had never seen him when he wasn't strung out on something. He had no doubt that every cent he'd ever paid Hotwire had gone straight into the pipeline of drug money he was trying to shut off, but he couldn't see any way around that. Sometimes you had to put a minnow on your hook to catch the really big fish.

The Ribbon was down at ground-level here; it ran through the sand at the back of the beach. On one side, towards the parking lot, was Kim's oyster shack; on the seaside there were about a dozen white-painted picnic tables underneath colored umbrellas. Hotwire was sitting at the one closest to the ocean. John sat down across from him. It was a couple of hours past lunchtime by then; there wasn't anybody else there.

"Afternoon, Boss."

"I thought I told you not to call me that, Asshole." It was funny; whenever John was on the way to meet Hotwire he told himself he was going to be nice to him this time, but as soon as the kid opened his mouth he wanted to kick his teeth in.

"Sure, Boss."

Christ. "Is that a blunt you're smoking?"

Hotwire took it out of his mouth and looked at it like he didn't know where it had come from. "Uh, no." He flicked it out into the sand for the crabs to toke on. "How about a plate of oysters, Boss?"

"Not for me, but you go ahead." John slipped him a five and Hotwire went away for a while. John would have considered that a good deal, except eventually the weasel came back.

"You know what these are good for, don't you?" he said with a lopsided grin. The sea breeze was blowing his stringy white-blonde hair around.

"Getting your daily supply of heavy metals?"

"Heavy metal? Didn't know you were into that, too, Boss."

"I'm not." *Way* not.

Hotwire was smirking. Oyster juice was dripping down his scraggly chin. "These are supposed to be better than Viagra, if you know what I mean."

Christ. The idea of Hotwire . . . John didn't want to go there. "No kidding? Look, how are things in the Underworld?"

"Swell, Boss."

Swell? John felt like he'd wandered into an episode of *Leave it to Beaver from Hell.* "Everybody on the street is happy?"

"*I'm* happy."

John thought: *tell me again what I'm paying you for?* "Listen Leroy," he said, ready to start in on him.

Hotwire stopped grinning. "I thought I told you never to use that name." He didn't seem so stupid—or stoned—anymore. For a second, in his eyes, you could see that he'd kill you if he had the chance and you gave him a good reason.

"Tell you what. I won't call you Leroy if we can get down to business."

Hotwire didn't say anything. John took that as a "yes." He wondered why it was that calling him Leroy always set him off. Maybe it reminded him of some used-to-be life when he had a real home and wasn't a junkie, when there was somebody who actually gave a damn whether he lived or died. Maybe that was a place he didn't want anyone else to touch. "I'll give it to you straight, Hotwire. We think there might be something new on the street. If you can find out what it is, you might save some lives."

He didn't look too impressed. "What's fucken in it for me?"

That's what it came down to for everybody these days, didn't it? "How's about I buy you another plate of oysters and don't beat the living shit out of you?"

Hotwire sat there, glowering. "Look," said John, "If you can find me something that turns out to be real, I'll make it worth your while."

Leroy's eyes went from dusk to daylight then. That was something he could understand. One time he'd helped bust up a prostitute-and-drug ring and John had paid him enough that somebody like Kim could have started out a new life with it. He didn't think it did Hotwire or his liver any good, though. If anything it probably just took him three hundred steps closer to the boneyard, but for somebody like Leroy that might be the best thing you could ever do for him.

Christ, did he really believe that? After Leroy left, John walked down through the sand in his work shoes to get a closer look at the Gulf, wondering what had ever happened to the cop he used to be, the one who thought he could actually save somebody.

Chapter 5

A few days went by. Some of the dust stirred up by Tad Wellington's killing spree settled down to earth again. Every now and then somebody would kick a cloud of it up, but for the most part people moved on to other things like they always did. Was there a reason why it happened? Nobody had found one, not even Tom Etheridge.

John spent most of his time sifting through paperwork. More and more, that's all he did anymore. When he was younger he would have rather died than be stuck in an office; he loved getting out in the field. But what happened to a lot of cops finally happened to him: one morning you wake up to find Forty coming at you fast and all the sudden a desk job starts looking like a soft place to land. You get to the point where you want more responsibility, too.

Once, when John was a teenager, his granddad had tried to talk him into joining the military. *I don't want anybody telling me what to do*, John had told him, seething, *and I don't want to be telling anybody else what to do, either!*

The old man had just smiled like he knew something John didn't. Turns out, that was true. You have a kid and have to start taking on responsibility whether you like it or not, whether you're ready for it or not. At work you take orders from enough assholes up the chain that eventually you figure you couldn't possibly do any worse. You get to the point where you want to be the one calling the shots instead of somebody else. John had nine people working under him now and he tried to treat them like human beings. He tried to give them the support they needed and let them do their jobs. Sometimes he had to rein them in but made sure it wasn't personal. He tried to be fair and always give them good reasons. They didn't always agree with him, and they didn't always like him, but at least they knew where he was coming from.

Saturday rolled around. John spent the afternoon at the zoo with Mick and Ham. That was a little strange, walking through the park with those two in their black clothes and eye makeup and dog collars. He kept having this feeling that the animals were looking at him instead of the other way around, and that they were laughing behind their backs.

Glad I'm not a member of THAT species, dude!

John kept on wondering about Mick Devereaux, what she—or he— really was to Ham. Usually he was pretty good at checking M or F based on all those things like body type or shape of the face, but not this time around. Usually, he didn't give a rat's ass what other people thought of him, but had to admit he got tired of being the center of attention after a while, after the seventeenth old lady had wrinkled up her nose. By the time they finally left the park, he'd been ready to go for a couple of hours.

"Thank you again for inviting me, Mr. Briggs," Mick said when he dropped her off at her house.

Had to be a girl; she was too damned polite. She lived in a nice part of town, for Palmer. John supposed he'd have to meet her folks someday, if she kept hanging around. Maybe by then he'd know which pronoun to use, so he wouldn't make a fool of himself.

It was dinner by the time he and Ham got home and after they'd split a pizza (half double pepperoni, half veggie extreme), they settled in for the night. Ham was in one of his moods and went upstairs with his headphones. John figured maybe he was embarrassed, too, by the whole zoo trip, though probably for different reasons. About an hour later, John was watching a ballgame when the phone rang.

"Hey, Briggs, it's Tom. Are you busy?"

"Not really. What's up?"

"I've got something here you might want to see."

Here, it turns out, was the Fishbowl. The Fishbowl was a bar—the owners liked to call it a "nightclub"—down by the Sherry River. John had been there lots of times before, and not as a customer. It was a drug and hookup joint. You could bust somebody there every night if you wanted to. Mostly, he didn't want to, because it was a little like trying to dig at the beach: every time you pulled out a shovelful of sand the hole would fill right back in. The only reason to go there was if you needed to meet your quota, or if something really bad was going down. John didn't think Tom was there for his quota.

Red and blue lights were flashing off the cars in the parking lot, and the windows of the bar, and the river. It was like the strobe lights inside had leaked out. John ducked under the yellow tape and asked where to find Tom. There was something strange about the whole scene and after a while he figured out what that was: there wasn't any music playing. Usually, the place was pounding like a heart. Tonight it had a creepy, empty sort of feel, though, like a Midway once the carnival has left town. John could hear somebody crying in one of the little side rooms where the waitresses did lap dances. He caught up with Tom.

"Hey, what you got?"

Tom grabbed him by the sleeve and steered him towards the bar. "Some kid with a knife went berserk," he said, under his breath. "I'm still trying to piece this together but it looks like it was over some girl."

No surprise there. People were getting knifed in this place all the time over drugs or sex or something they called "respect." There was only one word out of what Tom had said that got John's attention. "What do you mean, went 'berserk'?"

"See for yourself."

They were out on the dance floor. There was blood all over it. There was blood splattered on the big mirror behind the bar, too, and on the rows of bottles on either side. There was even blood on some of the fish tanks scattered around the room. "Jesus," said John.

"Fourteen people on their way to the hospital now. Six to the morgue."

"Jesus," John said again. "All that for one girl?"

"She didn't want to dance with him. Her boyfriend didn't want her to dance with him, either. Kid wouldn't take no for an answer, though. Grabbed hold of her tits."

John had heard the story plenty of times before, but it usually had a different ending. Two guys would duke it out in the parking lot. Sometimes they'd even have knives, cut each other up a little. Every now and then one of them would get himself killed. But twenty people in the mix? A half-dozen on their way to the morgue? That was *way* over the top.

"What happened to the guy who started it?"

"He's one of the six."

John was looking at all the knocked over tables and chairs and it reminded him of something. DeAngelo's. It looked like DeAngelo's after Tad Wellington's spree. He felt cold. "How'd it end for him, exactly?"

"From what witnesses are telling us, it took seven guys. One of them says he kept stabbing him, but it didn't seem to make much difference. Kid was shot a couple of times, too, and just kept coming."

"You talked to all seven guys?"

"The two that went to the hospital, yeah. The other five are at Dayton."

The morgue? "Jesus Christ! Who was this kid, O.J. Simpson?"

"That's the weird part," said Tom. "He was pretty scrawny. Came on like Superman, though, from what people are saying. Here, one of the waitresses took a picture with her cell phone and sent it to me."

The shot was a little blurry but yeah, there wasn't much to him. A hundred and fifty pounds maybe, after a big Sunday chicken dinner. Wasn't much to look at either, at least John didn't think so, but sometimes he had a hard time figuring out what got women interested. Kid's hair was buzz cut down to black stubble. Heavy eyebrows, black too. Skin tone you might call "Mediterranean." John could tell he had a chip on his shoulder. A lot of guys that age did. "You think there's a tie-in here to what happened on Division?" John knew Tom wouldn't have called him down here on a Saturday night if he didn't think so, but felt like he had to ask anyway.

"It crossed my mind."

John's, too. Not that the crimes had a lot in common, but there were a few strange things about both of them. To start with, a bunch of folks had been murdered all at once, in a town that hadn't seen a lot of that down through the years. There was the sex angle, too. Wellington had taken a break from killing long enough to rape a girl in broad daylight, while this kid wanted a woman so bad he went berserk when she said no and put his hands on the merchandise anyway. It seemed like both of them had this crazy Superman side to them, too: Wellington with that look of his, joyriding a machine gun, and this little scarecrow had killed five guys with what looked like a pocketknife, all while they were stabbing and shooting him. John came back to Chief Horsebreaker's "feeling" again. There were a lot of drugs that could make you think you were King of the World; that

39

was the main reason people took them. There were some, too, that made it so you didn't feel any pain. Was there something that could do both and on top of that make you want to kill anybody who looked at you cross-eyed?

John looked around the room. It was strange to be there with nobody at the bar and nobody out on the dance floor and nobody sitting at the little round tables along the perimeter. It was dark except for the lights inside the fish tanks. "How about the girl," he asked, "was she hurt?"

"No, she's all right," said Tom. "A little shook up."

"I'll bet. She in good enough shape that I could talk to her?"

"We took a statement already. You want to see it?"

"Sure." John skimmed through it. "You mind if I ask her a question or two anyway?"

Tom held out a hand towards the side room where a few minutes ago John had heard somebody crying. "Be my guest. But trust me—you're going to want me in there with you."

#

John knocked on the door and went in. The girl was sitting in the chair where customers usually did and she was smoking a cigarette. He didn't bother telling her that she was breaking a city ordinance or that he personally hated having to breathe that crap; instead, he wasn't as nice as he might have been.

"Evening, Miss. I'm Detective John Briggs. You've already met Detective Etheridge. Mind if I ask you a few questions?"

"You, too? Well shit, I guess I don't care. Go ahead." If she was the one John had heard crying, she wasn't crying anymore. He noticed that the hand holding her cigarette was shaking. She had long, curly brown hair. The top she was wearing was cut so low he had to keep making himself look someplace else. It was brighter in that room than it had been in the bar, but even so he couldn't tell what color her eyes were. Hazel, maybe. And cold.

"Mary Witherspoon, is that right?"

She nodded. "What you need two of you for?" Those eyes were little slits now.

"Standard procedure, Miss Witherspoon, so we can keep each other in line."

"He's the one you have to worry about," said Tom.

John gave him a look. *Thanks, Buddy.* The real reason was so they could back each other up. In case she was to say later that he'd done something he shouldn't have.

"Two foxes in the damned henhouse. Shit, that makes me feel a whole lot better. Can I just go home now?"

John glanced at Tom. "In a minute. I want to ask you a couple of questions."

"All right, get it over with."

That must have been somebody else doing the crying. She didn't look like she was torn up at all. She didn't seem like she gave a damn that six people were dead and one of them was her date. The only human thing about her was that one shaking hand, and maybe her bust line. John looked down at the report Tom had given him. "It says here you were with your boyfriend."

"Hold on," she said, cutting him off, "He wasn't my boyfriend. He was just some guy I met in the bar."

John looked up at her, then back down at the report again. "All right, so you were here with some guy you'd met ten seconds ago."

"More like ten minutes but yeah, you've got the idea."

It was like she was daring him to say he didn't approve. He wondered how long she'd been without a daddy, and how long she'd been looking for one. John wasn't him. "And then you met the one that went loco."

"He was there at the bar, yeah."

"Was he sending you signals?"

"Signals?"

Wrong word, maybe. John had a sudden picture of Horsebreaker with a blanket, sending puffs of smoke up over a mountaintop. "Like he was interested. You know what I mean."

"Yeah, I know what you mean. He was and he wasn't. He was just sitting there."

With that top of hers, *she* was sure sending signals—to every man in the room between nine and ninety. "So he was just there."

"Yeah, he was just there."

"Were you attracted to him?" Having seen his picture, and looking at her, John was finding that hard to believe.

"Yeah. There was something about him."

His aftershave? If that was it, John figured he needed to get some. "Can you say what that something was?"

She shrugged. "I don't know. The way he looked at me, maybe. The way he moved. Pheromones. Who knows why anybody gets lit up by anybody?"

Lit up? He hadn't heard that one before. It made it sound like she was a Christmas tree. And since when did a girl the likes of Mary Witherspoon start throwing around words like "pheromones?" Must have heard it in some ad for cheap perfume. John was thinking about that look on the kid's face, in the picture on Tom's cell phone. There was something about his eyes, and the way his lip curled, like Elvis. It lit John up, too, but not in the way Mary Witherspoon meant. What he felt was a warning. John looked at the report again. "So he came on to you and you tried to hold him off?"

"I guess so."

"That's what it says here."

"Must be true then, huh?" She took a drag on her cigarette. "He wouldn't take no for an answer."

"You wanted him to leave you alone?"

"Kind of yeah, kind of no." She laughed. John didn't know she had it in her. "I was afraid he was going to get into a fight with Jughead, and I didn't want no trouble."

John looked at the report. "You mean Jurgen?"

"I guess so. German guy. Skinhead, probably. I don't think he liked the idea of a Turkish kid trying to cut in on his action."

John didn't know about the Turkish part, or anything at all about Jurgen, but he was starting to get a picture in his mind of what happened. "So how'd it start?"

"It's in the report there." She sounded disgusted with him. He couldn't blame her. He was sure she didn't want to live it all over again.

"Yeah, I see it now. Jurgen pushed the little guy and that set him off?"

"You could say that."

"It says here he put his hands on you."

Mary had finished her cigarette and was looking for a place to put it out. Before either Tom or John could help her, she dropped it on the floor and ground it out with the pointy tip of one of her fake snakeskin high heels. "Look, can I go home now? It's way past my bedtime," she said sweetly.

John looked at his watch. Almost two in the morning. Christ, it was way past his bedtime, too. "Yeah, sure. Unless Detective Etheridge has anything else?"

Tom shook his head. "We know where to find you. You need one of my men to give you a ride home?"

#

After she'd left, John hung around with Tom in the bar for a few minutes more, wrapping up. It was creepy. The overhead lights were out. The tanks scattered around the room were still lit up, though, and colored fish were swimming back and forth inside of them, and bubbles were streaming up through the water, making gurgling sounds. A couple of cops were working the scene, bagging up evidence. When John and Tom finally went outside there were news trucks in the parking lot. All kinds of cameras were rolling. John shouldn't have been surprised by that but he was, a little, just because of where they were. The bad side of Palmer usually didn't get this much press, even when things went this wrong. But he guessed the networks were still riding the wave of the Division Street killings and didn't want that story to end.

"I'd better go talk to them," said Tom.

"Better you than me."

Tom walked off towards the white vans with the 4s and 7s and 9s on them, while John went on home to Ham, turning over in his mind all those pieces that sure seemed like they might've come from the same puzzle, but that right now didn't fit together too well.

Chapter 6

Six people are dead, the result of a knife fight overnight at a bar in Palmer.
That was the first thing John heard when he turned on the TV the
next morning. The anchorman was talking about what had happened last
night at the Fishbowl. *This comes hard on the heels of the mass killing last week at
the Division Street Mall.* Why was he trying so hard to tie those two things
together? Ratcheting up the fear maybe, hoping to boost his ratings. Of
course John was thinking the same thing, that the two incidents might be
related, but he wasn't so sure of himself that he'd say that in public!

Then the anchor said something John didn't know. Turns out one of
the dead guys was State Representative Joe Diddy. Well, he wouldn't be the
first politician to get caught in a sleazy dance club, though off-hand John
couldn't remember any others that had been killed in one. Diddy was a
family-values guy, too, which upped the ante. Why were those clowns
always the ones caught with their pants down? With one side of his mouth
Diddy was talking God-sanctioned marriage, while with the other he was
drooling over Mary Witherspoon's tits. He'd been going by the name
Jurgen, too, which was getting as much play on the other side of the
political aisle as her cleavage. People were saying he wasn't just a closet
adulterer but a closet Nazi. Which was worse?

"Hey, Dad." Hambone was coming down the stairs.

"Morning, Sunshine." It was almost eleven o'clock.

Ham went for the coffeemaker. At least that was one food he wasn't
holier-than-thou about. Then again, lately he'd been trying to get John to

buy fair-trade beans. "Did you have to go out last night?"

"Yeah, did I wake you?"

"Yeah, but I got back to sleep."

"Sorry about that," said John.

"S'OK. What was up?" He brought his coffee over to the couch and sat down.

"Knife fight at the Fishbowl."

"I hear that place is crazy."

"Can be."

"Is that what they're talking about now?" Ham nodded towards the TV.

"Yeah," said John. They watched it for a minute, together.

"So Diddy was there?" Ham laughed.

"Yeah, and now he's at Dayton."

That sobered Ham up. "I'm sorry to hear that. I couldn't stand the guy, personally, but I'm sorry he's dead."

John felt good about that, like he'd raised his kid right. Sad to say, plenty of people who disagreed with Diddy politically would be happy this morning that he was gone and wouldn't make any bones about it. Some would even start pointing at his death like it proved something, like it meant they were on the right side of that line they thought was drawn through everything. "I'm going to see Grandma here in a bit. You want to come?"

"Umm, well actually I was headed over to Mick's. I was hoping you could drop me off?"

"Two of you got plans?"

"Not really. Just hanging out."

"Tell me something . . ." John started to ask, flat-out, if Mick was a girl, but when it came right down to it, he couldn't. It would just embarrass them both. So instead he said: "What do her parents do for a living?"

He hadn't slipped that "her" in there to try and ferret out anything; you sort of had to pick one gender or the other, didn't you? And he'd been thinking of her as a her lately, probably because that was what he wanted to believe.

Ham didn't correct him. "They do people's taxes."

"That right? Sounds smarter than being a police officer."

"Maybe. A lot more boring, though."

"I guess that's one way to look at it. Well, if you can be ready in twenty minutes, I'll drop you off on my way to the Center."

#

A half-hour later they were driving through Palmer. Ham was sitting in the back seat with his headphones on, like John was his damned chauffeur. Sometimes he thought the day when Ham sat in the front seat with him would be the day he'd know that his son was finally a man. John wondered what sort of music he was listening to. Sometimes Ham would talk to him about the bands he liked, though usually John wouldn't have heard of any of them. Scalded Crab, Staple Gun, The Stone Lemurs: it was all just words to him. At least they agreed that rap was crap. John still couldn't convince him that *Green Grass and High Tides Forever* was the best Southern rock song ever made, but Ham would at least admit the guitar solos weren't bad.

They pulled up in front of Mick's house. John waited to be sure somebody would come to the door. Mick did, and waved to him. He waved back at her and watched while the two kids went inside. Was this the start of something real or just one of those things he and Ham would laugh about ten years from now?

Remember that little girl you used to date, and the two of you were dressed in black all the time? You never knew what was ahead of you, though, around the next bend.

When John got to the Center he parked in the pickup lane and went inside to get Grandma. Sunday was their day to go out to brunch, and most of the time they went to Trudy's. While he was helping her into the car he asked her if that was where she wanted to go today.

"Yes, I would, John. I've got a craving for those biscuits of hers."

They *were* awful good, even though Trudy didn't make them herself, anymore. She'd been dead for eight years and her daughter ran the place now. Word on the street was those biscuits came off an assembly line these days, but they still tasted fine with some butter and blackstrap molasses. They drove there, talking small talk the whole way.

"What's Hamilton Briggs up to these days?"

John knew she must be disappointed not to see him again. "I think he's got himself a girlfriend," he said. He guessed he must be feeling pretty bold to say that out loud.

"Well now, is that right? Is she cute?"

John pondered that for a second. "Yeah, I guess you could say that.

46

Nice girl."

"Is he with her right now?"

"That's where I left him."

She was sitting there with her hands folded on top of her shiny black purse. She was wearing white gloves. John realized that he loved her more than anything else in the world right then. "Well, you tell him to bring her out to see me sometime."

"Yes ma'am, I sure will."

They arrived at Trudy's. Ellen, the daughter, had saved them a table. They'd missed coming last week, so this was the first time John had been here since the Division Street shootings, perpetrated by one of the restaurant's employees. The place was still as busy as a dollar store in a recession, but the atmosphere seemed a little subdued.

"Afternoon, Detective Briggs, Miz Briggs. How are ya'll this Sunday?"

It was nice of Ellen to come by and see them in person. She seemed her usual, cheerful self, in spite of the fact that one of her busboys had shot nineteen people. "We're doing just fine, Trudy, thank you," said Grandma, "How wonderful to see you again!"

Grandma and Ellen had this arrangement Grandma didn't know about: Ellen never bothered telling her that she wasn't her mother, that Trudy had been dead for a good long while. John figured it made them both happy. Grandma liked to believe that some things never change, and Ellen liked to be reminded that she was carrying on her mama's dream.

"Did you go to church this morning, John?"

They were having their coffee, waiting for biscuits, when she brought up that usual topic. And John gave her his usual answer: "Well, I meant to." At least this time he had a good excuse. "I got called out in the middle of the night for a disturbance down by the river and didn't get home till after two. I just couldn't wake up after that." The truth was he hadn't been to church in ten years, but Grandma never seemed to notice that his answer to her question was pretty much the same week after week.

"That wasn't that business with the congressman, was it?"

John sighed. "Yes, ma'am, I'm afraid it was."

"Lord, isn't that something? I don't know what the world is coming to, these days."

Their food came and John gave Grandma her insulin. They talked for a long while about a lot of things, without her hitting any nerves. That couldn't last forever. The good thing about Grandma spending most of her time in the past was that some people, like Trudy, had never left. The bad thing was that some others—Jenny, mostly—kept leaving over and over again.

"I wish you'd get out of that business you're in," she said, poking at her scrambled eggs.

"Somebody's got to do it, Grandma."

"I know that, Honey, but why does it have to be you?"

John shrugged.

"Is it because of her, because of that Jenny?"

"Might have something to do with it," he admitted, "or maybe it's just all I'm good at." He laughed, hoping that might take her off track.

"Well now, I seriously doubt that, John."

"Maybe they need somebody here at Trudy's." That just sort of slipped out. He hadn't meant anything by it. He certainly didn't want either one of them thinking about the busboy Ellen had lost, and how he'd killed all those people.

Maybe I should just shut up for a while. He was concentrating on his biscuits when one of Ellen's kids came by and dropped off a Sunday paper. Every table got one along with the brunch; it was a thing Trudy started a long time ago. It used to mean more before the Internet, but was still a nice touch. The *Times-Call* was sitting there on the white tablecloth in between them. The headlines were all about Joe Diddy, of course, and his secret life. His file photo from the State Capitol was there, right next to a shot of the Fishbowl. There was another picture there, too, that one of Tad Wellington waving his machine gun around.

"Lordy, would you look at that, John? It's that son-of-Satan again."

He'd been hoping Grandma wouldn't see the front page. In fact, he'd been getting ready to cover it up with his napkin. "Don't say that out loud, Grandma. He used to work here, you know."

"That's right, he did, didn't he? Well, I apologize. Every time I see that picture, though, it sets me off just a little. It's that look on his face that does it."

John knew what she meant. That look didn't set him off, exactly, but it did bother him. Grandma was still looking at it. She was moving her glasses around, trying to find the sweet spot in her bifocals. "That look of his is saying something," John observed, "I just don't know what it is."

Grandma was still staring at the grainy picture. "Well, I'll tell you what it says," she announced, after a while.

John sat there with his elbows propped on the table, waiting to hear what she would come out with. *I'm a minion of Mephistopheles?* John realized then that he was giving her one of those little smiles men and women his age were always giving old people and he made himself stop it, just stop.

She let go of her glasses and looked back up at him. "What it says, John, is 'this is my time.'"

#

This is my time. His time for what, though? That's what John kept wondering after he dropped Grandma off at the Center. His time to go crazy, to shoot nineteen people? He would have asked Grandma what she meant by that, exactly, except he didn't want to spoil any more of their brunch by talking about anything ugly. Life was way too short for that.

This is my time. John didn't really know where he was going; he was just driving around. But after a while he found himself at the Division Street Mall. He parked his car and got out and started walking. The mess Wellington had made of the place had pretty much been cleaned up now. Business was good again, even at DeAngelo's. You couldn't tell that anything bad had ever happened here, unless you knew where to look. There were still a few bullet holes in the walls of some of the buildings. One parking meter that had been shot up was still broken, and somebody was using that as an excuse to leave his car there for free.

This is my time. What the hell did that mean? Wellington's fifteen minutes of fame, maybe. His moment on center stage. John thought about Grandma, moving her bifocals around. Life was like that: there was this moment when you were in focus but then, before you really knew what was happening, you'd moved off to the blurry edge again. He thought about his own time, wondering if it was over already. He wasn't a young man anymore. Ham's time was still coming, his whole life was ahead of him, but what about John's? He sat down on one of the green mall benches and watched people go by.

Grandma was always telling him he needed to meet somebody, and he knew that was probably true; he just didn't know how to go about it. He didn't much care for the whole bar scene; that was too much like going to work. Maybe he could find somebody online? Get out of town. That was like bobbing for apples with your eyes closed, in a tank of dirty water. Grandma kept telling him he should go to church, that he'd meet a nice girl there, but he couldn't seem to bring himself to do that, either. He thought of himself as a spiritual person, but he couldn't stand organized religion anymore. There was too much human bullshit in it. Every time he saw pictures from the Hubble telescope, he knew there either had to be some kind of God or he was too much of an insignificant piss-ant to even have the right to worry about it. He wasn't sure if that was a comfort or not.

Sure, he'd like to meet somebody. It had been a lot of years since Jenny. You would have thought he'd be ready by now, but when it came right down to it, it seemed like he never quite was. He remembered then that he never had asked Hambone whether he should pick him up, or if Mick's folks would be giving him a ride home. He took out his cell. It was turned off.

Damn. He tried never to let that happen when he and Ham were apart. You never knew what kind of emergency might come up. As soon as he turned it back on it started beeping at him. He had a voice message. He went to his mailbox, hoping Ham wasn't in trouble, hoping it wasn't the Center calling about Grandma. It wasn't either one. It was Hotwire. What the hell did *he* want?

"Umm, yeah, Boss, it's me."

Didn't even leave his damned name, just figured John would know who it was. And he did, but only because the voice sounded like a lovesick weasel's.

"Look, I think I might have something for you, man, you know, like you asked me? Umm, yeah, that's it. So maybe you could meet me tonight down at the Fairgrounds? How about eight? At the Ferris Wheel?"

Christ. He probably just had a craving for some cotton candy! You never knew, though; maybe he'd actually dug up something useful this time. John got up from the bench and headed back towards his car. There was one good thing about that call, at least. He wasn't feeling so sorry for himself anymore. He figured things could always be worse. He could be Hotwire.

Chapter 7

John figured he'd go home and catch one of the afternoon games on TV. On the way he called Ham. It took a while for him to pick up and when he finally did he sounded a little out of it. "Hey, Dad, what's up?"

A lot of things went through John's mind. Were he and Mick making out? Or doing drugs? Were her parents even home? In the end he did what you have to do a lot of when you're a parent: he didn't ask and hoped for the best. At some point you just had to trust your kid and hope you'd raised him right. Not to say that was easy, especially when he remembered all the things he'd done at that age! "We never did talk about how you were getting home, so I wanted to get that straight."

"I was going to call you, Dad. Mick's parents want me to stay for dinner. And they want to take us over to the carnival at Seaside afterwards. Any chance you could pick me up there?"

John didn't say anything at first and Ham probably thought he was pissed. He wasn't. He was just trying to figure out how all this could work, what with him meeting Hotwire there already. What if Mick or her parents saw him talking to the weasel? Did that matter? What if the weasel saw him there with his son? He didn't want Leroy Miller to even have a peek into his personal life!

"Dad?"

"I'm still here. Sorry, Hambone. I guess I could pick you up. What time?"

"Ten?"

He said that like he already knew it wouldn't fly. It didn't. After the night John had just had, he wanted to turn in early. "Make it nine. You've got school tomorrow."

"OK. Where do you want me to meet you, at the Ferris Wheel?"

Hell, no. Not with him meeting Hotwire there! "Make it the roller coaster."

"Which one?"

"El Diablo."

After he hung up, John wondered if this wasn't all a mistake, if he wasn't letting work and home get too close together. Ever since Jenny he'd tried to be careful about that, but it was hard to keep those two streams from ever crossing when they weren't all that far apart to begin with.

He followed the one stream back to his place. It felt empty without Ham there, even though they didn't interact a whole lot these days. Just having him around was worth something, though. Actually, it was worth everything. Was this what it was going to feel like all the time, once Ham went off to college? He would, one of these days. John knew that, and knew the day wasn't all that far off. He popped a Bilge Light and turned on the tube. The Braves were at the Marlins. He sat down on the couch and watched for a while. Top of the fourth, score tied, two men on base, one out. He should have just stayed there with his chips and beer, and the sun shining in through the window finally after an overcast morning, but turns out he couldn't leave well enough alone. It was just too good of an opportunity. He went upstairs to do one of his drug checks in Ham's room.

John always felt a little guilty for doing that, but it was like he couldn't help it. Blame it on Jenny. He'd trusted her. For years he thought she was clean and looked the other way while she was practically waving a syringe in his face. After she OD'd, he wished he'd been less of a husband and more of a cop; he wished he'd listened to that part of him that wasn't head-over-heels for her. He trusted Ham. He just didn't want to ever find himself in that spot again, in that place where you wake up one day to find that everything you care about is gone, knowing that you might have stopped it from happening if you'd been willing to man up a little. Still, he hesitated for a second there on the landing before pushing open the door. He didn't feel good about poking his nose into his son's private business.

The place looked like it had been bulldozed. In that way, at least,

Ham was your typical teenage boy. John tried flicking on the lights only to find they were out. He went into handyman mode and was going to replace the bulbs until he looked up and saw that they'd been unscrewed. What the hell was *that* all about? Maybe he liked pretending his room was his man-cave. John went over to the window and opened the blinds to let some light in. Where to even get started? He almost said to hell with it right then; it was easier to trust Ham than to try and dig through his mess. In the end, though, he decided to at least have a quick look in the chest-of-drawers.

Nothing. Nothing except—Jesus Christ, the women's underwear was still there. He stood looking at all that black lace for a minute, afraid to even think what it meant. Call him crazy, but just once he'd like to go through Ham's stuff and find a pack of condoms. What if it turned out his son was a cross-dresser? Would that really matter? It shouldn't, it didn't, he'd still be the same person, but John couldn't help feeling a little let-down. Why was that? Was he even more old-fashioned than he thought he was? Maybe. Maybe without knowing it he'd been hoping to have grandkids someday? John liked to think he was a tolerant man. Live and let live and all that. There were all kinds of people in the world and as long as they led stand-up lives, he didn't really care. At least he thought he didn't. At least that's what he'd always told himself. Did he really mean that or was he as much a hypocrite as Congressman Diddy?

John shut the blinds and stepped out of Ham's room and closed the door behind him. It was hard knowing when to push and when to just look the other way. What was he feeling so damned depressed about, though? He hadn't seen any evidence that his son was taking drugs. That was what really mattered, wasn't it? The rest wasn't any of his business. He went back downstairs and sat on the couch and tried to pick up the thread of the game. But it was like he didn't care who won anymore.

#

What do you wear for *this* occasion, John asked himself. You're meeting the lamest snitch in the city but you might also bump into—for the first time ever—the parents of your teenager's girlfriend. Or boyfriend, or just friend, or whatever Mick Devereaux was to Ham. In the end he just left on the Sunday suit he'd worn to please Grandma, and had never thought to change out of. He didn't want Leroy Miller to know what he usually wore on his day off anyway, to see him in jeans and a t-shirt. The weasel might start to get the idea that John didn't own him.

The Fairgrounds at Seaside. It wasn't as busy this time of year as it was in the summer, but still drew a pretty good crowd at night, on the weekend. John parked his car and wandered along the Midway. He was a good twenty minutes early. This place always reminded him of when he was a kid, even though it hadn't been built until he was on this side of thirty. It was like they took all the different parts of his childhood and stuck them together. There was the sound of waves in the dark. There were the colored lights of the Ferris Wheel and the Zipper and El Diablo, burned onto a clear night sky. There was the smell of popcorn. He walked along through the crowd, taking everything in. The carnies were there, undressing with their eyes every teenage girl who walked by in a halter top. A pickpocket was watching the parents who were watching their kids up on the rides, waiting for the right time to make his move. It was all part of the thrill, though, that seamy side of the Midway. The carnival, for a kid, was Life; it was everything that was just ahead you, everything that was out there waiting for you, and you knew going in that it wouldn't always be safe, or pretty.

Up ahead was the Ferris Wheel. It was John's favorite ride now, though it hadn't always been. When he was a young man he'd liked the coasters and the Tilt-a-Whirl better: anything that was fast and would sling him around a little. These days, though, he'd just as soon take that slow roll over the top of the wheel, with its chance to look out over the Fairgrounds and the sea and the city. These days his favorite thing was to stop up there with the breeze blowing and the cradle rocking and happy sounds drifting up at him from somewhere down below. It was like Time stood still for a while. John was looking up at the wheel with a crowd of other parents, acting like he had a kid up there, too, when a whiny weasel-voice reminded him that he'd come here for a different reason.

"Hey, Boss."

John turned around. It was Hotwire, all right, but something about him seemed different. Not his clothes. He was still wearing a dirty black Metallica t-shirt, maybe even the same one John had seen him in the last time at Kim's, that one with lots of skulls on it. His dirty white-blonde hair was blowing around in the night breeze coming in off the Gulf. "Hey."

Hotwire came up and stood beside him. They were both looking up at the wheel. "What've you got for me?" John asked, after a while.

Nervous: that's what it was. Hotwire seemed nervous. John wondered why.

"That's what I was about to ask you," snickered Leroy.

"I asked you first." That was cop-speak for *you tell me what information you've got and I'll tell you if it's worth anything.*

Leroy's eyes were darting around. The Ferris Wheel stopped to let somebody off, and take someone else on. After a while Hotwire must have figured out that he didn't have any leverage. "You asked me to find out if there was anything new on the street. Well, there is."

John lifted an eyebrow. He wasn't sure which thing surprised him the most: that maybe Leroy was about to give him some useful information for a change, or that the weasel hadn't tried to hit him up for a corndog first. "Yeah? Where's it coming from, Mexico?"

"Don't know." John slipped him a twenty and he took it, but then said "Don't know" again. John thought about taking it back.

"What the hell *do* you know, then?"

Hotwire sniffled. Did he have a cold or was he back using blow? "It hasn't been around long," he said. "I hear it has a real good front end but a real bad back end." All the time that he was talking he kept looking around, like maybe he was afraid of something. Or someone.

"I'll say it has a bad back end, considering the two people we think may have used it are both in a drawer out at Dayton." But John figured that was worth another twenty. "What do they call this shit?" The smell of funnel cakes came wafting by. Talk about something that had a good front end and a real bad back end!

"Must."

"Must?"

"That's what I said, yeah."

John chewed on that for a while. He'd never heard of it. Must like in musty-moldy, or must like in junkies must have it? They were talking illegal drugs here, so he thought he knew the answer to that one. "Anything else?" Then he froze. Hambone and Mick were coming towards them.

He'd hoped to avoid anything like this. Maybe they wouldn't see him? Christ, they *had* seen him. They were waving. There was nothing else to do but wave back. They were coming this way. Was that a skirt Mick was wearing? It wasn't even black; it was denim. She looked almost cute, if you forgot about the heavy eye makeup and dog collar. Ham still looked the way he did when John dropped him off: a cross between a pharaoh and a funeral home director. But she looked real cute. How the hell was he going to introduce them to Hotwire, though? He turned around to tell Leroy to get lost but the weasel wasn't there anymore; he'd run away like a cockroach in the kitchen when you turn the lights on. John was so grateful he would have given him another twenty if he could have.

"Hello, Mr. Briggs."

"Hi, Mick, how are you?"

"Hey, Dad, I thought we weren't meeting till nine?"

"We are, at the Diablo. I just got here a little early and thought I'd walk around. Don't you kids mind me." Ham would have taken him up on that and run off, but Mick seemed like she wanted to talk. John was starting to like her. She either cared what he thought or at least pretended to real well, well enough that maybe it didn't matter.

She chatted with him for a minute then the two of them got in line for the Ferris Wheel, and John wandered off towards the Octopus.

He was thinking again about what Hotwire had told him. Must? That wasn't anything he'd ever heard of before. Why was it called that, what did it mean? Must kill, must have Mary Witherspoon's tits, must have more of whatever this is that's making me feel like I'm king of the world?

John was wondering, too, what had happened to Hotwire. He didn't think he was coming back. Leroy hadn't been his usual asshole self, and that kind of worried him. Usually Hotwire was too much of a scrawny little punk to be afraid of anything, but just now he'd looked like he thought somebody might be after him. As John watched, the Octopus lifted off in front of him. It started spinning around. The kids in the pods at the ends of its arms started screaming.

#

Mr. and Mrs. Devereaux—Hank and Donna, they wanted John to call them—were nice enough people. Accountants, just like Ham said. Hank was about John's age, balding and overweight, which made John feel a little better about himself. He was carrying around a few extra pounds of his own, but at least he still had a full head of hair. Donna Devereaux was a helicopter mom, which was all right with John; in his opinion there were too many people out there these days who just didn't give a damn.

"We think the world of Hamilton," she said and then he liked her even better. How could you not take a shine to somebody who thought your son was a stand-up guy?

Now that John knew for sure Mick was a girl it was easy to tell her mom that she was a sweetheart, and mean it. They had a nice conversation there, under the scaffolding of El Diablo, though every now and then they had to repeat themselves when the roller coaster thundered by on the tracks overhead.

The only thing that kept nagging at John while they talked was that meeting he'd had with Hotwire over at the Ferris Wheel. He kept thinking about what the weasel had told him, that there was some new drug called "Must" out there on the street. He kept thinking about how those two kids who might have tried it were both on their way to the boneyard now, along with a whole lot of other people. That was the real scary part: all those other people. If junkies wanted to kill themselves with this shit, well that was one thing, but it was something else altogether if were going to drag dozens of innocent bystanders down to hell with them. If Must really was the cause of what happened at the Fishbowl, and down on Division Street, then Gulfport might be in for real trouble. It wouldn't take too much of that to turn his city into a war zone.

Chapter 8

Marianne Harding had known John Briggs for three years and had carried a torch for him for two of them. When they first met she was caught up in a bad marriage and a meth habit, and John helped her out of both of them. Her soon-to-be-ex was a Samoan football player named Leti Tulafono, or at least he used to be a football player, and it was his fault she got mixed up with meth to begin with. She'd never cared much about drugs one way or the other before she met him. Except in high school when she smoked pot for a while just to fit in with her circle of friends, creative types who wrote poems about Death and Love and Lovely Death and Deathly Love. She'd written that kind of crap, too, back then.

Those poems got a little too real, though, after she moved to the Gulf from Indiana and married Leti. What had she ever seen in him anyway? Maybe nothing. Maybe it was all about what he'd seen in her. He wanted her, or at least said he did, and she'd been flattered by that, probably because no one had ever really wanted her before. And he wasn't the kind of guy who would take no for an answer. He kept coming at you. Being married to him might have been all right if things had stayed the way they were that first year—Leti had his good points, like most people—but along about their anniversary he started coming home drunk, and beating her. That's when she first started taking pills, for the pain. And washing them down sometimes with Southern Comfort. And then one night Leti did what he did to Pearl.

Pearl was the white Persian cat Marianne had found on the street out in front of their apartment. Leti wasn't happy about having Pearl in the house, but he let Marianne keep her anyway. He let Marianne keep her and she felt better about things for a while. When she got home at night from the Quick & Ready and Leti wasn't there, at least she had Pearl to keep her company. When Leti came home drunk and angry, she could take Pearl into the kitchen and talk to her. Or hide away with her, upstairs.

But then one night . . . One night Leti had come home drunk again. He was sitting in the living room in his favorite chair. He was watching the game. It always meant things were bad when he watched the game. It meant he was remembering things he'd said he didn't want to remember. Marianne wondered: what kind of things? She and Pearl were in the kitchen, hiding out. They were talking. And then for some reason Pearl jumped down from the table and ran out of the kitchen, into the living room. Marianne ran after her, tried to stop her. But by the time she got to the doorway it was too late. Pearl was already there, on the floor, in between Leti's legs. She was rubbing up against his blue jeans, purring.

"Shut the fuck up, cat," he said.

Why did Pearl even like Leti? He hated her. Couldn't she tell? She kept rubbing up against his leg. She kept saying meow. Leti was drinking a bottle of whiskey. He was watching the game. Once he said "stupid son-of-a-bitch" to somebody on the screen. Pearl said meow. Leti kicked her out of the way, just a little push really.

"Pearl!" whispered Marianne.

The cat was too dumb to listen. Why did she like Leti anyway? Why did she want to play with him tonight of all nights, when he was drunk and angry?

"Fucking cat." Leti went back to the game.

Marianne kept trying to coax Pearl back to the kitchen. Pearl wouldn't come. She went back under Leti's legs. And then she jumped up onto his lap.

"Get away from me, fucking cat!" Leti swatted at her with one of those big hands of his. And Pearl went flying across the room, screeching. She hit the wall. Leti hadn't meant to kill Pearl. At least Marianne didn't think so. But when Pearl hit the wall it broke her neck. And Leti didn't even apologize. He hadn't meant to kill Pearl, but he did. And he didn't even apologize. He didn't even act like he'd done anything wrong. He acted like Marianne had. It was her fault for taking in the stupid cat. It was her fault for not keeping Pearl out of his way.

Marianne had never talked back to Leti but she talked back to him now. And he hit her, just the way he'd hit Pearl. He threw her against the wall. He didn't say he was sorry for that, either, not even the next day when he was sober again. Instead, he called her a fucking bitch. He did things to her that she didn't want him to do anymore. Marianne took Pearl's body and buried it in the flower bed in front of their apartment. She cried but then after a while she didn't care anymore. She didn't care about Leti and she didn't care about herself and she didn't care about their lives together anymore. That night she smoked Meth, for the first time. She didn't care anymore.

#

John Briggs saved her life; she had no doubt about that. He busted her and took her away from it all: away from the Meth, away from Leti, away from the dark cloud that had settled over her like . . . like Sylvia Plath's bell jar. Sylvia Plath was her favorite poet, in high school. She still was. Marianne had been a disciple from the moment she'd read the first line of the *Mad Girl's Love Song*: "I shut my eyes and all the world drops dead." Was that what she'd been trying to do with the Meth: close her eyes and kill the world that she hated now? Turns out it didn't work quite that way. Seems like the world just kept on coming at you. There was only one way to *really* get away from it. That's what Sylvia Plath must have finally figured out, too. That must have been why she stuck her head in an oven. Marianne might have gotten to that point, too, if it hadn't been for John Briggs.

What did he ever do for her anyway? That's what her friends wanted to know. *Put you in the slammer, that's all.* But he'd come by to see her in that slammer, a couple of times a week, for a year. A *year*. What other cop would have done that? What other man? Once she learned that his wife had died of an overdose, she figured it probably had something to do with that, that he was probably trying to save her to make up for having lost his Jenny. Jenny: she learned that name from somebody else; John never mentioned her. He wasn't much of a talker. But he'd ask her how she was doing, at least, which was more than Leti had ever done. He would ask her if she needed anything. And he pulled some strings to get her time reduced, to get her out from behind bars and into a halfway house. At least that was what she would always believe. He wouldn't admit it, swore he didn't have anything to do with it, but Marianne knew different. He was just modest, the way a man ought to be, not a big bag of brag like Leti Tulafono.

Leti. The good thing about her being in jail for a year (besides seeing John Briggs twice a week) was that she didn't have to see her husband.

That she was safe from her husband. That she could start divorce proceedings against him without having to be afraid. Leti was a scary man, but he couldn't reach her in prison. She filed for divorce. He didn't answer. No one could find him. John thought maybe he'd left town. But in Marianne's mind, she was free. At least that's what she thought at first, after she got out of jail. She was free in more ways than one. But then Leti showed up again. Something about her being clean, and interested in somebody else, must have got his attention. He started coming around again, pretending she still belonged to him. She kept on telling him she didn't and that kept on making him mad. And then he got even madder. She took out a restraining order. She changed where she lived, two or three times. That would work for a while.

During those whiles, when Leti wasn't after her, Marianne would try her best to figure out how to stay in touch with John Briggs. One day he gave her the answer himself. After the parole board was done, he came to her and asked if she'd consider working for him, undercover. She still had connections to the drug scene. There were still people out there who knew her as a junkie. She asked him: wasn't he afraid that she might go back to being one again, that she might go back on Glass? He looked at her with those big soft brown eyes of his, shook his head and said "no." And it was then that she knew two things better than she'd ever known anything before: that she'd be straight for life, and that she was in love with him.

"We both know there's only one reason why you ever went down that road," John had said to her, solemnly, taking her hands in his, "and I'm going to make sure that reason stays the hell away from you."

That was easier said than done. Leti wasn't anybody you'd ever want to be on the bad side of. He was six-foot-three and built like a truck, and had a temper that tended to boil over in a hurry. Even now, two years after their divorce became final, Marianne was still afraid of him. Even though she hadn't seen him in a good six months (that was part of what had made it a good six months), she knew he wasn't really gone from her life. She'd come to the conclusion that he never would be. He'd disappear for a while, sure, but sooner or later he'd turn up again—usually outside the Quick & Ready, watching her through the glass. That was just how she felt, sometimes: like she was under glass. Just as long as that glass didn't turn into the bell jar again. Just as long as she didn't find herself walking down that same dark road. That was what she was afraid of, even more than she was afraid of Leti Tulafono.

If John Briggs couldn't keep Leti away from her, though, and neither could a judge, could anyone? It didn't seem like it. Marianne kept hoping he'd eventually fall for some other girl, that he'd forget her, but one of the good and bad things about Leti was that he latched onto people. It didn't matter whether he loved or hated you; either way he never would let go. So she had no doubt, even this time, that he'd show up again sooner or later. Probably sooner, because it was already six months later, six months since she'd last seen him looking in at her through the window at the convenience store.

What were you going to do, though? One of two things. You could worry about it all the time, live your life in fear, or you could go on about your business. Every morning she got up and made a conscious decision to do the one, not the other. To put in her hours at the Quick & Ready. To use the contacts she still had in what John Briggs called "the Underworld" to get information for him whenever she could. Whenever he needed it.

He was the one who came up with the idea of planting her inside of a high school for the first job she did for him; he said she looked young enough that she could easily get away with it. She couldn't decide if she was pleased by that or not. On the one hand what woman didn't like being told she looked younger than she really was, especially after she'd been through what Marianne had been through? On the other hand, it made it seem like there was even more of a gap in between their ages. How old was he anyway? Forty? Forty-five? Either way he didn't look it with that full head of brown hair that she'd like to get her fingers into.

So the two of them were about fifteen years apart. Not enough to matter, really. She'd known plenty of women whose husbands were that much older than they were. But if he really thought of her as seventeen, that would make her young enough to be his daughter! She told him she'd do it anyway, just so long as he promised not to treat her like a high-schooler. Just so long as he would remember that she was a grown woman. She could have said that a lot of different ways; it seemed as though the way she did say it made him a little uncomfortable. After that it was like he was making an effort to be all business. Marianne took note of that and backed off, biding her time.

She sniffed out a dope ring for him at Palmer High. She was able to personally give him the good news that his son wasn't involved. That might have been the happiest day of her life. The happiest one in a while, anyway. She was hoping her happiest days were still ahead of her, though, including the one when John Briggs would finally see her as something more than a snitch. As something more than a one-time junkie. In the meantime this still seemed like the best way to stay close to him, to stay on his mind: help him out however she could, whenever he needed it. And judging by the look on his face when she met him down on The Ribbon, it sure seemed like he needed it now.

Chapter 9

So John thought there might be something new on the street, and that it might be coming from Mexico. Marianne figured that meant it was probably coming across the Gulf on a boat. So many Minutemen were patrolling the border these days, looking for illegal immigrants, that they were disrupting the pipeline. At least that's what she was hearing from some of her customers at the Quick & Ready, the ones that came in late at night. Which meant that if there was a new drug out there, the place to look for it might be down at the docks.

She'd been there plenty of times after she'd run away from Leti Tulafono, selling herself so she'd have money to buy drugs. She'd always had plenty of customers. She wasn't sure why; John had shown her pictures of how she'd looked back then, just to give her motivation to try and go straight, and no lie she'd looked like a character out of the Addams Family. Like somebody who hadn't slept in about three lifetimes. Some of those dock hands must've been necrophiliacs to have wanted her. There was one guy she met, though, who was a human being. His name was Jimenez and he had a thing for her. Not in that sleep-with-the-dead kind of way; he treated her like he thought she might be his daughter. She always thought it was because she had the same name as his ship. The *Mariana*: that much she remembered, though most of everything else from that time was buried under a black fog that had built up inside the bell jar.

It was easy enough to find out which ships were coming into port these days, and when; easy enough to find out that the *Mariana* was still making her every-other-Tuesday run out of Veracruz. That it was still bringing in sugar, officially. Seems like it would have been easy to slip illegal drugs into that kind of cargo, but she had a hard time believing that Captain Jimenez would get mixed up in something like that. Maybe he would, though. Maybe he had been, even back then. Marianne had been too strung out at the time to notice, or care. She'd take the money Jimenez would give her so she wouldn't have to sell herself at the docks, then go right back into town and pay to have Glass rape what was left of her. Glass: the drug sounded so clear, so clean, so pure. But it lowered itself onto you and suffocated you. It closed you into a tight little space where finally you couldn't breathe anymore. You could look through it and still see the world, still see life going on all around you, without you, but there wasn't any way out of it. It was the bell jar.

Crystal, Ice, Glass: they had such pretty names for it. Like it was something you might buy for yourself at the jewelry store. Like something you might wear to a party where all the men would be looking at you. Turns out it was the necklace you hanged yourself with, the one they would bury you in along with your smeared eye makeup and broken teeth, and the scars on all your faces, all those different faces you'd shown to different people just to get what you wanted. And there was only one thing you wanted: more Meth.

Just remembering all that now shook Marianne to the core, but there didn't seem to be any way of *not* remembering it, down here at the docks. She strolled across the weathered boards in the afternoon sun, listening to the sea gulls that were squawking and flying all around her head. She could hear wood creaking as the boats moved up and down on the water, lying there at anchor. Things were quiet. A few stevedores were unloading one ship, but most of that work took place in the morning. She counted off the numbered piers as she walked past: three, four, five. It was six she was looking for. That's where the *Mariana* ought to be anchored. It was. Was Jimenez still her captain? Marianne's hair was tucked up inside a baseball cap and she was wearing frumpy Atlanta Braves' gear—not so much because she was trying to hide that she was a woman as that she didn't want anyone to recognize her. It had been two years but there might still be a few lowlifes around who could. She put a hand on the Saturday Night Special she'd stuffed into one of the pockets of her windbreaker.

Pier Six. The *Mariana* looked pretty much the way Marianne

remembered her, though maybe she had a new coat of paint. There were little crystals of light sparkling their way out towards the setting sun. There was a sailor up top, cleaning the deck. She called out to him:

"*Hóla! Está aquí Capitan Jimenez?*" She never had learned a lot of Spanish; a whore didn't need to say much in any language. A drug addict, either. *You want it?* and *I need it.* That's about all there was.

"*Sí, señorita.*" The deckhand motioned for her to come up. She climbed the gangplank. A few minutes later she was in the wheelhouse with Captain Jimenez. Neither one of them much recognized the other.

"May I assist you, *señorita?*" He was an older man now, just like he was then, but she hadn't really remembered his face. It was a nice face, a gentle face, but she didn't remember it.

"I have the same name as your ship."

He gave her a funny look. She wasn't sure what it meant. "Mariana?"

"Marianne, yes. Do you remember me?"

He shook his head. "No, senorita. I am sorry if I should."

If she'd had a picture of Morticia Addams to show him, he might. "You helped me out once, no lots of times, a long time ago. I'm hoping you can help me out again now."

A light went on in his warm, dark eyes. "*Ah, Mariana! Sí, sí. Yo recuerdo!*"

He seemed happy to see her looking so well. She wondered if when she'd stopped coming around, he'd assumed she was dead. In a way that was true. Dead and then reborn, in the slammer. All thanks to John Briggs. She smiled at Jimenez. "I'm hoping you can help me out again now," she said, repeating herself. "I'm trying to . . ." What *was* she trying to do anyway? Gather information. Not for the police, though; she couldn't tell Jimenez that. That could be unhealthy, for an informant. And he might just clam up on her, too. No, what she had to tell him was . . . She didn't really want to do that, though. Here he was all happy that she looked so good, that she was finally clean and sober, and she was going to have to let him down. The way she'd let so many other people down before, herself included.

"I'm looking for drugs." His eyes clouded over. Her heart clouded over then, too. In a way saying those words was like going back there, back to that time in her life when she was continually strung out, when she was a junkie. Out of the corner of her eyes, she could see the bell jar. It was always there but it had been years since it had come this close. She felt her chest tighten.

Jimenez was shaking his head. "I no longer engage in such practices, Mariana."

Did that mean he had, back then? That he hadn't been so pure after all? None of that made her feel any better about what she was doing. It made her feel dirty, all over again. She wished she hadn't promised John Briggs she would do this. She wished he hadn't asked her to. "I don't either . . . Miguel." His first name had just come to her, out of the blue. She hadn't remembered that she'd ever known it. "*Tengo una amiga . . .*"

His eyes turned cold. Apparently, even in Spanish that line sounded like bullshit. She changed the story around. "I have a friend who is hooked on some new drug that's making the rounds. I don't even know what it is. I'm trying to find out, though, so I can help her. I know where she's headed because I've been there and I don't want her taking that trip."

His eyes went back to being soft again. He was buying it. Probably because he wanted to. She felt bad about that, about lying to him, but in a way it *wasn't* really lying, was it? She and John did want to help people out, just not any one person in particular. Yet. If this drug *was* out there and use of it spread, it wouldn't be long before she *would* know someone, given the people she knew. How bad was this shit, anyway? John had seemed like he was worried. When she'd asked him if there was a connection to what happened down on Division Street, he wouldn't say anything. But the way his body moved when she asked him made her think she might have hit a nerve.

Jimenez was looking at her, sizing her up. Was he wondering if she was working for the cops? Maybe the "I have a friend" speech was sounding lame to him in a different way now—not that she really wanted the drugs for herself but that she was a plant. If he wasn't still mixed up in the drug trade, though, why would he care? She felt a chill. What if she'd wandered blindly into the heart of the operation, what if Jimenez himself was one of those smuggling in the new drug? Finally, he said something.

"I . . . I have heard only rumors."

Now Marianne was the one thinking: *bullshit.* He'd heard more than that! He was just trying to make sure he stayed out at the edge of this thing, that he didn't get involved in it. "What have you heard, *Capitan*?"

He was looking around the wheelhouse like he thought there might be somebody in there with them, hiding. Marianne noticed through the windows that the sun was going down. *Shit*. The plan was to get in and out before dark. She didn't want to be anywhere near here after nightfall. She had too many bad memories from the old days, when she was a dock whore. A junkie. One of the living dead. It felt good to run down the person she'd been back then because it helped keep that person in her place. And her place was somewhere far away from here. A place so far away that Marianne could never go back there. A place so far away it was on the other side of the Looking Glass. It was in *there*, inside the bell jar.

"A few months ago," Jimenez was saying, still sizing her up, no doubt still wondering who or what she really was, "there was a strange shipment of something. I heard rumors only. Some of my fellow captains . . ." He looked around again for that imaginary eavesdropper. *Was* he imaginary, though? There were plenty of places inside the wheelhouse where somebody could hide. She shook it off. His paranoia was spilling over onto her now. "Some of my fellow captains were concerned that they might have, how do you say, competition?"

"They were running drugs?"

He looked around the wheelhouse. "They were smuggling, yes. I was not," he hastened to add.

"Of course." She waited for a minute but when he didn't say anything else, she tried priming the pump. "Were they selling the same stuff, is that why the captains were worried about competition? Or were they worried because they were seeing something new?"

Jimenez shifted his weight around. He was visibly uncomfortable. "I do not know if it was something new or not," he said. "There were rumors. I do know that what concerned the captains most was where the shipment was coming from. They were afraid there was a new source of competition for them."

Marianne's ears perked up. Now *that* was interesting. Where else might drugs be coming from besides Mexico? Even further south, maybe Honduras? "Where were those drugs coming from? Did anyone ever say?"

"Again, there were only rumors," said Jimenez. By now he must have figured out she was working for the cops. The questions she'd been asking weren't the questions of some addict's friend. They asked for too much detail. Why would a friend really care where the drugs were coming from?

Marianne was onto something now, though, something she could tell John Briggs. Something that might actually be of use to him. She had to press Jimenez some more. "What did those rumors say?" she asked him. "Where were these shipments coming from?"

Jimenez hesitated. Was that because he really shouldn't be telling her this, or because it was all just rumors and he didn't really believe it? "Africa," he finally said.

Africa? That sent Marianne for a loop. What was he talking about? Who would be bringing in drugs from there? It wasn't like it was right across the Gulf from here! That was more like halfway around the world, wasn't it?

"And now, Mariana, you must not ask any more questions," said Jimenez.

There was something in his voice that got her attention. It was getting dark outside. Suddenly she was feeling a little closed in, inside of the wheelhouse. It was like somebody had thrown a dark blanket over all those windows. "Right. I'd better be going."

Jimenez was looking at her. He seemed like he might be mulling something over. "Please, allow me to escort you."

Marianne hesitated. This man who had seemed so kindly back when she was a junkie, who had seemed so kindly up until now, suddenly seemed suspicious. He even looked different. Was that just because it was getting dark outside? He turned on an electric lamp inside the wheelhouse. It was suddenly very quiet. It must have been this same way before, with the ship's timbers creaking, with water sloshing against the hull outside, but it was like she was only noticing that now. Was it safer to let him escort her, or to leave here alone? Both sounded dangerous.

"All right." Better the captain she knew than the ones she didn't. The docks at night could be a scary place. There was a time when she had wandered everywhere, like she owned the wharf, like she was one of the bilge rats moving on and off of the ships unnoticed, on wires. In a way she had been one of them, one of those rats. She'd belonged. Well, she didn't belong now. Not anymore. Now the place made her nervous. She should never have come back here. When you've spent years climbing out of a well—or a jar—the last thing you should do is walk right up to the slippery edge of it again.

Jimenez led her out of the wheelhouse, onto the deck. It was not only getting dark but a little chilly. Or maybe that was just the mood she was in. There was a breeze coming in off the Gulf. The sailor she'd first seen when she came walking up was nowhere in sight. She tried to block it out, block everything out except for the information she had, these things she was going to tell John.

Yes, there is something out there. Jimenez hadn't confirmed that exactly, not in so many words, but she'd seen it in the way his eyes shifted.

And it's coming from Africa. He'd actually said that much. It wasn't just her reading things into his words, and expression. And the information was surprising, at least to her. Would John think so? She thought yes. She felt warm inside, just imagining herself telling him all this, feeling useful to him. She'd be his confidante, his right hand girl. Maybe he would think about her in a different way?

"Watch your step, Mariana, *por favor.*" Jimenez was leading her down the gangplank, in the dark. There was a bit of a moon rising now, a fat sliver. Clouds were passing in front of it. The docks would get darker then lighter then darker again, depending on those clouds and the moon.

They were down on the pier. "You have an automobile?" Jimenez was asking her.

"Yes." She nodded in that direction, down the docks.

"Come. I will make certain you reach it."

He seemed different in the dark. Maybe it was because she couldn't see his eyes. Those warm friendly eyes of his. Here he was just another man, one who had motives she couldn't see, didn't know. But it was either walk with him or walk off alone in the dark. If he'd even let her do that now.

"*Sí, gracias.*" Speaking Spanish to him was a conscious decision, a way of trying to connect with Jimenez, of trying to create even more of a bond between them. So much from the street was coming back to her now, all those things she'd learned, that she'd had to learn in order to survive. Whenever you could, you had to force others to see you as a human being. Not as a whore or a junkie, but as a real person. Someone named Marianne. That made it harder for them to toss you aside like a piece of trash.

They walked together down the dock, passing pier after pier. Five, four, three. The Gulf sloshed at them. The ships they passed creaked and groaned. She hadn't seen another soul since leaving the *Mariana* behind.

No one except Jimenez. And she was wondering now if he even had a soul. He was still who he was, in a way. He still smiled at her every now and then and when he did his white teeth glowed in the moonlight. She could no longer see his eyes, though. They were just wells of dark shadow, underneath the brim of his Captain's hat. She was shaking now, and it wasn't the cold. There was no damn cold. It was warm and she had on a Braves jacket. If only it could really do that for her, she thought: make her brave. The fingers of her right hand touched her gun.

She'd done the hard part already, though; she'd forced herself to come here again, to the docks. She'd made herself go and see the captain. She'd asked him questions she hadn't known she could ask. The worst was over. Now it was just a matter of getting back to her car, and leaving. And telling John what she'd found out. When? In the morning? She could call him on his cell. For that matter she could call him right now. She was tempted to, but that would mean stopping and she didn't want to do that, even for a minute.

She thought she heard something. Something that wasn't the Gulf sloshing, that wasn't a ship creaking as its weight shifted back and forth in the water. It wasn't Jimenez, either. In fact, he'd noticed it, too. He stopped. He stood there, listening. The cloud that had been in front of the moon passed on by, and now she could see the Captain's face again. He was frowning. "Come, *señorita*," he said, "let us hurry."

Yes. She was all for that, all for getting out of here as quickly as possible. They picked up the pace. Pier 2 was ahead. Just a little further now to the parking lot. She pictured herself getting her keys out, opening the door of her car. They were almost there. She pictured herself telling John Briggs what she had found out. She pictured him smiling at her. She pictured him reaching out with a hand to touch the side of her face. She saw those soft brown eyes of his.

"Wait." Jimenez had stopped again. She stopped, too, so suddenly that she ran into him. She stood there beside him, her breath coming fast. The moon was hidden again. Another cloud had moved in front of it.

"What is it?" asked Marianne.

"*No se,*" whispered Jimenez.

They stood there together, listening. The sloshing water. The creaking ships. Something that sounded to her like a footstep. *Shit.* Marianne stuck her hand inside of her Braves' jacket, looking for the

Saturday night special. She found it. She clutched it. She looked off to her right, then left. Nothing. She heard something else then, a gurgling sound. She turned towards Jimenez to ask him if he heard it, too. The cloud slid off the moon. And there was the Captain, eyes bulging, flailing in the air right beside her. It was like he was having a seizure. Like he was a marionette and somebody was jerking every one of his strings. Then she saw the long dark slash across his throat, the blood. He managed to gasp: "Run, Mariana!"

She ran. She turned and took off down the dock, forgetting about the gun that was still in her pocket. She ran into the dark. She crashed into something. Somebody. She couldn't tell who it was. He was wearing some kind of mask. He had his hands on her throat. She tried to scream but he had his hands on her throat. She wanted to pull out her gun but it was lost somewhere now, inside of the Braves jacket. She couldn't find it. She couldn't breathe. All the air had been sucked out of the bell jar. She couldn't find the gun. She couldn't scream. She shut her eyes, and the world dropped dead.

Chapter 10

Having stayed up so late the night before, John had expected to sleep like a rock, but instead he tossed and turned. He had too many things on his mind. About four in the morning one of those things—this new drug called "Must"—woke him up all the way. He went downstairs to the kitchen and fixed some coffee, then fired up his laptop. He sat down on the sofa in the den and called up Google, his late-night (or in this case, early-morning) friend. Searching the Internet, he'd decided a long time ago, was a lot like looking for something in Hambone's room: there was stuff everywhere and no real order to it and sometimes it was hard to know how to even get started. He thought about that for a minute, how to get started, then finally gave up and typed Must into the search box all by itself. He wasn't really expecting to catch anything that way, with a hook that simple, but it felt good to at least be casting a line.

WIKIPEDIA: **Must** *(from the Latin vinum mustum, "young wine") is freshly pressed fruit juice (usually grape juice) that contains the skins, seeds, and stems of the fruit.*

Well, he was pretty sure that wasn't what Hotwire was talking about. Enough wine could do bad things to you—he knew that much from personal experience—but he'd never heard of it turning anybody into a mass murderer before.

MUST - Management and Unions Serving Together.

Management and Unions: that sounded like a bad mix to John, like taking two drugs from that chart he and Tom used to have on their dorm room wall. But he was pretty sure that wasn't what he was looking for, either. Even when management and labor were at each other's throats they didn't usually kill each other.

DICTIONARY. MUST. "Must" is most commonly used to express certainty. It can also be used to express necessity or strong recommendation . . .

Hell, he knew what the word meant. You **must** be out of your mind to be sitting here in front of a computer screen at four in the morning. You **must** figure this out though, before somebody else goes berserk and gives the folks at Dayton even more business. They had all they could handle already.

NASA – Motivating Undergraduates in Science and Technology.
MUST awards scholarships and internships to undergraduates pursuing degrees in science, technology . . .

Christ. He didn't think this had anything to do with NASA, unless Must was coming from someplace one hell of a lot farther away than Mexico! Not a damned thing, then. That wasn't surprising. People who took this kind of shit probably weren't going to be posting to the web about it. They were too busy killing and raping and then getting blown up by a SWAT team. John leaned back on the couch and drank some more of his coffee. In the background, out of the dark, he could hear the refrigerator humming. The laptop kept humming at him, too. Then after a while he noticed a list of more searches at the bottom of the screen.

Searches related to MUST

Elephant must   *Must definition*

Must reads   *Must video*

Malnutrition universal screening tool

What the hell was "elephant must?" He wasn't looking for anything related to illegal drugs anymore; he was just hooked, like a lot of people were these days, on clicking one blue link after another. Something came up, though, that got his attention:

*Musth – Wikipedia, the free encyclopedia. Musth (alternatively spelled **must**) is a periodic condition in bull elephants, characterized by highly aggressive behavior . . .*

It was those last words, "highly aggressive behavior," that jumped out at him. If it hadn't been for that—and the fact that the sun still wasn't up yet—he might not have read on. But he did.

. . . accompanied by a large rise in reproductive hormones. However, whether this hormonal surge is the sole cause of musth, or merely a contributing factor, is unknown; scientific investigation of musth is greatly hindered because, during musth, even the most otherwise placid of elephants may try to kill human beings.

Well, that was kind of interesting. But it didn't have much to do with John's world, with kids going berserk in shopping malls and dance clubs. At least he didn't think it did. He shut the machine down. He flicked on the news. And that's when he found out that Marianne Harding had been found dead on the docks at Seaside.

#

"Why didn't anybody call me?"

Chief Horsebreaker was standing in John's office, leaning back against the closed door with his arms folded. "I'm sorry, John. I know she meant a lot to you."

Did she, though, really? Yeah, but not in the way most people in the department probably thought. There never had been anything going on between the two of them. But John felt responsible for her, all the same. He felt like he should have been looking out for her. And now she was dead, strangled on the docks east of Seaside. "Any idea who did it?" Christ, was that all he could say? It was the cop in him, he supposed, all those years of wanting to find out who was to blame and nail them. But right now that had kind of a hollow feel to it.

"Not yet." Horsebreaker was watching him closely. "What do you think she was doing down at the docks? That's not her usual turf, is it?"

"No." At least it hadn't been for two or three years, ever since she'd gone straight. Certainly, it wasn't any place he'd ever ask her to go back to.

"She was supposed to find out if there was anything new on the street," said John, feeling guilty and battered, "Maybe that trail led her out to Seaside, somehow." He kept seeing her flirty green eyes, kept thinking about the last time he'd been with her, out on The Ribbon.

"Do you think maybe she found something?" asked Horsebreaker.

John could see Rick, the intern, trying to peek in through the mini-blinds covering his window. Looking for the Chief, no doubt, so he could put in his daily quota of ass-kissing. "She might have." John told him what he'd heard from Hotwire, at the Fairgrounds.

Horsebreaker nodded, like he'd known all along that this was where they were headed. "And it's called 'Must'?"

"That's what Leroy said, yeah."

"Ever heard of it before?"

"Not until now." John kept thinking about what he'd read on the Internet that morning, about bull elephants and highly aggressive behavior, but he wasn't about to breathe a word of that to Horsebreaker. The Chief would think this thing with Marianne had really sent him over the edge, and it hadn't. He was feeling guilty about that. Her getting killed had shaken him up and he did feel sad about it, and responsible, but more than anything else he just felt numb. Was that what being a cop for twenty years did to you? Or just living in general? Whatever the reason, he didn't like it. If you forgot how to cry you might as well be in a drawer out at Dayton.

"What about the guy that was found dead with her?" asked John.

"Captain of one of the ships docked there, the *Mariana*. Don't know if that means anything or not."

"What's the connection between them?"

"Don't know."

What the hell was she doing down there? That was the question John wanted to ask next but it was basically the same one the Chief had already asked him. And he didn't like the answer that kept coming back at him: *Because I sent her there.* He hadn't really, though, had he? He'd never meant for her to go back to that world. Had he? All he'd asked her to do was to keep her eyes and ears open. Still . . . the docks used to be her turf. Where else did he think she'd go sniffing for drugs?

"Listen," said Horsebreaker, "if you need to take some time off . . ."

"No, I'm all right." John's head was spinning around and he tried to settle it down by focusing on something, anything. "Did we ever get a tox report on the guy at the Fishbowl?" At the moment he couldn't remember the kid's name. He must have heard it on TV a dozen times over the past few days, though mostly what the networks wanted to talk about was Congressman Diddy.

"Yeah. Little bit of alcohol in his bloodstream, but not enough to even keep him from driving himself home. Legally."

"Just like the other one, then." John was talking to himself more than he was to the Chief. "If there is something out there called Must, and these guys were taking it, why didn't it show up in their autopsies?" If he'd thought about it, he would have known the answer to that question without having to ask it.

"Because," said the Chief, "we don't even know what it is we're looking for."

#

Of course. How could the coroner check for something he'd never seen? Something he probably didn't even have a test for? John thought about that on his way out to the docks with Tom Etheridge. That was the Chief's idea, to pair him up with Tom; Horsebreaker didn't think he should be alone right now. John had tried to tell him he was OK, but now that he was sitting in Tom's car, watching the scenery go by, he wasn't so sure anymore. He felt sick to his stomach. He kept thinking about Marianne, and Must, and Hotwire. He kept remembering how scared Leroy had looked, last night at the Ferris Wheel. Maybe he had good reason to be. John wondered if he should tell Leroy what had happened to Marianne, just to make sure the little weasel knew that these Must dealers were playing for keeps, but after a while he decided he probably didn't need to. One thing about weasels: they might not know jack shit about anything else, but they did know how to take care of themselves.

"You OK?" asked Tom, after a while.

"Yeah, sure."

They parked at the docks. There were cops all over the place, still gathering evidence. Tom and John talked to one of them and got the details: seems Marianne had been strangled near a stack of crates on Pier 2, around eight or nine the night before.

Jesus, thought John; that was about the same time he was talking to Hank and Julie Devereaux, underneath the tracks of El Diablo! Somehow that made it all worse, knowing that he'd been out at Seaside, too, that he'd been right there going on with his life while hers was ending. It wasn't that he felt all that close to her, really, but he felt like he should have known something was wrong. Couldn't she have called him? Not with somebody's hands around her throat. He wished she would have called him earlier in the day, though, that she would have told him where she was going and what she was up to. If he'd known, he would have had one of his cops follow her. Hell, he'd have gone with her himself, if she'd asked him to!

John and Tom walked along the wharf together. "Why do you think she was here?" asked Tom. He knew Marianne, and that the docks weren't part of her turf. Officially, anyway.

John told him what he'd told the Chief: that he'd asked her to keep her eyes and ears open, to let him know if she heard anything about a new drug on the street. She must have heard something that led her out here, maybe that a shipment was coming in? From where would it have been coming, though? John and Tom checked the manifestoes of all the boats that had docked last night or this morning, knowing that it was probably a waste of time. It was. Who would put an illegal drug on their list of cargo? But at least it was something to do. It was better than standing around.

"What about this guy they found close by, with his throat cut?" asked Tom. He was looking through a report one of his cops had filed. "Jimenez. Ship captain. Do you suppose she'd come down here to meet him, or was he just at the wrong place at the wrong time?"

"Both," said John. He was trying to piece together what had happened. It seemed pretty obvious to him that Marianne had come down here looking for information. That maybe Jimenez had given her some. He wondered if he was somebody she knew from her past, from those days when she was a junkie? Whoever had killed her must have killed him, too, just a few minutes before or after.

"I've already asked my men to search his ship," said Tom, "You think we ought to have the rest of these searched as well?" There were six or seven others docked in the vicinity.

John was about to tell him not to bother but then wondered if that would sound cold, like he was willing to cut corners, maybe leave stones unturned. "Sure." Not that he thought they would find anything. All the ships that were docked here now would have been unloaded earlier in the day; any cargo, illegal or otherwise, would be in a warehouse by now. Or on the street.

The sun was beating down; it was going to be another hot day. At least there was a breeze coming in off the ocean. Gulls were wheeling and diving in the air up above him. One of Tom's boys in uniform came running up, out of breath.

"Yeah, what you got Simms?" asked Tom.

"Some guy wants to see you. Pronto. Name's telephone, or something like that."

"Telephone?" Tom looked puzzled. "Well, bring him over, I guess."

Telephone? That name sounded familiar. "Tulafono?" John asked Simms.

"Yeah, that's it."

"Shit, that's Marianne's ex," John told Tom. "He's a scary motherfucker."

Tom raised an eyebrow. "You think he might know something?"

"I doubt it. Well, maybe. He hates my guts, though. Thinks Marianne and I had something going on."

"Didn't you?"

"Don't tell me you believe that, too?"

"Not if you tell me otherwise."

"Otherwise," said John.

"That's good enough for me. It sounds like this guy Tulafono believes those stories, though. Do you want me to talk to him alone so he doesn't go off on you?"

John shook his head. "No, let's both go. If he knows anything he might let it slip out while he's shooting off his mouth at me."

#

Christ, he'd forgotten what a big guy Tulafono was, and how mad he could get. He was Samoan and had a neck as thick as the trunk of a palm tree. Long, crimpy hair that flowed free down his back. A face that looked like one of those Easter Island statues, with a mustache painted on it. He was a four-star football prospect out of high school until he got in with a bad crowd, until he started using. He played on the D-line, John seemed to recall. Tulafono was in a bad mood, as usual, one that got even worse as soon as he saw John.

"Briggs!" He practically screamed it. John was like a red cape flapping in front of him.

"Leti," John said, thinking maybe it might help if he used his first name, "I'm really sorry, man."

"You should be, cop asshole. You're the one that killed her!"

"Easy," said Tom.

Tulafono was holding back, at least for now, but John could tell he wanted to take him apart with his bare hands. He was breathing hard and his nostrils kept flaring and when John looked in his eyes it was like he wasn't all there. John wondered if he might be on something. Maybe, or maybe he just had too damned much testosterone for his own good. Leti was delusional; John knew that much about him. Before this, he still believed Marianne might come back to him, even though she'd said "no" ten thousand times. He thought that if it wasn't for John, he'd be back in the picture. The truth was, when he and Marianne were married, he beat her. The truth was she was flat-out afraid of him. But now that she was dead it was even easier for Tulafono to believe whatever he wanted to believe about her.

"I'm sorry, Leti," John said again, "I really . . ."

"Son-of-a-whore!" He charged at John.

Tom motioned to a few of his guys. They were coming but maybe not fast enough. Tulafono was so close now John could see white flecks of spit coming out of his mouth. It was like he had rabies.

"Bastard!" Tulafono's hands were up in the air, out in front of him. He was closing in. Then he saw that Tom had his gun out.

"Easy."

"You're not going to shoot me with that, cop asshole!"

Tom shot him, in his right leg. Tulafono screamed but kept coming anyway. There was blood on the docks. Tulafono kept coming. That's when four cops tackled him, which was a good thing because Tom was just about to shoot him again, in a body part with a higher profile.

"Son-of-a-whore!" Leti was fighting them, the four cops, and Christ, he was winning. Tom and John just stood there watching, like they couldn't believe what they were seeing. One of Tom's guys went flying.

Another one had been hit hard in the face; he was sitting down on the docks in a daze, with his nose bleeding.

"We need a fucking Taser," said Tom. He still had his gun out but John knew he didn't want to use it. Couldn't, with his guys all around. He might hit one of them. But if Tulafono was to break free and come at them again . . .

It didn't get that far. One of the officers hit Leti over the head with a nightstick and dropped him like a rock. He was lying there on the wharf, blood streaming out of both his right leg and the back of his head. Even though he'd been knocked out cold, it looked like he was still seething.

"Shit!" said Tom, taking a deep breath, "The guy is like a goddamned rampaging elephant!"

Chapter 11

They took Tulafono away in an ambulance, in handcuffs. "You were right," Tom said with a whistle, "That *is* one scary motherfucker!"

"Took too many steroids in high school," John said, but he was thinking about another drug, about Must again, especially after Etheridge had compared Leti to a rampaging elephant. That connection didn't make any sense, though. He had to let go of it. But he couldn't seem to because every time he tried, he started thinking about Marianne Harding, how somebody had put his hands around her neck and had choked the life out of her. Why? Because they were afraid she might find something. Because maybe they were afraid she already had. This wasn't like the Division Street killings or the ones at the Fishbowl; this was more the kind of thing John was used to seeing. Marianne had gotten in the way of the money. Question was: whose money?

Once Tom drove him back to the station, John told the Chief he wanted to take him up on his offer, after all. That he wanted to go home for the afternoon. Only when he left the office he didn't go home; he went out to the City Zoo instead. What was he hoping to find there? He didn't know. But after a while he found himself standing in front of the elephants. John had always liked them. To him they seemed like peaceful, intelligent creatures, maybe more intelligent, in some ways, than people. There was something about their eyes, and the way they moved, and the way they touched each other with their trunks, that made them being in a cage feel not quite right to him. Every now and then he would read about one of them going on a rampage and trampling somebody, but he always found that hard to believe. Sure, they were big but when they looked at you . . . Most animals' eyes were either flat or scared; you could tell they were thinking only about eating something or running away to keep from being eaten, but elephants always seemed to have other things on their minds.

After he'd stood there for a while, watching them, John decided to walk over to the building where the Zoo had its admin offices. Like most buildings these days it was too cold on the inside but that felt good after coming in from the blazing heat. John went up to the receptionist's desk.

"Good afternoon. May I help you?"

She was a redhead, maybe just out of college. She was a ways down the road from perky to jaded already; dealing with people day-in and day-out could do that to you in a hurry. John made an effort to be nice to her. "I hope so. I'm Detective John Briggs. I'm a police officer." John showed her his badge and she got a little perkier: frosted perky in all that air conditioning.

"How may I help you, Officer?"

"I was wondering if there's somebody here who's an expert on elephants. Somebody who might be willing to talk to me for a few minutes."

She looked a little surprised by that—who wouldn't be?—but had a quick answer. "That would be Dr. Relson. Shall I see if she's here?"

"Yeah, if you don't mind."

She picked up the phone while John wandered around the lobby, looking at pictures of Wildebeest and Caiman and Wild African Dogs. All those pictures were of animals in their natural habitat. John wondered if being a zookeeper was any different than what he did, always locking things up. Except that, as far as he knew, the animals hadn't committed any crimes. "Officer Briggs? Dr. Relson is on her way out to see you."

"Thank you. I really appreciate that."

In a few moments a woman came out of the corridor that led from the lobby into the back. She was brisk, business-like. She had long brown hair, straight, and light blue eyes that said she didn't put up with much. Brown skin like she was out in the sun a lot. With the elephants? She had on dark blue pants and a gray shirt with a button-down collar; together, they looked like they might be her zookeeper uniform. In fact, the shirt even had a nametag on it: J. Relson. John wondered what the J stood for. He hoped it wasn't Jenny.

"Good afternoon, Detective Briggs. I'm Jill Relson from CERES, the Center for Elephant Research. I understand you would like to talk to me about the animals we have here?"

They shook hands. "Yeah, thanks. Mostly, I just want to talk about elephants in general." What the hell was he doing here? He had to be out of his mind. If Horsebreaker had any idea as to where he was, and what he was up to, he'd have him set up some sessions with the Department's resident shrink. John decided Jill Relson was pretty. Almost as tall as he was, wearing sensible shoes. "Umm, do you have an office or someplace where we can talk in private?"

She hesitated and John could almost see what was running through her mind. "Is this official police business?"

John took out his badge again. "Yes, ma'am, it is. Though I do come here a lot with my son, as a private citizen. It's a nice place you've got." Why did he even say that? Maybe just to try and soften her up a little. It seemed as though it might be working.

"All right. Let's go back to my office. Marcy, would you give me a ring at two-thirty to remind me about that conference call?"

John wondered if that was her way of putting their talk on a timer. It was two o'clock now. That meant he had a half-hour, at most. It probably wouldn't take anywhere near that long, anyway. Chances were he'd know in about ten minutes that this whole idea was bullshit, and he'd be back out in the parking lot, trying to remember where he'd left his car. John followed the Elephant Doctor back down the hallway. There were rows of rooms on either side. It looked a lot like the police station, only less hectic. She led him into her office. She went straight to her desk. "Please, Detective," she said, "Have a seat."

"Call me John. Do you mind if I close the door?"

"If you think it's necessary."

In other words, don't. John did anyway. He closed it because he was already feeling stupid for being there and he wasn't sure he wanted anyone else coming to that same conclusion. She probably would, he couldn't help that, but why spread the word around to people who happened to be walking by? There was one armless chair against the wall across from her desk. John took it. On the walls there were plaques and certificates and diplomas. Jill Relson was good at what she did. There were pictures of her, with elephants, in a place that looked like Africa. There was a picture of some guy in a safari hat, with his arm around her shoulders. On the desk there was a portrait of two little girls, both of them younger than Ham. Hers?

"Well, Detective, maybe now you'll tell me why the Police Department is interested in elephants?"

In other words, get on with it. He took a deep breath. "Please, call me John. I was wondering if you could tell me about musth."

"Must?"

For a second John thought maybe she didn't know what he was talking about, that he'd made a complete fool of himself. He even thought maybe he'd imagined all that stuff he'd read on the web, about bull elephants going crazy. "Yeah, like m-u-s-t-h must, when elephants . . ."

"I know what it is."

That was a little icy. "Yeah, I expect you do. That's why I came. To learn more about it from you."

She didn't say anything for a minute, but there was a lot going on behind those blue eyes of hers. No doubt she was wondering why a policeman would be interested in such a topic. Officially.

"Well," she said, "it's a periodic condition in male elephants related to mating cycles . . ." She seemed to be having trouble deciding at what level to talk to him about it. Obviously, he wasn't a scientist but he wasn't exactly your typical zoo visitor, either. She made up her mind. "Musth is related to establishing dominance and to mating behavior but it isn't quite clear yet to those of us who study elephants exactly what that relationship is." She looked at him to see if that was answering his question. Kind of. "When you read stories in the newspaper about elephants going rogue, destroying things or attacking people, it's almost always related to their being in a state of musth."

John nodded. "And what do you think causes it?"

"The state of musth? We don't know, exactly. There's a surge of reproductive hormones, of course, but we're not sure yet exactly what triggers that physiologically."

"I see." OK, so what else did he want to know? He knew he'd better ask something soon or the interview would be over. What he really wanted to ask her was if there was something that could make human beings act the same way, but he wasn't sure if he was ready to go there just yet. "The word musth. When I first heard it I thought it was the English word 'must.' I thought it just meant the elephants had to do whatever they had to do, but with the 'h' added on there it must—" John stopped, and smiled, and corrected himself "—it has to come from some other language and mean something else, doesn't it?"

Jill Relson was leaning back in her chair, studying him. John wondered if the animals she watched out in the wild felt as uneasy about that as he did. "It's a Persian word," she said finally, "one which translates literally as 'intoxicated,' though I understand these days it's used more to mean pleasure, enjoyment, or gratification."

"Hmm." That was interesting. A lot of that definition could tie into drug use. Suppose somebody had figured out what triggered musth in elephants and gave it to human beings? Could you get some kind of crazy superman high off of that? A high that might send you off on a killing spree?

"Detective?"

"Sorry, my mind was wandering."

"Do you have any more questions for me, Detective?"

He could tell she was getting impatient. He couldn't blame her. "Please, call me John."

"If I do, will you tell me why you're interested in this topic? Because I'm at a loss. I don't understand at all how the police department could possibly be interested in elephant musth."

"Tell me something," John said, "do female elephants ever go into musth?" He was remembering that the two cases he was working both involved men as the perps, but then that was just two cases. Might be a coincidence. If there *was* a new drug out there on the street, though, you could bet it wasn't just men who were taking it.

"No." She looked completely disgusted with him. But then she softened again. "Females have their own cycle, estrus. The behavior is completely different."

"Not aggressive?"

"Not to that degree, no." She paused. "You never did answer my question . . . John."

It seemed almost like it pained her to say his name. "No, I didn't." John sat there for a minute, trying to figure out exactly how to do that. How could he tell her what he was thinking without sounding like he'd gone off the deep end? He took a deep breath. "Look, I know this is going to sound crazy . . ." Then he ran out of steam, or guts, or something.

She was watching him with one of her eyebrows raised, waiting. "Yes?"

Maybe he was better off telling her this than Horsebreaker, though; at least *she* couldn't put him on medical leave. "Did you see on the news about the shootings at the Division Street Mall?"

She nodded. "Of course. Just the latest indication that we live in a society that's gone completely insane."

"And then a few days ago that thing that happened at the Fishbowl?" She gave him a blank look.

"That business with Congressman Joe Diddy?"

"Oh right, yes of course. Another family values politician who turned out to be a hypocrite. As a behaviorist, I'm used to seeing that from the species."

It was John's turn to lift an eyebrow. He guessed he knew what side of the political fence *she* was on! "I've been investigating both of those killings as possibly having a connection to illegal drugs."

"You're a narc?"

That brought John up short. He thought about Hambone and his "narc-o-lepsy." He remembered his son's face hitting the cereal bowl, the Cheerios and milk spraying all over the kitchen. "Well, that's kind of old terminology but yeah, you could say that."

Her phone rang and she picked it up. "Yes? Right. Thank you, Marcy. No, it's all right. Thank you." She hung up. John figured it must be time for her conference call and that they were done with the interview. Maybe that was just as well. But she didn't get up right away. She went on talking. "You haven't said what any of this has to do with musth, Detective."

He gave up on the John thing. He took another deep breath. "Yeah, I'm getting to that. Like I said, I've been looking into those two killing sprees as maybe having a drug connection. I had an idea that maybe there was something new on the street. I've had a couple of my . . . informants working the underside of the city, trying to find out if that's true or not. A few days ago one of them told me that he heard there *was* something new out there, and that people were calling it 'Must.' When I was wandering around on the Internet I came across something about elephant musth and sort of went from there. I know there's probably no link between those two things, but I felt like I had to follow up on every possible lead. Eighteen people are dead and if there's any chance I can keep that number from going any higher, I have to take it."

While he was talking to her, John saw her face go through some changes. In the beginning she was thinking this was the most ridiculous thing she'd ever heard, but by the end she was at least willing to consider it. "The chances of there being any connection whatsoever do seem . . ." She was looking for a word; she found two of them. "Somewhat remote." She was tapping her fingers on the desktop. "You don't have anything to go on, really, Detective, except the fact that one of your informants has heard there might be an illegal drug called Must on the street."

"Yeah, that's about all I've got," John admitted.

"Otherwise, there's absolutely no link whatsoever to elephants?"

"Nope."

"Well, I'm no detective, um, Detective, but it sounds as though you're grasping at straws."

"Yep, that's pretty much it," agreed John. "Wild goose chase. Wild elephant chase. Something." He could see she was thinking about it, he just couldn't tell what it was she was thinking.

"So, the theory here is that the men who committed these crimes might have been on a new drug called Must, which might be somehow related to elephant musth, because the effect of the drug seems to be that it causes highly aggressive behavior?"

Listening to her, it was like the air was going out of him. "When you say it like that . . ."

"When I say it out loud? It does seem implausible, doesn't it? Maybe any connection here is purely superficial, Detective. Maybe people are calling the drug Must because what it does to you happens to look a lot like what happens to male elephants during musth?"

"Maybe. Though I'm guessing there aren't a lot of junkies and pushers who've ever heard of elephant musth. I hadn't heard of it myself until this morning. So it might be hard for them to make that connection, unless there really is a connection there, unless somebody already made that connection for them. You're probably right, though. I'm probably making too much out of a word. I do appreciate all your time, though, Dr. Relson." John started to get out of his chair.

"Wait," she said. "I was about to say there *is* a test you could do, if you have blood samples from the criminals."

John sat back down. "The coroner does. I'm pretty sure he keeps those for a while. In fact, I know he does."

"Do they routinely check for testosterone levels?"

"Not unless it's somebody in the NFL."

She gave him a strange look. Was it possible that she'd never heard of the National Football League? "If you could ask them to check those levels for you, it might prove revealing."

"Let me guess. Elephants in musth have pretty high levels?"

"Fifty or sixty times normal," Jill Relson said.

"Fifty or sixty?" John whistled. Just think if some defensive lineman *did* get his hands on that! Though he guessed it might tip off league officials when that lineman killed everybody in the other team's backfield. "Anything else I should tell the Coroner's office to look for?"

"Well," she said, "elephants in musth are continually dribbling urine. Which tends to make their penises turn green."

John thought she might be pulling his leg for a minute, but then he saw she wasn't joking. "Green penis, huh? I'll be sure to tell them to look for that."

#

When they went back out into the lobby the secretary, Marcy, was waiting for them. Or at least she was waiting for Jill. "A Dr. Casey from NSF keeps calling about something. He wants you to get back to him as soon as you can. He sounds like a jerk."

"So-and-so A, or B?" asked Jill.

"So-and-so B, for sure," answered Marcy.

"Give me his number. I'll call him back in a minute."

John looked at the clock. It was almost three. "You were supposed to be on that conference call at two-thirty. And now Dr. Casey is pissed."

Jill Relson looked a little sheepish. "Actually, the two things are unrelated, Detective. 'Conference call' is just a code phrase that I say to Marcy if I . . ."

"If you want to cut off meeting with somebody you'd rather not be talking to?"

"Yes. Something like that. Just in case you had also turned out to be a So-and-So B."

SOB. John finally got that. "But I didn't? Glad to hear it."

"The conversation was at least interesting, Detective. If a bit strange."

"I could say the same. Thank you for your time, Dr. Relson."

It seemed as though she made a special effort then to smile at him. "Goodbye, John, and good luck with your investigation. If you think of any more questions, please do give me a call."

"All right, I will. Thanks." John started for the door, but he was already trying to think up some excuse to come back.

"Oh, and Detective . . ."

John turned around. "Yeah?"

She looked like she was trying to decide whether she ought to say something else or not. Something else won out. "When you get those lab results from the Coroner's office, I'd be interested in hearing what they are."

"You'll be the first person I call," John promised.

Chapter 12

I must be out of my damned mind, thought John as he drove out to Dayton morgue that next morning to see Bill the Coroner. Was he actually taking this elephant shit seriously? He felt like he had to, at least for now. He didn't have anything else to go on.

Dayton was right next to St. Luke's, the big hospital in Mayfair, which John supposed was convenient—usually folks would spend a little time there, in the emergency room, before checking into Bill's place. Bill and Scotty's. John's flesh crawled every time he thought about *him*, about Scotty, but the morgue was his place, too; he had a right to be there. Still, John tried never to talk to the guy unless he had to. Unfortunately, today, he felt like he had to. Scotty was the one in charge of the bodies and he liked his job a little too much; he would slide the drawers out with a smile, like he was showing you specimens from his bug collection. And there was something about that smile, something wrong. It was kind of sickly-sweet and never changed, almost like the kid had been embalmed. He wasn't a kid, really, he was probably more like thirty, though it was kind of hard to tell what with the embalming and all. John decided to call on his boss first.

"John Briggs! How good to see you again," said Bill Meeks, coming out from behind his desk, "It's been a while."

"Yeah it has." John said he was sorry about that though in a way he wasn't. If he hadn't seen Bill for a while it was because he hadn't had any cases like this one, and that was a good thing for both him and the city.

Bill was a stand-up guy. He looked like one of those pipe-smoking, Brylcreemed men in magazine ads back in the Fifties, some agency's idea of what a grown-up man ought to be. His short hair was black, too black. You could tell he'd had it dyed on the cheap. He must have dyed his eyebrows, too; they really jumped out at you. The crow's feet and wrinkles said he was sixty, at least. Good guy, though, as hard-working as they come, and he cared what happened to people. He wasn't just sitting at his desk hoping an interesting corpse would show up to break the monotony. Once, John saw him barely get through an autopsy of a little twelve-year-old girl who'd been beaten to death with a hammer; sometimes he thought he could still see that one in Bill's eyes when they shook hands.

"To what do I owe this honor?" Bill talked a little like the Fifties, too. Today he was wearing a long white lab coat; he must have just come from an examination. He had that pipe of his cupped in his left palm, but it wasn't burning. Just a comfort thing, maybe.

"I'm here about a couple of your recent guests, so recent you might still be boarding them."

"Not just a social call, eh?" He let out a sigh. "This business is hard on the ego, John. Here you sit with nothing but a lot of dead bodies around you, yet it's always them people are coming to see."

"Well, I wanted to see you, too, Bill," John said. "That's the main reason I came."

He seemed a little surprised, and pleased. "Is that so? Well, why don't you sit down?"

They were inside his office. There was a window to the outside and the morning light was streaming in. The lower part of every wall was covered up with gray metal filing cabinets, and there wasn't much above them except one certificate that said he really was an honest-to-God Medical Examiner. John thought about all those framed papers on Jill Relson's walls.

Bill's desk was a wreck. It was like he was in the middle of doing an autopsy right now, on top of it. Spilled coffee was puddled up in one corner, and there were pens and paper clips mixed in with the liquid. It looked like a pile of robot guts. "Oh, that?" He laughed when he saw John staring at it. "Sorry. I was running out of here to do an exam this morning and must have knocked my mug over." He pulled a wad of Kleenex out of a box on top of one of the file cabinets and started mopping the mess up.

"Bill, I've got a question for you."

"Have at it."

"When somebody's been through here, do you keep blood samples around for a while? I mean, after you've done all your standard tests?"

Bill was still standing up, leaning over his desk, mopping up coffee.

"Not always, no. But many times we do. Why do you ask?"

"If I wanted another test done, and you still had those samples, could you do it for me?"

Bill finished cleaning up and threw the wad of wet Kleenex into a trash can. He sat down and pulled his pipe back out of his lab coat pocket. He knocked it out in a dirty stone ashtray. "Most likely. It depends upon the test, of course. Is this hypothetical or are you really asking?"

"I'm really asking."

He kept fiddling with the cold pipe cupped in the palm of his hand. "What would you like me to check?"

"Testosterone, if you can."

Bill shrugged. "Certainly, but I can tell you now it would come back positive. Everyone has some, you know," he said with a smile.

"I know, even women. But I mean could you check the levels? Could you tell how much there was . . . on board?" That didn't sound like the right way to say it, but John figured Bill would get the idea.

"Certainly. Whose body fluids might we be testing?" He was rummaging on his desk for something to write on and finally found a yellow legal tablet.

"Tad Wellington."

Bill looked surprised. "The Division Street killer? I was expecting you to ask me about some football prospect."

"I'd also like to get levels on the kid who stabbed a bunch of people at the Fishbowl last weekend. Aziz Assad is his name, I believe." It was more than a belief; John had finally looked it up.

Bill wrote those names down and then sat fiddling with his pipe for a minute. "We've still got samples for Wellington; I'm certain of that. Lawsuits have been coming in like mail order catalogs. The D.A. has asked me to hold onto everything related to his case, indefinitely."

"What about Assad? I'm surprised Joe Diddy's family hasn't sued yet."

"The Diddy family would like people to forget about this as quickly as possible. They don't want to call any more attention to it by going to court. Besides, this Assad fellow seems not to have had any money, or any connections whatsoever. Still, I think I'm holding onto his fluids, too, in case some reporter begins floating out theories about him and the congressman." He gave John a knowing look.

"So you've got them both?"

"I think so."

When Bill said "I think so" that meant yes. He was pretty thorough. "How soon could you find out their testosterone levels for me?"

Bill shrugged. "You know how backed up we always are. A week, maybe." He must have seen the look on John's face. "A few days, if it's really important."

"It might be," said John, "It just might be."

#

John had wanted to see both bodies as long as he was there, but when Bill checked for him he found out that Wellington's had already been released to his mother. Assad's was more recent and so far nobody had stepped forward to claim it, so his was still in the holding pen, aka Scotty's bug collection. John went down to the basement to see him.

"Hey, Scotty, how are things at the Hotel Cadaver?" With this guy John always tried to keep it light. Not that that mattered. Not that that helped much. Scotty was always smiling the same creepy smile, and his eyes were glassy, like a doll's. Something was missing there, something important, but he did a job not many other people wanted to do.

"Good morning, Detective Briggs."

John guessed it was still morning. Down here, underground, in a flood of florescent lights, it was hard to tell.

"May I be of assistance?"

They were in his little box of an office, outside the cold room. There was absolutely nothing on Scotty's white walls. There was nothing on his desk, either. John was standing in the doorway while he was talking to him. "Yeah. I wanted to see one of your customers, if I could."

Scotty stood up. He came out of the office and looked John over. He was wearing little wire-rimmed glasses that made his eyes seem even flatter, even colder. Like always, there was something twisting around inside of John, something that wanted to get away from Scotty. It was like being in somebody's house where there was this really bad smell, but to be polite you were trying not to let on that you noticed.

"Who have you come here to see, Detective?"

It was hard to describe Scotty's voice. He talked like there was something wrong with his larynx, like maybe he'd blown it out at a rock concert a long time ago, or had burned it out by drinking too much straight whiskey. Or maybe he just talked that way for kicks, to creep people out. It was working. "Aziz Assad," John said and handed him the slip of paper that came from his boss. Scotty probably would have let him in without anything from Bill; he'd been coming here for a lot of years. But with this sick clown it was always best to do things by the book.

Scotty led John into the cold room, muttering what sounded like random words under his breath as he went: "Murderer. Arabian, that's it. Either nobody or the son of a sheik. Could be Taliban. Bad teeth. Not much of a dick. Facial hair: still growing."

Jesus Christ. *When I die*, thought John, *I just want to be cremated as soon as possible.* Anything to keep this maggot from ever touching his body, even without him in it. It was freezing inside there, like always, and the lighting was strange. It kept flickering, like it might give up the ghost, too, like it was hovering on the borderline between this world and whatever comes next. John tried to focus. Scotty went straight for one of the drawers. How the hell did he know which one? There were dozens of them. He grabbed the handle and pulled. A body slid out into the quivering light. There was a sheet over most of it. All John could see was Assad's face and his feet, and a toe tag. He had a black beard and a black mustache, both of which looked a little ragged. They must still be growing, like Scotty said. If this guy had been headed for a funeral home, they'd have fixed him up a bit, but since it looked like he might wind up in Potter's field, nobody gave a damn.

"Good morning, Mr. Assad," said Scotty in that voice of his, "How are we today?" He turned his formaldehyde smile on John. "Would you like me to pull back the sheet, Detective?"

John nodded. "Yeah." Not that he really wanted to see the guy's privates, not that he really expected to find anything. But he kept thinking about what Jill Relson had said, about what happened to an elephant's penis when it was in musth. The sheet came off. The first thing John noticed was how scrawny Assad was. Not exactly your physical specimen. Not much of a dick, either, just like the clown said. But it *was* green. John felt his heart rate jump. Wait a minute, no . . . maybe it wasn't green after all. Maybe it was just the lights. Assad's balls looked green too, now, and so did his legs. Now that John thought about it Assad looked green all over. Maybe he was from Mars instead of the Middle East? John held his own arm out into the light. It looked sort of green, too. *Shit.* What a damned waste of time!

Scotty was watching him. "Would you like to handle it, Detective?" he said.

"Huh?" John looked up at him like he was crazy. "Hell, no. Why the fuck would I want to handle the dick of a corpse?"

Scotty looked a little taken aback. "I'm sorry, Detective."

He looked like he really didn't understand why John was so upset. Maybe that was why he was working here and John wasn't. Maybe that was why . . . Jesus! John didn't want to think about it anymore. He couldn't get out of there fast enough. But while he was climbing the stairs he couldn't help wondering again how this puny little chicken Assad could have killed five strapping guys, with a knife that was about as unimpressive as his dick was.

#

After that little episode, John had to drive around in the sun for a while, until the world started to feel right again. He didn't really want to go back to the office. Where the hell *did* he want to go, then? The truth was he wanted to stop by the Zoo and talk to Jill Relson. But he didn't have a good reason to do that, at least not yet. He didn't have anything new to tell her, except maybe that Assad's dick wasn't green. So instead he went to the Center to check up on Grandma.

She was on the couch in the common room, like she usually was, watching her programs. When she saw John come in, though, she broke away and they went outside together into the courtyard. The sun was still beating down but it wasn't too hot under the big shade tree. There was only one other family out there so it was quiet enough that they could hear the breeze blowing through the leaves of the live oak over their heads.

"This isn't your usual time, John," she noticed.

"I know," he said, "I just happened to be driving by, though, and thought I'd see how you were doing."

"Well now, that sure was nice of you. How's that Hamilton Briggs of ours doing these days?"

They talked about him for a while, and Mick Devereaux, and what the two of them were up to. John kept looking off into the distance at the puffy white clouds building up over the Gulf, wondering if that meant a storm was coming. He was thinking about other things too, though, and Grandma noticed.

"You met somebody didn't you, John?"

"What's that?"

She smiled. "You met somebody since the last time I saw you. A woman."

John didn't quite know what to say. "No, not really. Well, I guess maybe I did. But I don't know anything about her. Might be married and have seven kids." He was thinking about the picture on her wall of that guy in the safari hat, with his arm around her, in Africa.

Grandma was still smiling. "You like her, though, don't you?" she teased.

That made John smile, too. "Yeah, I like her. But . . ."

"But you don't know a thing about her."

"Yeah. We just met."

Grandma had on a little dark blue pillbox hat, the kind you didn't see much anymore except in places like this. She looked sharp, like always. "Well, Honey, why don't you just look her up on that Internet thing? From what I hear, that's about all it's good for!"

#

Grandma was a little behind the times, thought John, but at eighty-five he guessed she had a right to be. The Internet was good for all kinds of things, but it was probably true too that a lot of the traffic was people looking up other people. That night he took her advice and plugged "Jill Relson" into the search box. He wasn't expecting to be as nervous as he was about that. What if she *was* married? He didn't really think she had seven kids, but there *was* that picture on her desk of those two little girls . . . A lot of links came up.

Something about CERES, that Center for Elephant Research she said she was a part of. Three or four hits on different pages from the City Zoo website. One of them was a profile. It had a picture but not much of one: she was standing next to an elephant named Mitzi in the Africa Exhibit and she was wearing sunglasses that covered up those blue eyes of hers. The profile had a lot to say about her work with conservation, but not much about her personally. Seems she traveled once a year to some place called Tsavo, in Kenya, to study elephant behavior. Was that where the safari guy was? At least there wasn't one of those lines at the end that said something like this: "Dr. Relson lives in Mayfair with her husband Eric and their twin daughters, Sasha and Blair." If anything, it seemed as though she might be married to her work, to the elephants.

John kept on clicking but didn't come across much else: an announcement for a talk she gave at the University, two years ago. Some award she received from the conservation society. An obituary. Was that for her mother? It looked like it. The hit came up because Jill Relson was in the list of Survived Bys. Happened four years ago. Laura Relson. So they had the same name. These days, that didn't tell you much. It looked like Jill had a sister named Maggie who had a husband named Brad, but there was no guy's name in parentheses next to hers. So four years ago, at least, she was single. Could have had a guy even then, though, maybe the same guy, the one over in Africa. John started to feel uneasy along about then, like he was spying on her. This was all public record stuff, it was out there for anybody in the world to see, but just the same, after a while, it didn't feel quite right to him.

"Whatcha looking at, Dad?" It was Hambone, coming down the stairs.

"Nothing, really. Just surfing the web. You finish your homework yet?" John clicked back to his home page.

"Yeah. I'm just gonna grab a snack before I head off to bed."

"Sounds good."

He started rummaging around in the pantry. "You know, if you're looking at porn, that's OK. I understand."

John looked over at him like he was crazy. "What the hell are you talking about? I'm not looking at porn. Why would I want to do that?"

"Sorry." He sounded like he really was.

"Jesus!"

"Hey, Dad, by the way, is it OK if I go over to Mick's for a while after school tomorrow?"

"Yeah, I guess so." John was still a little pissed off. "You need a ride?"

"No thanks, we can take the bus."

"Just as long as you get home by dinnertime."

"I can do that. Thanks, Dad."

He sure seemed happy. "Hey," said John, "could you hit the lights on your way up?"

"Sure."

Every little bit helped, when it came to the electric bill. Ham went on up and John sat there in the dark a while longer with his good friend Google. He'd been wondering for a while now what an elephant in musth actually looked like—maybe there was some video footage out there? He tried "elephant rampage" for starters and got a lot more hits than he would have thought. Eeny-meeny.

He clicked on one that somebody had shot in India, a couple of years ago. A bull elephant was in the middle of a city street. Mumbai, the clip said, but there wasn't anything about how the elephant had got there, or why. Maybe in India elephants just wandered around loose all the time? Or maybe this one had been on a leash right before the clip started; maybe he just now broke free? Didn't matter. What mattered was that it was going crazy. Jesus Christ. You knew they were big and strong, but this was scary. He was rolling some guy—his trainer, maybe—around on the ground like a log. Now he picked the guy up with his trunk and threw him about thirty feet through the air. Then the elephant turned on the crowd of idiots that had closed in for a closer look. They scattered. They ran screaming through the streets. John thought about turning the sound up so he could hear them, but didn't want to bother Ham. He didn't want to stop and hunt for headphones, either. So he just sat there watching a silent three-minute clip of people getting trampled, of people getting tossed around like they were made out of straw.

Now the elephant met up with a car, some little van parked along the side of the street. Something about that vehicle must have pissed him off. He started ramming it. His tusks were breaking out windows and putting holes in the sides of the doors. He pulled back and one of those doors came with him, dangling at the end of his tusks until he shook it off and charged again. Shit, now he'd knocked the whole van over onto its side. Now he was pushing it down the street. How much did those cars weigh, five thousand pounds? Now he was lifting up his front feet and stomping the van, over and over, turning it into mashed potatoes.

Jesus Christ! Was that all coming from too much testosterone? Or was there more to it than that? In the dark, in the flickering light coming out of the laptop, the bull elephant kept stomping the van. It was like he was stuck in some crazy, mad-as-hell loop, stomping the van.

Chapter 13

John spent most of the next morning looking at police reports. He had this idea that maybe the Fishbowl killings and what the Press kept calling the Division Street Massacre weren't the only two cases with a possible tie-in to Must. He had to make some assumptions, though, before he ever sat down at his computer with a cup of coffee; otherwise, he might have been parked there all day.

He decided to look only at a month's worth of violent crimes, ones that had sent somebody either to the morgue or the hospital. You would have thought that would have narrowed it down more. It did, in that it dropped everything from petty theft to disturbing the peace from his search, but the database still came back with close to five hundred hits, just looking through that narrow window of time.

Christ, human beings sure were a species with a nasty streak! Men, in particular. John opened a few files just to get a feel for what was there and it took a long time before he got to one where the perpetrator was female. There, finally: some woman from Mayfair had shot her husband to death while he was asleep. Turns out the son-of-a-bitch had been cheating on her with half the neighborhood. Still, that was the exception that proved the rule, the rule being that men were violent assholes.

This guy from Palmer had shot his boss and two co-workers because he'd just been laid off from his job at a carpet store. Another one had beaten his wife to death after an argument over dinner at Seaside. Even Society Hill wasn't immune: some father-of-the-year there had shaken his girlfriend's baby until it was brain dead. That kind of stuff was hard to look at, even for a twenty-year cop like John. It was bad enough when you were focusing on one crime at a time, just doing your job day-to-day, but it was worse when you stopped and took a step back, when you got a glimpse of the big picture. The view from ten thousand feet wasn't pretty.

John leaned back in his chair and took a sip of his sludge. There had to be a way to shrink this pool down. He didn't have the time, or the patience, to look through four hundred and ninety-three records, one-by-one. What was he thinking he might find, anyway? He could word search pretty much anything in the database, but that didn't help if you didn't know which words to use. "Must" was worthless, at this point; none of the cops out there had even heard of it yet so how could they have put it in their reports? Multiple murders? Cases where the perp had been shot and killed by a SWAT team? Cases where there was both a rape and a murder? The phone rang, saving him from having to figure that out for a while. Maybe it was Bill with the test results he was waiting for?

"Briggs."

"Is this John Briggs?"

"Speaking."

"Good morning, Mr. Briggs. This is Vice-Principal Sleeper, from Palmer High School."

What now? He looked at the clock. It was after eleven. At least Ham had made it through most of the morning before getting into trouble. Must not be the Pledge of Allegiance this time. Then John noticed there was something else behind Sleeper's usual parent-teacher conference voice: there was anger.

"Your son Hamilton and his friend, Miss Michelle Devereaux . . ."

So Mick, nice girl that she was, was mixed up in this, too? How bad could it be, then? Sleeper let loose with it. Barbed wire and signs up all over the school, including one outside his office that read: "Herr Sleeper." Seems they'd turned the place into a Nazi *stalag* for the morning. Mick and some of her friends from drama class had dressed up in rags and shuffled through the halls like they were POWs. Ham had put on a helmet and boots and had goose-stepped into the Admin offices, where he apparently shouted out: "Heil Sleeper!"

By the end of the tirade, John was having a hard time not laughing, though he knew he had to hold it together. Sleeper was about to explode as it was. Couldn't they find a way to make this into what they were always calling a "teachable moment?"

"The signs they put up all over the building had swastikas on them," said Sleeper, and it was like cold air was hissing from between his teeth.

Well all right then. "Yeah," said John, trying to see it from his side, "I guess these days that's pretty much *verboten*."

That must have been the wrong thing to say. For a long time there was an icy silence on the other end of the line. Crap, thought John, now I'm in trouble, too. He needed to shift into concerned parent mode in a hurry or he was going to wind up in one of the files he was still looking at on his computer screen. "I'm sorry," he said, "I suppose that was insensitive. I share your concern, Mr. Sleeper, I really do." Only it was hard to get too worked-up about what was obviously a high school prank, when he was knee-deep in murder and mayhem cases. "What's our next step, Vice-Principal?"

"Our next step," he said, and each syllable was still an ice cube, "is that your son and Miss Devereaux will be serving detention all week. Will you be able to pick Hamilton up at five o'clock this afternoon?"

"I'll manage."

"Excellent. Good day, Mr. Briggs."

"Yeah, good day to you, too . . . Herr Sleeper." John did say that last part out loud, but only after the Vice Principal had hung up the phone. *What an asshole.* No wonder Ham loved to pull his chain. If he'd given them all points for creativity and had taken the chance to talk to them about how bad the Nazis really were instead of taking it personal, everything might have ended up all right. *But who am I to tell him how he should've handled things,* thought John, *I didn't do so well on the phone just now.* He could have at least pretended to be on Sleeper's side, instead of practically giving him the finger.

John went back to the grown-up world, where people were killing each other left and right for real. At least that's what his computer screen kept telling him. He gave up trying to narrow those four hundred and ninety-three files down because he couldn't figure out how to do it. He was flipping through some of the more recent ones, at random, when he came across Marianne Harding's. *Strangled on the docks, at Seaside.* Case unsolved. This was the first and only file where you would find the word Must, at least in reference to an illegal drug. John knew that because he was the one who had put it there.

He sat looking at that file for a long time, thinking about Marianne. It was hard to believe she was gone. It was like those green eyes of hers were staring out at him from the screen. Were they blaming him for what had happened? He didn't think so. Maybe they wanted to tell him something? He wished they could. He wished they could tell him why she was down at the docks in the first place, and he wished they could tell him who had killed her. If she even knew. He thought about what a long road she'd traveled, from being a battered wife to a drug addict to a model prisoner and then an informant. And now a dead body. He felt something twisting inside and it was like all kinds of things were being wrung out of him: guilt, for having asked her to be a snitch for him in the first place; sadness, because he really did care for her, if not quite in the way she'd wanted him to; and anger, that somebody could put his hands around that fragile neck and choke the life out of her.

After he'd stared at her file for a while, though, he eventually clicked on past it, just like he'd gotten out of bed on the morning after her murder and had kept right on living. Harsh, but what else could you do? .

The phone rang again but it was his cell this time, so at least it couldn't be Sleeper. Couldn't be Ham, either; it wasn't the right ringtone. "Briggs here."

"Boss?"

Christ, it was Hotwire. "Yeah, what's up?" He felt a sinking sensation in the pit of his stomach. What if Leroy was in trouble, too? He was surprised that even mattered to him.

"I need to talk to you."

"You got something for me?" John asked hopefully.

"Maybe."

"What do you mean, 'maybe'? Either you do or you don't!" He was starting to get pissed off, like always.

"I've got to talk to you in person."

Sure. John couldn't buy him any food over the damned phone, after all! "What'll it be tonight, Chinese?"

"Huh?"

Okay, so maybe Hotwire wasn't in on the joke. Maybe he wasn't even thinking about food, for once in his life. "Where do you want to meet?"

"Down on The Ribbon. Usual spot. Can you make it at ten tomorrow morning?"

"Yeah, maybe," John said, like he was doing Hotwire a favor. No sense letting the weasel think he was the one calling the shots!

Then the line went dead before John could even say "bye." Where did Leroy Miller get the idea he could just hang up on him? That was the last fucking straw! John was tired of sitting around on his ass. He needed to get out in the field. He wasn't sure what that meant right at the moment; he just knew he needed to get out in the field.

He'd already switched off his computer and had picked up his jacket when the Chief showed up in the doorway. "Sorry, John, were you on your way out to lunch?"

John glanced at the clock. "Yeah, I guess I was. You want something from the deli?"

Horsebreaker shook his head. The guy looked grim even when he was saying no to a sandwich. "Thanks, though." He kept standing there in the doorway with his arms folded.

"What's up?" John finally asked him.

"Leti Tulafono escaped this morning."

That didn't make any sense for a moment. Then it did. "How the hell did that happen?"

Horsebreaker's cheeks puffed out. "I'm not sure yet. They . . . we were moving him out to Morgan when he went berserk in the car. That's about all I've heard. Even with cuffs on he beat up two officers pretty bad."

Morgan was a prison a couple of hours inland. Better security, supposedly. Why the hell were they taking a raging bull out there in a squad car, instead of a paddy wagon? John didn't ask the Chief that, though. Horsebreaker didn't seem like he was in the mood. "Why tell me about it?"

"Because," said the Chief, "according to the two cops who wound up at St. Luke's, the last thing Tulafono said was that he was coming to kill you."

Great. "That's just great," said John, "Tell him he'll have to get in line behind Vice-Principal Sleeper."

#

It was another nice day, on the outside. Big white clouds were scudding by in the sky out over the Gulf. Heat and humidity were stacking up, even though it was a long ways to summer yet. Once July and August came around, you didn't want to be in this town unless you lived near the water. Unfortunately, unless you were in the drug business, you probably couldn't afford one of those posh townhouses along The Ribbon. How did that work, that people who were trying to tear the city down lived in all the best places, while cops had row houses in Palmer? It was a strange world, sometimes. John wouldn't have wanted to trade places with those people, though; he couldn't figure out how they slept at night. Out all day selling shit that wrecked people's souls, and then checking into the Quincy. The view from up there was great, he'd heard, but you had to be able to live with yourself. They must have figured out how to do that, somehow.

At the deli he got something with lots of mustard on it and then drove around without really knowing where he was going. But all along the way he was keeping an eye out for a big crazy Samoan. One who'd been shot in the leg, no less. How had he gotten away from two cops when he was handcuffed in the back of a squad car?

John found himself out at the docks. Was that stupid? He couldn't decide whether it was the first or last place Tulafono would look for him. He had a few hours to kill, though, before he could pick up Ham from detention and he was kind of desperate to pick up the trail of something. Must, or Marianne's killer? Both, maybe. He was sort of assuming now that either one would lead him to the other.

Things looked different than the last time he was here. It was still busy but in the usual way; today there weren't any cops—except John himself, of course. Ships, boats, whatever you were supposed to call them, were docking and leaving in a steady stream. There were lots of inspectors and port officials running around, but who knew how many of them were on the take? The hard truth was, even after 9-11, it was pretty easy to smuggle something into this country, if you wanted to badly enough. Somebody did. Unless, of course, this Must crap was homegrown. Unlikely. If that was true then what had Marianne Harding been doing down here at the docks? Mexico. This shit had to be coming down the pipeline from Mexico, from the wide-open spigot that was Mexico.

John walked back and forth for a while, trying to decide what to do. What was he hoping to find? A crane lowering a load of boxes with the word "MUST" stamped on the side? Jesus Christ, he'd been sitting behind a desk too long. He had all the instincts of a bloodhound without a nose. His phone rang. He wondered if he still knew how to answer it.

"Good afternoon, John. It's Bill Meeks."

The coroner. "Yeah, hi Bill. What you got?"

"I wouldn't have believed it, but it looks as though you may be onto something. Assad and Wellington both had elevated levels of testosterone."

"Elevated as in how much?" asked John.

"Forty times normal, give or take."

Jesus. "That's pretty high, isn't it?"

"That's damned high. Do you have any idea how it happened?"

"Maybe."

Bill grunted. "That means you do but you'd rather not say just yet."

"Right." A ship with a Mexican flag was coming in at Pier 8 now. Home port, Veracruz. John knew that because it was written right there on the hull: Veracruz. He stood watching as it came in.

"Tell me something, Bill. Some guy with testosterone levels that high—would he be more likely than the rest of us to waste a bunch of people without much of a reason?"

There was a long silence at the other end of the line. Then Bill said: "A man with that much testosterone in his system? He'd be like a stick of dynamite with a lit fuse."

Chapter 14

Next morning, John called the Zoo from his office. That was a little harder than he'd thought it would be. He told himself to relax, that this was just business, but there was a side of him—one he hadn't seen much of since he'd lost Jenny—that kept having other ideas.

"Jill Relson."

"Umm, yeah, Dr. Relson? This is Detective John Briggs. From the Police Department."

"Oh yes, hello Detective. I've been wondering if I would ever hear from you again." She paused. "You had promised to let me know the results of your tests."

Hearing her voice, John could see her sitting there at her desk, and it made his mouth go a little dry. What the hell was he, a sixteen-year-old kid? "Yeah, that's why I'm calling." He cleared his throat. "Umm, I was hoping you could find some time . . . ah, I was hoping we could get together sometime and talk about those results."

"You found something then."

"Yeah."

She didn't say anything for what was probably only about two seconds but seemed more like two minutes. He was afraid she was going to ask for those results right now and then there'd be no reason for him to stop by and see her in person. "I've got a pretty busy schedule this morning, Detective, but I'm free over the lunch hour. Would you be able to come by the park then?"

"Sure. How's noon?"

"Noon is fine. Let's meet at the Treetops. Do you know where that is?"

The outdoor café. "Sure. I've been there hundreds of times with my kid."

There was another long pause before she said: "I'll see you there, then."

After he hung up the phone John wondered if he'd blown it already. Was she thinking that since he had a kid he must be married? Or that even if he wasn't married, he wasn't completely free? Who the hell was? John was pretty sure he'd mentioned Ham when they'd met before, but maybe she hadn't picked up on that. The good news was that she at least seemed like she might be interested. Or had been, anyway, up until then. This was crazy. For all John knew she was married herself, and those two little girls in the picture on her desk were hers. Except that after looking her up on the Internet, he didn't think so. What was he feeling so down in the mouth about, though? If his having a kid could turn her off that fast, then the two of them weren't going anywhere anyway.

Listen to you! Here he was building a whole life around somebody he'd just met, somebody he didn't know a thing about.

John stopped and tilted back in his chair and laughed at what a stupid son-of-a-bitch he'd turned into. This was just business. *You'll probably never see her again, after today.* But he kept thinking about her all the same, as the morning wore on. He'd Googled her; he wondered if she'd done the same to him? If she did, what would she find?

He'd never looked himself up online before; that always seemed like a self-centered shithead kind of thing to do. But now he was curious. He typed his name into the search box. The first thing he found out was that there were a heck of a lot more John Briggses than there were Jill Relsons. It took a while to weed all those other Johns out. One of them, in North Carolina, no joke, was a circus clown. Finally he found a few links that pointed in the right direction: to a twenty-year cop who a few years back got a commendation. To a parent in a picture with his kid Hamilton, age seven, at a school play. Jesus, he looked younger back then! He still had the same amount of hair, at least, but there was some gray mixed in with the brown now. And he'd put on a few pounds. For at least the third or fourth time this month, he thought about cutting back on the fast food.

Then he clicked another link and a picture popped up of him and Jenny, at one of the Policeman's charity balls. That was why he tried not to take too many walks down memory lane; sometimes it took you places you couldn't stand to go back to. He closed his browser, watched her flicker out of his life again. He wasn't used to spending much time thinking about things like this; usually, he kept pretty busy just living. And maybe he was better off that way.

He looked up at the clock. Nine-thirty already, and he was supposed to be meeting Hotwire out at Seaside at ten. He'd never make it in time.

#

Traffic was bad, like it always is when you're in a hurry. John didn't pull into the parking lot until a quarter after. He could see Kim's, and the white picnic tables, and a few people sitting there eating oysters, but none of them looked like a punked-out little snitching weasel. *Damn!* Had Leroy come and gone already? John went over there anyway and sat down, as far away from everybody else as he could get. He was looking out at the Gulf, watching the gulls and waves, when out of the blue Leroy plopped down right across from him. "You're fucken late, Boss," he whined, sounding like he was pissed. John figured he had a right to be. Even a stool pigeon deserves a little common courtesy.

"Sorry about that. I got caught up in traffic." *And my own damned daydreams.* "You want oysters?"

"Nah, too early for lunch. Forget it."

John had to pick his jaw up off the table. "You said you had something for me?"

Leroy kept looking around, like he was nervous. "I might."

He didn't say anything else, though, so finally John had to ask: "What?"

Leroy looked around again, up and down The Ribbon. "I think I know where I can score some Must for you."

That was a lot more than John had hoped for. Maybe Leroy was a better snitch than he'd been giving him credit for? It sounded like he'd done some actual digging for once, instead of just scratching his ass by the sidewalk until somebody committed a crime right in front of him. "It would be real good," John said, trying not to get too excited, "if we could actually get our hands on some of this shit."

Hotwire nodded two or three times, fast, like one of those bobble-heads people put up in their car windows. "That's what I thought, Boss. That's what I'm saying. It's a little risky, though."

That was a snitch's way of saying it was going to cost something. "How risky?"

109

"Real risky."

Buying a plate of oysters now and then was starting to sound like a good deal. John took a little spiral notebook about the size of his cell phone out of his coat pocket and opened it to a blank page. He handed it to Leroy, along with a pen. "Write down a number."

Hotwire stared at the paper for a minute. You could see the little wheels—and hamsters—running around inside his brain. No doubt he was trying to figure out just how far he could go with this. A lot of people were dead already; he could go a long ways. But John wasn't about to tell him that. "This is *real* risky," Hotwire said again. "I heard one of your other snitches bought the farm."

That brought John up short. How the hell did he know that? Marianne Harding's murder was in all the papers, but how did Leroy know that she was working for the police? He sure wasn't supposed to! It made John wonder: if a little turd like Hotwire knew she'd been working for him, then who else might have known? No wonder she was dead. "Write down a number," he growled.

Finally the butthead did and passed back the notebook. John looked at it. Could have been worse. A whole lot worse. "All right," he said.

"That's not all, man."

Oysters, too? John lifted his eyebrows and waited.

"I want to wear a wire."

"I figured that was part of the deal already," said John.

"And I want you personally to hang close enough that you can pull my ass out of the fire, if I need you to."

"I'm touched, Leroy, I really am. That you trust me that much."

"Don't call me that, Briggs. I mean it."

John was a bit taken aback. He couldn't remember a time when Leroy had ever called him "Briggs." Son-of-a-bitch must really be on edge. "All right. I'll keep tabs on you myself, if that makes you feel any better."

Hotwire turned sideways on the bench and looked out at the ocean. "If anything goes wrong, just try like hell not to be late, would you?"

#

Friday night: that was when Leroy was supposed to score the hit of Must. John wondered if it would really happen. He wondered if the weasel would chicken out on him between now and then. He wouldn't blame him if he did. Wearing a wire was a dangerous business. As he drove to the

Zoo John thought about that, thought about Hotwire as somebody's kid instead of just a lovesick weasel. Leroy was a loser and had a knack for getting under John's skin, but even he had to matter to somebody. At least John hoped that was true. He promised himself then that if Hotwire did go through with this, he'd try and look out for him. As far as he could tell, nobody else was going to.

John pulled into the lot at 11:30, and showed his membership card at the gate. It was pretty busy for a Wednesday; three buses of school kids were running wild through the park. He wandered over to Treetops and bought a cup of fair-trade coffee, in a mug that was biodegradable. Ham would have been proud. It wasn't like he had much choice, actually; that was all they sold these days. He sat down at one of the tables alongside the wood railing that ran around the edge. The café looked like a tree house; it was built on a platform way up in the air. From where he was sitting he could look over the edge at the zebras and bongos and wildebeest down below. A whole lot of memories were there. Ham, riding up on his shoulders so he could see the animals better. Ham in his red panda phase, when he would tell anybody who would listen that he was going to save them from extinction. Maybe he still would, someday.

"Good morning, Detective."

John glanced at his watch. She was a bit early, too. She was wearing the same uniform as last time: dark blue pants and a gray shirt and a nametag. She was still just as pretty. That was mostly her eyes, John decided; they seemed an even lighter shade of blue today, in the sun that was filtering down through the trees. He took his sunglasses off. He didn't want any cop walls in between them. "Good morning. Can I get you something?"

"No, thank you. I've already had my caffeine. I'm eager to hear what you found out about your two criminals, though."

Right down to business then. Too bad. John wondered if he was on a timer again. "All right. First off, though, I have to ask you to keep this to yourself. I haven't even had a chance to tell the Chief yet." Well, that wasn't exactly true. He could have told Horsebreaker everything this morning if he'd wanted to, but instead he'd decided to wait and hear what Hotwire had to say.

"I assume their testosterone levels were high, then?"

Apparently, she wasn't about to promise him anything. Not that he was too worried about it. The chances of her running to the Chief, or the Press, seemed remote. Her eyes were telling him that she had good sense. That he could trust her not to be an attention-starved little celebrity wannabe like most people were these days. "Yeah, you could say that."

"How high?"

John told her.

She looked surprised. She looked like she was trying to process that information. "Quite high, then," she said finally.

"Yeah."

She was fiddling with a live oak leaf that had fallen onto the table. "What do you think it means, Detective?"

John shrugged. "Well, from a Law Enforcement perspective it means a couple of guys went crazy and killed a whole lot of people. Outside of that, I'm not too sure yet." He sipped some more coffee. "What do you think it means, Dr. Relson?"

She folded her arms on the tabletop. All the sudden the restaurant started piping in music over speakers that were hidden somewhere up in the trees. Rap, for Christ's sake. John couldn't believe it. "Jesus," he said before he could stop himself, "Do they have to play that crap even here at the Zoo?"

"I take it you don't care for rap music, Detective?"

"Hell no, I hate it." When he looked up she had this funny little smile on her face.

"Well, what kind of music *do* you like, then?"

They were getting into something besides business, at least. John was pleased. Was she interested in him at all, though? He couldn't tell. It had been about as long since he'd done anything like this as it had been since he was a cop who worked out in the field. He realized that he was seriously out of practice at both. "The Outlaws, the Marshall Tucker Band, Charlie Daniels . . ." Nothing he was saying was registering in those blue eyes of hers. "You've never heard of any of them, have you?"

"Nary a one, Detective. I'm sorry." She was giving him that funny little smile again.

"The Allman Brothers?"

She perked up. "Oh, is that the same as Greg Allman? Him, I've heard of."

"Well, he's one. Pretty much the rest of the band is dead now."

Jesus, what was he talking about? "I'm sorry," John said. "I'm off on a tangent."

"That's quite all right."

"Anyway, if you have any clout around here, could you tell them to change what they're piping in? Either that or they should start putting earplugs out on the tables."

She was outright laughing at him now. Probably because she was thinking he was a crabby old man. How young was she, anyway? Thirty-five at the most, probably closer to thirty. "If I have any clout at all," she said, "I'm afraid it's not in that particular arena."

"Too bad. Anyway, sorry about getting off-topic. Where were we?"

"You had asked me to comment on the fact that these criminals of yours had unusually high—absurdly high—levels of testosterone in their bloodstreams."

Why did she have to keep calling them "his" criminals? Like he had something to do with making them what they were! "Yeah, that sounds about right."

"Well, my initial thought was to wonder if they might simply be taking steroids?"

"Not a chance. I've never seen anybody who was doing steroids have levels like that. I think their hair would fall out and their balls shrivel up—or maybe it's the other way around?—long before they ever got there. Anyway, that's not something you need to buy off the street. There's plenty of sports doctors who will get it for you, if you ask."

"Is that really true?"

"Yeah. Sad to say."

She was still playing with that oak leaf with those brown hands of hers. "When we talked about this the first time, Detective, you said you had heard that some people were taking a new drug they called 'Must.' That's what led you to me. You had read about elephant musth and the aggressive behavior that is sometimes associated with it and wondered if there was a connection. I assume you're still thinking along those lines, or you wouldn't have come back to see me."

Well, there *was* one other reason, thought John. But yeah. "I know it sounds crazy, but it still seems like a lead I should follow up on."

"All right. Let's examine that theory more closely for a moment. Even though scientists all over the world aren't sure what causes musth in elephants, let's say that nevertheless someone managed to isolate out a substance—a hormone, perhaps—that triggers that condition, those particular behaviors. And this mysterious someone discovered that if this substance is given to human beings, it triggers similar behaviors. And this someone decided that there was a market for that, within the American drug subculture. And so he or she started selling it on the street . . ." She stopped and gave him a strange look.

"I'm with you so far," John said.

Jill threw back her head. "You're with me so far??? I was hoping you would see how preposterous this sounds!"

John sat there looking at her for a moment. He sure didn't want to seem stupid, but . . . "You know, there's a little white flower that grows in faraway places like Afghanistan. Somebody found out a long time ago that if you cut into the pod you get a substance that, after it's been cooked and processed a bit, well, I guess you could say it triggers certain behaviors in human beings. And they decided there was a market for that. So they started selling it on the street, here in America."

Those blue eyes of hers darkened a little. "I don't see how opium has anything to do with this."

John had been thinking more along the lines of heroin, but she had the right idea anyway. "I'm just saying that if there's something that gets people high, no matter what it is or where it comes from, there's a market for it here. Sad to say."

Jill was thinking about that. She dropped the oak leaf over the edge of the railing. John watched as it fluttered down towards the Wildebeest pen. "I think maybe I will get some coffee after all. And perhaps a bite to eat, as well. Would you care for anything, Detective? It's on the house."

"No, thanks. Well, maybe a refill." He handed her his mug. "And maybe a bag of chips, if it's not too much trouble."

She was gone for a few minutes and while John was sitting there alone he thought about what he'd said to her. Did he believe any of that himself? He thought about Jill, about how much he was starting to like her, about how stupid that was when his life was so settled. He had Ham to take care of, and Grandma Briggs. He had his job. He had Jenny's ghost. What more did a man need? But Ham would be leaving, one of these days. Grandma wouldn't live forever. Even she thought it was way past time he got on with his life, that he let go of Jenny.

Jill Relson came back with what he presumed was a fair-trade salad. And one little bag of corn chips. "Is this what you usually have for lunch, Detective?" she asked as she sat down.

"Nah, usually I have corned beef from the deli across the street from the station."

The look on her face fell somewhere in between amused and disgusted. "Your diet is atrocious."

"Tell me about it. Thanks for the coffee. I'm surprised you even sell these here anymore," said John, opening the bag of chips.

"We still sell a few little pieces of our soul to the corporate devils."

John laughed. "You sound like my son, Ham."

"How old is he?" asked Jill without missing a beat—or a bite of salad. "Fifteen."

"Teenage boy. Must keep you and your wife busy."

"His mom died a long time ago," John said solemnly.

Jill put her fork down. "I'm sorry. I didn't know. That must be difficult for both of you."

He shrugged. "Was. Still is, sometimes. We take pretty good care of each other, though. You got any kids?"

"Just the elephants." She laughed. "Well, I do have two nieces, my sister's girls."

That was interesting. He was finding out a few things about her. Too bad he couldn't think of a smooth way of asking about the guy in the safari hat. "You ever take them behind the scenes to see the elephants up close?"

"Now and then, yes. It's one of the perks of the job."

Neither one of them said anything for a few minutes. Jill was eating her salad and John was finishing off his bag of corn chips, wondering how he could manage to set things up so he would get to see her again. He really didn't want to leave here with that still up in the air.

"One thing I don't understand, Detective."

"Just one?"

"Well, lots of things, of course, but at the moment what I'm wondering is this: why are people taking this drug?"

"Why?" John shrugged. "I guess for the same reason they take any other drug. It makes them feel good."

"Killing people feels good? And I remind you that both of these men who supposedly took the drug are now dead."

"True," said John, "but I'm guessing they felt pretty good right up until then. I'm guessing they felt like kings of the world, like they were invincible, maybe even immortal. Right up until they got killed."

"That's a rather abrupt end to a high," said Jill.

"Yeah. Obviously, neither one of them saw that coming."

She picked at her salad. "I experimented with drugs a little when I was much younger. I do understand why people take them, though for me I think it was more about fitting in with my peers than it was about trying to experience reality differently. Now that I'm a long way away from that, it seems silly. It's especially hard to understand why anyone would take something that powerful. If you know the end might be this bad, why would you ever start?"

"Nobody ever thinks much about the end at the start," John said, and he was thinking about a lot more than just drugs: relationships, marriages, having children. "This is a new drug, too, so maybe people don't know how bad it is yet. On the other hand, there are plenty of drugs already out there that will almost guarantee you a trip to hell or the cemetery and people keep on taking them anyway. I guess they must think the worst will never happen to them. They do it a few times, like the high they get, and the next thing they know they're hooked. Then they're driving down a road with the accelerator stuck and the brakes aren't working anymore." Saying all of that was painful; it was like living his life with Jenny all over again. It was like she was the one stuck behind the wheel of that car and there was no way for him to get to her, no way to stop her. "What worries me is there may be a lot more people out there, already driving, who just haven't crashed yet."

"Is there anything I can do?" asked Jill, and she looked like she really meant it.

"Maybe." John finished off his coffee. "You could put some feelers out. Maybe one of your scientist friends has recently figured out what triggers musth, or knows somebody that has?"

"If that were the case, I'd have heard about it already. There aren't that many of us and we're a fairly close-knit group. And this would be enormous news, in our world." She paused, and looked at John. "But I'll contact some of them and ask. It certainly couldn't hurt. What do you plan to do in the meantime, Detective?"

"I'm going to try to buy some of the drug, off the street."

Jill looked alarmed. "Won't that be dangerous?"

"Not for me," John said with a laugh. "I'm having somebody else actually do the buying. Somebody young and kind of edgy. I'm not sure they'd even sell it to a guy like me, to somebody who looks like he just came from a PTA meeting."

Jill Relson smiled. That felt good: making her smile. "Well, then," she said, matter-of-factly, "Will you call me next week to let me know what you found out? Maybe I'll have something to report by then, as well."

It wasn't exactly a date, but John was just happy that things weren't ending right there. "I will," he promised her. "When's a good time to reach you?"

"I never know," said Jill, "but Marcy will."

Marcy? Oh yeah, the little red-headed secretary. "Right," said John, "your bodyguard."

Chapter 15

There was a guy from the Projects who told Leti Tulafono he could hole up with him for a while. Said his name was Jermaine. Said he'd played ball with Leti once. Must've been back in junior high, before Leti started showing up on top 50 lists at places like Rivals.com. Leti didn't remember him, but that didn't matter. He needed a place to crash, a place where the cops wouldn't think to look for him. A place where he could make plans for how to take out John Briggs, the son-of-a-whore who had killed Marianne.

"You all right, man?" asked Jermaine, while Leti sat seething on his ratty-ass sofa.

Tulafono nodded, without saying anything. His leg was all right. The cops had made sure it got fixed up before they'd tried to cart him off to prison. Tried, and fucking failed. Because there was something about this new shit he was on that made him feel the way he used to feel, back when recruiters from USC and UT and FSU were stopping by his mother's house in Ridgway, Texas every weekend, promising him the moon.

He'd been on top of the world then, the man everybody wanted to be, or at least be with. He'd felt like he could do anything, fucking fly if he had to. Guys from ESPN and Sports Illustrated kept dropping by like they were neighbors. Hell, even Coach Bobby Bowden paid him a visit. The top prospect at defensive end in the state of Texas, third best prospect overall. That was saying something in a state where football came second only to religion. Hell, it *was* a religion in Ridgway, where they'd worshipped every quarterback sack, every bone-crushing tackle he'd ever made on a running back. There was more money passed under the table in those days than scraps for his dog, Tiny Loco. There were girls behind every door, practically begging him to fuck them. Usually he did. A least until his uncle got hold of him. To'afa had actually played a few years in the NFL, so he was one of the few people Leti felt like he ought to listen to. Even though To'afa was a has-been now, even though he'd washed out and was working at a natural grocery store in Austin, where the kids all called him "Tofu."

"You watch it man, or you find yourself with five kids from five different women and all the money you make going to them instead of to Leti."

After a while Leti figured that just might be good advice. One girl was already saying he'd fathered her son. Another one was saying he'd raped her. Bobby Bowden stopped calling. He was making headlines for all the wrong reasons. Plenty of offers were still coming in, but some of the best ones were gone. He still got his chance to play, but it wasn't with one of his top three picks. SI said he was damaged goods. ESPN said Tech was "rolling the dice" with him. A steely-eyed coach named Greer sat down with him in the weight room one day and told him he needed to shape up if he ever wanted to make it in college, much less the NFL. The world was full of guys like him, Greer said, who thought they were something special but now they were bagging groceries. Leti thought about his uncle To'afa, and that scared him. He promised he would work hard. That he would keep his head on straight. That he would keep his eye on the ball.

It was a different game, though, in college. Everybody was big. Everybody was fast. Running backs were able to turn the corner. O-line guys as big as Polynesian boars were pancaking Leti on a regular basis. Or tying him up for what seemed like hours while the QB looked over the field like he was window-shopping. Twenty yards over the middle. Fourteen, end around. Eight up the gut. Touchdown.

"Get some pressure on the quarterback, goddamn it Tulafono, or you'll be riding the bench for four years!" said the line coach. Leti was already second on the depth chart, slipping towards third. He spent more time in the weight room, more time with the playbook, but none of that was helping. At least not fast enough. Then one day he met a man who had all the answers.

It's not that those guys are better than you, he said, *they've just got the right equipment.*

What was he talking about? Leti strapped on his helmet and shoulder pads like everybody else.

No, I'm talking about something extra. An edge. They've got the edge on you, man.

An edge you could get for money. Money was no problem; he got all he needed from boosters. Boosters who were already getting impatient with him, calling him a bust on the fan blogs. A paper tiger. Man, those guys were savage. Fat balding white guys who had never played a fucking down in their lives. Or did in high school and thought that made them an NFL coach. They'd been all happy after he made the decision to come to Tech; he was like the second coming of Jesus Christ. Now they'd turned on him. They wanted his head on a fucking platter. They wanted his scholarship pulled. Leti decided to take the pills. Just for a while, until he got his feet under him. Until he adjusted to the speed of the game.

It helped, for a while. Leti felt stronger and faster. He was mad all the time, too, which seemed like a good thing, at least at the start. He wanted to kick the shit out of everything that moved. He felt like a wild animal out there on the field. He broke a quarterback's wrist in the seventh game, which Tech won to turn their season around. There was a world of difference, the sportswriters said, between 4 and 3, and 3 and 4. A bowl game was still not out of the question. Maybe even a conference division title, if somebody ahead of them would lose. Leti was a big man again. Everyone on campus knew him, knew his long, flowing black hair. They only saw him on game days. More and more there was no reason to go to class. People handed in his assignments for him. Professors looked the other way. For Leti there was just the weight room and the locker room and the practice field. And on Saturday the stadium, with 50,000 people screaming his name. 100,000 on the weekend when they played at Ohio State, and every one of those fucking Buckeye fans wanted his blood. They got it.

Leti's team won but he was injured and spent the next few weeks with trainers and doctors, just hoping to get back on the field for the bowl game. He took more drugs. Legal ones, this time, shit his doctors prescribed. Seems they didn't mix too well with the other one. But he was afraid to stop taking it, afraid he might lose his edge. So there he was on the sidelines, on crutches, watching his team get ready for the last conference game. Still too injured even to work out with the scout team. Pissed off about that. Ready to mix it up with anybody who gave him shit about anything. And then there was this guy . . . Who the hell was he, anyway? A booster? Maybe just some stupid kid, who never should have been there in the first place.

"You're fucking fakin' it, ain't you man? Cock-sucking Samoan!"

Leti hit him in the head with one of his crutches. He went down. Blood was spurting out of his ear. It wasn't as bad as it looked, but it looked pretty bad. The sports reporters on the sidelines were all over it. All the sudden it was bigger news than what was happening on the practice field. Bigger news than the upcoming game. *Assault and battery. Charges filed. Defendant arraigned. Tulafono suspended. Star loses scholarship. Defensive end dismissed from team.*

Just thinking about it now, how it all played out, made Leti sick all over again. And mad. Washed out, washed up, just like Uncle To'afa. Worse, because at least Uncle had played two years in the NFL. At least he walked away with his signing bonus. Leti walked away with a limp and fucking nothing. He was back in his mother's house in Ridgway, trying to figure out what to do. Everybody was looking at him but on the sly now, staying out of his way. Maybe that was good because he wanted to kill every fucking one of them. He did kill Tiny Loco. The Chihuahua bit him on the ankle one night, under the fucking table. Why the hell did he do that? Because Leti was no good to anybody anymore. Even a fucking Mexican dog felt like he could take a shot at him. Leti reached under the table and grabbed him like a football. Grabbed him hard. Tiny Loco was yelping, twisting to try and get away. But Leti had always had big hands, strong hands, and all the sudden Tiny Loco was what was wrong with the goddamned world. The little fucking dog was everything that was wrong with the world. Leti threw him into the hutch behind his mother's head. The glass front shattered. His mother's dishes on the inside shattered, too. Pictures of Leti in uniform. Pictures of Uncle To'afa. Silver cups and gold trophies went flying. Tiny Loco's blood went everywhere. The dog was just a dead piece of meat. And there was this look on the face of his mother ...

#

Leti couldn't stay in Ridgway no more. He left home, left town, moved a few hundred miles away to the Gulf. To a city where no one knew him. Where everyone had already forgotten him. And that was where he met Marianne. Not right away. That was a good thing, because he might have killed her, too, like he did Tiny Loco. He met her six months later, after all the drugs had washed out of him. After he'd finally found a clear place where he could stop and look back at everything that had happened, everything that he was. A fucking train wreck. A pile-up. He was lucky he'd even walked away from it. Leti got a job stocking shelves at Home Depot. He was trying to put his life back together. He was talking to his mother sometimes, on the phone. He was trying to hold it together. He met Marianne. She hadn't been in town too long, either. She didn't know anything about football, didn't give a damn about football. She didn't know anything at all about the man who used to be Leti Tulafono.

She wasn't like those girls in high school and college. She didn't like him just for the money he might make someday. To her, he was just some guy who stocked shelves and swept floors at Home Depot. And she liked him anyway. For a while, Leti was happy. But it was hard, man, it was hard. Just like it was tough to adjust to the speed of the game in college, it was tough to adjust to the speed of life now. It was like everything moved in slow motion. The days at work seemed to last forever. Nobody paid any attention to you. The weekend would come and nothing was different— there was no game waiting for you. You could watch one on TV but that made things worse; it reminded the new Leti of the old Leti, the one he didn't want to remember. He and Marianne would watch old movies instead.

It was life, it wasn't a bad life, but there was always something burning Leti up inside. There was something inside of him that hated this. There was still a part of him that was a four-star prospect, number three overall in the state of Texas. The Leti that everyone remembered and wanted. He had to drown that out somehow, kill it. He couldn't let that Leti come out. He started drinking whiskey. He drank on the weekends at first, to forget there was a game. Then at night, too, on the weekdays, to forget about Tiny Loco and Uncle To'afa. To forget about everything that had happened at Tech, and in Ridgway. To forget that he was a nobody now, working at the fucking Home Depot. Wearing that shitty little uniform of theirs, like he was really part of some team. He'd played in front of 100,000 fans once, at the Horseshoe at Ohio State! Even whiskey couldn't drown all that out. Leti would try, though. He would sit in his armchair at home, drinking. Thinking about what Leti had been, and what Leti was now. And the world kept on getting darker. Marianne's white cat Pearl jumped up on his lap. He swatted the fucker away with the back of his hand. She crashed into the wall. She broke her neck. There the cat was, dead just like Tiny Loco. And there was this look on the face of his wife, Marianne . . .

What the fuck are you looking at? said Leti. He didn't like the way she was reminding him of his mother. Of all the bad shit that had gone down before. He didn't like that she was crying. That she was looking at Leti like he was some kind of monster. That she was begging him not to drink anymore. That she was saying she couldn't stand to live with Leti no more.

Leti hit her too, then, with the back of his hand. Swatted her just the way he'd swatted Pearl. She hit the wall, too, but got up and left the room. The next day, when he was fucking her, he saw she had bruises. Big bruises on her back and arm. Maybe that would teach her not to mess with Leti. Not to get another fucking cat. Not to talk to him about the whiskey. To leave Leti alone. Leti was watching the games on the weekend, now. Leti was remembering the Leti that he used to be. He was drinking in the daytime now too, at the Home Depot. He ran into a wall with the forklift and lost his damned job. He gave them back their shitty little uniform. There had to be a fucking better way.

Leti went home to Marianne but Marianne wasn't there anymore. Where the fuck had she gone, the bitch? In the kitchen, Leti found Pearl. What was left of Pearl after Marianne had dug her up from the flowerbed: Pearl's bones and what was left of her flesh and a note that said *Fuck you, Leti.* What was left of Pearl's body was stinking to heaven. Leti ground it up in the garbage disposal, thinking *Bitch! Bitch! Bitch!* Then Leti went out looking for Marianne. Nobody said fuck you to Leti Tulafono! Nobody walked away from him. Especially not Leti's woman! He went looking for her, on the street. Leti was looking for her for days, for weeks. Leti was finally sober now but he didn't have no place to stay. He'd been kicked out of his apartment. Not that she cared, the bitch. She'd run away from him! He finally found her. Leti found her working the docks like a whore. She looked so bad it scared Leti. She looked like Pearl in the kitchen. Leti had gone to the docks to kill her but when he found her she looked like she was already dead. That's when Leti left, to go home to Texas.

#

Leti went to Austin to work with his Uncle To'afa, at the natural foods grocery store where they called him Tofu. The people were nice. Nobody wore any shitty uniforms. They were mostly kids who went to UT.

Younger than Leti, but cool. Leti began to fit in with them. They called him "Lettuce." He had dinner sometimes at Uncle To'afa's. Uncle's wife was nice. She was Chinese. To'afa seemed happy, even though he'd washed out of the NFL. He helped Leti out. Got Leti a car, an apartment. He was forgetting the old days now: the drinking, the football, the cat, that junkie and whore, Marianne.

But in the fall, on Saturdays, he had to walk past Texas stadium. He had to listen to the roaring crowd. *Go Horns,* the rednecks were screaming, *Go, fucking Horns!* He saw the players walk by in their white helmets and orange uniforms. That part of his life was over. Leti knew he could never go back there. He thought about another part of his life that was over now, too, that one happy year he spent with Marianne. Marianne Harding Tulafono. He was still married to her. She was still his woman. He wondered if she was still a Meth junkie and dock whore. He wondered if by now she was dead. How long had it been since he'd seen her? It seemed like only a few weeks but then Leti realized it had been almost a year. A fucking year! How could that be? He liked what he was doing at the natural food store. He liked all the people. Marianne would like them all, too. Leti started thinking about going back to the Gulf, to see her. He was thinking about bringing her home with him. He decided to take a long weekend and drive there, to see her. To find her again. If she wasn't already fucking dead.

#

Prison. His woman was in prison! That was what Leti found out. For some reason, that made Leti happy. It was like they were saving her for him. If she was in jail she wasn't being a whore. She wasn't being a junkie. They were springing her soon so she would be ready to start out a new life with Leti. He would take her away with him, to Austin. They would be happy together, like Uncle To'afa and his wife, the Chinese woman. Leti would buy Marianne a new cat, a white cat like the one she'd had before. They would start over again. And things would be different.

Leti was happy. He went back to Austin but came again soon, to the Gulf, to see her. By then, Marianne wasn't in prison no more. Leti watched her for a while and then one day he went to see her, where she worked at the Quick & Ready. It was early on Sunday. There was no one else in the store. Marianne's eyes got wide when she saw him. She was surprised, but Leti could tell she was afraid of him, too. Leti couldn't blame her. He'd beat her sometimes in the old days. He'd killed her cat, Pearl. He told her he was sorry for that, for everything. He told her she was still his woman. He told her he wanted to start over again, he wanted them to have a new life. Leti was there with his hat in his hand. Leti had come to apologize. Leti was asking her to please forgive him. And what did she say?

Go away. Marianne told Leti it was over between them. She told Leti she'd divorced him, while he was in Texas. She told Leti she was happy now, that she was . . .

Leti asked her if she was seeing another man. She said no but Leti knew that was a lie. In her eyes, there was a different answer.

Who the fuck is he? Leti had told himself he wouldn't get mad. He'd told himself he wouldn't call her things like *bitch* and *whore*. But then he did. He told her he was going to take her back to Austin with him, whether she wanted to go or not. Then the bell on the door rang. Another customer came in, to buy smokes. Leti left but told her he would come again, soon.

He was going to take her back with him. It wouldn't be easy, though, because she was making sure she was never alone. She was with friends. She was with customers. She was with the man she wouldn't tell Leti about, a cop named John Briggs. She met him every once in a while. They never did anything together but talk, as far as Leti could tell. The way Marianne looked at him, though . . . She looked at him in a way she had never looked at Leti. And that made him mad. He wanted to be with her, sleep with her, to have their old life back. He had a right to her. She belonged to him. She was still his woman. Leti wanted to bring her back to Austin with him. He had told her that, at the Quick & Ready, but she'd said she didn't want to go with him. Why, because she wanted to be with that cop, John Briggs? He didn't love her. Leti could tell. He was using her. Leti tried to tell her that, once, but she wouldn't listen. She didn't want to believe it. And then she was dead.

Just like that, she was fucking dead. They found her strangled, down on the docks where she'd once been a whore. Leti felt himself getting angry again, angrier than he'd been in a long, long time. The papers were saying they didn't know who killed her, but Leti did. It was John Briggs. Maybe he wasn't the one who put his hands around her neck, but he was the one who killed her just the same. And the son of a whore had to die for it. He never should have let Marianne go down to the docks alone. He never should have used her to do his damned dirty work. Now Leti was without his woman. Now his woman would never come back to him, never go with him to Austin.

Leti sat on the ratty-ass sofa at Jermaine's place in the Projects and thought about one thing and one thing only. That one thing was all that mattered to him anymore. All that mattered was how soon he could kill the fucking cop, John Briggs.

Chapter 16

John had been on the back end of a wire before, lots of times. Those were all drug stings, too, but this one was different. He wasn't after some Mr. Big this time, at least not yet; for now all he wanted was to get a sample, to find out what this drug *was*. It'd be nice to know an origin, sure, but that might have to wait. Any pusher who was far enough down the food chain to be talking to Leroy Miller probably didn't even *know* where the shit was coming from. So this was Sting Lite, he guessed you could say. Maybe that's why he wasn't too worried about either his hide or Hotwire's, in spite of the fact that so far everybody who had gotten within snorting distance of Must was dead.

They were inside a van in the warehouse district in Palmer. Off and on, it was raining. The deal was supposed to go down in a park, a block and a half away. Two techs from the Department were there, outfitting Leroy with his wire. John had worked with them before. Their names were Curtis and Dennis, though the guys at the station called them Cob and Corn, not always behind their backs. John tried to stick with their real names. As long as they were good at their jobs he didn't really give a damn what they did with each other in their spare time.

"There we are, young man," said Curtis, fiddling with Hotwire's collar, "That's better now, isn't it?" How old was he? John's age, give or take. He had a neatly trimmed brown mustache and was wearing a billowy yellow shirt, one John wouldn't have cared to be seen in at a funeral home.

"You sure this thing will work, dude?" Leroy looked even more nervous than usual. He looked even more like a loser punk weasel than usual, in blue jeans and a black Iron Maiden t-shirt. John had this picture pop into mind then of a parent getting his kid ready for prom night, and what he was looking at was so far away from that he almost choked on it.

"Are you all right, Defective?" That was Dennis, over at the van's instrument panel. He was Middle Eastern, had really short hair, and was in his mid-twenties. He had some kind of speech impediment, or at least John assumed that was why he was always calling him "defective." Or maybe he just did that to pull John's chain. If so, it wasn't working; he'd been a parent for fifteen years, after all.

John waved a hand at him. He was glad these two clowns weren't his only backup. Tom Etheridge and one of his men were in an unmarked car, somewhere in the vicinity.

"Of course it will work," Curtis was saying to Leroy, "but if you'd like we can run a little test. Just step outside the van before I turn it on. We wouldn't want any nasty feedback loops, now would we?"

Leroy gave John a look that said he couldn't quite believe these two either. John just shrugged at him. Leroy slid the panel door open a little and stepped out through the crack. Not much light spilled in after him. John looked at his watch. Six-thirty. Plenty of daylight left, but the rain made it seem like there wasn't.

"Is it working?" yelled Hotwire.

Jesus! Why didn't he just let the whole world know he was a plant? Why not just tattoo *I'm a police informant* onto his forehead? Then John realized that Leroy's voice was coming at him over the wire, through the speaker inside the van.

"I apologize, gentlemen. That volume needs a little toning down." Dennis fiddled with the dials.

They had video inside the van, too, coming from a security camera on one of the buildings on the square, a webcam that Dennis had been able to patch into. Once Leroy got to the park they'd be able to see him, at least from a distance.

"Any chance the rain will short this thing out?"

Idiot. They couldn't answer him over the wire; the transmission was a one-way feed. Curtis could have outfitted him with an earpiece so they could talk back to him, but that might've been a little obvious to whoever was on the other side of the drug deal. And pushers didn't usually take it too well if they found out you were wearing a wire. John leaned out through the open door and gave Leroy a thumbs-up, just to let him know that everything was squared away. He looked like a drowned rat standing there in the rain. John motioned for him to scoot, to get started.

"You'll be right there if I need you, Boss?" he whined, over the wire.

Hotwire was already halfway to the park by then so there was no way John could answer him, but he said "Yeah, I'll be right here" anyway, to himself and the two techs inside the van.

"Hones-ly, Defective," said Dennis, with his hands on his hips, "Is he *really* the best you could do?"

John gritted his teeth. "Maybe you'd like to be out there instead?"

Dennis didn't look like he wanted to. They settled in to watch the show. Leroy had just now come into the picture. The park, McAdams, was just a few trees and some grass, inside a square drawn with streets. Right in the middle there was a statue of some Confederate hero, on horseback. There were a couple of green painted park benches. On one of those benches there was a wino—drunk, or asleep, or dead for all John knew. There was a flock of pigeons strutting along the sidewalk. The view was grainy, in the rain, and it came from high up: they were looking down at the park at an angle. John wondered if the wino could be Leroy's hookup. He wondered if Leroy was one of those pigeons. He felt a little guilty then. If anything went wrong, John could be there to bail him out in a couple of minutes, but that might not be fast enough. If somebody wanted him dead he'd be a corpse before John could even get out of the van. It didn't seem like there was much chance of that happening, but he kept thinking about Marianne.

The wire was doing its job. John could hear cars driving by on the main street that went by the park. He could even hear the sound of pigeons' wings as they scattered when Leroy came walking up to them. The wino hadn't moved. Hotwire went straight for the statue, like he was supposed to, and stood there trying to look like he wasn't meeting a pusher. He wasn't doing a real good job. Christ, if you showed footage of this to a class of fourth-graders, most of them could have told you what was about to go down! John looked around the edges of the feed, waiting for somebody else to walk into the picture. The wino was still lying there, with a newspaper tent covering his face up. It was drizzling but apparently not enough to interfere with anything: not with your sleep, not with your pecking up crumbs along the sidewalk, not with your basic drug deal.

"Where the fuck is he?" said Leroy.

"Come on, man, shut up," John said through his teeth, "Don't blow your cover!"

From somewhere behind him, inside the dark van, he heard Dennis say: "Asshole!"

"Just stand there and wait for it," John was telling Leroy, under his breath, even though he knew the weasel couldn't hear him.

Leroy lit a cigarette. He smoked. The minutes ticked by. Then somebody came into the top of the picture, riding a bicycle. Could he be the one? It was just a kid. A least that's what it looked like from a distance. The bike he was riding had swooped handlebars, like what you might see on a chopper. It was red and white and had little blue plastic streamers hanging down from the pedals. The kid was wearing a brown hooded sweatshirt. He rode all the way up to Hotwire, at the statue. Could he be the hookup? He looked too young. You never knew, though, these days. Seems like John was busting everybody from babies to grandmothers, lately. Couldn't anybody get through life anymore without a little helper?

"Hey, man, got a light?"

"Sure," said Leroy, fumbling through his pockets eagerly.

It helped to have the video feed but it wasn't exactly like you were there with them; it was more like they were down on the diamond and you were up in the bleachers. But the sound was good. The kid was standing next to Leroy now, smoking.

"You got the stuff, man?"

Too soon! That's what John's brain was screaming, but maybe it wasn't too soon after all. Hotwire had done this a lot more times than John had. Leroy probably knew what he was doing. Sooner or later, John just had to trust him. Hell, he had to trust him right now—he was too far away to do anything else.

"You got the money?" Once John heard the kid's voice he knew for sure he was way too young for this. He was way too young to even be smoking. John was kind of surprised he didn't still need training wheels on his bicycle.

Leroy slid the envelope John had given him a few inches up out of his pants pocket, just enough so the kid knew it was there. "You got the shit?"

"Nope." Kid shook his head. "I'm just supposed to tell you to meet a guy. Over there, inside of that warehouse." He was pointing somewhere.

Shit. That wasn't part of the plan!

"Where?"

"That red door. See it?"

"Yeah, I see it," said Leroy, but John couldn't. It was somewhere off screen. This wasn't how things were supposed to go down. John wasn't liking the way they were going down. But there wasn't much he could do about it from here. Leroy was on his own. What would John tell him to do, anyway, if he could? Bail? Probably. That would be the safest thing to do right now. John wanted to get his hands on some Must, bad, but this was starting to feel like a set-up.

"Go through it," said the kid. "What you're looking for is on the other side." He took one last drag on his cigarette and flicked the butt away. "Gotta run, man. Thanks for the light!"

He went pedaling off. What'd they pay him to do this: a Snickers bar? Pack of cigarettes, probably. Leroy stood watching him go. Then he looked back towards the warehouse. John was guessing he was looking at that red door. "What do I fucken do now, man?" said Leroy. He tossed his cigarette. "I'm not going inside any fucken warehouse." He said that but he was still looking at it. Probably thinking about the three hundred bucks John had said he would pay him, if he could get his hands on some Must. That'd buy a lot of blunts and oysters. He started walking in that direction. John wasn't sure he wanted him to. If he went through that door, John would be blind. Hell, he'd be blind even before then; Leroy was almost to the edge of the camera's range now.

"I don't like this," John said to Curtis and Dennis. "I'd better follow him."

"Would you like me to move the van?" Curtis asked.

"No, stay here. But can you wire me up and patch me into the audio feed?"

"You bet." He clipped a little pad to John's collar. He ran a cord from there up the side of John's neck. He slipped the bud at the end of it into his ear.

The video feed was telling John that Leroy was about to cross the street on the other side of McAdams. Sound was coming over his wire now. He could hear Leroy muttering a steady stream of crap, under his breath.

"You'd better have my back on this, Boss," he was saying, "This wasn't part of the fucken deal. Cover me, man, cover me! I want more money for this, do you hear me?"

Better shut up or you won't be alive to spend it, thought John. Somebody might be listening. "Am I ready to go?"

"Almost," said Curtis.

"Come on!"

"All right, you're good," he said, pulling his hands away.

John stepped out of the van. The rain was still falling but lighter now; it wasn't much more than a mist. Over the wire, John could hear Leroy take a deep breath. "There's the red door."

John was walking fast, towards McAdams. Then he was running. He had to slow down to cross the street. Was Leroy inside the red door yet? John didn't have eyes anymore. He was in the park, running again, past the wino and the gang of pigeons. Leroy wasn't talking. That was probably smart, but it meant John didn't have ears now, either. He didn't know what the hell Leroy was doing. John was close enough that he ought to have been able to see him by now. Had Leroy gone through that red door? John reached the other end of the park. He could see the door now, on the other side of the street, but there was no sign of Leroy Miller. John stopped. He looked around. What the hell should he do? Follow him in? That was sure to blow the deal up. John stood there at the edge of the park. There was no point in crossing the street unless he was going to go through that red door. Should he?

"Anybody home?"

It was Leroy. John started breathing again. He stayed where he was. Nobody had wasted the weasel yet. That was good news. John wondered what it was like inside there. Was it all dark or was there light coming in through those dusty windows, up on the second story?

"Please, remain where you are." Another voice was coming over the wire. It was deep and gravelly and sounded like one John had heard before. It sounded a little like the actor James Earl Jones. Not James Earl when he was Darth Vader in *Star Wars*; more like James Earl when he was the king in that movie *Coming to America*. An African king. That was what the guy sounded like: an African king.

"Sure, man, sure. Look, I'm stopping." Leroy sounded like he was about to wet his pants. John was itching to follow him in there, but if James Earl had wanted to kill him he'd have done it already. If John ran in there now, he still might.

"So you want to be a man, eh?" the voice said. John wondered if Leroy could see him. He doubted it. If the guy was smart he was hanging back in the shadows.

"Umm, sure, yeah," said Hotwire finally. "Is this shit gonna do that for me?"

"Oh, yes, my friend."

"Better than oysters?" laughed Leroy.

"Better than oysters on Viagra." The deep voice laughed, too.

"You take it yourself?"

"I do not need to," said James Earl Jones, "I am already The Man." He laughed again. Sounded a little crazy, to John.

"Where the hell are you?"

"That is not your concern. Have you the money?"

Hotwire said: "Yeah."

"Place it on the floor then, please, in front of you."

"On the floor?"

"That is what I said, yes."

For a few seconds there was nothing coming over the wire. John was there, in the park, on the other side of the street, looking right at that red door. He was wishing he could see through it. Then the deep, African voice said: "Now, please sir, back away slowly."

A pause. "OK man, I'm away. Now where the hell is my package?" Maybe Leroy was a better actor than John had given him credit for. Or maybe he really was worried about getting stiffed here. If he didn't get the Must, he didn't get his money.

"One moment, please," said James Earl Jones. "Step into the light."

"Huh?"

"Please, step into the light."

"What the hell for?" snarled Leroy.

John wasn't sure if the weasel was following orders or not. He wasn't sure if he should or not. Why did James Earl want to see him better? Did he suspect something? The seconds were ticking past. Nothing was coming over the wire. Outside, John was a basket case. Should he barge on in there, in case Leroy was in trouble? That might blow the whole thing sky high. It might get Hotwire killed. It might get them both killed. Better to cool it. Better to just stay where he was. There wasn't anything coming over the wire. What the hell was going on in there? John reached inside his jacket, felt for his gun. Then he heard James Earl Jones's deep voice again.

"Are you one of the zero-zeros?"

"What?" said the weasel.

"Are you one of the zero-zeros? Have you followed me here?"

"I don't know what the hell you're talking about, man!"

John could hear the panic in Leroy's voice. He was panicking a little bit himself. Zero-zeros: what the hell was that? Did James Earl suspect that Leroy was working for the cops? He'd never heard cops referred to as "zero-zeros" before, though.

"I am not your enemy," said James Earl then, almost sadly, "We have a common enemy."

"Where's my shit, man!" Leroy barked out. "I paid for it, now where's my shit? Give me my shit man!" he shouted.

John got his gun out. If Leroy kept this up, he was going to get himself shot. Hell, if he kept whining John might have to shoot him himself! He jogged across the street, heading for the warehouse.

"Look behind you," said James Earl then.

John stopped short of the door. He heard something that sounded like scratching, or scraping. He wasn't sure what the hell was going on. "This it?" asked Hotwire finally.

Nothing else was coming over the wire.

"Hey, man, you still there?"

Nothing else was coming over the wire.

"Shit," said Leroy.

John stood right outside the red door, holding his breath. He could hear Leroy flapping his beak so James Earl must not have wasted him. Sounded like James Earl might be gone. But why then wasn't the weasel coming out of the warehouse? John had just about decided to risk going in after him when Leroy came waltzing out through the red door, his head of stringy white hair, his cotton-top, bobbing up and down. He saw John. He came walking up to him. That was probably the stupidest thing either one of them could have done, meeting like this right outside the warehouse. What if James Earl Jones was still watching?

"Did I do all right, Boss?" His voice was coming from two places at the same time: right out in front of John and inside his left ear, through the wire. John unhooked his speaker, just ahead of a blast of feedback that could've blown out his eardrum.

"Did you get the shit?" It was stupid for them to be talking like this, out in the open, but the damage was pretty much done already. John looked past the weasel, at the warehouse. He halfway expected somebody to take a shot at them from one of those second story windows. But nobody did.

"Yeah, I got it," Hotwire said with a grin.

"Then I guess you did fine."

"You got something for me?"

"Yeah, sure," said John.

"Funny how that works," said Leroy, grinning, "I give him money, then you give me money."

"Yeah, but it would be a whole lot cheaper for me if I just gave him the money myself."

"Sure, but you don't have the street cred, man. They'd know you were a cop from a mile away. Just look at you!" Now that it was over, Leroy had all kinds of balls. Now he was downright slap-happy.

"Yeah? Well, let's hope he's not watching us now. He might not take too kindly to you being a fucking plant."

#

It was dark by the time they were back in the van, driving through Palmer. The rain was pouring down again. Leroy had given John the shit, which turned out to be a little bottle of what looked like water. That in itself was interesting. John hadn't even known how you took Must, if it was something you swallowed or smoked or injected. Looked like injected. John asked Hotwire where he wanted them to drop him off.

"As long as you give me the money, I don't give a shit, Boss."

"The county jail then?"

"Very funny."

"Curtis here will take you wherever you want to go, as long as it's in the city."

"How about the Fishbowl?" said Leroy.

That seemed like a real bad idea to John. He knew it had opened up again; it would take more than a few homicides to run a place like that out of business. But that didn't mean Leroy needed to be going there. Who was John to stop him, though? He wasn't his daddy. "Sure, just promise me you won't blow all your cash there." John wanted to think he'd have a little left over for food, or to buy a new t-shirt, or to fix up that grimy little shack of his, out at the Landfill.

"No more than half of it, Boss, I promise," Leroy said with a grin. "But a guy's got to get laid every once in a while!"

They pulled up in front of the Fishbowl. Leroy got out of the van but then just stood there for a moment, looking back at John. "Hey, Boss," he said.

"Yeah?"

"What the fuck do you think that guy was talking about with that zero-zero shit?"

John shrugged. "Don't know. Maybe he was stoned."

Leroy looked like he didn't believe that, but maybe didn't have a better theory. Finally he just waved a hand in the air and wandered off towards the Fishbowl, looking for an STD. John sat there for a minute with the sliding door open, watching him go. The colored strobe lights inside the building were flashing again, like nothing bad had ever happened there. John couldn't help thinking, though, about that night when Joe Diddy was murdered, all the blood he'd seen on the fish tanks and dance floor. A steady stream of people was flooding in and out of the place now, and music blared out through the doors whenever they opened and closed.

He couldn't believe what he was thinking right then, that he was hoping he'd see Leroy again, alive. That he was actually worried about him. John slid the panel shut and everything outside went away: the music and the lights and the cool night air coming off the river, and one white-haired, soon-to-be laid and wasted weasel. Curtis was in the driver's seat and Dennis was sitting beside him, and they were a little too close together. The only light inside the van was a green one, coming from the dashboard panel.

"The station?" asked Curtis.

"Yeah, the station." He'd left his car there. "Thanks." As they drove along the river he pulled the vial of Must out of his pocket again and looked at it like it might tell him something. Too bad he'd have to wait until Monday to get it into the lab.

Dennis must have been thinking the same thing, that John would have it in his possession over the weekend. "Just don't sneak and take any of that yourself, Defective."

"Yeah, right." That's all he needed, to bump up his testosterone. He was having too many crazy man-thoughts about Jill Relson already. If anybody needed a boost, thought John, it was the two clowns in the front seat. Or maybe they didn't. Maybe that would be a waste of time, like doping up a donkey at Churchill Downs.

Chapter 17

Off John's bedroom there was this little balcony he almost never used, but on Saturday morning he found himself out there with a cup of coffee, taking in the view of Palmer. There wasn't much to see, just a bunch of streets and buildings that hadn't held up too well in this Gulf-coast weather. Across the street there was a construction site, a motel they'd started building last year but had given up on after the economy went into the tank. He was still in his bathrobe. The door on the other side of his bedroom was open and he could hear the sound of cartoons coming up the stairs from the den. He liked that Hambone still watched those; it was like his son was still holding onto a piece of his childhood, which meant John got to hold onto it, too. Sounded like Ham was watching Bugs Bunny this morning. Man, those *never* got old!

John looked up at the sky. Just a few white clouds. It ought to be a nice day. He wasn't as relaxed as he sometimes was on the weekend, though, because last night kept butting in. The pusher, for one thing, that guy he thought of as James Earl Jones. Was he really African or had John just imagined that? If he *was* from Africa, did that mean Must was, too? Maybe. Maybe this did have something to do with elephants, after all. Crazy as that sounded. What he couldn't figure out, though, was this: if somebody really was bringing in drugs from Africa, why were they bringing them here? Why not New York, or Miami? That would make a whole lot more sense. There were some good reasons why Gulfport was at the end of the Mexican pipeline: the Rio Grande wasn't all that far away and it was a straight shot across the water from Veracruz. But Africa?

John set his mug down on the two-by-four railing. He pulled the vial of Must out of his robe pocket. What was he doing carrying it around with him? Did he think if he took it out every now and then and looked at it, he'd figure out what it was? John thought about last night again, remembering how James Earl had asked Hotwire if he wanted to be a man. Was that how they were marketing this shit to kids? Maybe when James Earl saw what a scrawny-assed little weasel Leroy was, he just figured that would be the best way to pitch it to him? John wanted to open the vial up, smell what was in there, maybe even taste it, but then he decided he'd better not. Might contaminate it. Better leave it just the way it was, for the lab techs to look at on Monday.

He heard the phone ring, downstairs. "I'll get it!" said Ham. He was talking to somebody. Mick, probably. John wasn't paying much attention. Then Ham called up the stairs: "Hey, Dad, it's for you! Somebody named Jill!"

That turned John's head around. "On my way," he yelled. He tucked the vial of Must back in his pocket. Jill? Relson? He didn't know any other one. Why was she calling him here? How did she get his number? Well, there *was* this little thing called the phonebook! John walked down the stairs. His heart ran on ahead of him.

Slow down. You probably just left something on the table at the Treetops and she's calling to see if you want it back.

He took the phone. Ham winked and pointed a finger at him. Smartass. "Hello?" That part, at least, was easy.

"Good morning, Detective. It's Jill Relson." She paused. "From the Zoo?"

Like he wouldn't remember! "Yeah, hi Dr. Relson. How are you?"

"I'm fine, thank you. Listen, Detective, I'm sorry to call you at home. I realize this is probably all very improper, but . . . well, we had said we would meet sometime next week anyway, in order to discuss . . ." She took a deep breath. "Tuesday morning is my time to work with the elephants and I thought perhaps you would like to meet them, that perhaps you would enjoy meeting Mitzi and Lola."

John didn't say anything for a few seconds. He guessed he was out of practice, or in shock, or something. Was she asking him out?

"Strictly from a professional standpoint, of course. As a means of gathering information for your ongoing investigation."

John snapped out of it. If he wanted to see her again he needed to help her out a little. "Yeah, I'd like that. When did you have in mind?"

"Well, Tuesday morning. That's the time I set aside each week to work with them."

Right. She'd said that already. Jesus, he wasn't much good at this anymore! "Well, it's a workday for me, too, but I think that qualifies as being part of the investigation. What time do you want me to be there?"

"Usually, I like to work with them first thing in the morning. Could you be there as soon as the Zoo opens, at nine?"

John was finally on the right bus. "Yeah, I'll be there. What'd you say their names were? Mitzi and Lola? Which one of them is the painter?" In the gift shop, for years, he'd been seeing canvases with swipes and blotches of color on them, and a sign saying they were elephant artwork, on sale for thirty-five dollars. To tell the truth, he liked them better than most of that modern crap in the museum up on Society Hill.

"That's Mitzi," Jill said with a laugh. "She's a real sweetheart."

"And the other one?"

Jill laughed again. She had a nice laugh, one that made you want to jump right in there with her. "Lola? I'm afraid she's a bit temperamental!"

#

After he got off the phone with Jill, John tilted his head back and let out a long breath. He'd forgotten that Ham was still close by. "You got a date, Dad?" he said from the den, grinning.

John shot him a look. "No. Just business." That was kind of true, wasn't it? It was kind of bullshit, too, though, at the same time.

"Hey, it's all right with me if you do. I think that's great. Who is she?"

"Works at the Zoo," was all John could think to say.

"Oh yeah? That's cool! Have we seen her there before?"

"I don't think so."

"Hey, maybe next time you and Mick and I go there for a visit we can make it a foursome?"

John shot him another look. "Don't count on it," he growled. "I don't even really know her yet."

"That's true for everybody, at the start."

Who was the parent here? "Aren't you supposed to be getting ready to go over to Mick's?"

"That's not till noon."

"Well, don't you need to be putting on some black clothes or something? Go take care of that, would you? I think I'll take a shower."

"Cold one?"

Smartass. John went back upstairs without bothering to answer.

\#

Jill Relson. Tuesday morning. That gave John something to think about besides Must, for the rest of the weekend. He kept remembering those blue eyes of hers, and her laugh, and how she kept calling him "Detective." What was up with that? It was almost like a little joke between them now. He was thinking about her while he was driving Hambone to Mick's house on Saturday, and he was thinking about her that afternoon while he was watching the Braves' game, and he was still thinking about her on Sunday when he stopped by the Center to take Grandma to lunch at Trudy's.

"Well, I'll be," she said when John came walking into the common room.

"You'll be what?" he said, teasing her. She looked sharp, like always. She was wearing her green outfit, this time. That dress always looked sort of Chinese, to John. It had a pattern that was either there or not, depending on how long you looked at it. Maybe there was something like that about him, too; maybe that was why she kept staring.

"You really are serious about this one, aren't you, John?"

"This one?"

"This girl you've been seeing. The one you won't tell me anything about!"

John rolled his eyes. "Grandma, I'm not seeing anybody right now."

"Hmm," she said, "You could've fooled me! Well, if you're not seeing her yet, then you'd like to be!"

That much was true, but he wasn't about to admit it. "Tell you what, Grandma," he said, "If I do start seeing anybody, I promise you'll be the first one to know!"

"You'd better do more than that, John! You'd better bring her out here to meet me!"

He laughed. "If I ever do bring anybody out here to meet you, Grandma, then you'll *know* it's serious!"

She fixed her little brown eyes on him then. "I just hope this one's better for you than that one you married."

That one you married. He wished Grandma would just say her name. Lord knows Jenny wasn't anywhere near a perfect human being, but John didn't know anybody who was. He still missed her. He still wondered whether he could have done anything else to save her. He tried to put all of that out of his mind, though, and started ushering Grandma towards the door. They'd almost made it when Mr. Covington caught up with them.

Lester Covington was one of Grandma's friends at the Center. He was about ninety years old and had Alzheimer's, though his hadn't gotten too bad yet. He was bald on top and had eyebrows that looked like barbed wire, but he still took good care of himself. Wore natty suits. Every now and then John was tempted to tease Grandma about him, to ask her if she had herself a boyfriend, but he never did because in the end that never felt quite right.

"Good morning, John!" Lester called out.

John was surprised he remembered his name. Must be one of his good days. "Morning, Mr. Covington. You're sure looking sharp!"

"Why, thank you, John. I thank you. Listen, I was wondering if I might borrow that phone of yours? I've been wanting to call my wife and nobody here will let me!"

His wife had been dead for twelve years. John didn't feel like it was up to him to tell Mr. Covington that, though. He fished through his pockets until he found his cell and gave it to Lester even though he didn't really want to.

"How do you work this thing, son?" Lester asked, turning it over in his wrinkled hands.

"Like this, Mr. Covington." It was a flip phone. John opened it up for him. He saw how tiny those buttons were, next to Lester's shaky fingers. "Why don't you let me dial the number for you?"

"Well now, yes, that'd be right nice," he said, looking down at John through his glasses. He was a good six foot seven. "Would you do that for me, son?"

"Yes, sir. You just tell me what to dial, Mr. Covington."

"Well, let's see now." He thought about it for a minute. "Five-five-one . . ."

It took him a few tries, and he never did get enough numbers. John was still waiting for the last one when Lester took the phone away from him. "That's it, son! Thank you! I'll carry the load from here."

John was about to tell Lester that he still needed another digit, but the phone was already up to his ear by then and he was talking into it. His wife Gertie was on the other end of the line, or at least he thought she was. John wished he really did have that kind of phone, one that could put you through to somebody in Heaven. If he did, though, who would he call? He looked over at Grandma but she was staring off into space, like she did more and more these days. It was like she'd gone somewhere else for a while. Maybe she had. Maybe John was the only one left here, the only one out of the three who was still stuck wrestling with earthly things. Right now the main one he was wrestling with was this: how was he ever going to get back his damned cell phone?

Chapter 18

John had forgotten how much better everything feels when you're interested in somebody. Especially if you think she might be interested in you, too. He was up on a cloud when he went in to see the Chief Monday morning. It took about two seconds, though, to come back down to earth, to figure out that Horsebreaker didn't give a damn about his weekend. He just wanted to know what happened with the Friday night sting. John dug out his Must sample. The Chief took it from him and held it up to the light. It didn't look like much, just a clear liquid with a few white crystals that had settled down to the bottom of the vial.

"Nice work, John. You'd better get this down to the lab and have it analyzed." Ed handed it back to him. "I'll call down there myself and tell them to move this up to the head of the line. I've got Commissioner Egan and the Mayor both leaning on me on this. They want us to get a handle on it yesterday." He gave John a look that said maybe the Great White Higher-ups were all assholes. "Lot of talk lately about butts and hides and political footballs. Me, I'm just tired of turning on the TV and seeing dead people."

He wasn't the only one. The news coverage had died down a little—it had been more than a week now since the Fishbowl killings and people's attention spans weren't all that long—but you could still see the whole thing playing itself out, over and over, on cable.

"You haven't seen any sign of Tulafono, have you?" the Chief asked.

John shook his head. "Nope. But I've been keeping an eye out for him, believe me."

"Maybe he got smart and left the city."

"Maybe."

Horsebreaker shrugged. "Anyway, we've got bigger fish to fry."

For just a second John had this picture come to mind of Tulafono as a fish, and he had to say Leti was a pretty big one himself: a shark, at least, or maybe even a killer whale, an orca with long, crimpy, Samoan-style hair.

#

John went down to the lab. He dropped off the sample. Then he went back to his office and sat down at his desk. He was having a hard time shifting gears from the weekend. He sat there for a few minutes on the taxpayers' dime, thinking about Jill Relson. He wondered what she was doing right that minute. Was she sitting at her desk, too? After a while he shook all that off and started looking through the case files that had stacked up electronically over the weekend. Robbery, robbery, murder, misdemeanor: all the usual human mayhem. It looked like nothing over the top had happened for the past few days, though, nothing that looked like another Must rampage. Sometimes no news really is good news. John was still worried, though. Twenty people dead, altogether, if you counted Marianne Harding and Miguel Jimenez, and what if that was just the tip of the iceberg? What if there were more Must time bombs out there, just waiting to go off? The one thing he was still having trouble figuring out in all this, though, was the business model. If he was a pusher or a dealer he wouldn't want to be killing off all his customers. The idea was to keep them hooked and alive, wasn't it?

He remembered something like this from back in the day, when he was still wearing his badge on his shirt instead of carrying it around in his wallet. There was a shipment of heroin that was too pure making the rounds, and people who used it were dropping like flies. The cops had warnings out all over the city. They were even offering to check people's dope for them, no questions asked. Not that very many junkies ever took them up on it. After a while, the whole thing blew over. Either that shipment ran out or the dealers started cutting it with something. Dead junkies weren't much good to anybody. John wondered if that was what would eventually happen here. Maybe it was too soon for him to even be worrying about it. So far, it was only two people: Wellington and Assad. Trouble was those two people hadn't just taken themselves out; they'd dragged a whole lot of innocent bystanders down to hell with them. Didn't that make all of this a little more urgent?

After a while lunchtime rolled around and John still hadn't heard anything back from the lab. So he went out to get his hit of ground beef at McBypass, hoping like he always did that it wouldn't kill him this time. It was a bright, sunny day. He couldn't see going right back to the office afterwards, so he drove around for a while with the windows rolled down and the radio on, thinking about Jill Relson. The Zoo was where he really wanted to go right now but he knew he had to stay the hell away from there until Tuesday. The last thing you wanted to do when you were in a situation like this was let the other person think you were too eager. Bunch of stupid rules, but anybody who'd ever dated learned pretty quick that you'd better follow them. He was starting to remember now why he never went out anymore.

John didn't think he was going anywhere, really. He thought he was just driving around. But the next thing he knew he found himself out at Eastlake, at the cemetery where Jenny was buried. Well, not exactly buried—they'd had her cremated. That was what she said she wanted. They had her cremated and then scattered her ashes in the trees alongside the lake. That was what she said she wanted.

John parked his car in the lot in front of the gravestones but didn't walk out through the field to see them; there wasn't much point. Instead, he followed the red dirt path that circled the lake, winding its way through pines and live oaks and cypresses. It seemed like she was still there, at least a little, in the light breeze that was moving through the leaves and needles. John could almost imagine that her ashes were still floating around in the air, years later, that they hadn't quite reached the ground yet and maybe never would.

Grandma thought it was awful that they'd had her cremated; she thought everybody deserved their own little patch of ground. Even Jenny. She told John if he even *thought* about doing that to her, she'd come back and haunt him. But cremation suited a free spirit like Jenny. John walked through the trees where he'd left her, thinking about her, wondering why it was that so many people who thought of themselves as free spirits were so quick to climb inside a cage of drugs?

The breeze swirled around like it was trying to tell him something. But what? That she was all right with him moving on? That if he wanted to care about somebody else, he ought to go ahead and do it? Or maybe that was what he wanted her to say? John wasn't getting any bad feelings from her, at least. Not that he expected to. Jenny never did think she owned him. She didn't believe people owned each other at all, didn't even believe all that much in marriage. It was a wonder she'd ever married him.

It was a wonder the two of them had ever got together at all, a wonder that what they'd had ever lasted. Maybe it wouldn't have, if Jenny had stayed around much longer, if she hadn't—

John thought he saw her then, on the path behind him. He stopped and turned around and looked back through the trees. There wasn't anybody there now. If there ever had been. It was probably just somebody else doing what he was doing, somebody else taking a walk down memory lane. John stood there for a minute, watching, before he went on. He was most of the way around the lake now. There was still a bit of a breeze coming off the water, but it didn't seem like it had anything to do with Jenny anymore. It was just wind. He came out of the woods into the field that was the graveyard. He had to cut across it to get to his car. He walked past row after row of headstones, looking at them as he went along. He read the dates and names. Some of those people had been there a while; others had just arrived. But all of them had been laid to rest Grandma's way, the old-fashioned way. Every now and then, as he went, John would look behind him. It still felt like there might be somebody back there. It still felt like there might be somebody following him. He didn't know who it might be; all he knew for sure was that it wasn't Jenny.

Chapter 19

Since when did he start caring about what he wore? John stood in front of his closet Tuesday morning and actually thought about it for once. He had seven work shirts, three pairs of good pants, and two sport coats. That didn't make for a whole lot of combinations. He couldn't see wearing any of those this morning, though, not if they were going to be inside elephant pens. One spray of piss and he could lose a third of his wardrobe. He didn't want to wear what he usually did on his days off, though; he didn't want to show up there in nothing but shorts and a t-shirt. He wanted to look halfway presentable. Maybe some jeans that weren't too ragged, along with a purple polo shirt?

I'll think about that while I'm in the shower. Jesus, he knew there was a reason why he didn't date anymore!

After John got dressed (the jeans and polo shirt won out) and had breakfast, he and Ham headed into town together so John could drop him off at school. Ham had his headphones off for once and John wondered what was up with that. Did he actually want to have a conversation with his old man?

"Are you meeting that lady at the Zoo this morning?"

John shot him a look in the mirror. "Yeah, but it's just business, remember?"

"Is that why you're wearing cologne?"

John shot him another look. "That's for the elephants."

Ham laughed. "Good one, Dad. I'm glad you're taking a little break from work, though. You could use it."

John shot him a different kind of look. He thought: *he's growing up on me.* How much of that was Mick and how much was just Ham getting older? "Thanks. Yeah, I'm kind of looking forward to this." That was probably enough. He didn't much like talking about himself to anybody, not even his own son. So he did what he always did when anybody started asking him questions about himself: he threw those questions right back to them like they were hot potatoes. "What about you? What's your day look like?"

"Test in Algebra."

"You ready for it?"

"As ready as I'll ever be. Today's the last day of detention with Sleeper too, remember?"

"Yeah, I remember. I'll be there to pick you up at five."

"Unless you get delayed."

John laughed. "Yeah, unless I get delayed." That was a little bit of a running joke between them; in police work it seemed like something unexpected was always coming up. Over the years John had left Ham stranded in all kinds of places. That was the main reason why the two of them finally got cell phones.

Ham laughed, too, and it was one of those laughs from when he was younger, one that took John back to those days when they used to hang out together more, when Ham was just finding out about the world and John was along for the ride. He felt both sad and happy at the same time, then: sad that those days were gone but happy that they'd come this far together, that Ham was growing up into somebody he liked, somebody he knew was going to be a good person.

John dropped him off at "Alcatraz," which was what he'd been calling Palmer High ever since the detention started. Then he drove on to the City Zoo, just him and his butterflies. He asked himself again what he thought he was doing. He told himself again that this was just business. *Right.*

You can feed that nonsense to Hamilton, but don't you dare try to feed it to me! It was like Grandma Briggs was inside his head, like the straight-talking part of him that came from her was warning the rest of him not to tell any more whoppers.

I can see right through you, John Briggs, she used to say when he would try to give her the business, back when he was a kid. He was lucky as hell she'd been there to raise him. No telling where he might be now if she hadn't been.

There was the Zoo, up ahead. John had enough butterflies now that if people could see them, he'd be a walking exhibit. He sat there in the car for a minute, just trying to calm down.

Finally he got out and started walking across the parking lot and the exercise helped a little. He went through the gates. They hadn't really said anything about where they would meet, so John went into the Admin building where he'd met her before. Marcy, the little red-headed secretary, was sitting behind the desk.

"May I help you?"

"Umm, yeah, I'm Detective John Briggs and I . . ."

"I'm just teasing; I know who you are," Marcy cut in with a smile, "She's been expecting you. Hang on, I'll give her a call."

She did and a few minutes later Jill Relson came out of the back, looking as good as she always did. She had on another uniform but this one was made for work in the trenches: short sleeves and short pants that both looked a little ragged. Nice legs, though.

"Good morning, Detective."

"Morning, Doctor."

Marcy let out a long sigh then and took off her computer glasses. "When are the two of you going to stop calling each other Detective and Doctor? Here, let me introduce you. Jill, this is John. John, this is Jill. There, isn't that better?" She was sitting behind the desk with her arms folded across a polka-dot blouse, giving them pretty much the same look Ham had given John that morning after he'd told him this visit was strictly business.

"Thank you, Marcy," said her boss, "We'll be with the elephants."

"She's got a point you know, Jill," said John as they walked out of the Admin Building into the public part of the Zoo.

"Of course she's got a point; that's why I'm annoyed with her," she said with a smile.

He followed her over to the new Africa exhibit. There were lions and zebras and rock hyraxes in their own displays, but all the habitats were designed to look the same, like one continuous savannah. "Was that your son I talked to on the phone on Saturday?" Jill asked as they went along.

"Yeah, that was Ham."

"Seems like a nice kid."

"Yeah, he is."

They reached the elephants, which were on the opposite side of the new exhibit from the lions, in a space that wasn't too bad: a big open area full of dirt and grass and boulders. There was a deep, dry moat in between the two big animals and the public, which for the moment included John, but then Jill took him behind the scenes.

"The secret entrance," she said, using her keys to open a door that was out of sight on the side. John followed her down a sterile-looking hallway. He could hear water running. There was a strong smell of elephants in the air. "You can get to the hippos and rhinos this way too," she said, her voice echoing off the gray metal walls. Then the hallway opened up into a room that looked like it could have been a pen for King Kong. There was a cage with bars that went about fifteen feet in the air. Those bars looked as thick as John's arm. There was nothing in there right now, though.

"Mitzi and Lola are outside."

"Yeah, I saw them."

"Down that way there's a part of the pen that can be seen by Zoo guests. Sometimes we bathe the elephants out there so people can watch."

"Yeah, Ham and I have done that before. It's fun."

"Should be even more fun today. You get to actually hold the hose."

John raised his eyebrows but didn't say anything. He wondered if he was ready for this. Didn't matter whether he was or not. That was just one of those things about being a man; sometimes you couldn't let good sense get in your way. Whenever that happened to him he knew why male animals did what they did, why they danced and bellowed and strutted around; sometimes Mother Nature just got inside your car and took the steering wheel from you. "Let me know when."

That's it, he thought, *try to act like this isn't any big deal!* But he was already wondering whether he'd be spraying them from outside or inside the cage. Jill answered that question when she slipped through a door that was too little for the elephants to get out of. She was in there, hooking up what looked like a fire hose.

She said: "Come on in, John."

Yeah, sure. She looked good standing there, so he went in after her. She pulled her hair back into a ponytail before turning the water on. That ponytail looked good, too. The jet was strong enough that it kicked her back a little, until she got both hands on the hose. "They'll hear the water and come," she said, and in a minute they did. "Hey, Girls, there you are.

Nice to see you today!"

Damn, they were big when you saw them up close! Nine or ten feet high at the shoulder. And mean-looking tusks. "I thought you said they were girls."

"They are." She was already blasting the side of one of them, like she was washing a truck.

"What about the tusks?"

"In African elephants, both males and females have them. In Asians, it's just the males." Spray from the hose was blowing all over the place. It was loud, too, so John had to concentrate just to hear her. She was moving the hose back and forth. The elephant she was washing seemed to like it. The other one wanted in on the action, too; she kept trying to move into the stream. Jill gave her a shot. "This one is Mitzi," she shouted over the sound of the water, "She's the painter. Lola seems pretty calm today but I'd keep an eye on her. Sometimes she can get a little testy."

Oh yeah? John made sure he knew where the testy one was, from then on. He didn't like the way those tusks looked or the way her trunk kept moving around. She was trying to drink from the hose. Now she was touching Jill's shoulder. That was nice. He'd known plenty of people who weren't that affectionate! Jill's girls must like her. "You want to try it?"

"Sure." He had a Y chromosome; he couldn't say no. He stepped up to the plate. He'd done a gig as a volunteer fireman once, so at least he knew how to hold a hose to keep it from getting away from him.

"Why don't you rinse off their legs, then I'll try to get them to lie down for you."

She was talking to them like they were horses or something. "Come on, Mitzi, there you go, Lola, good girl, do you want to lie down?"

They did. Now John was hosing off their bellies. He was starting to like them. There was something calm and old about them, and maybe even an "I've seen it all" kind of sadness. Jill was behind him now, turning off the hose. It died in John's hands.

"They're going to want their dust baths now," she predicted and sure enough, as soon as the water stopped they got up and shook off a little and moseyed towards the front of the pen where there was an open gate to the outside.

"How did you like it?" she asked with a grin while she was winding up the hose.

"I like *them*," said John. He was thinking about their eyes.

"Come on, let's watch." Jill walked on ahead of him, through the gate.

John went after her, towards the light. When they got there he could see that Lola and Mitzi were scooping up dirt with their trunks, and dropping it onto their backs. "Man, I just got you clean!" John couldn't help saying.

Jill laughed. "It's good for them. Protects their skin from the sun and insects."

"I guess it's cheaper than Deet. Smells a whole lot better, too." It was along about then that John noticed he was as much on display as the elephants, that there were people on the other side of the moat, watching. Maybe wishing they could be in here with him. Every now and then down through the years he and Ham had seen zookeepers in the animals' pens and they'd always said to each other that it seemed like a fun job. Washing Lola and Mitzi in the back room *was* fun, but he wasn't so sure he liked it out here, having so many people look at him.

"Can you help me with their food, John?"

She was dragging a bale of hay out of the back room and John could see five more in a stack behind her. He grabbed two, one by the strap with each hand. "They eat a lot, don't they?"

"Three or four hundred pounds a day, between them," said Jill.

John whistled. "All hay?"

"With some alfalfa mixed in." She'd pulled a knife out of her belt and was cutting one of the bales open. She started spreading the hay around with a rake.

"You want me to bring out some more bales?"

"Yes, please, all of them."

John did that while she did the cutting and spreading. Then afterwards they stood there together watching the two elephants eat. "It's hard to believe they can turn so violent," he said, thinking about that video he saw of the one stomping the van, "But I guess that's just the males, huh?"

"Usually. Though the females can get pretty riled up, too, if you mess with the herd, especially the young. Elephants are matriarchal so the lead female in particular is very protective."

John thought about Grandma, how she'd kept the family together for years, how she had a fire in her belly that you'd never guess was there, just to look at her.

"Whoa!" said Jill then, watching them, "Right on time. You want to help me clean up some elephant poop?"

"Sure, why not?" said John, looking around. "You got a snow shovel?"

#

After they cleaned up they had lunch at the Treetops again, and it felt a little more relaxed this time around. "Thanks for sharing that with me," John said as he sat down with his fair-trade, free-range veggie burger. Or whatever it was. The fries tasted good, anyway.

"I'm glad you enjoyed it," Jill said in between bites of her salad, "A little different from police work, I imagine."

"Yeah, though the part where we were cleaning up crap seemed kind of familiar."

She laughed. "I wanted you to see for yourself, up close, what peaceful creatures elephants are."

"Except for the males, when they're in musth."

"Even that's not a problem if humans aren't involved. Out in the wild it's just a natural part of the breeding cycle. Certain males go into musth and other males know how to react to that, and the females know how to react to that, too, instinctively. As usual, though, we enter the picture and throw everything out of balance. Poachers kill off the largest elephants because they have the largest tusks and suddenly there aren't any fully mature males around. Without any adult males present the younger ones enter musth prematurely and often as not go rogue, killing hippos and each other and sometimes human beings. The entire breeding cycle is completely disrupted."

"Sounds kind of like what's been happening here for a while, in the inner cities." John ate a few fries. "Did you ever hear back from any of your friends overseas, about whether or not anybody has figured out what makes elephants go into musth?"

"Some of them wrote back right away, the ones who are working at universities and have easy access to email. As I suspected, none of them knows anything. As I was telling you earlier, it would be very big news in our world if someone had made that sort of discovery. There are still a few colleagues I haven't heard from, though, the ones who are working out in the field. There isn't any access to the Internet out at Tsavo, for instance; you have to go into Nairobi or Mombasa, which we don't often do. So I sent my colleague, Cynthia Jones, a letter instead. Even that takes longer to arrive than you might think, given the state of mail service in Kenya. So I won't be surprised if it takes several weeks to hear from her."

John was watching her face the whole time she was talking. He could tell something was bothering her. "This really has you worried, doesn't it?"

She'd only finished about half her salad and was poking a plastic fork at the rest. "Suppose all you suspect turns out to be true, John. It wouldn't be the first time that elephants had something we humans wanted, something people were willing to pay enormous sums of money for. The ivory trade drove elephants to the verge of extinction . . ." She poked at her salad. "I guess I'm worried this might be the end for them, should poachers start killing every elephant that goes into musth, just to extract some substance they can sell as a drug."

John thought about that for a minute. "It wouldn't have to work that way, though, would it? I mean, if somebody was to figure out what chemical was in an elephant's body that made him go into musth, and then made more of that chemical in the lab . . . Seems like that's the way you would want to do it, if you could, to really make money off this thing. Even if you couldn't do that it wouldn't make sense to kill the elephant; you'd want to knock it out somehow and take the chemical, wouldn't you? That way you could do it again, next season. No need to kill the goose that lays the golden eggs."

"I suppose it could be done, if you knew what you were looking for and how to extract it," said Jill. "It would be a bit dangerous, though, getting close enough to a musth elephant to tranquilize him and take his blood. If this drug of yours does come from elephants, I hope that's how they're getting it, rather than killing them."

This drug of yours. There she went again. Like John made the shit himself. He guessed he knew what she meant, though. "Has poaching over there gone up at all, recently?"

"That's something I asked Cyn, too, in my letter."

John looked down at his plate and realized he'd eaten every last bite of his fair-trade burger. Must not have been that bad, after all. "That might tell us something, if things have gotten worse lately."

"What happened on Friday, by the way?" Jill finally asked him.

"Were you able to get your hands on the drug?"

He'd been waiting on that one for a while. He was surprised it had taken her this long to ask. "Yeah. It's still in the lab, being analyzed. Even that may not tell us much, though; about all they can do is give us back some chemical formula."

"That might provide a signature we can trace, though," she said, thinking out loud, "That might tell us whether or not the drug can be linked back to elephants."

We? Us? John guessed maybe it wasn't just his drug anymore! He smiled. That was good to know. Maybe they'd be working together on this for a while. "One thing I thought was interesting," he said, remembering how the sting had gone down. And then he told her about hearing the voice of James Earl Jones, how he'd thought the man sounded African.

"Lending credence, perhaps, to the theory that the drug does come from Africa," Jill said, taking that out to its logical conclusion, "Which may lend credence to the theory that it comes from elephants."

"Maybe."

"What sort of accent did this man have?" asked Jill.

John gave her a blank look. "What sort?"

"Yes. Not everyone in America speaks English the same way; you wouldn't expect everyone in Africa to, now would you? The continent is vast."

John was still giving her the same blank look. "I guess not."

"Well, the way South Africans speak English is distinctly different from the way they speak English in Kenya. Just for example."

"I guess that makes sense," said John, "But to me, it all sounds the same. Sorry."

"Don't be. I wouldn't expect you to be able to pick up on such nuances." She drank a little of her diet soda. "Too bad you don't have it on tape."

"Actually, I might," John said, almost to himself, "I'll bet Cob and Corn recorded it."

"What's this about a corncob?"

John snapped out of it. "Sorry. It's just that the kid who bought the drug for us was wearing a wire. I'm wondering if the two techs who were helping me to listen in might have recorded the whole conversation."

"Well, if you find out that you do have such a recording, could you

156

let me hear it? I'm no expert in linguistics but I know someone who is: Thomas Mbele, who teaches African Literature at Emory, in Atlanta. We met in college and got to know one another through my work at the research station in Kenya. He's originally from Tanzania."

"I'll check into it and let you know," John said, though he wasn't exactly sure what that would buy them, pinning down James Earl's accent. For just a moment he thought he might tell her about the zero-zeros thing, but then decided to drop it. It didn't mean anything. The guy was probably just high on his own damned drugs.

He and Jill concentrated on their food for a minute. They were both about done. John realized they were coming to the end of their morning. He'd had a good time. He didn't want it to end. At least he didn't want it to end without knowing when he was going to see her again. She'd made the last move; he figured this one was up to him. "Listen, Jill . . ." he said.

She was listening.

"Umm, yeah. I need to head into the station here, but . . ."

She was still listening.

John took a deep breath. "OK, I know this is going to sound crazy because we just met but I don't want to walk away from here today not knowing when I'll see you again." How could that have been as hard as hell to say but at the same time so easy? The toughest part was waiting to hear how she would answer. At least she didn't make him wait long.

"Well, perhaps we should decide on another time and place now, before you go?" She had a nice smile on her face. "What did you have in mind, Detective?"

So, were they all the way back to that again? But she wasn't saying "Detective" the same way she had at the start. It wasn't like she was saying that to keep him at a distance now; it was more like she was teasing him. What *did* he have in mind? Nothing really, except for that part about making sure he would see her again. He tried to come up with something, fast. "Are you doing anything Saturday night?"

"Not yet."

She was smiling at him. He couldn't stop looking at those blue eyes of hers. He had to clear his throat a little. "Maybe we could have dinner together, somewhere out at Seaside?"

"That would be nice. Shall we say around seven o'clock?"

Those butterflies were still with him when he left the Zoo, but this time it seemed like he was floating through the air along with them.

Chapter 20

By the time John got back to the station, it was afternoon. He sat down at his desk and tried to pick up the threads of all his pending investigations, but was having a hard time thinking about anything else besides Jill. He just sat there staring at his computer screen like that might get something done all by itself. *How's about opening one damned file?* Finally, he managed to do that. He looked through the specs of what they were calling the Carter Case, three brothers who were cooking and selling methamphetamine. Christ, that shit was bad news. Made him long for the good old days when people just smoked reefer or snorted cocaine. Every now and then, back then, you'd come across somebody with no soul left, somebody who was just bones and hollowed-out eyes, but drugs like Crystal and Crack had really upped the ante over the past ten years. Now you routinely ran into people you had to scrape off a rock like a fungus, people who weren't even really people anymore but had turned into something else, people whose only purpose in life was to take whatever drug they were hooked on. And they'd kill their own mothers to get more of it.

Compared to shit like that, was Must really so bad? Maybe they were all just scared of it because they didn't know much about it? Maybe it was like one of those exotic African diseases you read about every now and then in the papers. A bunch of people would have died in an almost unbelievable, end-of-the-world kind of way that scared the living shit out of you, but in the end it would turn out to be maybe thirty villagers. Meanwhile the regular old flu was wiping out millions. Which one were you going to spend your time worrying about?

The phone rang. It was Chief Horsebreaker. He said: "I need you to come down to my office right away."

"What's up?"

"I just got results back from the lab."

On the Must sample? That was fast. He guessed the Chief really did have more clout than he did! He walked down the hall. Horsebreaker's door was open but he knocked anyway and stood there until the Chief said: "Come in."

John sat down in the chair beside his desk. Horsebreaker was standing there in his gray three-piece suit, with his hands behind his back, looking out through the window. "Glucose and H-two-oh," he said without turning around.

Huh? John was trying to think what that was, what the hell the Chief was talking about. He was wishing he'd paid more attention in Chemistry class. Then something finally got through the cloud of stupid that was swirling around his head. "Sugar water?"

"Yeah."

What the hell did that mean? John had heard of kids getting sugar highs and then crashing, but he couldn't remember anybody going off on a killing spree after drinking a soda. Then the stupid cleared out the rest of the way. "The sample was a fake?"

Horsebreaker shrugged. "Either that or Must is."

John thought about that for a minute, stunned. It didn't make any sense. "A boatload of people are dead and we found something in the blood of both of the killers. I don't think the shit is fake. Maybe somebody tipped off our hookup?" He could see how that might have happened, how James Earl might have switched vials on them, giving Hotwire Kool-aid because he'd figured out that the weasel was wearing a wire.

"Maybe."

"Either that or . . ." He wasn't sure why this one came to him last. Maybe at heart he was just a trusting bastard. "Either that or Hotwire switched out the real stuff right before he gave it to me."

The Chief turned around. "Your guess is as good as mine."

"But how would he know ahead of time what the package would look like?"

Horsebreaker just stood there looking at him, waiting for his brain to kick in again. "Oh, right. We didn't know what the package would look like ourselves, going in. We'd never seen it before. He could've given us a box of Jujubes and we wouldn't know the damned difference." John felt his blood pressure start to go up. He was getting pissed, which was something he tried hard not to let happen. It was almost like letting yourself get drunk—you tended to do things you wished later you hadn't. But the motherfucking weasel had played them for suckers! Now he was probably out there trying to sell the real stuff on the street and double his money. "I think I'll go have a talk with Leroy," John said, gritting his teeth.

The Chief had been standing there watching while the change came over him. "Just try not to lose your cool, OK? Try not to beat the shit out of him unless he really deserves it."

#

John was pretty sure Hotwire really deserved it. All he could think about as he drove through Palmer out towards the weasel's shack by the Sherry River was how he took three hundred bucks of the Department's money and gave them a bottle of damned sugar water for it. Horsebreaker was right though. He needed to simmer down. This wasn't L.A., where you could kick some punk's teeth in and expect to get promoted. John saw a drugstore up ahead and decided to stop in for some Tums. His heartburn was killing him. Either Leroy was to blame or the veggie burger he'd had for lunch at the Zoo.

He parallel-parked alongside the street and went into a Walgreen's. He bought four rolls of antacid and crunched one of them down while the girl at the register was ringing him up. Then he went outside and got back in his Nova. He tossed the bag with the rest of the rolls in it onto the seat. It slid off onto the floorboard.

Damn. He leaned across the bench-seat to pick the bag up and that's when he heard what he thought might be a car backfiring. Then somebody screamed. He felt little pieces of something showering down all over him. What the hell was going on? He turned and looked up without actually getting up and saw that his driver's side window was missing. Somebody had shot the glass out. He heard more screaming then, and honking horns, and what sounded an awful lot like gunfire.

BLAM! BLAM! BLAM! John reached inside his coat and pulled out his Smith & Wesson. He came up out of his hole, slowly. A lot of cars parallel-parked on the other side of the street were missing their windows, too. There was a woman sitting inside one of them. Her head was slumped on the wheel. There was blood in her hair. There was blood on the side of her face, too, and she wasn't moving. She was done moving.

Jesus Christ! John could hear more screams and more gunfire, coming from somewhere up ahead. He stuck his police light on top of the car. He turned it on and pulled out into the street. Little pieces of glass were still falling from what was left of his driver side window. What the hell was going down here? He saw a yellow Ford Mustang turning right on Division a couple of blocks ahead of him. Some guy was leaning out the passenger side. He had a handgun. BLAM! John heard more screaming.

He slipped on his hands-free and called the station, while he was roaring down the street toward Division. The light had just turned but he barreled through anyway, hoping like hell that the cars going east and west would hear his wimpy little siren.

"Dispatch, Shirley."

"Shirley, this is John Briggs. Can you tell me what's happening down on Division? The cross street is Mercer."

"I don't show anything, John. Have you got a situation?"

"You could say that, yeah. Some asshole is shooting people out of his car. He's headed east now. Ford Mustang, yellow. He's hanging out the passenger side with a gun. Semi-automatic. I can't tell who's driving him."

"Have you got a plate?"

"Not yet, can't get close enough."

"I'm calling for backup. Stay on the line. Let me know if he turns off of Division."

John saw somebody else dead in a car that was parked alongside the street. And another one dead on the sidewalk. *Jesus Christ.* How could he be the first one calling this in? It must have just happened. The guy in the yellow Mustang had seen him now; he leaned out the window and fired. The Mustang was speeding up. It blew through a red light, taking John with it. People were honking and cursing at the cross street behind him, not knowing how lucky they were just to be alive.

BLAM! A bullet hit the front of John's Chevy. He wanted to shoot back, but needed both hands on the wheel. They came out of downtown to where Division Street opened up. Out here it was called Highway 19. They were still headed east. There were stores on both sides of the road, even here, but at least they were spread out from each other, and you didn't have crowds of people standing around on the sidewalks.

BLAM! Who *was* this son-of-a-bitch, anyway? All John could tell was that he looked like a punk. After what had happened at the Fishbowl and down on the mall, that made him feel a little sick to his stomach.

BLAM! Whoever was driving the Mustang for him had opened up the throttle. They were starting to pull away. John stomped down on the accelerator, hard, trying to keep up with them. He thought he heard sirens in the distance now, but it sounded like backup was still a ways off. Could he take out this punk before he killed anyone else? John couldn't see how. The faster he had to go to keep up with the Mustang, the less safe it was for him to let go of the steering wheel, even for a second, even with just one hand.

Shirley was back on the line. "Confirming . . . suspect . . . east . . . Division." John was having a hard time hearing her with the air rushing in through his busted-out window.

"Yeah, though now it's Highway 19. And he's up past eighty, most of the time."

"Backup . . . try . . . cut him off . . . Horan."

Horan was the next real town east out the highway. At least there were fewer people out here. John locked in behind the Mustang, chasing it. Every now and then the guy on the passenger's side would get off a shot at him. Now the driver swung out into oncoming traffic.

Shit! He just missed hitting a pickup truck head-on. John fell back, waiting for the lane to clear. He lost some ground. The Mustang was a good ten car-lengths ahead now. John gave it the gas. He was gaining. He was back on his tail. BLAM! The S.O.B was shooting at him again. John's windshield shattered. He couldn't see. He was up above eighty-five and suddenly he couldn't see. He slammed on the brakes. He was skidding. The Nova turned sideways across the highway. He was fighting to keep the wheels on the road, fighting to keep the car from flipping over. He was sliding towards a swamp. There wasn't a damn thing he could do about it. He hit the water. His head snapped forward into the steering wheel and the airbag came out. His face was buried inside a balloon. For a second he couldn't breathe but then he managed to pull out of it, just enough so he could suck some air back into his lungs.

The car was sinking. Water poured in through the busted window. He started to panic, thinking he might drown, but turns out the swamp had a shallow bottom. The Nova had sunk up about as far as it was going to go. There was water inside, up to his waist, but the good news was that made it easy to open the door. He stepped out of the car and staggered. Things were spinning around. He grabbed onto the door to keep from toppling over. Then he looked up the road that led to Horan. It was empty. The light on top of his car was still flashing, red-blue, red-blue, but the siren was busted. Smoke was coming out from under the hood of the Nova. John was waist-deep in the swamp and the car was sunk up in it too, as far as the top of the wheel wells. There were little yellow flowers blooming up and down the side of the highway. He realized then that his left arm wasn't working. It was hanging down limp at his side. He could feel it; he just couldn't move it. It was hanging down at his side.

John was standing there in all that bright sunshine, holding his gun in his right hand, wondering what the hell to do next, when he saw it. The Mustang was headed back this way. Had they run into a roadblock up near Horan or were the sons-of-bitches so crazy they were coming back to finish him off?

BLAM! John guessed that answered his question. There was a splash in the swamp right in front of what was left of his Chevy. The Mustang was coming at him. John lifted his gun.

BLAM! A bullet hit the water just off to the left of him. He propped his Smith & Wesson up on top of the open car door to steady it. He sighted along the barrel. His left arm was still hanging limp at his side. It had been a long time since he'd had to shoot anybody. He still went out to the range twice a month to keep his cert up, because he had to, but that was different than actually trying to bring somebody down.

BLAM! John wasn't trying to kill anybody; he didn't *want* to kill anybody; he just wanted to stop that kid in the Mustang from shooting at him. He just wanted to blow one of the tires out.

BLAM! Another shot whistled by in the air over his head. He blotted that out. He blotted out everything now except the gun barrel and his finger on the trigger and how slow and easy that finger was squeezing.

His shot, when it came, sounded more like a BOOM than a BLAM, and he felt the recoil in his arm all the way up to his shoulder. The Mustang's front left tire blew. It went into a skid. It fishtailed back and forth on the highway. Then it flipped over. It flipped over and slid along on its top for a while, and sparks showered up onto the pavement. It went off onto the shoulder. It hung up there, though, instead of sliding all the way into the swamp like John's Nova had done.

WHOOM! Not the sound of a gun this time; it was the sound of the car catching fire.

Jesus Christ! John scrambled up out of the swamp and ran across the highway towards the Mustang. Was anybody inside still alive? He knew he had to get there fast or there wouldn't be. He had to get in there before the fire really took hold, before the whole damned thing blew up on him. With the car upside down and the top flattened and flames leaping out of the windows it was hard to see anything. But it looked like somebody in there was still moving. Not the punk on the passenger's side, the one who had been doing the shooting; he was hanging out the window and there wasn't much left of him. John ran around to the other side. The driver was trying to crawl out of the wreckage. Christ, he was burning. John tried to pull him out, tried to beat the flames off him. That was when he screamed bloody murder. When *she* screamed bloody murder and then tried to attack him.

It was a woman. It was a woman and the back of her shirt was burning and her hair was burning and she was coming right at him. "Ma'am, I have to ask you to stop," said John, "Ma'am . . ." He wasn't even quite sure what the hell he was saying. She looked like she might be from hell herself, come to think of it, what with all that screaming, what with her hair burning. She turned her head a little and now John could see that part of her face on the left side was missing, that the flesh there had been scraped off the bone.

"Wait just a minute there, Ma'am, now just hold on . . ." Shit, she was still coming at him. She had something in her hand. It looked like a butcher knife. "Hold on, would you, Ma'am? Just hold on. Stop, or I'm afraid I'm going to have to shoot you." John lifted his gun up in front of him. "Stop!"

She kept coming. She was younger than he'd thought at first, maybe only about seventeen. "Stop now or I really am going to have to shoot you!"

She kept coming.

John squeezed off a shot in the air, hoping that might snap her out of it.

She kept coming. She was screaming again. She had a butcher knife and a face that looked like a zombie's and she just kept coming at him. He heard sirens. They weren't all that far away now. If he could just hold her off for another minute or two . . . She rushed him. She rushed him with the knife out in front of her and he only had a second to decide what to do, if he could take her with only one good arm or if he was going to have to shoot her. He didn't want to have to shoot her but she was still screaming like she was from hell, and she still had the knife and she was still coming at him. He shot her.

He tried to shoot her in the leg like you're supposed to do if you can, to bring the suspect down without killing her, but because she was moving the target kept changing and the next thing he knew she'd dropped to the ground like he'd hit her OFF button. She was lying there, bleeding and burning. John couldn't tell where the stream of blood was coming from, if that was because he'd shot her or because of the wreck but in the end he guessed it didn't matter. His legs gave out on him. He sat down in the middle of the highway. It wasn't like he fell; it was more like he just couldn't stand up any longer. He was sitting there smack dab on the double yellow line. Good thing there weren't any cars coming. Well, there *were* cars coming now but they were all cops and troopers; their sirens sounded like they were right on top of him.

The yellow Mustang was upside down on the side of the road, burning. The woman who'd been driving it was lying there in the westbound lane, burning. John was shaking. He was shaking so hard he couldn't even hold his gun anymore. It slipped out of his hand. It hit the pavement. The sun was beating down and there was smoke rising from the Mustang and he still couldn't move his left arm. Sirens. John looked back at his car. It was halfway sunk up in the swamp and the front fender was crumpled and the front and side windows were busted out and there were bullet holes in the hood. Then it was like Hambone was there with him; it was like the two of them were sitting there together, talking. It was like he was there with John, waiting for the ambulance to come. It wasn't hot anymore. John felt cold. He was trying to tell Ham what had just happened.

"You know how I said you could have this car in a year or two?"

Hambone was looking at him like he was afraid he'd gone off the deep end. "Yeah, Dad?"

"Well, I don't think you're gonna want it anymore."
And that's when the whole world went black on him.

Chapter 21

Tom Etheridge was the first one to come see him in the Emergency Room. "Hey, man," he said, "How you feeling?"

"I've been better," confessed John. His left arm was still numb but according to the EMTs ought to heal up in a day or two. Just a stinger, they said. He had a cut on his forehead but they'd already stitched it up; he couldn't even feel it anymore. Now that he could stop worrying about himself, though, he was starting to worry about Hambone.

"He's all right," Tom said with a grin, "When you didn't pick him up at school, Sleeper called me as the backup, just like he's supposed to."

"That's good. He may be an asshole, but he's a thorough asshole. Or maybe just thoroughly an asshole." John was starting to relax a little.

"Anyway, Ham's out in the lobby, if you want to see him. I wouldn't let him come back because I wasn't sure what kind of shape you'd be in."

"Can you bring him back now?"

"You bet, man."

Tom ducked out but came right back, with Hambone behind him. Poor kid looked scared. "Dad!" He came running over. He gave John a hug.

"I'm OK," John said, "It's good to see you."

"Good to see you, too, Dad."

Tom turned on the TV set above the bed and just as he did they broke in with a newsflash about the shootings out on Highway 19. The camera was looking down at the burning Mustang from somewhere above.

"Where'd they get this footage, Tom, a chopper?"

"Yeah. Once all this started Channel 4 sent Eye-in-the-Sky, the traffic lady, out there to cover it."

They watched for a while. Black smoke was rising up from the Mustang. A body was burning in the middle of the highway. Some guy was squatting right on the double yellow stripe, like he'd sat down there for a picnic. John knew he was that guy but that guy didn't really look like him, somehow. Police cars were blocking the road, lights flashing. The crawl underneath the picture kept saying the same thing over and over again: *High speed chase ends with two dead and police officer injured. Suspects went on killing spree in Mayfair. As many as 15 shot with semi-automatic pistol.*

John remembered the rest of it then, how the whole thing had started. It all came rushing back at him. He remembered the woman in the car across the street from the drugstore, her head slumped forward, her face bleeding. "Jesus Christ, Tom, did they really kill that many people?"

He nodded, grimly. "Would have been a whole lot more, I'm guessing, if you hadn't of been there. Bet you get a commendation."

"A suspension, more likely."

"Well, that too. You shot somebody. Horsefucker won't have any choice."

"I guess I could use a few days off," said John.

"I'll bet you could."

They kept showing footage from the copter cam, over and over. They kept running the same crawl. *Fifteen people.* John felt cold. He was thinking that at least he didn't need to wait for any tox report this time. He was pretty sure he knew already what those two kids in the Mustang were high on.

They were showing something else now. Either new footage had just come in or maybe they'd had this all along and were only now deciding to go with it. It was the same scene but a few seconds earlier. John and the zombie girl were still there but now he was up on his feet and she was alive. Her hair was on fire. The camera shot was coming from far away at first but then, without warning, it zoomed.

"Jesus Christ!" cried Ham.

You could see the girl's face burning; you could see part of her skull showing. Who the hell had let this get on the air? Tomorrow, that guy would get a promotion.

"Dad!" Ham sounded like he couldn't breathe. John wanted to turn the

TV off, wanted to keep his son from seeing this, but he didn't have the remote and Tom Etheridge, who did, was standing there hypnotized.

"Dad, they've got to do something!" Ham said while the girl burned, and when John turned to look at him he was a little kid again, one who was little-kid scared. "They've got to do something or there won't be anything left but a city full of dead people!"

John wished he could say a few words to calm him down but right at that moment couldn't think of any that would. Because he was a little scared himself. Because he still didn't know what this drug Must really was, and he didn't know how the hell they were ever going to get a handle on it.

Part Two

Darkest Africa

Chapter 22

"Tell me again why I need to be here?" It was the morning after the shoot-out on Highway 19, and John was meeting the Chief on the Capitol steps. But he wasn't real happy about it.

"Because Mayor Crawford specifically asked me to bring you." The Chief seemed to fit right in with all those suits walking in and out of that big gold dome, but John felt like a fish out of water.

"You just got some good publicity at the wrong time," Horsebreaker explained with a tight little smile, "Crawford is probably feeling like he needs a hero to help save his political hide."

"Swell."

"How's the arm?"

"Swell." It was still in a sling; what was he supposed to say? They finished climbing the steps and went into the building. John looked up at the high ceiling inside the rotunda, wishing the hell he could fly. The Chief led him through a set of tall double doors. Why couldn't he just go back to his office, thought John, feeling miserable; meeting with the Mayor wasn't going to solve any damned crimes!

"Good morning, Chief!" the receptionist said with a smile that seemed different from the one she showed the public. "Mayor Crawford is expecting you." She just nodded at John.

Horsebreaker led him back to Moses' office. That really was the Mayor's first name, Moses, a hard one to say without rolling your eyes. Still, John had voted for the guy in the last election, though right at the moment he was having a hard time remembering why.

"Ah, Chief Horsebreaker. Glad you could make it, Ed. And this must be the famous Detective Briggs?"

The Mayor was a tall, thin man with a smile that came easy and seemed a bit phony. He had salt-and-pepper hair and a skinny mustache that looked like a matching accessory. Brown eyes that were warm and friendly up front but said *don't fuck with me* underneath. He was wearing a gray three-piece suit that made the Chief's look shabby, and that took some doing.

"I take it you know the Commissioner?"

John knew him well enough to stay out of his way. Fat guy, balding, son-of-a-bitch. James Egan was his name. He was one of about forty reasons why John would never want Horsebreaker's job. Egan used to be a wrestler in college and had a wrestler's torn-up ears; even when he was wearing a suit he looked like he was about ready to come across the table and kick the Greco-Roman shit out of you. Why didn't they just turn *him* loose on whoever was out there dealing Must? Maybe they would. Maybe that was the plan. No such duck-fucking luck.

"Have a seat, gentlemen, please," said the Mayor.

The four of them sat down around a table that was big enough to hold eighteen, made of some kind of dark wood you'd never find in a house in Palmer. There were glasses and a carafe of water almost within reach— John would have loved to have had some but wasn't about to call attention to himself. With only one good hand, he figured he'd probably spill the damned thing anyway.

"I think you all know why we're here," said Crawford, "We have a bit of a crisis brewing." Funny how when he was dedicating a new mall it was always "I this" and "I that," but as soon as the shit hit the fan it was "we" who had a problem. Now why was it he'd voted for this guy?

Crawford recapped for them what they already knew better than he did. "Mass, unpredictable violence," was how the Mayor characterized what had been happening. "That's one thing that can cripple a city in a hurry. There's a certain level of crime that most of us can tolerate, that you might even say is part and parcel of urban living, the trade-off, if you will, for having all the comforts of civilization close at hand. And hell, it keeps the news people busy!" he added, laughing.

Not to mention Law Enforcement, thought John. Which was worse, he wondered: a politician or a goddamned Must dealer?

"We have reached a point, however, where people are starting to panic. They're closing up, shutting down."

Was he talking about people or businesses?

"I know the police are doing their best," Crawford said, in a way that let John know he didn't think they were, "yet clearly we have to step up our efforts. We've got to shut this drug traffic down. We're making national news, gentlemen, and not in a good way. That's especially unfortunate with the summer tourist season right around the corner. That's especially unfortunate, coming as it is on the heels of so many reports of drug violence in Mexico. All those crazies who want to build a Berlin wall along the Rio Grande will be using us for ammunition; they'll be saying the drug cartels have finally crossed the border onto American soil, that they're taking control of our cities."

Finally, John was starting to remember why he'd voted for Crawford: the guy who had run against him last time was worse. He'd been one of those wall builders

"Clearly, Mr. Mayor," said Commissioner Egan, scratching one of his cauliflower ears, "drastic measures are called for. I say we bring in the Guard."

Crawford winced. "Nonononono!" he said, spreading his hands on the table, "That's the *last* thing we should do. Think about it, Jim—would you take your family on vacation to a city that's under martial law?"

"Well now, I might," said Egan. "At least I'd know the town was safe."

"It seems as though you have a different plan in mind, Mr. Mayor," said Chief Horsebreaker diplomatically, "What would you like us to do?"

"What I would like you to do is your jobs!" he said, in a tone of voice that was rapidly taking a turn for the worse. "Let other things go if you have to. Stop writing so damned many parking tickets!" he thundered. John wondered how many the police force had written *him* lately. "Look, we're this close to losing the city!" snarled Crawford, holding up a thumb and forefinger like he was ready to pinch something off, "We've got to get a handle on this drug—not next month, not next week, fucking now!"

Well shit, *that* was a directive, thought John. Nearly impossible to follow in the real world, but it was a directive. The Chief and Egan and John looked at each other across the table, each one knowing his butt was now officially on the line.

The Mayor's feathers were finally starting to unruffle. "This is what we're going to do," he said calmly. "Tuesday, when I hold my regular press conference, I'm going to announce that I personally am launching an all-out war on this drug Must and I'm going to promise the citizens of this fair city of ours that we'll have it off the streets by June first. Detective Briggs, you'll be standing at my side, as a symbol of the commitment our city's finest have pledged to provide. Jim and Ed, all you have to do is look grim. But I hope that long before any of us gets to Tuesday, you'll have both rolled up your sleeves and dug in, because I'm serious when I say that by June One either Must will be a thing of the past, or our Police Chief and Commissioner will be."

#

"Well, the Mayor was pretty clear in there, wasn't he?" said Egan, once the meeting was over and the three of them were standing outside on the Capitol steps.

"Crystal," the Chief said.

"Umm, where exactly are we on this Must thing right now, anyway?" It sounded like the Commissioner was out of the loop and had just found out that he needed to get back in, in a hurry.

"Not much of anywhere, to tell you the truth," shrugged Horsebreaker, "Right now we don't even know exactly what it is . . . or what it looks like."

"I guess it would be good to know what we're dealing with," said Egan, "but maybe in a way it doesn't matter. What matters is that we shut it down. Go after the pushers. Cut off the supply. See if we can find out who Mr. Big is. There has to be one, right?" He looked off across the steps towards downtown. "You know, this just might be a golden opportunity. Maybe it gives us a chance to clean up drug traffic in this town once and for all. We don't know what Must looks like, so we confiscate everything that isn't an aspirin. Make a clean sweep. In six weeks we have this place looking like Disneyworld!"

"Or Singapore," the Chief muttered.

"What's that?"

"Look, Commissioner," Horsebreaker said, "we can't just lock up every drug user in the city. We don't have that many cells. And most of those are full already. I don't think it's going to help us, either, to try and confiscate everything that even smells like a drug. We'll just open ourselves up to lawsuits and lose the trust of the people we're trying to protect. Once we've searched a few dozen junkies, I'm guessing we'll know what Must looks like and we can focus our efforts there. If we let word get out that

176

that's all we're after, and why, we may even get some of the airheads on our side. They're always wondering why we don't leave them alone and go after the people who are selling shit that kills souls; let's tell them that's the new campaign."

Egan looked like he was thinking it over. John could tell he really hated letting go of the idea of cracking down and cracking heads, but he'd been in the business long enough that he had to know the practical limitations of the job. You only had so much time, so many resources. You had to pick and choose your battles. "All right," he said, nodding, "Well, what are you two still standing here for?" And then he stomped off to look for his white Cadillac, leaving John and the Chief to commiserate.

Horsebreaker took a deep breath. "Oh-kay," he said.

John felt that way, too, like they'd dodged a bullet. "What about Leroy Miller? I'll bet I can still get that hit of Must from him."

"Don't bother. Like I said, we start busting junkies and we'll know what we're looking for within a few days. Or hours, depending on how much of this shit is out there."

"All right. What do you want me to do next, then?"

Horsebreaker was giving John a funny look. "What I want you to do is give me your badge and gun."

"What?"

"You shot somebody, remember? The Mayor may think you're a hero but there's this set of regs I have to follow. They say if you use deadly force I have to put you on Admin Leave while the investigation plays out, unless maybe the guy you shot was Satan himself."

John handed them over. "Any idea when I might get these back?"

The Chief grinned. "Now that I *do* have some control over. We know for sure you've got to be reinstated by Tuesday, don't we, for the Mayor's press conference? So why don't we shoot for Monday morning. That means this may be the quickest internal investigation on record, but given what you've done for the city, I don't think that'll be a problem."

"Thanks," John said, and meant it. He wasn't sure what he would do if he had to hang around the house for much longer than that.

Chapter 23

It was late morning by the time John got back to the house, driving the crappy Dodge rental car they'd given him while his Nova was in the shop. He climbed the stairs and then stood looking around the empty den, wondering what the hell he was supposed to do all day on a weekday. There ought to be *some* way he could move the investigation along, even if he was stuck at home with a busted wing! He sat down on the couch. He thought about what Commissioner Egan had said, that they needed to cut off the supply of Must and run down Mr. Big. Easier said than done. Whoever was pulling the strings probably didn't live in the city. Might have even come here from overseas. Africa, maybe. Sunlight streamed in through the window. It was quiet, so damned quiet. Was this how things were going to be all the time, once Hambone went off to college? That'd happen sooner or later, probably a lot sooner than John would be ready for it. Then it'd be just him and his good buddies, Web and Boob, just him surfing the Internet all day long or watching TV.

He decided to hang with Web for a while. He fired up his laptop. Then he sat there staring at the white search box on Google, wondering what to throw in there. Africa? That was the big question mark in all of this, wasn't it? James Earl Jones sounded like he might have come from Africa. Must might be coming from elephants, and they lived in Africa. At least some of them did. There wasn't any point in typing in "Africa" by itself, though; it was a continent, for Christ's sake! What about "Must?" He'd tried that once before and had struck out swinging. If it was coming from over there, though, wouldn't some of those people be using it, too? Maybe they called it something else? How was he supposed to know what they *did* call it, though? He felt like he had to type something just to stop the damned cursor from blinking at him, so finally he threw "Africa" and "illegal drugs" in together to see what would happen. Eleven million hits came up. Looked like things were just as bad in that neck of the woods as they were over here! John skimmed the first page.

Illegal narcotics trade in South Africa.
BBC report: Does Africa have a drug problem?
Kenya: the war on illegal drugs has flopped.

That third one kind of caught his eye, maybe because it mentioned Kenya. Wasn't that where Jill went every year, to work with her elephants? John clicked the link. He started reading the article. There wasn't anything in there about Must, but as he scrolled down the page words kept jumping out at him.

. . . *documented evidence reveals that drug barons have a firm grip on law enforcement machinery . . . worse still, rumours suggest that some of those drug barons may be government officials . . . meanwhile use of heroin, not to mention local products such as changaa and khat continue to rage unabated.*

What the hell were changaa and khat? Could one of those be their name for Must? He got a little excited for a minute, until he looked them up on Wikipedia. Khat, it turned out, was just a weed some people chewed on to get a cheap high. Changaa was a little more hard core:

Changaa or *Chang'aa* (literal meaning "kill me quick") is an alcoholic drink which is popular in Kenya. Its production and distribution is controlled in many cases by criminal gangs like the Mungiki and Nzige. The alcoholic content of Changaa is sometimes increased by adding substances like jet fuel, embalming fluid or battery acid, which has the effect of giving the beverage more 'kick'. In Nairobi slums like Korogocho, the water used to make the drink is often contaminated with feces, and women's underwear along with decomposing dead rats have been found in the drink during police raids.

Now *that* shit sounded like bad news! But it wasn't what he was looking for. John leaned his head back on the sofa and let out a long breath. So, he hadn't learned much of anything except that Nairobi was a rough town. It was hard to imagine Jill over there but then she probably just flew into the airport and drove straight out into the wild. *The Wild.* Funny that people called it that. Sounded like the slums of Nairobi were one hell of a lot wilder than anything you'd find in the bush! John looked back at that original article about Kenya's war on illegal drugs. It was embedded in an online newspaper called *Daily Nation.* He used the links to back out to what looked like the front page. There were the same kinds of headlines you'd find anyplace else: Train Wrecks! Politicians! Weren't those pretty much the same damned thing? Then something else caught his eye.

It wasn't an article this time, it was an ad for some local outfitter called "I Safari." John wouldn't have given it a second thought except for the picture that went along with it: a photo of the owner, the big Bwana himself, a guy John could have sworn he'd seen somewhere before. The caption underneath read: *Roger Sutherland, Proprietor and Big Game Hunter.* Wasn't that the guy in the picture on Jill Relson's wall? The same guy who had his arm around her? So that was his name: Roger Sutherland. John looked at him. Big smile, straight white teeth. Blue eyes with crows' feet around them. He looked like he spent a lot of time out in the sun. Well yeah, he led safaris for a living! Photo safaris, John found out when he read a little more on the website. Apparently, they didn't do the other kind anymore. John clicked further in.

"I Safari" took tourists out to some place called Amboseli, and there were lots of pictures: cheetahs on a grassy plain that looked like it went on forever; an elephant herd with Mount Kilimanjaro in the background; wildebeest crossing a river. A row of khaki-colored tents. People sitting in a circle, at dusk, around a sparking campfire. And there, in the center of that circle, holding court, was Big Bwana Roger . . . and Jill. Or somebody who looked an awful lot like her.

Well, suppose it *was* her? She was a grown woman. She'd lived a life. It was just interesting, that was all. John clicked on a link labeled "About the Bwana." Born in Wimbledon, England. Played tennis for a while for a living before finding out that his "true passion" was Africa. Oxford educated, photographer, writer . . . he sounded like a damned renaissance man! John had to remind himself that this was written for the express purpose of pumping the Bwana up, to sucker tourists in. He had to remind himself that if Roger Sutherland and Jill had anything going on she'd be over there more than once a year. It wasn't any of his business anyway.

The phone rang. John picked it up, thinking it might be the body shop with some bad news about his car. Instead, it was Jill.

"Finally!" she said. "I've been trying to reach you since yesterday afternoon, ever since I saw the news story. Are you all right?"

John said he was, except for his arm. Even that was getting better. He could move it a little now and it was doing a lot of tingling.

"Good, that's all good," said Jill, but then it was like she didn't know what else to say. "Well, I won't keep you. I was just a bit worried and wanted to be sure you were OK."

"It was nice of you to check up on me." John was feeling better about the Bwana business now: Roger Sutherland was halfway around the world, and Jill was on the phone with him. "How were the girls today?"

"Rambunctious," she said, with a laugh. "Mitzi knocked me over, accidentally."

"You all right?"

"Just a few bruises. It's an occupational hazard, I suppose, sort of like gun-toting criminals are for you."

John laughed. "Usually not. Most of the time, I'm a desk jockey. I was just in the wrong place at the wrong time, I guess."

"That happens. Say, were you ever able to get a recording of that drug dealer's voice for me?"

Drug dealer's voice. For a second, John drew a blank. Then he remembered: James Earl Jones. "You know, I forgot to ask the techs about that. I'll give them a call."

"Great. Are we still on for Saturday night?"

"I'll be there if I have to pick you up in a wheelchair," said John.

Chapter 24

First thing the next morning, John phoned the Station and had them patch him through to Curtis Livingston in the tech lab.

"Well, good morning, Detective, how are you? We've all been watching your exploits on the news! People here have been calling you 'Dirty Harry!'"

Christ, thought John. He told Curtis why he was calling.

"Always business, aren't we? And I was hoping this might be a social call! Well, let me check into that for you. We *may* have kept a copy."

He went away for a few minutes while John sat on the couch watching a talking dish mop tell him how to clean up his kitchen. Who the hell needed to take drugs when you could hallucinate just watching TV? Then Curtis came back on the line. "Why, yes, we do have that. Would you like me to burn a CD for you?"

John said he would. He asked the tech when he might be able to pick it up.

"This afternoon, if you'd like."

"I'd like." It would give him something to do, at least, a reason to get out of the damned house.

"We're all hoping you feel better soon, Detective," said Curtis, in a voice that to John sounded sickly-sweet, "Just know this: that you truly *are* a hero!"

"Just burn the damned CD for me, would you?" said John, and hung up the phone.

#

After lunch John drove out to the station to pick up the CD, but along the way decided he'd stop by the Center to see how Grandma was doing. When he got there he found everyone crowded around the big TV

182

in the common room, watching the news. The anchor was talking about the killing spree out on Highway 19, and how that had put the whole city on edge. John didn't know that the city *would* be on edge if they didn't keep telling it that it was. If they'd just stop replaying clips of that crazy woman with the knife in her hand people might have a chance to catch their breath. How many times were they going to show her on fire? How many times were they going to let the camera zoom in on that missing part of her face?

"Lordy, John, just look at what they've done to you!" Grandma came running over and started checking up on his sling.

"It's not anything, Grandma. Don't you worry about it."

"Well now, I will if I want to! Are you all right, Honey?"

John said he was. He found himself watching TV along with everyone else. That burning woman was about the last thing he wanted to see, but at the same time he couldn't take his eyes off her. That's when he realized this wasn't the local news, that the story must have gone national. The Mayor was right. They didn't need this kind of publicity.

"Young man? Oh, young man? I wonder if I might borrow your phone again?"

Oh hell, it was Lester! He looked sharp in his white shirt and red bow tie, like he belonged in a Norman Rockwell instead of an old folks' home. John felt sorry for him but not sorry enough to lend him his phone again. Last time he liked to have never got it back.

"I'm sorry, Mr. Covington, but you know I think I must've forgot it this morning. Left it at home." John made a show of searching through his pockets with his one good hand, at least the pockets where he knew for sure he wouldn't find it.

"I'd really like to call my wife."

"Yes, sir, I know. She does like to keep track of you, doesn't she?" Even from the Promised Land. John's heart went out to him, but he wasn't about to give him his phone. Then the damned thing went off. John couldn't believe it. It started playing "Free Bird" right there in the common room! It took Lester a few seconds to figure out what was going on, but he did. Then he put his hands on his hips and gave John the evil eye.

"Liar, liar, pants on fire!"

Christ, how bad could one week get? Shot at out on Highway 19, wrecked his car, got roped into the Mayor's press conference, and now some ninety-year-old with Alzheimer's was calling him a fibber right in front of his own grandmother!

"Well, what do you know?" John said. "There it is! Guess I didn't forget it after all. Hold on there for a minute, though, Mr. Covington; I need to take this call." He did, actually; the ringtone was Ham's. John caught a glimpse of Grandma's face as he was digging the cell out of his pocket and she was laughing at him. She was telling him with her eyes what she used to tell him out loud the whole time he was growing up: *Never lie, Honey. People always find out!*

Turns out Hambone wanted to know if he could ride home with Mick after school. John said OK. "You want me to pick you up there later on?"

"Nah, I think they can give me a ride."

"Just make sure it's not too late. Tonight's a school night, you know."

"I know. How about if I get home by nine?"

John had to stop and think about that for a minute. It was a little later than he'd really like, but . . . "OK, if you can get all your schoolwork done while you're there."

"Can do, Pops. Thanks."

What was this "Pops" business? Kid was making him feel old! Grandma came up close to John then and whispered in his ear: "You'd better get out while you can, Honey. I'll see what I can do with good Mr. Covington."

#

John drove down to the station. He sneaked into the tech lab through a side door, hoping nobody would see him. Whenever he went in there, he always felt like he'd stepped onto the set of a James Bond movie, except the gadgets they had weren't anywhere near as cool as Q's: no machine gun umbrellas or exploding shoes or anything that might *really* come in handy when you were in a tight spot! Just your everyday boring, real-world police stuff like phone taps and tracers and wires.

John found Curtis in his cubicle and put a finger to his lips before the tech could say anything. "I'm trying to keep a low profile," he whispered, "I'm on Admin Leave, you know, until Monday. Not even supposed to be in the building."

Curtis's eyes got wide. "Oh, right. Understood, Detective," he whispered. He looked like he was having way too much fun with this. "I have the recording for you right here." He handed John a CD.

"Thanks."

"Don't mention it, Detective!" He winked.

John couldn't get out of there fast enough. He went back to his car and put the CD on the seat beside him, thinking he'd listen to it once he got home. That's when he realized he didn't have to wait. His Nova just had a cassette player, but apparently most cars that had been built since The Flood came standard equipped for CDs. John popped the disc in and pushed play. As far as entertainment value, the CD was just a step up from rap: lots of long silences (that was the part that made it better), and static (actually, that made it better, too), and in between there was a bunch of useless talk from that weasel, Hotwire. It took a while before John got to the part where James Earl Jones came in.

"Please, remain where you are."

James Earl still sounded African to John, even through all that static. He barely said a dozen words, though, the whole time, so it was hard to know for sure. At least it was hard for John. Maybe it would be easy for Jill's professor friend in Atlanta.

"Place it on the floor then, please, in front of you."

"On the floor?"

"That is what I said, yes."

And then John came to that weird part where James Earl had asked Leroy if he was a "zero-zero." What the hell did that mean? John had to admit it was a pretty good description of the weasel, that when you came right down to it he wasn't worth squat, but you could tell James Earl had something else besides squat on his mind.

"Have you followed me here?"

That didn't make any sense unless James Earl thought Hotwire was somebody else. And how could you think that? Leroy was a one-of-a-kind weasel. Now John was at the part where the drug deal went down. And he found himself getting mad all over again, thinking about how Hotwire had swindled him, how the weasel had given him a vial of sugar water and kept the Must for himself.

John listened closely, thinking there might be a clue as to how and when that had happened. But of course Hotwire didn't say anything about switching the shit out. He was a prick but he wasn't stupid. At least not that stupid. He'd had plenty of time to make a trade, though: he could have done it while he was picking up the drugs that James Earl had left on the floor, or in those few minutes before he came out of the warehouse to meet John.

Thing was, either way he had to have planned this out ahead of time. That's what was really making John mad. If Leroy had done it on impulse, because he was a greedy little weasel, John could've understood it better. But Hotwire had to have brought that vial of sugar water to the sting along with him, which meant he had to have planned this all along.

Scrawny son-of-a-bitch! John was tempted to drive out to his place right then and take the Must back from him, no matter what the Chief said, and kick Leroy's ass while he was at it. He kind of hesitated, though, on account of not having two good arms. John looked down at his left hand, poking out of the sling. He tried to make a fist with it. He was surprised that he could. The feeling was coming back. The arm still felt weak, though. John didn't think he could count on it for much.

At the same time, if he was going to pay Leroy a visit he didn't want to wait too long to do it. Every day that went by meant Hotwire had another chance to sell the Must to somebody. It was pushing a week now since the sting. Maybe he *should* head on out there? He didn't even have a gun right now, though! The Chief had it. Maybe that was a good thing. Maybe if he didn't have a gun he wouldn't be tempted to kill Leroy with it? Maybe he'd work harder to keep his cool? John weighed the pros and cons. The Chief didn't seem to think they needed that hit of Must anymore. But it seemed to John that the sooner they knew what it looked like, and the sooner they could have the lab rats run some tests, the better off they'd be. Maybe none of that mattered though, when you came right down to it. Maybe all he really cared about was that Leroy Miller had duped him and was thinking he'd gotten away with it. John gritted his teeth, imagining that smug little weasel out on the street, bragging how he'd pulled a fast one on the stupid cops.

About the time John pulled up in front of his row house, he'd decided to do it. He'd decided he would drive out to the Landfill and pay Leroy a visit. It would be a good time, since Ham wasn't coming home until nine. He didn't have anything better to do. But before he headed out that way, towards the Sherry River, John went inside to get a little something for the road: a can of mace he'd taken away from Grandma back when he moved her into the Center. He'd practically had to pry it out of her hands, which he hated to do, but he was afraid if he didn't she'd use it on the staff there the first time she got pissed off at them. And he'd known for a fact that, sooner or later, she *would* get pissed off at them.

What about me, he wondered, *will I use it, if I get pissed off at Leroy?* Hell, he was pissed off already!

Chapter 25

John drove out past the Fishbowl into the cruddy little neighborhood that some people called The Landfill, along the banks of the Sherry River. Shacks and houseboats, mostly, with a few trailers thrown in. It took him a while to find Leroy's place, even though he knew where it was, because so many of those shacks looked alike. He parked his rental car about a block away and walked from there, so that hopefully the weasel wouldn't see him coming. John didn't want him slipping out the back before he could get his hands on him.

Try and keep your cool. John knew he had to keep his anger under wraps but a little bit of red kept surging up behind his eyes anyway, every time he thought about how Leroy had taken three hundred dollars of the Department's money and had given them a bottle of sugar water for it. He left his sling in the car. He didn't want anybody knowing that his left arm wasn't much good yet; he didn't want Leroy thinking he could get the jump on him.

It was four o'clock by then, still hot as hell; you'd think being so close to the water would have helped a little. It didn't. John stood there at the cross street looking down the alleyway that led to Leroy's shack, taking in the scene. There was a dirty wooden fence on the left, with some dirty wooden houses on the other side of it. On the right there was a silver trailer with a clothesline out front. Nothing on that line was moving. No breeze at all, just dead air. John could feel sweat building up along his hairline already. He could hear an invisible dog barking. Down past the end of the alley, at the bottom of the slope, was the Sherry. The late afternoon sun had set fire to it, which was kind of what John thought needed to happen to the whole damned neighborhood. He started walking.

Leroy's place was at the dead end, a crappy little cracker box that looked like an outhouse. The walls were just planks that didn't fit together too well. There was one little window on the side facing the river, but it was so dirty you couldn't see through it. John knew because he tried. Then he walked around to what passed for the door, wondering if he should knock or just break it down. That wouldn't be too hard. It was a sheet of plywood with a wire handle on it.

John decided to knock. He didn't have a warrant, and wasn't even here on official police business. Just a social call, really. Nobody answered. John knocked again, then pounded a little. Still, nobody answered. John tried peeking through the cracks in the walls. From one angle he thought he could see Leroy in there, lying face-down on what looked like an army cot. That's when he got worried. Maybe the weasel was dead? Maybe he'd OD'd on Must? Or maybe James Earl Jones had figured out that he was a snitch and had followed him back here and wasted him? Warrant or not, John figured he had to get in there.

There was cause, he practiced telling the Chief, for later; *I had reason to believe Mr. Miller might be in need of medical assistance.*

One good kick broke the latch. Hell, it wasn't even a good kick. "Hotwire?" John was halfway expecting him to jump up from the cot and whip out a Saturday Night Special, but Leroy didn't move. Shit, maybe he *was* dead? Either that or strung out real bad. John walked over to the cot, leaned over, and shook him. Leroy came up fast then, his white-blonde hair flying all over the place like dandelion tufts and he reached for something under the covers. John grabbed him by the arm before he could get it, and yanked him up to a sitting position.

"What the fuck?"

"Relax, Hotwire, it's me."

"Boss?" His eyes were all bloodshot to hell. The son-of-a-bitch *was* stoned! "What the fuck are you doing here, man? How the fuck did you get inside? You got a fucken warrant?"

John had told himself he wasn't going to get mad but as usual the sight of Leroy just naturally pissed him off. That, and his potty mouth. "Yeah, I got a warrant—to kick your sorry weasel ass to Kingdom Come."

"What the fuck do you want with me, man?"

"I want the shit I paid you for, Asshole."

"What shit?"

"You know what I'm talking about," said John. "That bottle of Must you got me last weekend was nothing but sugar water. I figure you palmed the real shit."

Leroy looked a little less stoned now. Adrenaline surge must have sobered him up. He was sitting on the edge of the cot and John was standing over him, waiting for him to make a run for it. "Why the fuck would I do that?"

"Because you're stupid. And greedy. You figured you'd sell it on the street and double your money."

"I wouldn't do that to you, Boss!"

"Glad to hear it. Then you won't mind if I look around?"

"Suit your fucken self."

John started kicking through a pile of clothes on the floor. He'd seen better stuff in the throwaway bin at the thrift store. The whole time he was looking, John was keeping one eye on Leroy. He figured sooner or later the weasel would make a break for it. There was nothing in the clothes but Leroy's bad smell. John took a step back. Then he remembered how Hotwire had been reaching under the covers for something. Maybe he hadn't been looking for a gun after all? "Stand up."

"What for?"

"Just stand up, Asshole." Leroy did, but John noticed that he tried to stay close to the cot. "Step over there for a minute." Leroy backed up a little and John bent down to reach under the sheet, keeping one eye on him. After he'd groped around for a minute, he came up with a little clear plastic bag. "Hello. What's this?"

"That ain't nothin', man, just a little meth I've been holding onto for a friend of mine. I don't use the shit myself, honest."

"It's not meth," John said, looking at the pile of rocks inside the bag. "Meth isn't blue. Little different texture, too." He stuck a finger in. It was a different consistency from either Crank or Crack; more like caked sugar than soap or wax. "I don't remember ever seeing shit like this before. You know, Leroy, I'm thinking this might be our missing Must. I'm thinking I ought to run you in."

Hotwire's eyes got dark when John called him "Leroy." Asshole and Weasel he could live with, but he had this thing about his real name. "On what fucken charge?"

"Possession, for starters. Unless you've got something you want to tell me?"

"I don't have shit to say to you, Boss!" He bolted. John was still ready. He kicked Leroy's legs out from under him. "Son-of-a-bitch!" screamed the weasel. Leroy was down on the floor. John had a knee in his back before he even knew what hit him.

"Are you using, Leroy?"

"Hell, no!" He was coughing down there in the dust and cobwebs.

John leaned down to where Leroy's face was mashed flat against the floor. "You going to tell me what you've been up to?"

"Fuck you, man!"

"All right. Then I guess I put the cuffs on you." At least the Chief hadn't taken those away! John whipped them out but in that second when he let go, Hotwire broke loose. He was on his feet, punching and screaming. The little asshole was wiry strong. John was having a hard time getting control of him. His left hand still wasn't much good. One of Leroy's haymakers got through, clipping John on the shoulder. That sent a bolt of lightning down his bum arm. *Jesus Christ,* he thought, *I'm losing him!* That's when he pulled the can of mace out of his pocket and sprayed Leroy full in the face with it.

"Ow, fuck. God *damn* it, Boss! Fuck you, man, fuck you!"

"You shoulda come quietly, Leroy."

"I can't fucken see!"

"With this shack of yours, that might be a blessing."

"Asshole!" Tears were streaming down Leroy's face and he had his hands over his eyes. John might've started to feel sorry for him except that's when the dirty window blew out, when bullets started ripping through the shack like the walls were made out of paper.

"Shit!" John dragged Hotwire back down to the floor with him. Leroy hit his head on the corner of the cot. He was bleeding.

"Fuck, man, just shoot me if you want to fucken kill me!"

"I don't but it looks like somebody out there does." John reached for his gun but couldn't find it. Then he remembered it wasn't there. Son-of-a-bitch! He was looking through the open plywood door to the outside, but couldn't see much of anything. Whoever was shooting at them was smart enough to have made sure the sun was behind him. Was it just one guy? A hell of a lot of bullets had just torn through the walls of Hotwire's shack, but the sound John kept hearing was the same one; it seemed to him that all those shots might be coming from the same damned gun. Crack!

There went another one. Assault rifle, maybe? One guy with an assault rifle, shooting at them from somewhere up there in the sun.

"Is there a back way out of here?" John asked Hotwire. Getting out the front door was looking dicey.

"It's a fucken *shack*, man!"

"Help me out here a little, wouldja? I'm trying to save your hide!"

"Yeah, so I can be a damned blind beggar for the rest of my fucken life!"

"Stop whining, Asshole. It'll clear up after a while."

"Fuck you, Fucker!"

Leroy was so pitiful John might have laughed at him if somebody hadn't been shooting at them right then. He crept a little closer to the open doorway, dragging Leroy along with him. There hadn't been any shots for a few seconds now; maybe the guy was out of ammo? Maybe he'd decided to split? Who the hell was he, anyway? James Earl Jones? Why would James Earl come after them, though, even if he'd figured out that Leroy was a snitch? Unless . . . Unless this had something to do with that zero-zero shit James Earl had spouted. He'd almost sounded like he was afraid of Leroy, when he said that. John remembered something else, though, remembered James Earl saying *I am not your enemy*. Well if this was how he treated people who weren't his enemies, John would hate to see how he treated folks who weren't his friends!

There were some toppled over aluminum garbage cans about eight feet away. John wondered if they could make it that far. From there it looked like they might be able to slip around the north end of the shack, where there was another fence and some more houses. If they could get there, and turn the corner, they'd at least be out of the line of fire. "I think we're gonna need to make a run for it, man."

"You run for it, Boss. I'm fucken blind!"

"All right, I'll leave you behind to meet up with this guy."

"Fine. You're probably the one he's after anyway, Boss!"

"You sure about that? It's your shack he came to. If you stay here alone you really are blind; if you go with me at least we've got one pair of eyes between us. And one brain," John couldn't help adding.

"Yeah, mine. Fine, Boss, fine, goddamn it. Let's just go, let's just fucken go already!"

John went. "Stay low!" He had Leroy by the arm. Just as they dived behind the trash cans the guy up there let loose with another volley. John heard bullets ripping through the aluminum.

"Shit, shit, fuck, shit!".

"Shut up man, we made it." John looked around. They ought to be able to get to real cover, he figured, if they could just shoot the six foot gap between here and the next alleyway. No hope of getting back to his car, though; it was parked along the same line as the guy with the gun. "Be ready to run when I say go," he told Leroy.

"Shit, shit, fuck, shit!"

"Go!" They were up. They were running. Bullets were hitting all around them, ripping up the trash cans and blowing little craters of splinters out of the fence. But they made it around the corner. Now where the hell should they go? "This way," John said, tugging Leroy behind him. He ran until there was a cross street and took a right on it. Then he ducked behind another fence and leaned up against it, trying to get air back into his lungs. Leroy was breathing hard, too, but not as—he was twenty years younger, after all, even if he did get a face full of pepper spray.

"Did we lose him?" asked Hotwire.

"I don't know."

"Is he still coming after us?"

"I don't know."

"Well, what the fuck *do* you know, Boss?"

"That you're a stupid little greedy asshole." Now that they finally had a second, John reached into his pocket for his cell phone. He started punching buttons.

"What the fuck are you doing, man?"

"Dialing 9-1-1. That all right with you?"

"You've got a fucken cell phone? Why didn't you do that ten minutes ago?"

"I was sort of busy." Dispatch picked up. It was Shirley.

"You're having one hell of a week, John," she said.

"Tell me about it." John kept looking along the alleyway, wondering if the guy with the gun was still after them. At the end of the street the sun was starting to go down; it was turning orange, burning up the river. Where the hell should they go from here? If James Earl came around the corner right now they were dead. They were still out in the open. They had to find a better place to hide. John looked down the street the other way. He saw a car parked by the side of the road. From here it looked like a piece of crap, but at least it wasn't up on blocks. It might run. They just had to break into it and get it started somehow.

"Let's see if we can make it from here to that car without anybody killing us."

"What car, Boss?"

"Oh right, I forgot you're blind. Here, I've got you—see if you can keep up!" John grabbed him by the arm and ran. He kept expecting to hear shots, to feel something burning besides his lungs; he kept thinking that whoever was after them would flat finish them off. It didn't happen. They made it to the car. Rambler, yellow, should've been in a museum. John looked back down the street, breathing hard, but couldn't see anybody. Maybe they'd lost him? John tried the car door. It was locked. What else would it be? He scanned the pavement underneath. He found a rock. He picked it up with his good right hand and smashed the driver's side window.

"Shit!" Cut his damned self.

"You all right, Boss?"

"Yeah." His hand was bleeding. They had bigger problems than that, though. John reached in and opened the door. "Get inside." He gave Leroy a shove. "Can you see yet?"

"Not really, man. Just a little light out at the edges."

"It'll get better."

"Says you."

John slid in after him. "Keep your head down." The car wasn't half bad. Somebody had taken good care of it. Up until now. "See if you can get it started."

"What are you talking about, Boss? I can't even see the fucken key!"

"There is no damned key, Asshole. If there was a key, I could turn it myself. I need you to get the car started."

"I. Can't. Fucken. See!"

"Well, tell me what the hell to do then!"

"How the fuck should I know? Yank some fucken wires!"

That's when it hit John. "You don't know how to do it, do you?"

"Why the fuck should I?"

"Because your damned *name* is Hotwire! Now you're telling me you don't know how to hotwire a car?"

"Well, man, it's been a long time," whined the weasel.

"Jesus Christ!" Just then the back window exploded, showering the insides of the car with bits of glass. "Shit man, he found us!"

"We're fucken dead!"

"Shut up!" Another one of the windows blew out. John thought he saw somebody back there in the rear view, running down the street towards them. He wasn't moving all that fast, though, and there was something strange about the way he was doing it. "We've got to make a run for it again," John said, "We can't just sit here!"

"Don't leave me behind, Boss!"

"You've sure changed your tune!"

John heard bullets chunking into the back of the car. He heard one whistle through the air above them as they hunkered down in the seat. He heard . . . he heard something else then. Sirens. Was there any sweeter sound in the whole world? Sirens. They were echoing across the river. They were closing in, fast. "Cavalry's here," he said to Leroy, and let out a long breath. He let go of his arm. In the rearview, which was about the only piece of glass in the whole damned car that wasn't smashed to smithereens, John could see the guy who'd been shooting at them turn tail and start running the other way. And that's when he realized a couple of things. That the guy had long, crinkly black hair; and that he was limping.

"Leti Tulafono!" John said, under his breath.

"Friend of yours, Boss?" asked the blind mole that was Leroy.

"Shut the fuck up, Asshole," said John.

Chapter 26

John hadn't been in the ER long, maybe forty-five minutes, when the Chief arrived. That was long enough for them to get him into one of those damned gowns of theirs, though, the kind you never can figure out how to tie shut in the back. He guessed that was so they could do a rectal exam on you any time they were feeling happy.

"You keep showing up here," said Horsebreaker, "they'll start charging you rent."

"I think they already do."

He laughed. "Yeah, I guess that's right." The Chief glanced around the room like he was trying to figure out how much the place would cost. "I thought we decided you *weren't* going to drop in on Leroy Miller."

"Yeah, we did. That was stupid, I know. The little weasel pissed me off, though." John was sitting on a table on a sheet of butcher paper that rustled every time he moved his ass. "Please tell me that none of what happened is going to show up on the ten o'clock news?"

Horsebreaker grunted. "Fortunately, nobody too much cares what happens out at the Landfill, unless you throw in a politician and a stripper. Not so many folks out there walking around with cameras in their pockets, either. All of which is good because I don't want to have to explain why an officer on Admin Leave decided to do some off-duty breaking and entering." He let John squirm for a minute before he pushed on. "You're lucky we got there when we did. A few more minutes and you and your sidekick might have been on your way to Dayton. Seen a doctor yet?"

Sidekick? For a second he had this picture come to mind of Hotwire as a bleached-out Tonto and almost choked on it. The only thing more ridiculous than that was the idea of John Briggs as the Lone Ranger. "Yeah. He said that except for my bad attitude, I'd be fine. A few cuts and scrapes; I'm just waiting for the nurse to get in here with some antiseptic."

Horsebreaker nodded. "I saw the statement you gave Tom Etheridge. So you think it was Tulafono that tried to kill you?"

"No doubt about it."

"You think he's mixed up in drug trafficking, or was this personal?"

"Hell if I know. Personal, probably. Did you take him into custody?"

"Not yet. But we will."

"So he's still on the loose? Jesus Christ, the man's the size of a whale and he's got a gimp leg!"

The Chief had his stony face on. "We'll get him."

"Hopefully before he puts a damned bullet in me." John shifted on the table and the butcher paper rustled again. "How's Hotwire?"

"Checked out already. They flushed his eyes, bandaged his head, and sent the little peckerwood home. Not that he's likely to go back to his shack for a while. I don't think I would either if somebody had shot my house full of holes. You think we should've held onto him?"

"Nah, he doesn't know anything. He's just a greedy little asshole, and stupid to boot. Always getting mixed up in shit he ought to be avoiding like bubonic herpes. I did find something at his shack, though. I think it may be our missing hit of Must."

The Chief frowned. Probably thinking about how John hadn't had a warrant. He didn't say anything, though. "You sure this time?"

"Pretty sure. Look in the pockets of my pants over there."

Horsebreaker went over to where John's pants lay folded over the back of a chair and dug through them. He found the clear plastic bag with the pile of blue rocks in it. He took one of those rocks out and turned it around a few times in his hand. He smelled it. "You think this is it, the real deal?"

"I'm guessing. Leroy tried to tell me it was Crystal, and that he was holding for somebody else, but it doesn't look like meth to me."

"Me, either. Let me get this analyzed. Maybe the lab guys can tell us something." He popped it into a neat little pocket inside his blue vest, one that looked almost like it was made for something like this. "Are they going to let you out of here anytime soon?"

"Any minute, they say."

"You need a ride home?"

John hadn't even thought about that. They'd brought him and Hotwire to the hospital in an ambulance, even though neither one of them was all that bad off. Standard op. John didn't know where his rental car was; probably still where he'd left it, down by the river. "I guess maybe I do," he said, "I can always get a cab, though."

"I've got you covered," Horsebreaker said, then added "It's on my way" before John could act too grateful.

Chapter 27

After the shootout down by the Sherry, Leroy went underground for a while. Had to, man; somebody was flat out trying to kill him. Who was that fat ass with the machine gun anyway? *Lady Toolaphono.* That was what Briggs said. Didn't look like any woman to Leroy, though, even with all that hair. Looked like some fat ass guy with a limp.

I can take you, though, thought Leroy, checking to see if the gun in his pants pocket was still there. *If I see you first you're dead, man.*

Leroy wandered the streets. *Shoot up my fucken shack, will you?* He got pissed off all over again, thinking about that. No way was he going back there now though, when it had more holes in it than a fucken Swiss cheese. Hey man, that sounded good right about now: cheese! But that wasn't the fucken point, was it? The point was the shack, man. Leroy wasn't going back there and not just because it was full of holes now. It was because the fat ass that made it that way might come back again. As far as Leroy could tell, the cops hadn't caught him. Son-of-a-bitch must be bad ass. Had a bad-ass gun, anyway. And now he was after Leroy K. Miller. The K stood for Kickass, he thought to himself as he wandered the streets, sleeping under the boardwalk along The Ribbon, sleeping in doorways and dumpsters.

Life on the street sucked, man. Leroy was missing his shack. But he couldn't go back out there now, not with that fat bad ass still walking around. *Hey, man, if I see you first . . .* Leroy checked to see if his gun was still there. He was on the lookout for that fat bad ass. He was looking out for the Boss, too. Not to kill him or anything, but Leroy wouldn't mind shaking his ass up a bit, spraying some mace in *his* face for a change, shooting him in the fucken foot just for fun. Or the dick. Where the hell was he, anyway? Lived in Palmer. Leroy remembered that much. Couldn't remember where he'd heard that, or when. Briggs could've moved six times since then, but Leroy doubted it. He was one square-ass straight shooter, the Boss; he just went along and did what he did. Maybe that was why Leroy liked him. Maybe that's why Leroy was looking for him now. There hadn't been too many things in his life that had ever stayed the same, but John Briggs was one of them.

There had to be some way to find out where he lived. If only Leroy had one of those new smart-ass phones. Look it up in a fucken second. Surf the web for girlie pictures, too. He'd done that a few times at the public library before they chased his ass out. Now he went to convenience stores to look at the Sports Illustrated swimsuit issue instead. Chick on the cover this year had tits, man, like you wouldn't believe. They chased him out of there, too, though; said he was drooling all over the cover. Shit, man, he wasn't drooling! It had just been a long time. Seemed like forever.

Palmer. Scaly-assed place, really. Not much better than the Landfill, if you asked Leroy. They just thought it was. Lots of broken-down buildings and row houses. Better than shacks, maybe, but didn't none of them have a view of the Sherry River. Only water in sight was a puddle of piss some dog had left on the sidewalk. Leroy stopped and bent over laughing.

You're not much better off than me are you, Boss?

Leroy looked up and down the street. The sun was going down. Had to find a place to crash, man. Some place where the fucken rats wouldn't get him. Leroy looked around. Where the hell was he, anyway? Someplace in Palmer. Looking for the Boss, John Briggs. But it was getting late already, getting dark. He checked his pocket to see if the gun was still there.

Leroy kept walking, kept looking for a place to crash—alleyway, dumpster, somebody's yard. They didn't even have yards, out here. With these row houses it was just a sidewalk and then the fucken street. There was a store up ahead, though, a Quick & Ready.

Too bad I don't have any cash, man.

All he had was one fucken quarter. He was saving that for something. One condom or one phone call to the Boss. What was he supposed to do with a condom when there weren't any fucken chicks around? There was a phone up ahead, though, at the Quick & Ready. He thought about calling the Boss right now. What for, though, man? He didn't have anything to tell him, nothing to sell. But what was that, hanging down underneath? Fucken phonebook. That's right, they still made those things! You could look up somebody's address in them, too. Leroy moved in, watching out for rats and fat bad asses toting machine guns. This part of town was worse than the Landfill, man, mostly because Leroy didn't know his way around. Didn't know who or what to watch out for. Leroy picked up the book. He flipped through it. Now how the fuck did you spell Briggs?

Leroy flipped through the white pages. There it was! Only, there were three of them. Just John. John B and John P. Which one was it? Three fucken numbers and three fucken addresses. Only one was in Palmer, though: John P. Leroy wondered what that P stood for. Prick? He bent over, laughing. Didn't matter. What street was he on? Figueroa Road. What kind of a name was that? He wasn't even sure how you said it. It looked like Go Figure. Or maybe Fucken Road. He didn't have anything to write it down with. He tried to remember what it was after he'd closed the book but it was hard, man. When you'd smoked a lot of blunts, when you were smoking a blunt right now . . . Things kept slipping in and out on him. Go figure, Fucken Road. Something like that. How the hell was he supposed to know where it was though, man? Leroy looked over at the Quick & Ready. What street was he on now? Mercer? Vane? What was that thing running into the bushes, over there in the dark? Fucken rat! Son-of-a-bitch was fucken *huge*! Leroy started walking towards the market. He needed to go inside, ask the guy at the counter. Leroy looked in at him through the window.

Some old black guy with buzz-cut white hair. Face looked almost as bad as the bucked-up asphalt out here in the parken lot. Not the kind of guy you'd want to mess with, though. Looked like he might used to have been a Marine. Leroy toked up the last of his blunt and threw the butt towards the place where he'd seen the ratzilla.

Get yourself high, motherfucken rodent! He laughed. He went inside the store.

"Hey, man." Leroy was looking out the side of his eye at the SI swimsuit issue that was up on the rack. There she was, that chick with the tits that wouldn't quit.

"Whatchyouwant?" said the Marine behind the counter.

What kind of fucken customer service was that? Dude was supposed to be waiting on Leroy and he might as well have called him an asshole just now! "Directions, man, if you don't mind. How do I get to Fucken Road?"

"What say?

Dude looked pissed off. Looked like he was about ready to come over the counter. Leroy reached into his pocket to see if the gun was still there. "You heard me, man. Fucken Road. I'm looking for this street, man, it's called Fucken Road. Right here in Palmer."

"Look, man, you and I both know you're stoned. Why don't you get the hell out of my store before I call the cops?"

"I just want directions, man, that's all. No gas, no smokes, no bullshit."

"If I wasn't on duty right now, I'd come out from behind here and whoop your little ass."

"You and how many other ninety-year-old pussies?" said Leroy.

Shit, man, the dude was coming over the fucken counter! Leroy split, in a hurry. Ran out the door and in between the gas pumps and across the street without looking back. Almost got hit by a fucken car! On the other side he stopped and turned around. The pussy Marine hadn't come out of the store after all. Musta thought twice about it. Good move. Didn't want to be getting his ass kicked by some young stud. No, wait a minute, here he came! He was coming out of the fucken store! Had a gun, man! Leroy started running again. He ran down the bucked-up sidewalk. He heard a shot, behind him. This was a fucken bad part of town, man!

Shit. Leroy tripped on the sidewalk. Went sliding off into the grass. Scraped his fucken arm up. What the hell was going on? He sat up and looked back at the Quick & Ready, breathing hard. He couldn't see the pussy Marine, though. He musta gone back inside.

I oughta come back there and cap your ass! Leroy looked at his arm. Scraped up but not bleeding. He checked to make sure his gun was still there. Where the hell was he, anyway? It was dark already. He saw a green sign then, on the other side of the street, at the corner. Figueroa. Well, shit, what do you know! That was the Boss's street, wasn't it?

Man, you live in a sorry-ass part of town, Briggs! Leroy had seen worse, out at the Landfill. But at least out there you got a good view of the river. This place was just two steps better than a hell-hole, with nothin' to write home about. Seaside was halfway across the city. You'd need a bus to get from here to the Sherry.

What do you know? Fucken Road! Leroy had figured out how to get here without the help of that pussy Marine, without even having a fucken map! Leroy Miller was a street rat, man, a *survivor*! Now he just needed some place to crash. He lit up a blunt and started looking around. More row houses right up ahead. Leroy started walking. There was a number he kept thinking about but couldn't remember what it was. The Boss's house had a number. Every house did, even Leroy's shack out by the Sherry River. 426. That was it, that was his number. That was the one he couldn't forget. But what the hell was that one for Briggs comma John P? Leroy couldn't fucken remember. He took another toke on the blunt. He kept on walking down the bucked-up sidewalk. Row houses right up ahead. Lights on. It was getting dark, man.

Shit! Almost tripped again on the fucken sidewalk! Thought he saw another rat the size of a dog. Here he was, at the row houses, looking for a place to crash. Shit, there wasn't nothin' there. No alleyways; houses all ran together. No dumpsters; where the hell did they put their trash? Leroy looked around, up and down Fucken Road.

There was a construction site on the other side of the street. Looked like a motel they were building. One they'd started building, anyway; didn't look like anybody had been in there for a while. Didn't look like there was anybody in there now. Place was probably full of fucken rats, but if he could just get upstairs into one of those rooms . . . No windows, everything was all open in front. Place looked like an empty wine carton somebody had tipped up on its side. There was a chain link fence around it, but if you could get over that, man, then it looked like you might be home free. Unless they had fucken dogs inside.

Leroy got closer, scoped the place out. Chain link fence but no fucken barbed wire. It looked to Leroy like he could take it. It looked to Leroy like there wasn't nobody there. They musta stopped working on this place when everything went to hell last year. Leroy looked both ways down Fucken Road, then fifteen ways through the chain link fence. Nobody. Not even a dog, man. He looked up and down the street again. Nobody coming.

Wait a second. Leroy was standing there with his hands on the chain link fence, about to climb over, when he saw headlights coming at him. He was about to climb over anyway, but thought he'd better wait those lights out. Backed up against the fence then, tried to stay out of sight. Better wait until those headlights went by, man. What if it was the cops?

Keep your cool, man, you're just out for a walk. That ain't no fucken crime!

He tried to stay out of the light. Fucken car was slowing down, though! Some chick, maybe, checking him out? Leroy tried to keep his cool, tried to look like he was just hanging out. That chick with the tits on the SI cover, checking him out. The car was slowing down. It was pulling up right in front of one of those row houses on the other side of the street.

Leroy put a hand on the gun inside his pants pocket. Then he saw the sign on the side of the car door. Green and black sign that said Panda Li's. Had a picture of a panda bear on it, too, holding a pair of fucken chopsticks! Leroy started to laugh. It was just a delivery car for a fucken Chinese restaurant! Leroy had the munchies, man, bad. Blunts'd do that. Thought about holding the guy up, stealing his chicken. Leroy's mouth was watering. He had his hand on the gun inside his pants pocket. That shit smelled good even from all the way over here, across Fucken Road! The Chinese kid was ringing somebody's doorbell. Leroy pushed off from the fence and started walking across the street. He had his hand on the gun in his pocket. One of the doors over there swung open. It was dark on the street but when that door opened it let some light out. An old fart was standing there in the doorway.

"Delivery!" the kid called out.

Leroy was halfway across the street, thinking about how fucken good that chicken smelled, wondering if he could take the old dude and the delivery boy, wondering if it was worth it to hold the both of them up for Kung Pao. He might as well rob the two of them while he was at it; if the cops caught you they'd throw you in a cage for ten years for armed robbery, either way. Didn't matter if you took wallets or chicken.

"Thanks, here's something for you."

Shit, he was missing his chance, man! The deal was going down! If he didn't get across the street in a hurry, he was going to miss out on all of it, the cash and the fucken chicken! Hang on, though. Wait a minute. That voice, man, that dude over there in that lit-up doorway. It sounded like . . .

Boss?

Leroy stopped and backed off. He couldn't fucken believe it. That was the Boss, man! That was John Briggs standing there with that chicken pusher! Leroy backed off. He was on the other side of the street again, back in the shadows alongside the fence.

Shit yeah, that was him! Leroy leaned against the chain link fence, smoking his blunt, thinking what a fucken stud he was. Went looking for the Boss all the way across town and found his way right to his door!

The delivery guy got back in his car and drove off. The Boss had already closed his door. He was back inside now, munching on his Kung Pao. And Leroy wasn't getting any. And he was hungry enough now that he could eat a fucken rat. But he had a place to stay for tonight. For a whole lot of nights, if he could just climb the fence. And if they didn't have fucken dogs inside. What do you know! It was right across the street from the Boss's row house! If Leroy could just get up there, he might even be able to look across the street right into his window. See what the hell he was up to. Fucken shoot him from there, if he wanted to. Not that he wanted to, man. The Boss was alright. Leroy was still pissed off about the mace, and his shack, and getting shot at by that fat bad ass, but he thought about the three Benjamins the boss had given him, too, after that sting a while back. If he could come up with something else about that drug, Must, then maybe . . .

Man, he needed cash like nobody's business. Nothing but a fucken quarter left. Nothing to eat all fucken day. And now his last blunt was history, too. He flicked the butt off into the dark. It bounced around for a while on the bucked-up sidewalk, kicking up sparks. Leroy started climbing the chain link fence.

Chapter 28

"How do I look?"

"Hang on." Ham blasted a few more slugs from outer space before pausing the video game and turning around. "Like you're trying too hard."

"Better than not trying hard enough." Finally, it was Saturday night and John was getting ready to go out with Jill Relson.

Ham was sitting on the sofa, still holding the controller. "Maybe. I'd lose the tie, though. And wear your sport jacket."

"What are you now, Tommy Hilfiger?" This from a kid who'd been wearing nothing but black t-shirts for the last six months! But John went back to his room and changed anyway. When you haven't been on a date since the Bush Administration, he thought, you'll take fashion advice from anybody, even a Visigoth.

"Better," the Visigoth said when John came back into the den.

He still felt like a fish out of water but there probably wasn't any way around that. There was a time in your life when the whole dating thing made sense, but once that was over you'd just as soon turn on the game and order a pizza. If it was anybody else but Jill . . . "You'll get something to eat while I'm gone?"

"I think I can forage, paterfamilias."

Fashion consultant, spoke Latin, killed slugs from alien worlds: John was raising a damned renaissance man! "Got any homework?"

"Did it already."

"OK. Guess I should just go then."

"Yeah. Have fun."

John drove across town. It was good to have his car and his left arm back, even if they both were clunkers. Jill lived in Mayfair, in a townhouse complex between the Zoo and the Woodlands. Some place called The

Remington. John had never been there before. There was a guard house out front, one of those that never has anybody in it. The buildings were nice: used red brick and white siding and lots of glass. Jill was in 7C. John knocked at the door. He felt like a damned vacuum cleaner salesman again. That was a job he did one Saturday when he was seventeen, for all of about five hours—which was four and a half longer than it took to find out he wasn't any good at it. Turns out you actually had to care whether you sold your product or not. At least he wasn't selling anything now. At least he didn't think he was. Damn, he was nervous! The door opened.

"Hi, John, how are you?"

"Good. You look nice." She did, too. She was wearing tan pants and a purple top and dangly silver earrings that looked like little wind chimes.

"Thanks. You look nice, too." She locked the door. "I love that it's still light outside, this late."

"Yeah, me too. Glad to see the sun finally starting to go down though. Maybe it'll cool off now." Just a few hours earlier, it had been ninety degrees. Jesus, those blue eyes of hers looked right through you! John thought maybe he should have brought her some flowers, but then decided that might have been too much. He did have something to give her, though, when the time was right: that CD with James Earl Jones on it.

"So, where are you taking me?"

"I didn't say?"

"No, you did not."

John didn't know whether to open the car door for her or not. This used to be easier, a long time ago, back when everybody followed a script. "It's the blue jalopy," he said, pointing to his Nova. Straightaway, she walked around to the other side and he let her go there alone. "Piece of junk, basically."

"As long as it gets you where you want to go," she said when they were inside.

"The Catamaran."

"What?"

"That's where we want to go: the Catamaran. It's a nice seafood place down at Seaside. Ever heard of it?"

She shook her head. "I don't eat out very often."

"Me, either, unless you count fast food. But I busted somebody there once and it looked nice."

She laughed. "So you're taking me to a crime scene?"

"Well, just about every place is, sooner or later. Sad to say."

John pulled out of the parking lot. They were driving across town. He could smell her perfume on the other side of the car. She was an interesting lady. Worked with elephants all day but smelled nice when she wanted to. Looked nice without even trying.

"So, John, how long have you been in Law Enforcement?"

He laughed. "Sorry. Whenever I hear somebody say 'law enforcement,' I think about garbage collectors calling themselves 'sanitary engineers.' It always sounds like you're trying to doll the job up."

"All right," she said seriously, "how long have you been a cop?"

"Too long, probably. Twenty years? Give or take. How long have you, um, how long have you been working with elephants?"

"Since I was nineteen."

"Oh, just a year then?"

She laughed. "John, there's sweet and then there's ridiculous!"

"Five?"

"Let's just say it's been a while. It hasn't gotten old yet, even if I have. I still look forward to it every day."

Man, if she was old what the hell was he? "Wish I could say the same," John said. "But I guess there's still times when it feels good, when it feels like you might be making a difference."

"It's certainly important work."

"Dirty job but somebody's got to do it." He shrugged. Up ahead he could see a red neon sign on the right. "There's the Cat, at the end of the street."

They pulled in. Judging by the number of people hanging around on the deck, there was a wait. Good thing he'd called ahead. It was dusk by the time they got out of the car and walked across the parking lot. There were plenty of people wearing suits and ties, but a lot of tourists, too, in blue jeans and t-shirts. It was a good mix and he and Jill were somewhere in the middle. He didn't feel out of place. They went inside and right away the hostess took them to their table, a nice spot by the windows overlooking the sea. The sun had gone all the way down by then but there were lights along The Ribbon in between the restaurant and the water, and lots of people were walking the path, or riding in bicycle rickshaws. You could see the Gulf out there in the distance but not the exact line of the shore; where the sand sloped down to the surf there was a trough filled up with shadows.

John ordered a beer—for once, some brand that was civilized—and Jill had a glass of white wine. "You know what I'd like to hear more about?" John said, "These trips you take to Africa."

"Well, I usually go once a year, as part of my work with CERES, the Center for Research on Elephants. We conduct studies related to conservation."

"Where exactly in Africa do you go?" he asked her, "Somewhere in Kenya, right?"

She nodded. "A wildlife preserve called Tsavo. Have you heard of *Out of Africa?*"

"Oh yeah, there was a movie. Redford and Streep, right?"

"Well, before that there was a book. But yes, either way, Tsavo is the place where some of that happened."

"I remember there was a lot of beautiful scenery. Does it really look like that? I mean, the way it does in the movie?"

"Yes. The landscape is amazing."

John didn't say anything about what he'd just been reading on the Internet, about all the drug problems they had over there. No need to spoil the mood. Before they could order their fish, Jill had to check with the waiter to see which ones were sustainable. "You're as bad as my son Ham," John told her.

She laughed. "Don't you mean 'as good?'"

"Yeah."

"He sounds like an interesting person."

"He's a good kid."

"What's he interested in?"

"Killing zombies and slugs from outer space," John said.

"What's that?"

"Video games."

She laughed. "Oh, I see. I meant, what's he interested in, school-wise?"

"Well, the environment, I guess it would be safe to say."

"That could be a good career choice, given where we're all headed."

"Could be." John looked out the window at the ocean and thought about the future: the next few years and then beyond that, to a time when he might not even be here. What would Ham do with his life? It was out there, somewhere, but like the waves breaking on the beach it was down in some trough where he couldn't see it. Ham was such a good kid.

The waitress brought their fish. "So, do you have any other family?"

"My grandmother on my father's side is about the only relative we have. At least, she's the only one still alive. She's at the Center in Palmer, these days."

"Oh, is she in poor health?"

"She has diabetes and a bit of heart trouble, but she's in pretty good shape for eighty-five. She's a real sweetheart, but tough as nails, too. She's the one who raised me, really." John was starting to feel like maybe he was talking too much. He tried to flip the conversation back the other way. "How about you, Jill, you got any family?"

"One younger sister, Maggie. She and her husband Brad and their two girls live in Nashville. My father still lives there, too, in a house down the street." She shrugged. "Other than that, a few aunts and uncles and cousins, scattered all over. Nobody who lives here in town, though."

"How's your Catfish?"

"Sustainable."

"Ouch. That good, huh? This Halibut's not too bad."

Dinner went by way too fast. There are people you kill time with, thought John, and people that, when you're with them, the time just flows past without you even knowing it's there. They weren't talking about anything special, but he was figuring out a lot of little things about her along the way: that she had enough self-control to switch to water after just one glass of wine. That she was a big soccer (she called it "football") fan. That she liked to get up early every morning, even on the weekends. But she said OK when he asked her if she'd like to take a walk with him along the ocean, even though it was getting late by the time they were done and he'd paid the bill.

They left the restaurant and picked up The Ribbon. It was busy right along that stretch: lots of rickshaws flying by like they owned the walkway. "Geez," said Jill when one almost hit her, "Isn't there any speed limit here?"

"Five miles an hour, but I can't be busting people *all* the time!"

She laughed. "I didn't really expect you to. It would just be nice if people thought about what they were doing every once in a while."

"Wouldn't it, though?"

After they'd walked a ways the crowd thinned out and so did the noise, and then they could hear waves breaking down at the shore. The chain of streetlamps gave out then, too. It got darker. Not all the way; there was a half moon hanging out over the Gulf. Right up ahead of them, too, were the Fairgrounds: lots of green and yellow neon burned onto the sky.

"You ever been on any of the rides here?" John asked her.

"No, not here. And not at all, really, since I was a kid."

They kept walking. "What was your favorite one, back then?"

She thought about that for a minute, while John listened to the roar of the roller coaster, and people screaming as they went down the big hill. "The Ferris Wheel."

"No kidding? That's mine, too. You want to ride it now?"

She was thinking about it. John thought she might say no, but then she must have changed her mind. "Sure, why not?"

John bought tickets and they stood in line. There was a nice cool breeze coming off the ocean. He thought about the last time he was here, when he'd met up with Hotwire and the weasel had first told him about this new drug called Must. They'd come a ways since then.

"Here we go," she said.

They stepped up to the platform and slid into the seat, Jill first. The carnie lowered the bar. Then they were moving, backwards, up through the cool night air.

"Whoa!" said Jill as they went over the top but John wasn't sure if she was saying that because of the view or the feeling you get in the pit of your stomach. For a few seconds the Midway was spread out underneath them, and The Ribbon leading back to the Catamaran, and all the lit-up buildings in the business district at Seaside. Then they were falling back down towards the beach, and the people waiting in line, and the carnies.

The second time around, they stopped right up top. "I was hoping," John said.

"What a view!"

The car was rocking back and forth. John could hear the coaster behind them and breaking waves on the shore and people's voices floating up from somewhere below. He hadn't felt like this in a long time. He was with somebody he wanted to be with. He was thinking about something else besides Ham, or work. "You know, if this thing was to get stuck for a while right now, I think I'd be all right with that."

"Me, too," said Jill, looking down, "as long as the weather doesn't change!"

But the wheel lurched and they started falling, and then John felt like he was chasing after that moment, trying to grab it out of the dark before it got away from him.

#

After they were done with the Ferris Wheel, they took a slow walk back to the parking lot by the Catamaran. The half moon was still hanging up there in the sky, though it was a little higher now and there was a cloud in front of it. Neither one of them had much to say. John didn't know if that was good or bad. All he knew was he felt all right about it, he felt comfortable. When they got to the car he opened the door for her this time, without even thinking about it. Old habits died hard.

"Thank you."

"I've got something for you," John said once they were inside. He opened the glove compartment. The butterflies came back when he reached in front of her to do that, when his hand crossed into what seemed like her space. He took out the CD and gave it to her.

"Oh, is this . . .?"

"Yeah, it's the recording of the drug deal that went down." How romantic. But she seemed excited to get it.

"Why don't we listen to it on the way home?"

John laughed. "You're not going to believe this, but my car is so old it doesn't even have a CD player."

"You're kidding." She had to look for herself. She poked a finger into the cassette slot. "What's this?"

"Well, it's . . ." Then John realized she was pulling his leg. She knew what it was, she just couldn't believe it. Jesus, he didn't want this night to be over with! At least not without knowing when he would see her again. He started up the car and pulled out of the parking lot. It was a little easier to talk about things like that when he had to concentrate on something else, when he had a reason why he couldn't look at her. "Once you've had a chance to listen to that, Jill, we should get together. I'd like to know what you think."

"Should we plan on having lunch again on Monday then, at the Treetops?" She paused: "Or is that too soon?"

"No," John said, "that's not too soon."

That was one good thing about dating somebody when you both were older. You didn't do so much dancing around. You tried to make things a little easier for each other. John drove. The highway stretched out ahead of him. It seemed like it was taking him someplace he wanted to go.

Chapter 29

On Monday morning John finally went back to work, having served
out his suspension. He'd only been gone a few days, but it felt strange
walking into the station.

"Hey ya'll, look, it's Dirty Harry!"

John just waved them away. *Christ.* He'd forgotten about that
already, about what had happened out on Highway 19. At least he'd tried
to. But there was Rick, the butt-kissing intern, holding a hand out in front
of him like it was a gun, mouthing the words *blam blam blam* as John walked
by on his way to the Chief's office.

"Come on in," Horsebreaker said when he got there. "How was
your time off?"

John sat down in the chair beside his desk. "I managed to keep
busy."

"That's what I hear."

Christ, he was hard to read sometimes!

Horsebreaker pulled John's badge and gun out of the top drawer of
his desk. "Welcome back," he said, handing them over.

"Thanks. I sure could have used one of these last Thursday."

"Let me guess which one."

John didn't say anything. He was thinking how strange it was that
the whole world knew what had happened on Highway 19, but his run-in
with Leti Tulafono was their little secret.

"By the way, I got the lab results back this morning," the Chief said.

"On Leroy's bag of blue rocks?"

"Yeah."

"Let me guess: it was bubblegum."

Horsebreaker didn't even crack a smile. "A lot of Cs and Hs and Os, with funny little numbers beside them."

John stared at him. "A formula? What the hell does that mean?"

"How should I know?" shrugged the Chief, "I'm not a damn chemist. But the point is I don't think it's sugar water this time around."

Didn't sound like it. "Can't the lab guys tell us anything more than that?"

"Just that it's not any of the usual suspects. It's not anything they've ever seen before. They'll keep looking into it."

John thought about that for a minute. At least they knew now that there really was something out there. They'd been pretty sure before, but this clinched it. He slipped his gun back into the shoulder holster inside his coat. "Did you ever hear anything back from the coroner about Bonnie and Clyde?" That was what he'd been calling those two kids in the yellow Mustang who'd gone on the killing spree.

"Their T-levels were through the roof. Even the girl's."

John nodded. No surprise there.

#

"Hey."

"Hey, there," said Jill, "How are you?"

And that smile of hers lit up his whole world. "Never better." That just sort of slipped out but as soon as it did John realized it was actually true. They were at the Treetops, standing in line for their food.

"Good to be back at work then?"

That wasn't what John had been thinking about but yeah, sure. "Yeah, sure. I'm not much good at sitting around the house. How are the girls this morning?"

"Just fine. They told me to tell you they missed you."

"Is that right? They must've liked how I shoveled up their poop for them."

She laughed. While they were standing there, the Allman Brothers came over the loudspeakers. "I see you had a talk with folks here," said John, nodding up towards the trees.

"What's that?"

"About the kind of music they pipe in."

She listened for a minute. "That does sound better, doesn't it? But I'm afraid I can't take any credit."

"Well, I'm sure grateful to somebody," said John, floating along to the music. *You're my blue sky, you're my sunny day* . . .

"What are you having today?" Jill asked him.

"You know, I was lying awake all last night thinking about that black bean burger they serve here."

"Good deal. Maybe Ham and I are converting you?"

"Maybe. I think I'll still check 'carnivore' on the census form, though."

Jill got her usual salad. She picked out a table at the far edge of the restaurant, away from people. As soon as they sat down, she said: "I found out a couple of things, John. One of them is interesting, the other quite disturbing."

"Let's hear interesting first. I've already had a few doses of disturbing this morning."

"All right." She put down her white plastic fork. "I emailed a clip of that recording you sent me to my friend Thomas Mbele, who teaches at Emory. He seems very certain your drug dealer is Tanzanian. And I'm inclined to believe him."

"Because he's a professor?"

"Well, yes, there is that. But he also happens to *be* Tanzanian."

"Hmm. That's interesting. Where is Tanzania, anyway?"

"Just next door to Kenya," said Jill, "South, southwest."

John ate some of his fries. "I don't know much about it."

"Mount Kilimanjaro, which you've probably heard of, is there—not too far across the border. I've been a few times, following the elephants' migratory paths."

"That's interesting," John said again. He remembered something else. "Say, what did you think about that part where the drug dealer asks . . ." he almost said Leroy, then decided he'd best not give out his real name, "asks my snitch if he's one of the zero-zeros? Is that anything you've heard of before?"

"I wondered about that, as well. It seems as though I *have* heard of it, and that I was in Africa when I did, but I can't remember in what context."

John filed that away. Jill was looking serious all the sudden.

"You're thinking about the disturbing stuff now."

"Yes. I finally heard back from Cynthia Jones, my colleague I work with at the elephant research station in Tsavo. You remember I wrote her a while back, asking about musth, if she'd heard of any new research that had been done?"

"Yeah, I remember."

"Well she hasn't, but she did have something else to report, something related." Jill looked off in the distance. John could tell this was hard for her.

"You know, for quite a while now we've been seeing a decline in elephant poaching. I think the public outcry about ivory, people's heightened awareness, has had everything to do with that. As well as the fact that the Kenyan government has come to see elephants as a valuable resource in terms of Tourism." Jill had picked up her fork again but was just stabbing things with it. "Well, according to Cyn, elephant killings are back on the rise. It's not a huge increase, at least not yet, but it *is* significant. And what's really disturbing about it is the kind of elephants that are being slaughtered. It's the ones that are in musth."

She looked at John like she thought that should bring down the house. He *was* thinking about what it meant, but more along the lines of what was going on here, not halfway around the world.

"The problem there," Jill said, once she saw that John wasn't following her quite all the way, "is that killing off elephants in musth disrupts the reproductive cycle. It has the potential to stop that cycle altogether. Which means no more elephants, eventually."

John frowned. "Are they taking blood from the elephants after they kill them?"

"Cynthia didn't say. She did say, however, that the poachers took the tusks."

"They took the tusks?"

"That's what Cyn said, yes."

"Then how do we know they weren't just doing regular old poaching?"

"I suppose we don't. Many of the males who are in musth are the largest ones anyway, which means they have the largest tusks. Which means they're the ones poachers tend to go after. What Cyn does say, though, is that every elephant the poachers have killed in these past few months was in musth, and that *is* unusual. As you know, the females have tusks as well, and some of them can be quite large. It seems unlikely to me that every last elephant these poachers chose to kill should be male, and that they all should be in musth."

"Is it breeding season over there right now?" asked John.

"There isn't really a season for it, for elephants. Males go into musth at different times, throughout the year."

This was sounding more and more suspicious to John now, too. "And we don't know what causes them to go into musth, do we?"

"No."

John thought about that for a minute. "How can Cyn be sure all those males were actually in musth? I mean, she wouldn't have seen them until after they were already dead, right?"

"Elephants in musth are continually dribbling urine, so that would leave a telltale trail. And because of that their penises tend to turn green, as well."

"Oh, right. I remember. The green penis thing." From what John had read on the Internet, those penises were four feet long. That would be hard to miss. "If the poachers were just after their blood, though, or whatever it is they're taking from them to make Must, why would they go ahead and cut off their tusks?"

"Maybe they figured they might as well," said Jill. "Why not make a profit off that at the same time? It's considerably harder to sell ivory now than it was in the old days, yet people still manage to do so."

John drank some iced tea. "Maybe they're just trying to cover their tracks."

"What do you mean?"

"Well, maybe they don't really care about the ivory, they just want people to think that's the reason they're killing elephants. Maybe they just want to throw everybody off the trail."

"Maybe."

They sat there and ate for a while. John wasn't sure what else to say. Whatever was happening over there in Africa, there wasn't much he could do about it. He was still having a hard time connecting the dots, too; he was having a hard time drawing a line from Kenya, or Tanzania, to Gulfport. So poachers took something from elephants and made it into a drug called Must—that didn't explain why it was winding up here. He could see why you might want to sell it in America, hell, we'd buy anything that made us feel good, but why wasn't it showing up anyplace else? Finally, he thought of something he could—and should—ask Jill. "Are you worried about Cynthia?"

"A little." She laughed. "Cyn's been dealing with people like this for decades, though. She's a tough customer. Most of the folks over there are afraid of her."

John smiled. "Is that right? God help the poachers then, huh?"

Jill laughed again. "Yes, I do feel a little sorry for them, actually!" But then she sobered up. "I really am worried, though, John."

"Yeah," he said, "Me, too." But it seemed to him that they might be worried about different things.

#

That night, after Ham had gone upstairs, John tried to do some more Internet sleuthing, this time putting Tanzania and zero-zeros into the mix. A lot of links came up, like they always did, but none of those links looked promising in the least. For a lot of them, he couldn't even tell why they were hits:

Kenya, Tanzania zero in on looters

Tanzania's bold war against HIV

Weak limits of zeros of orthogonal polynomials

He'd just about decided to give up, to move on to something else, when he caught sight of one interesting teaser near the bottom of the page, a link to a YouTube video:

Tanzanian albinos targeted for their body parts

What the hell? John frowned. The thumbnail was a flat-out strange picture. It was just a man and a woman standing around, but there was something different about them. Hats and dark sunglasses hid most of their faces, but you could tell they weren't just regular people. They looked washed-out. *Albinos*, he realized, and felt the same kind of wonder he'd experienced the first time he saw that white tiger they had at Jill's zoo. The man was wearing a black cowboy hat. Something purple and floppy covered up the woman's head. Both of them were obviously Black, but over the tops of their sunglasses their eyebrows looked white, almost bleached out. Leroy. That was who these two reminded him of, John thought with a jolt: they reminded him of Leroy Miller. That was enough of a reason for him to go ahead and click the start arrow.

Some woman from the BBC was doing a voice-over, in a British accent. She was talking about how these people she called "albeenos" were being hunted down for their body parts, all because some crazy witch doctors in Tanzania thought they had magic powers. Thought they could be used to ward off evil. Thought a hand or foot hanging around your neck on a rope could protect you from the demons they were just sure were running loose all over the countryside. John shook his head. This was all bad shit, but did it really have anything to do with anything?

Now the BBC lady was interviewing one of the natives, a regular-looking Black girl who seemed like she might be in her mid-teens. Kid was in pretty bad shape, crying in front of the camera. She was talking in a language John couldn't understand. What he did understand was that she was on the verge of breaking down, that she'd seen things little girls were never meant to see. That maybe nobody was meant to see. The BBC lady started translating for her, in the voice-over.

"They came for my sister one night. They took her out of our hut. They had guns, and machetes. Right in front of my family, they chopped off her arms and legs. Then they cut off her head. They slaughtered her like a goat."

John let out a long breath. He wanted to stop watching right then and there. He told himself he didn't need to be seeing this. It didn't really have anything to do with him, or with Must, or with what was happening here in Gulfport. Or did it? His finger hovered over the mouse for a minute but he couldn't make himself click it; he couldn't seem to make himself look away.

The BBC lady was talking to somebody else now, to that same grown "albeeno" man in the black cowboy hat, the one who was in the thumbnail. He'd taken off his sunglasses. He looked even stranger now because you could see his pink eyes. Those eyes were human, though, thought John, and full of pain.

"When they see us in the street," he said, "They call us 'zero-zeros.' Some of them fear us; others simply hate us. Either way, they wish only to kill us, to hunt us down like wild animals."

The voice-over was droning on but John wasn't hearing much of it anymore. *Zero-zeros.* He knew now why this link had come up. He knew now why James Earl Jones had asked Hotwire if he was a zero-zero: he must've thought that Leroy was one of these albinos. He tried to remember exactly what it was that James Earl had said to him: *I am not your enemy. We have a common enemy.* Something like that. What the hell did he mean? Did he think Leroy had followed him over here from Africa? Well, if they really believed these albinos had magic powers maybe that made sense. Maybe James Earl really did think Leroy had spirited his way across the ocean, tracked him halfway around the world? The way this video was presenting things, though, it didn't sound like the albinos were the ones doing the tracking; it sounded like they were the ones being hunted down.

John tuned back in. The camera was panning away to some white building in the middle of nowhere, out on a wide open plain that looked like Kansas. Had to be the savannah, he thought, that landscape they'd tried to copy for the Africa exhibit down at the zoo. The white building, according to the BBC lady, was a hospital. It was a place where they were committed to caring for and protecting as many of these "albeeno" children as they could, "offering them sanctuary, as it were."

"And yet the lure of one thousand British pounds for a hand or foot," she continued, "is a powerful incentive to engage in these horrific practices, in what is a brutally impoverished land."

While she was talking, the camera was zooming in on some kid who was standing in the hospital doorway, looking out from the shadows inside. If he'd been normal Black you wouldn't have been able to see him at all, or maybe just the whites of his big, soulful eyes, but he was one of those albeenos. He was sort of glowing there in the doorway, whitish-yellow, like swamp-gas. And then he stepped out into the sunlight. And you could see that he didn't have any hands. The kid didn't have any hands. Then a girl stepped out of the shadows, too, and stood beside him. She was a little older, a little taller. She put her arm around his shoulder. John wondered if she was his sister. She put her arm around his shoulder and there wasn't any hand there, either. There wasn't anything at the end of her arm but a stump. It was the look in her eyes that got to him, though, more than the missing hand: her little brother's eyes were big and sad and lost but in hers there was something else altogether. There was something that dug its way into John's heart so deep that he wasn't sure he'd ever be able to get it out. It was a look that said she knew how the world was. A look that said she didn't trust anybody. A look that said she knew she was on her own, that it was up to her to take care of herself and her little brother. That maybe the world really was full of demons.

John got this sick feeling in the pit of his stomach then, the kind of feeling he always got when he found out about bad things happening on the other side of the world. There was so much evil out there and nothing you could do about most of it, most of the time. You couldn't do much except try and keep it out of your own backyard, if you could. So far, he reflected, thinking of all those Must murders, he hadn't been doing a real good job of that.

The clip ended, having spewed out its 2:35 of Hell. John sat there looking at the Start arrow that was hovering out in front of the original albino man and woman, those two who were trapped in that thumbnail. Did any of this have anything to do with what was going on over here? John really wanted to decide "no," but couldn't quite make himself believe there wasn't some connection.

He leaned back on the sofa. What was really bothering him, he decided, was the fact that—more and more—it was looking like James Earl had come over here from Africa. That he'd brought this drug Must along with him. That some other people—people who were maybe even worse than drug dealers—might have followed him.

John didn't believe in magic or witch doctors, but the one thing he did believe in was Evil. Evil that could cut off a little girl's feet and hands. Evil that dealt in soul-killing drugs. Evil that turned kids like Tad Wellington into killing machines. It was one thing if that Evil was loose in Africa; that was bad enough. But he was afraid now—deep down afraid—that that Evil might have spread over here.

Chapter 30

If there really is a place called Hell, thought John, they're holding a press conference there right now. *No, come to think of it, Hell IS a press conference, one that lasts for all time.* The only thing he couldn't figure out while he was standing in the background in his badge and blues was who here was playing the role of Satan? The Press? They were more like a fiery pit of yelping minor demons. Mayor Crawford? He was an asshole, sure, but not nearly evil enough to qualify as Mephistopheles. Must itself? Maybe. The drug was behind everything that was going on, but there had to be somebody behind it, too: a person, or maybe a group of people. Maybe that's where you would finally find the real Devil.

"I want to assure all of you that we are doing everything in our power, and using every resource at our disposal, in order to stem the outbreak of violence that has so recently plagued our fair city."

The Mayor's words sounded fine in the air, and in the clips that took over the news channels for a while after that, but not everyone was buying what he was selling. John wasn't sure he was buying it, either. It was one thing to say you were going to cut off the flow of drugs, another to actually do it. It was one thing to say you were going to put an end to the violence, another to make any headway at all when a hundred fuses might have been lit all over the city, in places where you didn't even know to look.

"Mr. Mayor, can you tell us more about this new drug, Must?"

"Mr. Mayor, how do you plan to . . ."

"Mayor Crawford, do you feel that these violent episodes . . ."

"Mr. Mayor, Mr. Mayor, Mr. Mayor!"

John had to hand it to the guy: he kept his cool. Grandma always said people were put on this earth to do different things, and Crawford was doing his different thing now. That didn't mean John would vote for his ass again the next time around, though, not after the Mayor had made him stand inside the Capitol rotunda for an hour and a half! Not after he'd almost passed out several times from the heat and a continual stream of bullshit.

"Detective Briggs! Detective Briggs!"

Crap. Now they wanted to talk to the Mayor's designated pet hero. John wasn't biting. "I'm sorry," he growled, "but I can't say anything that might hamper our investigation."

That was a nice (well, sort of nice) way of saying *you're not getting the time of day out of me, Bubba!* Or Beelzebubba, to keep going with the same theme. By then John was ready to sell his soul if it would end this thing. When it was finally over he tried to get out of there as fast as he could, but wasn't quite able to before the Mayor came up to him and shook his hand, whether John wanted him to or not. Flash cameras were going off all around them like bombs.

"Well done, Detective," Crawford said under his breath, "Now see if you can get me some actual results!"

John would have told him what he thought of him right then and there, but he wasn't sure how much those fifty live microphones nearby might be picking up. The last thing he wanted was for Ham or Grandma— and now Jill Relson, for Christ's sake—to hear him on the six o'clock news, telling the Mayor of their fair city to go *bleeeeeep* himself!

#

"You did all right in there," said the Chief after the press conference was over, while they were standing outside on the Capitol steps, mingling with their fellow pigeons. At least those lucky fuckers had wings, thought John; they could fly away anytime they wanted to.

"Just don't ever ask me to do that again, all right?"

"I didn't ask you to this time."

"Yeah, I know. You have to do this kind of crap for Crawford all the time; how the hell do you stand it?"

Horsebreaker grinned. "You get used to it."

"How?" John didn't really expect an answer and the Chief didn't give him one. Instead, he changed the subject.

"So, where are you off to now?"

That was a happier topic, one John had been thinking about all morning. "I'm going to go out in the field like everybody else," he said.

"See if we can't put the heat on. That's the idea, right: all hands on deck? To tell you the truth, I'm looking forward to it. I don't get to work the street much anymore these days."

Horsebreaker nodded. He looked like he understood. He almost looked like he wished he could get out there himself. "Just don't go it alone, all right? Do things by the book."

"Don't I always?" asked John, innocently.

Horsebreaker gave him one of his stony looks.

"Don't worry," said John, "I've got it all worked out. I'll be riding patrol with Mona Greer, starting tomorrow morning."

The Chief's stone-face broke down then and he shot John a look that was somewhere in between disbelief and respect. "Damn," he said, "you're even braver than I thought you were!"

John grinned. Mona *did* have a bit of a reputation.

#

That evening, Jill called just to check in with him. "I saw you on television this morning," she said, "You looked cute, if a bit disgruntled."

"Jesus." John was sitting on the couch, hoping the Kung Pao chicken he'd had for dinner and the five alarm chili from lunch wouldn't team up to bore through his stomach lining. Ham was upstairs doing his homework. It was good to talk to Jill, but what he really wanted to do was see her. That might not happen until the weekend, though; he'd already told everyone in his unit that he intended to work them like government mules, and that only went over if you jumped in there with them.

Jill laughed. "You know, I'd never seen you in uniform before. I thought you looked rather dashing."

"It wasn't the uniform I minded so much," grumbled John, "It was being served up on a platter for all those . . . Well hell, you know why I hated it!"

She laughed again. "Yes, I do." There was a moment of silence on her end of the line then she said: "Say, you'll never guess who came out to see me at the Zoo this afternoon."

Out of the blue, John felt a rush of fear. He had visions of Must dealers or witch doctors or God-knows-what coming out of Africa to put Jill in danger, all because he'd asked her a few questions about elephants one day, a few weeks ago. "I can't imagine," he said, holding his breath.

"Your son and his girlfriend."

John started breathing again. That was a whole lot better than what he'd expected, but still . . . "Ham and Mick? Why?"

Jill laughed. "They said they wanted to meet me. I showed them around. They're nice kids," she added.

John was still in a state of shock. Ham knew Jill's last name, of course, and he knew that she worked at the Zoo, so it would have been pretty easy for him to track her down. Why would he, though? It sounded almost like something Grandma would have put him up to, except Ham hadn't seen her in months. "How'd they even get out there?"

"Took the bus, they said."

"I'm sorry they bothered you at work, Jill."

"No bother at all. It was nice to meet the two of them. I hope I'll get to see them again."

After they'd said their goodbyes John sat there alone in the dark for a while. Something about this was worrying him. It wasn't really that Ham had gone out to the Zoo to meet Jill, or even that he'd taken Mick with him. In a way, he was glad that had happened. He wanted his life to get tangled up with hers. But maybe he was just now realizing—or remembering, from his time with Jenny—that what went on between a man and a woman went way beyond just the two of them, that it had a way of causing ripples all across the pond.

Chapter 31

When Leti Tulafono woke up in the morning, on that ratty-ass sofa at Jermaine's place in the Projects, the first thing he remembered was that John Briggs got away. That was the first thing he remembered every morning now: that Leti had shot three clips of bullets at the son-of-a-whore at that shack down by the river and still the fucking cop got away. Now he would be on the lookout for Leti. Now it would be even harder to kill him. Leti gritted his teeth. The second thing he thought about was the dream. Every night now he had the same one. Marianne Harding Tulafono, dead, but still walking around. She was a dead dock whore, strangled. Somebody had strangled her. John Briggs? No, that wasn't right. There was somebody else. Captain Jimenez? Who the fuck was he, anyway? Marianne's new man, her old man, her drug dealer hookup? He was dead now too, though. He couldn't have killed her. Got his throat cut, down at the docks. In Leti's dream there was always somebody else there, somebody else that slit the Captain's throat, somebody else that strangled Marianne. There was somebody else there, but he always stayed back in the shadows.

Leti took out his Must pipe and smoked a few rocks. After a minute or two he felt better, he felt like the old Leti again, that Leti who was such good friends with Coach Bobby Bowden. That Leti who was on the top 50 list at Rivals.com. Leti felt something red, like blood, stacking up behind his eyes.

"Hey, man, don't you think it's a little early to be smokin' that shit?"

Jermaine was standing there. Leti stared at him, but didn't say nothing. There wasn't nothing to say. Leti was feeling like he could do anything, though: fucking fly if he wanted to.

"Hey, man, is you all right?"

Leti finished his pipe. He was still thinking about all those dreams. Pearl, Marianne's white cat, was there, still walking around. Her face was rotting but she was still walking around. You could see her bones, but she was still walking around. Tiny Loco was in the dream, too, that fucking dead piece of Chihuahua. Tiny Loco was chasing Pearl, and they were both running from Leti. Marianne was running away from Leti, too, just like in real life. A dead dock whore, a dead Chihuahua, and Pearl with half her cat-face gone. Leti looked up at Jermaine. He shook his head. Where the fuck was that cop, John Briggs? Where was he right now? Leti stood up and walked across the room.

Where the fuck is that cop, John Briggs?

"I don't know, man," said Jermaine, backing away. "Why don't you forget about that damned cop? That's just going to get your ass in more trouble!"

That red was stacking up behind Leti's eyes. He wanted to grab John Briggs by the throat, just the way the motherfucker had grabbed Marianne . . . No, that wasn't right. He didn't. There was somebody else. That's right: there was somebody else there at the docks, somebody else that had strangled her. But it was still John Briggs's fault! He sent her down there to the docks, to do his dirty work! He sent her back to that same place where she'd been a whore and a junkie. He *knew* what would happen, the son-of-a-bitch! So it was his fucking fault. But there was somebody else there too, that did all the killing. There was somebody standing over there in the shadows. Still, Leti wanted to kill the fucking cop. Leti wanted to grab John Briggs by the throat and crush his windpipe, choke the life out of him.

"Shit, man, let go of me! Is you crazy?"

Leti looked up. Through the red cloud he could see that he had his hands around Jermaine's neck. He was choking him, just the way somebody had choked Marianne. Leti was choking him just the way he wanted to choke John Briggs for killing his woman. Leti had to fight to make the red stand down, to make his hands open up, to let Jermaine start breathing again.

"Is you fucking crazy?" Jermaine said again, rubbing his neck. "You don't need to be smokin' no more of that shit. It does bad things to you, man!"

Days went by. Leti wasn't sure how many. Everything was mixed up in the smoke and the blue rocks in his Must pipe. The red was always stacking up behind his eyes. The same damned dream was always there. Nothing but dead dock whores and cats that were zombies and fucking rotting Chihuahuas. Coach Bobby Bowden . . . Rivals.com.

It was morning again. Leti walked into the kitchen. He stepped into something wet. He looked down at the floor. He was standing in a puddle of piss. Where was that fucking dog, Tiny Loco? Leti would throw his sorry little Mexican ass through a window! Leti was standing, in his sock feet, in a puddle of cold piss. What, the fucking dog wasn't house trained no more? Then Leti remembered. Tiny Loco was dead. Dead dogs don't piss on the floor, man. What the fuck was happening to him? Then he remembered last night. Was it last night? Maybe it was the night before that. Maybe it was a week ago, who the fuck cared? He remembered Jermaine, though, yelling at him.

"Is you crazy? Man, I ain't cleaning that up!"

Leti laughed. He remembered it then, remembered pissing on the floor himself. Remembered pissing all over himself. Just because . . . just because. That red was stacking up behind his eyes.

I'll piss wherever I fucking want to, man!

There it was, on the floor. And now his fucking socks were all wet. He kicked them off, watched them slop against the white wall. He walked around the tile floor, then the carpet, barefoot, leaving big yellow tracks. Where the fuck was Jermaine? Where had he run off to?

Days went by and Leti didn't see him no more. Last time Leti saw him, he looked scared. The place was empty now. Jermaine went someplace else. Marianne went someplace else. So did the fucking Mexican dog and the white zombie cat. Let them all go. Leti didn't give a shit no more. Leti was on the top 50 list at Rivals.com. Leti was on the cover of Sports Illustrated. Leti . . . Leti felt that red stacking up again, even harder, behind his eyes.

Where was that cop, John Briggs? There wasn't nobody left who could fuck with Leti Tulafono! Not Jermaine. Not that dead dock whore, Marianne Harding. Not Tiny Loco, the shitty little Mexican dog. And not Pearl, the fucking rotting white cat. John Briggs. There was just that one cop, John Briggs. Leti went looking for his rifle, wondering where the hell he had left it. Wondering if maybe Jermaine had run off with it. It had to be here somewhere, man. If Jermaine took it Leti would tear off his arms and legs!

Then he found it. He found his gun on the floor of the closet, by the door. Leti found clips of bullets there too, inside a shoebox. Enough ammunition to start a fucking war. Leti scooped it all up, laughing. Leti wrapped clips of bullets around his waist, and hung clips of bullets over his shoulders. He put on a leather jacket to cover it up. Jermaine's fucking jacket. Son-of-a-whore owed him that much. Leti tucked the rifle inside that leather jacket, too, but it didn't fit in there too well. It was sticking out like a bad hard-on when he opened the front door of Jermaine's apartment in the Projects and looked outside for the first time in maybe a week.

The sun was shining down. It was blinding him. There were big white clouds out towards the Gulf. What day was it, man? Leti didn't know, didn't care. All he could think about was John Briggs. Where the fuck would he find him, man? Police station? Leti thought about going down there and had to stop and laugh, thinking about walking into the police station with bullets practically coming out of his asshole, with the barrel of an AK-47 hanging down in front of his pants like a dick.

Briggs! I'm coming for you, man!

Fucking cop. There wasn't nobody around, out here on the street. Cars passing by. Couple of buses. The piece of shit superintendent for the Projects was over there by the flower beds, some Hispanic guy with a black mustache. He was looking at Leti like he knew something was up.

Something IS up, man!

That red. It was stacking up behind his eyes. Leti tried to remember the super's name. Something-Juarez. Leti laughed at him then and opened up Jermaine's leather jacket. Showed him what he had inside. Something-Juarez got real wide eyes. Something-Juarez took off running, maybe back to Juarez. Something-Juarez ran away like a fucking rabbit. That red was stacking up again, right behind Leti's eyes.

#

The world was red now, and it was Leti's. Wasn't nobody going to fuck with him no more. He drove around town in his white Volkswagen Beetle, stuffed into it like a fucking sardine, looking for his chance to kill that cop, John Briggs. How had Leti missed him the first time, at that shack down by the river? Now Briggs was onto Leti. Now Briggs was watching out for him. Now it would be a lot harder to kill the son-of-a-whore.

Leti drove around in his little white car. His rifle was on the seat beside him. He was looking for John Briggs, all over the city. There were too damned many people though, man! It was too hard to see him, too hard to find him. Leti kept on driving around. Leti drove and drove, looking for that bastard who had killed Marianne. Where the fuck was Leti now? Some part of town that Leti had never been before. Mexican side of the city. Tiny Loco side of the city. He pulled off onto the side of the road. Man, it looked worse here than the fucking Projects!

Leti pulled out his Must pipe. He smoked a pile of blue rocks. Where the fuck was he? Shit, man, was that a cop car right behind him? Leti looked up into the rearview mirror and there was a cop car right behind him. Flashing his red and blue lights. Leti put the pipe down. Leti rolled down the window to let the smoke out. Leti felt cold, all cold on the inside. Except for that red right behind his eyes. The cop got out of his car. The cop was walking this way. Nobody was going to fuck with Leti Tulafono, man! Especially not John Briggs. Was that Briggs back there now? Leti stared at the cop in the side view mirror, through the clouds of white smoke that still hadn't cleared out of his car. The cop was getting closer. He was slowing down. The cop knew something was up. He could tell. The cop knew this wasn't just going to be no routine traffic stop. Leti picked up his rifle. The cop looked back at his partner, who was still inside the squad car. He said something to him. The cop wasn't John Briggs. Leti didn't give a shit, though. He hated this cop, too. He hated all the cops, man.

"Get out of the car with your hands up!" the cop was yelling.

Leti laughed. He turned around in the seat and shot at the cop, emptied a full fucking clip at him. Glass was busting out everywhere. Bullets were dancing off the sidewalk. Leti was laughing at everything. The cop was running, man, running for his fucking life. There was blood on the sidewalk. The cops were shooting back at him! Leti emptied another clip of bullets at them. One of the cops was down. Leti couldn't stop laughing.

Don't be fucking with Leti Tulafono, man!

The quarterback was John Briggs, though. That's the one Leti had to get to. These cops were just fucking linemen. If Leti wanted to stay number one on the depth chart, if he wanted to stay friends with Coach Bobby Bowden, if he wanted to keep showing up on ESPN, he had to get to the quarterback. Leti got out of the car. Leti had to get the quarterback by the throat, just the way John Briggs did to Marianne. No. That wasn't it, man. It wasn't John Briggs who strangled her. Briggs was just the son-of-a-whore who had sent her back down to the docks in the first place. He was the one who had turned her back into a junkie and whore. Who was it that had strangled her, though? There was somebody else.

Leti went back behind the Volkswagen Beetle, looking for the cops. One of them was dead on the sidewalk. Blood was flowing into the gutter. Where the fuck *was* Leti anyway? Some part of town where he'd never been before. Leti saw the other cop now. He was inside the squad car. He looked like he was still alive, but he wasn't shooting at Leti no more. He was sitting there behind the steering wheel, looking up at Leti the way Marianne used to sometimes, the way his mother used to, sometimes.

What the fuck are you looking at, man?

The cop was just sitting there, inside the squad car. Leti walked towards him, holding his rifle. Leti thought about shooting the son-of-a-bitch. But he wanted to get closer to him, he wanted to get to the quarterback. Maybe this cop *was* the quarterback? Maybe he was John Briggs? Leti got closer. The cop was sitting there, looking up at him, but something was wrong. Leti smashed out the side window with the butt of his rifle. The cop was just sitting there looking up at him. There was blood coming out of his chest. The cop was alive but there was blood coming out his chest. The cop wasn't the quarterback. He was breathing hard. Leti looked down at him, looked down at the wounded cop.

"Where the fuck is this place, man?" Leti looked up, looked around. He'd never been in this part of town before. It was shitty. Bunch of buildings that looked like they'd been hit with bombs. Bunch of houses that looked like rat traps. Leti saw some Mexican kids, some punks on the street corner a long ways off.

"Tr . . . Tr . . ." The cop was trying to say something.

Come on, man, spit it out! Fucker was about to die on Leti.

"Tristy City," the cop finally said, with a wheeze.

Tristy City. Leti had heard of it. Hispanic part of town. Leti thought about his little Mexican dog, Tiny Loco. Leti laughed. Then Leti strangled the cop. How was he supposed to find the quarterback now? How was he supposed to find John Briggs in a place that was as shitty as this? Leti looked at the two cops. One of them was dead on the sidewalk, in a puddle of blood. His partner was dead now, too, inside the squad car.

Fucking cops! Leti got back into his Beetle. There were some Mexican punks on a street corner a block away. They were pointing at Leti now. They were coming this way. They were running this way.

Fuck them, man!

There was blood on the steering wheel of the Beetle, blood on his hands. There was blood stacking up, too, right behind his eyes. Leti laughed and then drove away, fast. Where was he going to go now, man? What was he going to do?

#

Who was that girl by the side of the road? She looked like Marianne. Couldn't be her though, thought Leti through a cloud of white smoke: Marianne was a dead dock whore.

Fucking John Briggs!

The girl was at a bus stop, inside of the shelter. Leti wasn't in Tristy City no more. He wasn't sure where the fuck he was, man. The Gulf was right over there, though: he could see whitecaps and waves. Leti made a u-turn right in the middle of the road, right there on the Gulf Highway. Now he was going back the other way, to get the girl who looked like Marianne. The girl in the bus shelter. Leti pulled into the turnout, right in front of the shelter. The girl was still there. She took a step back when she saw him. The girl looked scared. Leti laughed and got out of the Beetle. He started walking towards the shelter and the scared girl inside. She was looking around, looking for someplace to run. She didn't have no place to run. There wasn't no place she could go where she wouldn't be Leti's. She looked more and more like Marianne. Maybe she wasn't dead after all, man? Maybe it was all just a trick, a set up? Maybe she and John Briggs had planned it that way, hoping Leti would forget about her? Maybe the two of them wanted to be together, without Leti getting in the way?

The girl that looked like Marianne, that maybe was Marianne, ran out of the shelter. She bolted. Leti ran after her. She didn't get too far. Leti caught up with her on the sand, in between the shelter and the shoreline. Where the fuck was he anyway, man? Somewhere in Seaside. On the sand. Near the water. At the beach. Leti didn't give a shit no more.

There were people out there, though, lots of people. There were lots of people there at the beach. Leti didn't care no more. He had Marianne by the hair. He had his rifle. Leti showed it to her, showed it to everybody else around. They started running. Leti laughed. Marianne wasn't running, man; he had her by the hair. She was crying. She looked scared. She was screaming now, the bitch, making all kinds of noise. Leti picked her up with one hand the way he used to pick up Tiny Loco. Leti carried her back to the shelter. She was screaming. Leti hit her hard on the side of the face.

Shut the fuck up, bitch!

He could see people outside of the shelter, running. Marianne was still screaming. Leti grabbed her by her white throat . . . There was somebody else there that night, at the docks. There was somebody else who had strangled his woman. Unless it was all a pile of shit. Unless John Briggs had staged it so Leti would think his woman was dead. Unless John Briggs had fixed it so that he and Marianne . . . Leti looked at her and that red was stacking up behind his eyes again. She wasn't saying nothing no more. She wasn't screaming no more. There was blood everywhere, man. He had her by the throat. She wasn't screaming no more. She wasn't even Marianne no more. She didn't look anything like her. Marianne was a dead dock whore. So was this bitch. Leti slammed her up against the side of the shelter. Leti slammed her up against the side of the shelter again and again. She was covered with blood. She wasn't Marianne, though; she didn't even look like her, man. She was knocked out, dead maybe, lying there on the ground. There was somebody else there that night, at the docks, in the shadows. That somebody else was the one who had strangled her. Not John Briggs. But it was still his fault, man!

Leti came out of the shelter, waving his rifle around. There wasn't nobody on the beach no more. They'd all seen what he did to the girl. They'd all run away. He looked out across the sand. Where the fuck was that cop? There wasn't nobody that could stop Leti now, not even John Briggs. Where was he right now, though?

Leti saw something up ahead, on the beach. It was the Ferris Wheel! Spinning around. Leti laughed. He knew where he was now. There was the roller coaster, too; he'd been on that one before. Almost lost his lunch there once, man, a long time ago. On the new one, the big one they called El Diablo. Leti laughed. He could hear the sound of people up there. He could hear the sound of little girls. Lots of little girls. If he couldn't find the fucking cop, then maybe the fucking cop could find him?

Come on, Briggs, I'm waiting for you right here, man!

Leti went walking across the sand towards the Wheel, waving his rifle around. That red was stacking up right behind his eyes. That red was everywhere now, shooting out of his eyes.

Chapter 32

"So I get to ride around with you, huh, JB?" Mona said with a grin when they met at her car, an unmarked Ford Taurus. It was light blue and seemed to suit her.

"Yeah, just while Bill's out on Medical." Bill Henderson was her partner, out with a twisted leg that John still wasn't sure how he got.

"Lucky me, huh?"

"Yeah, lucky you."

"Say, you looked real good on the TV yesterday," said Mona.

John swore. "If I never have to do that again, it'll be too damn soon."

He and Mona both were in plainclothes. John never wore his uniform—except during press conferences, of course—and neither did Mona; blues tended to make it real hard to mingle with junkies, and that was most of what she did. She was wearing green pants and a white Houston Astros t-shirt, and a funky hat that looked like it was made out of leopard skin. Her dyed red hair-sprayed hair was poking out underneath, so solid that it wasn't going to move for anything short of a Gulf hurricane. She looked like somebody's mother and maybe that was the secret to her success; junkies tended not to see her as a threat. They might feel guilty as hell, thinking about how they'd let their own mothers down, but they tended not to scurry away from her like cockroaches from a kitchen light, the way they did when they saw cops like John.

"Mind if I drive?" she said.

"I figured you would."

"We working my usual beat?"

"That's the idea—everybody's responsible for his own turf."

"All right. We setting our sights on pushers or junkies?"

"Forget the users for a while," said John, "We don't have enough cells to lock them all up, and if we take their shit and let them loose, they'll go right back to the tit of the dealers. Users aren't going to lead us to Mr. Big, either, and that's where we need to be. Cut off the head and the whole operation dies, pretty quick."

"All right. Just don't expect them to be happy to see us."

John nodded. Why would they be when the idea was to confiscate any unsold Must he and Mona could get their hands on? Pinch off the pipeline, turn off the spigot, however you wanted to say it. John was glad the Chief was holding off Egan, that he wasn't asking them to go after drugs of all flavors. If word of that ever got out on the street, all the traffic would go underground. But if folks knew they were just hunting the little blue rock, and that they were doing it because people who were smoking it were blowing up, then they might even get some of the street rats to help them. Especially once those rats knew he and Mona were handing out money for information.

Mona was driving them towards Tejon, a well-known junkie boulevard on the west side of Palmer. The weather was fine. Mona had been talking about something the whole way there, but mostly John had been tuning her out. He'd been thinking about Jill and that letter she got from Cynthia Jones, and everything that might be going on over in Africa. He was thinking about that YouTube video he'd watched, the one about albinos and body part snatchers. Then Mona said something that broke through all the walls he'd thrown up.

"This Must crap is different from other drugs, isn't it? If I was a pusher I'd be loving that. Hell, you don't even have to push it, really. Sells itself to just about any man on the planet. Look at how well Viagra is doing! And it's not just you old guys that are buying it, either. I read this article the other day in *Cosmo* about how these Spanish bullfighters were taking it just so they could last longer with all their girlfriends."

John was looking out the window, rolling his eyes, watching stone cold parts of Palmer go by. He was remembering now why cops in his unit—Bill Henderson, mostly—complained about having to work with Mona; seemed like she never shut up. She was a talker and didn't seem to pay too much attention to whether you really wanted to hear what she was saying or not. John was starting to wonder if maybe Bill had twisted his ankle on purpose.

"It's kind of pitiful when you think about it," she kept on, "Like there's nothing else in life but being able to get it up once in a while. I feel sorry for ya'll, really. That's the difference between men and women, though, I guess: we've got all kinds of reasons to live; you've just got the one."

"If we only had that one," said John, getting drawn into the conversation against his better judgment, "I'd have been dead years ago. You forgot about beer."

"All right, two reasons then."

"And don't forget sports, either."

"Damn," she said, "ya'll are lot more complicated than I gave you credit for!"

"I don't know as I'd go that far."

She kept on driving and John tuned her out again. He didn't need to hear any more about how stupid men were. Hell, he knew that already. He was one.

Something was coming over the squawk box now; Mona picked up the transmitter with her right hand, keeping the left one on the wheel. "Hey, Shirley, what's up?"

You anywhere close to Seaside?

"Not too far away. Is something going down over there?"

You could say that. Shirley sounded like she was on the moon, what with all the static coming over the box. *Two cops are down in Tristy City and we're getting reports that the perp has shown up at Seaside, that he raped and killed some girl there.*

John felt like he'd been hit between the eyes. He had flashbacks to Division Street, the Fishbowl, and Highway 19. It had been a while since they'd seen anything like that. He'd been hoping they were past seeing anything like that. He took a deep breath.

John Briggs still with you? asked Squawk Box Shirley.

"Yeah, he's sitting right here," said Mona, "You want to talk to him?"

Nah, just tell him to be careful. The guy who's off on a rampage, the way people are telling it, he sounds a lot like John's old friend Leti Tulafono.

#

Jesus Christ, thought John.

"She said . . ."

"Yeah, I heard her."

Mona turned the car around and started heading south towards Seaside. What the hell was going on over there? It sounded like Shirley wasn't quite sure herself. John had a pretty good idea, though. Leti had an assault rifle; he knew that much from personal experience. If the big Samoan had shot a couple of cops already, how long would it be until he started wasting people at random? John wondered if this meant Leti had been using Must all along. He remembered that day at the docks when Tulafono had charged him and Tom, and Tom had shot him in the leg just to slow him down. Had he been smoking blue rocks even then? John whistled.

"What is it, JB?"

John shook his head. "I was just thinking: if Tulafono is on Must, and he's gone off the deep end, then he's going to be one hell of a load to bring down."

"You don't even know it's him yet."

"It's him," John said grimly, "If the descriptions people are giving Shirley are making her think of him, then it's got to *be* him. There aren't that many Samoans the size of whales running around loose in the city."

"Then I hope she's calling for backup."

"You know she is. Probably has every car within ten miles on its way there right now. And a SWAT team."

"I think I'll pick up the Gulf Highway. Shirley didn't say exactly where this is going down, maybe she doesn't know yet, but I figure we can just keep driving east until we see someone crazy."

Or a pile of dead bodies, thought John. But he wasn't going to say that out loud. He didn't think he had to.

They were on the highway now, with the sun behind them and the water off to their right. John had his window rolled down, on the lookout for anything out of the ordinary: dead people, crowds running along The Ribbon in a panic, some drugged-up Samoan waving an AK-47 around. Out here, though, this far west, everything seemed normal. He saw a half-dozen bicycles, a handful of joggers, a young couple walking along holding hands. John could hear waves breaking; the Gulf was right there, on the other side of a narrow strip of white sand. As they kept going east, that strip of sand got wider. The water got farther away. They passed a pier where some people were fishing. The Fairgrounds were just up ahead. Then something didn't feel quite right to him.

"Slow down," he told Mona.

"You see something?"

"Maybe." The Fairgrounds were right there. The Ferris Wheel was spinning around, like it always did. While John watched, some people went backwards over the top. "Slow down."

"If I go any slower the redneck in the truck behind us is going to give birth to a live cow."

"Pull over, then." John pointed up ahead. "I see a spot right there."

"It would have to be parallel!" grumbled Mona.

"You can do it if you put your mind to it."

"If you say a word about women drivers, JB, I'm going to kick your ass to the curb."

"Actually, I was thinking it was just you."

Eventually she got them backed in. She cut the engine. John sat there hanging out the window, listening.

"What is it, JB?"

"Shhh!" Cars were zooming by on the highway. That made it hard to hear anything. But every now and then sounds of screaming would come from the Ferris Wheel and the Zipper and the roller coaster known as "El Diablo." Only, the Zipper wasn't zipping. And the Diablo had stopped, its train stuck at the top of the biggest hill. The Ferris Wheel was still spinning around so it couldn't be a power failure, but there was something not quite right about that, too. After a while John figured out what it was. The wheel hadn't stopped turning the whole time he'd been watching. Usually, the carnies would let people off and put new people on every few minutes; you were lucky if you got three full turns around. John started counting: four, five, six . . . it was still spinning around.

"What is it, JB?"

"Something's wrong at the Fairgrounds," said John. Then they both heard it: gunfire. He turned and looked at Mona and said: "Come on!"

They got out of the car. They cut across The Ribbon to the sand on the other side. It didn't seem like anybody else had heard what they had; a steady stream of bikers and joggers was coming at them, but nobody acted like they were in any hurry. *Pop, pop, pop*: the gun, wherever it was, was still firing. John heard screams again and they weren't the right kind.

"Come on!"

They were running across the sand. They were heading for the entrance to the Fairgrounds. By the time they got there the crowds had thinned out and then the crowds were gone altogether. John felt the hairs on the back of his neck stand on end. All the booths where they sold hot dogs and funnel cakes were empty; the lights were still on but there was nobody home. It was like one of those end-of-the-world movies where the only guy who survived the plague is walking around through an empty town, wondering if he'll ever see another live human being.

"There he is!" cried Mona.

Shit, it *was* him, Leti Tulafono, down at the end of the Midway where the booths gave way to the rides. Leti hadn't seen them yet and John wanted to keep it that way. He herded Mona in between a couple of abandoned booths. Then they peeked around the corner together to see what Leti was up to. He was spinning around on his heels like he was drunk, or high, and he was waving his rifle around. Every now and then he'd squeeze off a shot but it was hard to tell what he was aiming at.

"We've got to get closer," said John, "See if we can take him down."

He led Mona back out onto the main street of the Midway and they ran past a few more booths before ducking in behind one that sold candied apples. And that was where they found the first body.

"Looks like Leti's not just shooting blanks," said Mona, bending down to check the guy's pulse at his neck. He looked about fifty, judging by the amount of gray hair. Tourist, judging by his cheap t-shirt. Right in the middle of that shirt there were two bright red stains.

"I never thought he was," said John. He wondered how long this had been going on. He wondered how long those people had been stuck up on El Diablo, how long the Ferris Wheel had been spinning around with nobody at the controls.

"What're we gonna do now?" whispered Mona.

John looked around the corner of the candied apple stand. Tulafono was still there. He was twenty yards away and as far as John could tell hadn't seen them yet. That much was good. They couldn't just keep hiding out here, though, watching; they were going to have to try and take him down. John saw a couple of bodies on the main street up ahead and more in between the booths on either side of it. The Midway was starting to look like a morgue. He wondered if he could squeeze off a good shot from here, or if he ought to try and get a bit closer. If he did take a shot and missed, he and Mona would find themselves in a gun battle and Leti had the bigger

241

gun. Way bigger. But people up on top of the Ferris Wheel must have seen them now; they were yelling for help. Tulafono heard them. He let out with some kind of crazy laugh, one that curdled John's blood. He lifted his rifle. He pointed it into the air.

Crack! Somebody on the Ferris Wheel pitched forward and fell out of the sky. John watched helplessly as the body tumbled down in front of the flashing lights and landed with a thud on the wood ramp sloping up to the platform of the ride. The people who were still up there on the Wheel started screaming. Maybe thinking how they might be next. Maybe thinking how there wasn't anyplace to hide. Maybe thinking how there wasn't any way to get off. Some of them were trying anyway. A couple of kids had climbed out of their seats onto the spokes.

"Got to take him down now!" John barked at Mona. They couldn't wait for the SWAT team. He ran out into the Midway. He went down on one knee. He lined up his handgun. He sighted along the barrel. Mona was there with him, doing the same.

Maybe between the two of us we can bring him down. He drew a bead on Tulafono.

Then Leti saw him. He called out "John Briggs!" and smiled like he was happy to see him. It was almost like this was what he'd been waiting for, all along.

John was deep in his trance already, concentrating on squeezing the trigger. Leti whipped his rifle around. Leti was coming towards him. Leti was laughing now and that laugh sounded like it came from the Devil. John pulled the trigger. He saw his bullet rip into Tulafono's chest, but the big Samoan just laughed again and kept coming.

Shit! A bullet from Mona's gun hit him in the chest, too, but the son-of-a-bitch was still coming. He was lifting up his assault rifle.

"Take cover!" John yelled at Mona and then dived behind a booth that sold cotton candy.

She'd come up from her crouch but was still standing there in the Midway like she couldn't believe what she was seeing, like she didn't want to believe it. There was blood streaming down Tulafono's chest but he was still coming towards them, still laughing, still holding his assault rifle out in front of him. He let loose with a volley. Not at Mona, at least; not at Mona. John had only a split second to be glad of that—bullets were ripping through the stand he was hiding behind. One of them singed his leg. John rolled out from behind the stand into the Midway again, hoping to get off another shot between volleys. Leti was standing there with his leather jacket open, still laughing like the Devil. Inside of that jacket there were enough clips of ammo to fuel a small war.

"Briggs!" Leti screamed out when he saw John again, "Come on, Motherfucker!"

John squeezed off another shot. This one clipped Leti's left arm. Leti looked down at it like he'd been bitten by a mosquito. A trickle of blood was running down the black leather of his jacket. He laughed again. John could see Mona on the other side of the Midway, behind a couple of stacked crates of Coke cans. She let off another shot, too. John couldn't tell if she hit anything or not, but it got Leti's attention. He turned towards her. He'd reloaded now. He fired off another spray of bullets. They ripped into the crates. Mona dropped to the ground. Coke cans were exploding above her, sending sprays of foam into the air. That gave John a chance to line Leti up in his sights again. *Better make this one count*, he was thinking. He was aiming for Tulafono's head this time. The leather jacket was hanging open and John could see streams of blood pouring from Leti's chest, staining the white t-shirt he had on underneath, and flowing over the belts of ammo that crisscrossed it, that made him look like a Mexican pistolero.

John was aiming for Leti's head. He was squeezing the trigger. And then three guys came out of nowhere. Three guys came out of nowhere and tackled Tulafono.

What the hell? Three skinny Black guys had tackled Tulafono. Were they crazy? He'd never in his life seen anybody so brave—or so stupid. They'd get medals for this, if they lived. They had Leti down, on the sand, but he was fighting back like an animal.

John looked over at Mona. Was she seeing this, too? She was peeking over the top of the crates of Coke cans. She'd lost her leopard hat and it looked like there was cola all over that stiff red hair of hers. John stood all the way up. "Come on!" he said, waving Mona towards the fight that was going on in front of them. They started running down the Midway.

The three guys had taken Tulafono's rifle away. They had him down on the ground. How the hell had they managed to overpower him? There were three of them, sure, but they were scrawny little sons-of-bitches and

Leti was bad-ass even under normal conditions. With Must in his system you had to figure he'd be as strong as the Hulk. He'd taken a couple of bullets to the chest, though—maybe that was slowing him down. Something flashed in the sun. Those three heroes had knives.

John felt a surge of adrenaline. *Don't fucking kill him!* Not that he'd blame them much if they did. Leti had just shot a whole lot of people. But there *was* such a thing as carrying vigilante justice too far. "Hey!" he called out, moving in, "Hey, that's enough! Police officers! Let us take it from here!"

They still had Leti down on the sand. The big Samoan wasn't moving. All three of the vigilantes were bent over his body. What the hell were they doing? John could hear Mona shouting behind him. It sounded like she was trying to warn him about something. He already knew he was wading into a creek full of snakes, though.

"Cover me!" he yelled back at her. She was still trying to tell him something, but he wasn't listening. He was focusing on what was in front of him. "Hey, you three, back off! Police officers!"

They weren't backing off. They had Tulafono pinned to the sand. Then finally John got close enough to see what was going down. They'd cut Leti up bad. There was blood all over his body. And those three vigilantes looked like they might be lapping it up. It looked like the sons-of-bitches were drinking it.

Jesus Christ! It was like his own blood ran out of his body then, like it was trying its best to get the hell away from here, away from *them*. John fired his gun in the air. "Back off! Now!" They weren't listening. They kept on doing whatever it was they were doing. John didn't want to think about what they were doing. He fired again, this time right over their heads. And then, finally, they did stop. Finally, they turned around and looked at him.

Their mouths were all covered with blood. And there was something about their eyes. Those eyes looked hollowed-out, empty, and they were glowing red in the light of the bright midday sun. John felt cold. He was scared in a way he'd never felt scared before, all the way down to his bones. But his twenty years of being a cop didn't fail him; that part of him that could do this in its sleep kicked in.

"Back away from him!" he yelled, pointing his gun at the chest of the kid who was closest.

That's when all three of them screeched and came at him. John didn't hesitate. He shot the first one point blank. The guy kept on coming. John shot him again. He kept coming. And then Mona was shooting him, too. They must have hit him with five or six rounds each before the kid finally dropped to his knees, and even then he kept crawling towards them for a while, leaving a bloody streak across the white sand. The other two vigilantes finally turned and ran. John knew he ought to go after them, put the cuffs on them if he could, but it was like his legs had turned to rubber. It was all he could do to make it over to the one guy who lay stretched out on the sand. John knelt down, checked his pulse. He was dead all right— assuming he'd ever been alive to begin with.

Don't be going off into Bullshitland, he told himself, trying to run off any crazy notions that the kid might not be human, that he might be a vampire or zombie. He looked at the corpse. Young guy, in his twenties maybe. He didn't look like he was from around here. He looked African.

"I didn't think we were ever going to bring him down," said Mona, out of breath, as she knelt beside him. "What's going on? Is this one loaded up on Must too, do you think?"

"I don't know." John was coming out of his stupor now. He stared at the kid's red mouth. He checked his pockets. He didn't find anything except the wicked-looking knife he'd been using to stab Tulafono with. Then he noticed that the kid was wearing a necklace. More like dog tags, he decided once he'd looked at it a little more closely, but it wasn't like any set of dog tags he'd ever seen. It was a chain with a little metal tag at the end, sure, but that tag didn't have any names or numbers on it. Instead, there was a picture of something black, a picture that looked like it had been stamped or burned onto the metal.

"What the hell *is* that?" wondered Mona.

"I don't know, what's it look like to you?"

"Let me get a closer look." She took it from him and stretched it out as far as the chain would go. "Looks almost like a grasshopper," she said after a while.

"Yeah it does, doesn't it? A black grasshopper." He took it from Mona and then did something that surprised even him: he yanked the dog tag clean off. Broke the chain. Probably left marks on the back of the dead kid's neck.

"What the hell are you doing, JB?" hissed Mona, "That's evidence!"

"I don't know," he said truthfully. It just seemed like something he ought to do. He put the tag in his pocket. And that's when he heard a groaning sound. It was coming from Leti Tulafono.

"I thought he was dead," said Mona.

"Yeah, me too. Three or four times." John got up and ran over to where Leti was laid out on the sand. The big Samoan was in bad shape. He wasn't dead yet but maybe wishing he was. He looked up at John with glassy black eyes. His breath was coming slow and hard. There were at least a dozen knife wounds in his chest, and bullet holes, and what looked like a few bite marks. There was blood everywhere, soaking his shirt and the sand underneath.

"Hang on, man," said John, "You're going to be all right. I'll call for an ambulance."

Leti just looked up at him with those black glass eyes of his, breathing hard. Then finally he said: "Briggs?" It was like he was coming out of a stupor.

"You're going to be all right," he said again, "We'll get you to St. Luke's."

Tulafono reached up and grabbed his arm. "Briggs," he whistled, "There's something I've got to tell you, man."

"Sure, Leti, sure." John leaned in close but stayed on his guard, ready to fight Tulafono off if he had to, if what Leti had in mind was dragging him down to hell with him.

"It's important."

"I'm right here."

"There was somebody else there that night," whistled Leti, "Somebody there at the docks." He winced. He was in pain. "There was somebody else there that killed Marianne."

John frowned. Well, yeah, sure. He already knew that. But he was glad Leti wasn't blaming him anymore. "Yeah, I know."

"No you don't, man," Leti said, shuddering like he was seeing something he couldn't quite believe, "Briggs, I think it was me."

What the hell was he talking about? Did he mean he'd done it himself, cut Jimenez's throat and strangled Marianne? Or did he just feel responsible somehow, the way John did? "Leti," he said then, "who were those guys who attacked you just now?" It seemed like that was what was important here, not whether or not he felt guilty about Marianne Harding.

Tulafono wheezed.

"Leti! Who were those guys who attacked you just now?" John grabbed him by the shoulders. "Leti!"

The big Samoan groaned. His head turned to one side. "Leti!" John started shaking him. It was too late, though; Tulafono had already left the world behind. John turned and looked up at Mona then and saw that her eyes were wide.

"Just what is going on here, JB?" she whispered.

"Damned if I know," John said under his breath. He looked back down at Tulafono's shot-up and cut-up and mauled body and then said it again: "I'll be damned if I know."

Chapter 33

Horsebreaker must not have slept too well last night either, thought John, noticing the dark circles underneath the Chief's eyes. Berserk drug addicts shooting up your town would do that. And there was so much more to it now.

"I was up late reading your report," explained Ed, "and watching the news. And I still don't know what the hell is going on."

"Join the club." John was sitting in the chair beside the Chief's desk, while he did his usual rain dance around the office.

"I'm not even sure where to start." Horsebreaker picked up a manila folder, opened it and read for a minute. "Leti Tulafono," he finally decided, "You think maybe he was walking down the same road as the rest?"

John knew what he meant: the rest of the Must-fueled killers. He nodded. "Smoked himself into testosterone overload. Got his hands on a gun. Assaulted a girl. Shot up a bunch of people because . . . hell, I don't know, because he didn't like the way they looked at him."

"I was really hoping we were past all that, and so was Mayor Crawford. I actually saw him smile yesterday for the first time in a week." He had his back to John, looking out the window. "He's not smiling now."

"I can't think of anybody who is."

A few seconds ticked by. The Chief finally turned around. "What's worse, now we've got citizens trying to do our jobs for us."

"You mean those three vigilantes?"

"Hell yes, I mean those three vigilantes!"

It wasn't everyday Horsebreaker lost his temper. John couldn't blame him. This case was slipping away from them in all kinds of ways. "I don't think they were citizens, exactly."

"What do you mean?"

"There's no record of them, at least no record of the one Mona and I brought down. No ID and his fingerprints aren't in any of our databases, not even Interpol's. He might as well not exist."

"Oh, he exists all right," said the Chief, "People who don't exist don't kill other people." He had his stony face back on. He looked out the window, staring into his favorite alleyway. "What's this in your report about him drinking some of Tulafono's blood?"

John wasn't sure how to answer that. He'd witnessed the whole thing but still didn't quite believe it himself. "It is what it is."

"The Press is having a field day with that," said the Chief, like it was somehow John's fault. "Satanic ritual, they're saying. Gang initiation. Fucking vampires or aliens."

John raised an eyebrow. You didn't hear Ed Horsebreaker use the F-word too often. This must really be getting under his skin. It had been under John's for a while. "Illegal alien, maybe."

The Chief looked back over his shoulder, gave John a skeptical look. "The corpse I saw on the news last night didn't look Mexican to me."

"Not Mexican, African."

"Come again?"

John had wanted to have some actual evidence before taking this to the Chief, something more to go on than just a hunch, but there wasn't time for that anymore. He took a deep breath, then told him about the trail of musth breadcrumbs that seemed to point towards Tanzania, and elephants.

Horsebreaker just stood there, processing it all. "Why didn't you tell me about this before?"

"About the elephants?" asked John, raising an eyebrow.

"All right, never mind. I wouldn't have believed you. Shit, maybe I don't believe you now. Tell me something, though: why would somebody in Africa be selling drugs here? Not in America, I get that, I mean in our piss-ant town?"

Not that they lived in a backwater, exactly, but John knew what he meant. It wasn't Miami, either. "I've been asking myself that for a while now."

"Come up with an answer yet?"

"Nope."

Horsebreaker came over and sat down in his chair, heavily. He ran his fingers through his thinning black hair. He stared at John so intently that after a while he started to feel uncomfortable. "What's up, Chief?" he asked nervously.

"I get the feeling there's something else you're not telling me."

John hesitated. There were lots of things. Not because he didn't want the Chief to know about those things, he just hadn't figured out how they fit into the narrative. "Those three vigilantes," he finally said, grabbing for the loose end that was closest, "I don't think they killed Tulafono just to help us out."

Horsebreaker pondered that for a moment. He was sitting in his armchair, hands folded across his stomach, like he was in the middle of some strange, Native American prayer. He sighed. "I don't either. You think maybe they were a hit squad?"

"It crossed my mind."

"Why would they have wanted to take out Tulafono, though?"

John shrugged. "Well, that's the sixty-four dollar question." He *had* come up with at least one theory, last night: that maybe Commissioner Egan had gone rogue on them, that he'd decided to solve this Must problem his own damned way. That wasn't something John could float out to the Chief, though, not without a least some shred of evidence.

"You think maybe there's a rival cartel involved?"

"Maybe," said John, "but as far as we know Tulafono was a user, not a dealer. Why get rid of the customers you're fighting over?"

"Well, the chances of Tulafono ever buying any more product from anybody went way down as soon as he started shooting people but yeah, I see what you mean." Horsebreaker rocked back and forth. "What I can't figure out is why those vigilantes felt like they needed to kill Tulafono at all. I mean, even if they did want him dead—for whatever reason—why not just wait around and let you and Mona do it?"

John had been thinking about that, too, and always came back to the same answer. It was one he didn't like. "Unless drinking his blood played into it."

The Chief grunted. John could tell he didn't want to go there, but it wasn't like you could pretend it hadn't happened. Or that it wasn't significant somehow. "Any other reports of blood-drinking around town?"

"Not that I've heard." As he was processing that, John realized that his suspicions about Egan wouldn't hold water; even if the Commissioner

250

MUST

had decided to take the law into his own hands, would he have really hired three African vampires to do his dirty work? Not when there were plenty of sick cops right here on the Force, cops who were just waiting—hoping, really—for the chance to be unleashed. Well then, who was responsible? He was back to square one.

"Once I get back out in the field with Mona," he said, thinking out loud, "I should be able to . . ."

Horsebreaker held up a hand, cutting him off. "That may be a while," he said, "for the both of you. Remember: unless the guy you shot was Satan himself . . ."

Right, shit, that damned deadly force policy! John thought: *Not again!* The idea of hanging around the house watching dish soap commercials actually sounded worse than trying to track down a blood-drinking hit squad! "Maybe you can make a case to the Commish that this vampire vigilante actually *was* Satan himself?" he asked hopefully.

Horsebreaker had his stony face on. John sighed. He reached for his badge and gun.

#

"I really need to run a few things by you," John said to Jill. She was sitting across the table from him at the Treetops Café.

"I'm listening."

He took a sip of iced tea. "Some pretty strange things have been going on since the last time I saw you." He brought her up to speed. What did he expect Jill to do with that information, though? Tie it all up with a red ribbon? Maybe he was just hoping she'd see something he hadn't, or that she'd put the pieces together in a way he hadn't thought of—a scientist's way instead of a cop's.

"I saw something on the news this morning about those shootings at the Fairgrounds," she said, "Is it really true what they're saying, that the killers drank some of the victim's blood?"

"I'm afraid so, yeah." He still had this picture in his head of that one nameless vigilante coming at him, mouth so red it looked like he'd been eating a cherry snow cone.

"Why do you think they did that?"

"No idea. I don't believe in vampires, though."

"Me, either." Jill seemed to ponder that for a while, then said: "If it was just anybody's blood the three of them were after, why would they

251

attack the only person on the scene who had a gun in his hands?"

A really big gun, thought John. Jill was right: why would they attack the one guy who was holding an AK-47, if all they wanted was plain old type-O blood? There were plenty of easier targets around. "Now that you mention it, I guess that doesn't make much sense, does it?"

"Not unless there was something unique about the victim's blood."

John stared at her. She knew that there was. She, maybe more than anybody else, knew that there was. "Must," he said, "Tulafono had Must in his bloodstream."

She nodded. "Presumably, yes."

"You think maybe that's the whole reason why they attacked him? That the three of them were after the Must in his blood?"

"It's a theory, anyway."

"Yeah, but I'm not sure how you test that." Maybe wait around until the two remaining vigilantes jumped somebody else then check that victim's blood for Must? Then John thought of something else, something he'd forgotten to mention to the Chief this morning. Or maybe he hadn't forgotten it, exactly; maybe he'd thought about it but had decided to keep it to himself for a while? "The one guy I took down at the Fairgrounds was wearing a necklace," he told Jill, fishing through his pockets, "More like a dog tag, really."

"A dog tag?"

"Yeah, you know, like soldiers wear?" Finally, he found it and put it on the table in between them, broken chain and all. "Usually these have names and numbers on them, but all this one has is a picture."

Jill looked intrigued. She reached across the table and picked up the tag with her rough brown fingers. She studied it and the more she did the more troubled she looked. "A dark locust," she finally said.

"Locust? I was thinking grasshopper. They're the same thing, though, aren't they?"

"Sort of." She was looking intently at that black picture engraved on metal.

"What are you thinking about?" John finally asked her.

"The Nzige."

He didn't know what that was, but there was something in the tone of her voice that got his attention. "What's that?"

"Nzige means 'locust' in Swahili, the language most people speak in

East Africa. When I was in Kenya last, almost a year ago, Cyn mentioned them to me, these Nzige. They're a very mysterious group, apparently. According to her, some believe them to be criminals, sort of like an African mob. Others say they're ghosts or demons. I didn't give any of that too much credence, for obvious reasons."

Because it sounds like bullshit. "This tag is making you think maybe those stories might be true, though?"

She shrugged. "Well, it makes me wonder if there isn't at least some basis in fact."

"Do you know anything about them, these locusts?"

Jill shook her head. "Not much, I'm afraid."

"You think maybe this vigilante was one of them?"

"I don't know. It seems a bit farfetched, doesn't it, that one of the Nzige would show up over here? Yet given that so many other clues are pointing back to East Africa, I don't think we can discount it."

John ate a couple of French fries. They'd gotten cold. He frowned and pushed the whole plate away. "You know, for a while now I've been thinking that whatever is happening here is probably just a little spur off of something bigger that is happening over there. Just why there's a spur here, I don't know. That's the part that doesn't make any sense."

Jill handed the dog tag back to him. "There *is* someone I could ask, someone who might know about this if anyone does."

John tucked the tag back into his pocket. He had a bad feeling about where this train was headed. "Is he over in Africa?"

She nodded. "He owns a photo-safari outfit, so he travels regularly throughout both Kenya and Tanzania. He knows practically everyone in East Africa. If these Nzige are real, and they've come over here, I suspect Roger Sutherland will know about it."

The Bwana. John had to work hard to make sure that only the right emotions showed up on his face. So, Jill was still in touch with him. He shouldn't have been surprised by that—after all, she had a picture of him on the wall in her office! He had to stay steady here, though; he had to keep on an even keel. "Yeah, sure, ask him. Ask him why the hell a swarm of dark locusts would be over here in America, killing a junkie." *And drinking his damned blood.* John was in a bit of a bad mood now, but that didn't have anything to do with either grasshoppers or drugs.

Chapter 34

"How about I order pizza?" John asked Ham and Mick, once he found out she was staying for dinner.

"Sure, Dad," said Ham, "Veggie Extreme?"

"For the two of you maybe. I've gotta have my pepperoni."

"Stuff'll kill you, you know."

"Something's bound to sooner or later," said John. Better spicy Italian salami than a few other things he could think of right now!

"Did you want to watch the news, Dad, or is it OK if Mick and I play a video game?"

"You go on ahead." About the last thing John wanted to do right now was watch the damned news! "I think I'll just sit here with my laptop."

A few minutes later they were killing zombies on the streets of San Francisco, while John sat staring at Google. What the hell was he looking for? While the cursor in the search box blinked at him he ran through a list of the words that seemed like they mattered to this case: Musth, Elephants, Drugs. Kenya and Tanzania. Dark Locusts, the Nzige. Hell, maybe even Vampires and Zombies. *Bullshit!* He looked up from the screen without having typed anything in, and watched Ham and Mick for a minute. Their war was going about as bad as his investigation. They were stuck inside a bombed-out building in what looked like the Presidio, trying to hold off a dead army.

John turned his attention from the Zombie Apocalypse back to his laptop. The search box was still waiting for him. Finally he typed in some of his words. Nothing much came up in the first go-round; mostly a bunch of scientific articles. *Blood Volume in the African Migratory Locust.* What a damned waste of time! He didn't have much else to do, though, except wait for his pizza, so he kept tinkering with different combinations, throwing words into the pot together to see if any of them would make soup. Meanwhile on the other screen, the one that was Ham and Mick's, a horde of zombies was attacking them from all sides. Then one of his searches turned up something.

Men without souls destroy my village.

Men without souls. That reminded him a little bit of what he'd seen at the Fairgrounds, of those three blood-drinking vigilantes. There was a link to a YouTube video. John stared at the thumbnail. Something about it made his blood run cold. A mob of shadows was packed into that Pandora's Box, shadows that looked like dark human shapes with red eyes. Leti Tulafono eyes. Tad Wellington eyes. Those shadows were coming at him, out of the dark. In the background of the still frame big white clouds boiled up against a navy-blue sky. There were silhouettes of trees that looked like flattened umbrellas. Somehow John knew that what he was looking at was Africa, even before he followed the link to a description that read: *Atrocities committed in Malalongo, Tanzania.*

John read that again: *Atrocities committed in Malalongo, Tanzania.* It had been uploaded less than a month ago, by someone who called himself "Kili14." John tapped on his mouse a few times with his index finger, trying to decide whether or not he ought to watch this, wondering if he would regret it if he did. Sometimes you were better off if you just didn't know anything. He made up his mind. He clicked the start arrow.

In a heartbeat those shapes were on the move. They came flooding out of the dark. John couldn't see much of anything except their silhouettes and of course those red eyes. How many men without souls were there: a hundred? It was hard to tell. The camera was moving with them now, it was part of the army. That army poured into Kili's village. Cows and goats strained against tethers, mooing and bleating. Men, women, and children ran for their lives. The dark wave crashed over them. Those men without souls were shooting off guns. They were swinging machetes. Now some of them had torches. They were setting fire to the grass roofs of huts. Towers of flames shot up into the sky, illuminating what was quickly becoming a slaughter.

John watched as a woman with a baby at her breast was trampled. He watched as two boys, both younger than Ham, were shot at close range.

The camera zoomed in. In the midst of the carnage and chaos left behind in the wake of that dark wave, one of the men without souls had pinned a young girl down in the dust beside a burning hut, and he was brutally raping her. John wanted to look away but couldn't seem to. It was more like a bad dream than something caught on film; it was like it was all happening inside his head instead of scrolling past in front of his eyes.

The camera zoomed in. The screen shot was even tighter now, a close-up of the rapist's right arm. Everything else had turned blurry, just a smear of up and down motion. The girl's screams weren't blurry, though; those kept on ringing out clear as breaking glass. What the hell was Kili up to, why was he fixating on this? John kept on wanting to look away, kept on not being able to. The camera zoomed in. The man's arm filled up the screen. There was nothing there but his wrist now, and the girl's blood-curdling screams. And that was when John figured out what the point of this was, that was when he saw the dark picture burned onto the man's wrist. On the underside, where the skin was lighter, there was a black tattoo, a tattoo that looked like a locust.

John's blood ran cold. So, these were the Nzige! But what did that mean? What the hell were some of them doing over here, on this side of the Atlantic Ocean? There wasn't time to think about that now; the camera had zoomed out again, taking him along for the ride. He was back inside the dark wave that was washing over Malalongo.

Now he could see beyond the village, beyond the burning grass huts; there was a white building in the background, a two-story structure that reminded him of the Alamo. It looked out of place there and yet somehow it didn't, and John had the strange feeling he'd seen it before. Red and orange flames were reflecting off its white plaster front. Enormous shadows of victims and killers flickered across it like characters in some low-budget drive-in movie. And then the dark wave of men without souls reached the base of the building; that dark wave broke against it. The windows of the white building began to explode. Flashes of light emerged from them. Whoever was inside was fighting back. John heard gunfire, and screams. Then he heard a shout from Hambone, too; it was almost like he was inside the YouTube video

"Mick, watch out! They're trying to come in through the bedroom window!"

John tore himself away from Malalongo then, saw that Ham and

Mick were under siege, too, inside their virtual Presidio.

Mick mowed down a line of zombies with a machine gun. She lobbed a grenade. "Got 'em, thanks!" she yelled back at Ham.

John looked down at his own little screen again, his own little faraway war. Was it any more real than Ham and Mick's was? The firefight went on. Chips were being blown off the front of that white plaster building, as the Nzige laid down a withering fire. More flashes came from those dark first floor windows. And then something strange caught John's eye.

Up on the second story there was one window on the left side of the Alamo that was still intact. At that window he saw two faces. White faces. He leaned in a little closer. It looked like those faces belonged to a little boy and girl, eight or ten years old maybe—it was hard to tell from such a distance, by the firelight. John caught his breath. They were albinos. They were the same two albinos he'd seen before, in that video by the BBC lady, that documentary about children who were being hunted down for their body parts. And that's when he realized, too, that the building he'd been calling the "Alamo" was the same one he'd seen in that documentary, that it must be the hospital where they were providing sanctuary for these poor persecuted kids. What did that have to do with the attack of the Nzige? Had these men without souls come here looking for the kids, was that what they were after? One of them, the girl, put her hands up onto the inside of the glass. Only, she didn't have any hands. For the second time, John saw that she didn't have any hands. What she put up onto the inside of the window were just the stumps at the ends of her arms. And John felt the bottom drop out of his stomach again; again, he felt sick at heart. Who could *do* such a thing? *The goddamned Nzige.* He gritted his teeth. Then other strange things started to happen.

A shriek came floating up out of his laptop, something he thought at first might have come from Ham's game. It sounded like something dead, and yet it also sounded like something that was afraid. On the screen in front of him a torch lit up the face of one of the Nzige. It was enough to freeze your blood, maybe even enough to freeze your soul. There wasn't a damn thing in those eyes, once you saw them up close. They looked dead, undead, empty.

"Shit, Ham, we're toast!" John heard Mick cry out then, from the other side of the room, but he didn't bother to look up to see what was happening.

Run! John was yelling inside his mind, to those two little albino kids in the window, *Run!*

But of course they couldn't have heard him even if he'd said it out loud. They didn't move. They just stood there staring out at the scene with those pink eyes of theirs, those eyes that made them look like they came from some other world. One by one the dark locusts down below were stopping in mid-rape or mid-murder to watch; one by one they were looking up at the two albinos in the second-story window. Then something happened that John didn't expect: those dark locusts started running. Not towards the hospital; they were running *away* from it. The dark wave was receding. Behind them they left what looked like the wake of a storm surge: burned huts and broken bodies. The ground was littered with the dead and dying, men and women and children and beasts; those dark locusts had killed anything that moved, anything that got in their path. Anything, that is, except these two children. From them, they had fled. Why? They *were* a little scary-looking, John had to admit, standing up there in the window, by the firelight, with their strange white skin and their alien eyes. But why would an army be afraid of kids?

Fires were still raging in some of the huts, still casting an eerie orange glow over the scene of destruction. The white building, the hospital, still stood, its broken windows looking like gouged-out eyes. A trail of white smoke drifted slowly upwards out of one of them. The two albino kids were gone. And then, as abruptly as it had started, Kili14's video ended; the clip reset itself and went back to the start, to that still frame of the shadows with the burning red eyes.

Ham and Mick's game was over now, too; John could hear the zombies on the TV set laughing and moaning the way they always did when they won, when they managed to take over the city.

Chapter 35

Leroy Miller moved into a room on the fourth floor of what he called the Motel Winecarton, out on Fucken Road. There wasn't much to the place because they'd stopped building it last year, when the economy went to hell for a while. He'd been there four days and it was starting to feel like home. Nothing like having a roof over your head again, even if it was just a slab of concrete. The three walls were concrete, too, man. The fourth wall wasn't even fucken there. The front of the Motel Winecarton wasn't even there. Place was just open to the world, and the weather. If they'd ever finished it, Leroy was guessing they'd have closed it in with windows on that side, but as it was you didn't want to get too close to the edge because it dropped right off into fucken nothing.

Leroy sat on the concrete floor, on the blanket he'd found in a dumpster, looking out at John Briggs's row house on the other side of the road. The sun was going down and lights were coming up; it looked like the Boss was at home tonight. Son-of-a-bitch usually was. He was about as square-ass as they come. Cop by day, boob tube addict by night. He was either watching TV or doing something on that laptop of his, on the sofa. Leroy wondered what kind of shit he went on there for: porn? Guy's love life sucked about as bad as Leroy's. Usually he was home all night long, just him and his kid. And sometimes the kid's little skanky girlfriend, dressed in black with a lot of eye makeup. Still, she kind of turned him on. One night she and the Boss's kid were making out on the sofa before the Boss got home and Leroy got so hot he had to take care of his own business.

Shit, man, he had to find himself a woman! This was getting old. Tough, though, when you lived in a place like the Motel Winecarton. When you didn't have a car and no fucken money. When all you had to eat was the shit they were throwing out at the Quick & Ready.

Leroy looked out through the open front of his fourth floor room. It was getting dark. The lights were on across the way, and the Boss was at home. Was he cooking tonight or calling for pizza? Seems like he had take-out about every other night.

That can't be good for you, Boss.

About every other night, Leroy thought about holding up the delivery guy, taking his cash and food. They came flying in there so fucken fast, though, that by the time Leroy could run down three flights of stairs and climb over the chain link fence, they were gone. If he could already be down there when they pulled up, it'd be easy, but he never knew when or if they were coming. Looked like Briggs might be eating in tonight. Leroy could see him and his kid, sitting on the sofa, chewing on what looked like spaghetti. Hard to tell from here. Shit, that made Leroy hungry, just thinking about it! It was almost like he could smell it.

Leroy sat there on his dumpster-blanket, looking at the lit-up row house on the other side of the dark ditch that was Fucken Road. Made him think about how much he missed his shack out by the Sherry. Wasn't much of a place, but it was home. Made him think about the place where he grew up, in Arkansas, with his mother and brother. And then his aunt and uncle, once his brother George got himself killed by those fucken hillbillies, once his mother ran off chasing that guy that later on got to be President. At least that's the way Leroy heard she was telling it. He didn't believe a word. The guy she ran off with wasn't the President; he was just some fucken used car salesman.

Leroy wondered where she was now. Dead, maybe. You can't be drunk that much of the time and live forever. Weed was better, man. They said bad things about reefer, but even the cops knew it was minor shit, really; even the cops had better things to do than run around busting you for a couple of blunts. Shit, Leroy wished he had a blunt right now! But that was one thing you never found in a dumpster, man. That told you something, didn't it? Food, money, sometimes even babies, but man you *never* found weed in a dumpster! Nobody threw their fucken dope away!

Leroy sat there on that nasty blanket, looking out at the lit-up row house across the way, thinking about Arkansas, that place he'd lived in with his aunt and uncle, after his brother got his ass shot and his mama ran off with that dick. Made him think about nights in the summer when you'd look out across the open field that ran down the hill to the woods and the reservoir and you'd see lightning bugs all over the place. It was fucken beautiful, man! That was a good place, a good time, even if he did hate that school they had him in.

There were assholes in the hallways, kicking the shit out of him every day. Same bunch of hillbillies that shot his brother George. Cops never could find out who did it; they didn't fucken want to. Leroy knew who did it: those fucken hillbillies. Wasn't much he could do about it though. Cut out of school a couple of times but his aunt was a hard-ass woman. She made him go back. Probably would have kept on making him go back if she hadn't of got that cancer. Throat cancer, maybe from yelling at Leroy too much.

Leroy sat there on the blanket, looking out. He was remembering how she went downhill in a hell of a hurry. How his uncle shot himself one night, after that. How Leroy found him with the smoke still coming out of a hole in the side of his head. How he'd stood there for a minute, looking down at his uncle lying there on that bloody throw rug. How he'd gone into a panic, figuring the cops would think *he'd* fucken done it!

Leroy remembered picking up that gun and running out of the house with it, running down the hill through the clouds of lightning bugs, thinking to himself that he was done with all of this shit, done with school, done with Arkansas, man. By the time he got down to the reservoir he was out of breath, fucken crying, mad as fucken hell. He wanted to go after the hillbillies that killed his brother George. He wanted to go find his mother and beat the shit out of that used car salesman she'd run off with, the one she told everybody was the dick who went on to be President. Leroy wanted to take that gun and do what his uncle did. Except he wasn't that stupid or brave. He sat there in the dark by the reservoir, looking at the moon coming up over the water, trying to figure out what to do next. He turned and looked up the hill and there was his aunt and uncle's house, all lit up like somebody still lived there.

Leroy was holding his uncle's gun. What he really wanted to do was get away from there, go as far away as he could go. Away from the cops and the hillbillies and the smell of fucken death. Get away from his dead brother and his dead aunt and uncle. Get away from Arkansas. What a shitmeat state! Find his mother and the car salesman that thought he was the President. And do fucken what? You know what? To hell with it! Leroy didn't give a shit anymore. If his mother wanted to fuck some car salesman on a mattress in the back of his pickup truck, and then run off with him to Little Rock or the White House or wherever they went, Leroy didn't give a shit anymore. He was getting out of here. Heading to Texas. Or Mississippi. Some place, any place that wasn't fucken here.

He looked back up the hill at his aunt and uncle's house, at the lights that were still on even though there wasn't nobody home. Nobody alive, anyway. He'd had a lot of good years there. But all of that was over with now. Leroy put his uncle's gun in his pocket. He found the dirt road that ran by the reservoir and he started walking.

#

Leroy sat in the Motel Winecarton now, looking out at the lit-up row house on the other side of Fucken Road. The Boss and his kid were eating in tonight. No chance to hold up the delivery guy, then. But there was always the Quick & Ready. Leroy reached into his pocket to find his uncle's gun. It was there. He was tired of living like this, man, sleeping on a fucken rat blanket, eating shit out of a dumpster. He couldn't even afford to buy any blunts, man, couldn't afford fucken weed!

Leroy started thinking about that old pussy Marine at the Quick & Ready. Ought to be easy pickings. If he had to shoot that old pecker's ass, then he fucken deserved it! Had one foot in the grave already. Just thinking about it got Leroy's heart racing, though; it made his palms sweat. Had to break out of this somehow, though; couldn't live like this forever!

Leroy got up and stood there, looking out. He backed away from the edge a little so he wouldn't fucken fall off. The wind had kicked up and it was blowing in through the front of the Motel Winecarton. The Boss was over there with his kid, eating spaghetti.

I don't want to live like this anymore, man. Leroy reached into his pocket and felt of the gun. He went down the dark concrete stairs, working a plan.

#

Leroy had seen the same white car a few times before. He was walking along the bucked-up sidewalk, heading for the Quick & Ready to rob it, when he saw the car again, coming at him. Same one that drove by last night. And the night before that. At first Leroy figured it was just somebody that lived around here, like the Boss. But the car never pulled in anyplace, never stopped. Well, once it did. Once it pulled over to the curb and just sat there, like the people inside were looking for somebody. There were two of them, two guys; Leroy could see that once they rolled down the

smoky windows. They looked like they were looking for somebody. Two
Black guys, one up front and one in the back. What was it, a fucken taxi?
Hell, no. Didn't say anything like that on the side. It wasn't any taxi, man.
They were cruising the streets, looking for somebody.

Leroy reached into his pants pocket, found his uncle's gun. The
white car was coming right at him. Didn't stop, though, didn't even slow
down. Leroy let out his breath, figured he was safe. Then he heard the car
turning around.

Shit! Leroy looked over his shoulder. It was back there, a block
away, following him.

Shit! Leroy thought about making a run for it. There wasn't any
place to go, though, man; there were fucken row houses on both sides of
the street. If he could just make it to the next corner then maybe . . . he
was going to turn right there anyway, to get to the Quick & Ready. To rob
it. Leroy wasn't thinking too much about that right now, though, because
that white car that wasn't a taxi was following him. Had to be. Leroy held
onto the gun. He'd shoot the motherfucker if he had to, man! If he even
got the chance to.

That was the thing: would he even get the chance to? Cat could
shoot him out the window without even slowing down. The car was still
back there. It seemed like it might be closing in. Leroy had his hand on his
gun. He could hear the fucken window rolling down! Leroy pulled the gun
out of his pocket, held it down by the side of his leg. He looked left out of
the corner of his eye, trying to figure out what was about to go down.

"Excuse me, Mr. Miller?"

What the fuck? Leroy looked around. How did this cat know his
name? It was the back window of the white car that was rolled down.
There was a Black dude inside. Man, his voice sounded familiar, somehow.
Maybe Leroy had bought weed from him? Deep voice, different voice, not
from around here. What the fuck did this black guy want with him,
anyway? For just a minute he thought about this TV ad he'd seen a few
times: *Might you have any Grey Poupon?*

Leroy couldn't help himself; he started laughing. The cat inside the
white car was laughing, too, like he was in on the fucken joke. Leroy's hand
that was holding the gun started twitching, down by his leg.

"Mr. Miller?"

"Yeah, man, what do you fucken want?" Dude sounded like he

might be from out of the country.

"I would like to engage your services, Mr. Miller."

What did that mean, a job? "I'm listening, man."

"Would you please join me inside?"

What, did he really expect Leroy to get inside his fucken car with him? Leroy looked at it. Deathtrapmobile, man. If he got in there he might never get out. "I'd rather not, man. We can talk just fine from here."

Cat looked nervous. He was looking around. He was on the lam from somebody. The cops? "It is not safe for me to stay here for long. Please, Mr. Miller, join me inside. I am willing to pay you a great deal of money."

What the fuck for? What if he was some pervert, wanted Leroy to suck his dick? Leroy didn't want to get in the car. But what was that about a shitload of money? Leroy was thinking about it. Then he remembered who this cat was. He'd seen him before. Well, he hadn't really *seen* the man, just heard him. On that drug sting, the one Leroy worked for the Boss. The guy that sold him the bag of blue rocks. That was the voice he'd heard that night, in the dark, at McAdams Park! Leroy started feeling better about him. Drug dealers he knew how to handle. Perverts? That was a something else. Cat must want him to sell dope for him. Leroy could do that. If it meant getting a shitload of money. He sure as fuck needed money right now. Didn't want to live in the Motel Winecarton forever. Didn't want to have to rob no ninety-year-old pussy Marine. Not unless he fucken had to.

"All right, man."

The car door in back swung open. Leroy climbed inside. It smelled like leather in there. It smelled fucken rich. There was another black guy in front, ugly little son-of-a-bitch with a mustache and rat teeth. Didn't turn his head around, didn't even look at Leroy. Just started driving. Leroy looked at the black cat in the seat next to him. Looked respectable. Had on a suit and tie. Wore glasses. Had a beard that looked like he paid some attention to it. Looked high end. Leroy started to relax. Figured this cat might be on the level. Drug dealer, sure, but on the level.

"What do you want with me, man?"

The black cat grinned. Man, was he *ever* black! When he smiled it was like a spotlight, his fucken teeth were so white. "My name is Yusuph.

May I call you Le Roy?"

Something welled up inside of Leroy. He didn't want anybody using his fucken real name! Except this guy—what'd he say his name was, Joseph?—this guy Joseph didn't say it the way most people did. Not LEE-Roy but Lay-Roy. What the fuck was up with that? He kind of liked the way it sounded, though, kind of high end. The cat was looking at him now, smiling. "Le Roy. In French, it means 'The King.'"

Leroy was starting to like this black cat! "The King, huh? Well, yeah, I guess that's all right then." He was still holding his gun down by his leg, but had kind of forgotten about it. This cat seemed alright.

"Le Roy, I would like to engage your services," the cat said.

Leroy was trying to think what services those would be. But getting paid for it, whatever it was, sounded good. "What do you need, man?" As long as the guy didn't want him to suck his dick . . .

Joseph, or whatever his name was, was looking out the window as they drove around in his white car. "There are certain . . . individuals who are pursuing me," he finally said. "They have pursued me here from Africa. Initially I had thought you were one of the zero-zeros, Le Roy, that you might be helpful in fending them off."

"I ain't no zero, man," said Leroy, indignant, "I'm a good number one or two at least." *Wait a minute,* he thought, *that sounds kind of bad.* "Make it a three."

It was like the black cat hadn't even heard him. "But there may be another way. You work for the police, do you not?"

Shit. Leroy slipped his finger back onto the trigger of his gun. Was this a fucken set up? Cat knew he was a snitch and now he was going to waste him! Only . . . if that was true then what was he talking about paying him for? If he'd wanted to waste him he could have done that already, from the fucken car, without even slowing down. "Sometimes," said Leroy.

"You purchased the drug Must for them once, did you not?"

Leroy thought about that night again, that sting, that deep voice in the dark. How had he figured out that Leroy was working for the cops? Must have seen him talking to the Boss, afterwards. Must have figured it out. "Yeah, just once." Leroy had the gun ready, down by his leg, but it was looking like he might not need it. Cat didn't mean to waste him. What *did* he want, though?

"This may seem like a strange request, Le Roy, but I have need now to . . . to communicate with the police."

What say? Leroy looked at him. That didn't fucken make sense! It was like when he was stoned and things people said were coming at him through a fog—he'd have to try and fan the smoke away just to hear what it was they were saying. Only Leroy wasn't stoned. Couldn't afford fucken weed. Leroy was about as straight as he'd been in two years and this still wasn't making much sense. "What do you mean, man?"

Cat smiled big and white again. He laughed. "I certainly understand your confusion, my friend." He turned and looked out the window like he was watching out for something. Or somebody. The other cat in the front seat, the one with the rat teeth, drove. Where were they now? Across town, in Seaside, driving up and down the Gulf highway.

"I realize this may seem strange, Le Roy," he said again, "but I need to discuss certain matters with your police."

They ain't MY fucken police, thought Leroy.

"It has to do with this drug Must," the cat said.

I hear you, thought Leroy. "Yeah, well, the cops can be assholes sometimes, man."

"Are they really, all of them? It is my hope that I might make an arrangement with them. Is there not one among them whom you would trust, whom you may have trusted before?"

Leroy laughed. "Are you . . ." He was about to say "fucken crazy," then changed his mind. Maybe this wasn't the time or place to shoot his mouth off? "They're the cops, man!"

Cat named Joseph looked disappointed. "Not one?"

Leroy was looking at him with his mouth hanging open. "Well . . ." What about Briggs, man, the Boss? He was an alright guy, really. Bastard for spraying Leroy in the face with mace, but mostly he'd always played things straight-up. Paid the bill when it came due. Leroy kind of liked the guy. Square-ass as they come but that's why you could trust him. About some things, anyway. "Well," said Leroy, after a while, "yeah, there is this one."

Cat named Joseph perked up. Rat-teeth kept on driving around. Leroy was wondering if he'd be willing to go through a drive-through, get him something to eat. Man, he was hungry! Only thing we wanted more was a blunt. Could he work this to get that, too? Maybe. Or maybe just hang in for the cash. If he got enough cash, he could buy food and dope for himself.

Cat was talking now about what he wanted Leroy to do. Sounded easy enough. Set up a meeting with Briggs comma John P. Secret location and all that. Nobody else could know about it. Leroy wondered if this cat Joseph, or whatever his fucken name was, wanted to meet the Boss so he could waste him? That didn't make any sense, though. So what did this black cat want with the Boss, anyway? Oh yeah, said something about people being after him. Somebody that had come over from fucken Africa. Cat needed protection. Now that Leroy thought about it, cat looked a little scared. Always looking out the window. Didn't want to stay parked in any one place for long. Had Rat Teeth keep on driving him around.

Ain't none of my fucken business, thought Leroy. *Don't know, don't care. Just show me the money.* That's when he thought of something else. Something happy. The Boss would probably pay on his end to set this meeting up. Double dip! Yeah, sure, the Boss would pay to meet this cat, to meet Must's Mr. Big. If that's who the cat was. Close enough. Leroy could play both sides of the fence here, make out like a fucken bandit!

"So, do you think he will meet with me?" the black cat was asking.

"Yeah, sure" said Leroy. "If it's got anything to do with this Must shit that's been going down, he'll talk to you. He'll help you. I know the man."

Damn, thought Leroy Miller, *this must be my fucken lucky day.*

Chapter 36

When John woke up Saturday morning, early, he was having a real bad dream. Pretty easy to figure out where *that* was coming from! There were zombies in it. Men without souls and eyes. Had to be either the living dead or agents from the IRS. He got out of bed and went downstairs to the kitchen. He got the coffeepot going. The sun wasn't up yet but it wouldn't be long, this time of year. As soon as he had his mug ready he sat down on the sofa in the den and fired up his laptop. Then he tried like hell not to click his way back to Kili14's YouTube video. He lost out.

Next thing he knew he was sitting there with the sun coming up, staring at that thumbnail again, at those red-eyed shadows flooding out of the dark. Next thing he knew he'd clicked on the arrow and had watched all four minutes and nineteen seconds of it over again. He wondered if what he was seeing was real, or if this was just Kili14's own little *Blair Witch Project*? After a while he decided to click his way over to Kili's personal channel, to see if he'd posted anything else.

He had. There were lots of clips there. Most of them were videos of routine stuff, though, at least routine stuff if you happened to live in Africa: elephant herds and lions at night, their eyes glowing yellow like they were possessed. The landscape almost knocked his socks off: a grassy savannah that seemed like it went on forever, more of those flattened umbrella trees, outcroppings of rock that looked like little monuments, and in the background that mountain called Kilimanjaro. After a while John started to wonder if maybe that's where the handle Kili14 came from, if maybe the guy who had filmed all of this had taken his name from the mountain? If that was true, though, why the 14? Were there thirteen other Kilis out there? Not that that mattered. All the zebras and cheetahs and warthogs didn't matter, either. John liked to look at animals as much as the next guy, but that wasn't why he was visiting this channel. What he'd hoped to find was a clue as to why some of those dark locusts, those men without souls, were showing up over here, in America.

Then he came across a clip that didn't star herds of animals. Kili had labeled this one *Mama's Hospital.* It was almost a year old and had almost no hits. No surprise there. People wanted to see cute pet tricks or kids without hands, not some building out in the middle of nowhere. That's what was in the first frame: a woman standing in front of some two-story white building in the middle of nowhere. John had seen that building before. It was the same one from Kili's "Men Without Souls" clip, the same one from that BBC documentary about "albeeno" children. The woman—Kili's mother, maybe—looked almost like an albeeno herself, what with her white-white hair and bleached-out skin. She couldn't be one, though; she had dark blue eyes. Pretty eyes. In fact, she was a pretty woman. Fairly young-looking. Made John wonder just how old this Kili person was, if maybe he was just a kid. Was that where the 14 part came from? John clicked the arrow.

"Good morning!" the pretty white woman said. Her accent was a little strange. It didn't sound like the BBC lady's, but it didn't sound American either. "My name is Dr. Annika de Groot, and this is my hospital in Malalongo, Tanzania."

As she talked, John began putting together a timeline for her: Annika de Groot had arrived in Tanzania about a year ago, to open this hospital in the back of beyond. She wanted to bring healthcare to the natives, many of whom she already knew from her work with *Doctors without Borders.* The building had been something else before she got there, some sort of Christian mission. It hadn't been occupied in ten years, though, and had fallen into disrepair. She'd fixed it up herself, something she was obviously very proud of.

"Come," she said, smiling, "let's take a tour, shall we?"

Annika de Groot led him through the narrow front door. Inside, there were lots of little rooms and halls. It looked like a rabbit warren. There were cots everywhere and not a one was empty. Plenty of sick people to go around. None of them looked too bad off, though. Dr. de Groot must be taking good care of them. Now she was talking about what she was up against: the lack of medical supplies, the malnutrition, the indifference of the local government. John kept expecting to see some of those albino children inside the rabbit warren but didn't. There were plenty of kids mixed in with the adults but all of them were Black; in fact, Dr. de Groot was the only White person there.

When had the albeenos come into the picture? When had Annika de Groot's hospital become a sanctuary for them? If she'd only been there a year, it had to have been pretty recently. When had that come to the attention of the Nzige?

She sure seemed happy back then, in this video. She seemed like somebody who was living out her dream, doing exactly what she'd always wanted to do. What she knew she was meant to do. John felt a little uneasy then, maybe even a little guilty. Here this woman was, putting it all on the line. She'd given up the safety of her practice in someplace called Rotterdam to move here, to the back of beyond, and treat people who could probably only afford to pay her with smiles and goats. And she'd believed so strongly in what she was doing that she'd brought her son the filmmaker with her. Meanwhile, here John was living the life of Riley in America, even complaining about it sometimes. Just hoping that what he did every day made a difference. This woman had guts. And so did her son. John wondered where Kili had shot that attack on the village from, how close he'd been to the action? And he wondered, too, what was happening to Annika de Groot now, one year after she'd opened her little hospital, now that crazy zombie men were trying to tear it apart?

The clip was ending. John was ready for it to end, ready to go back to his own little insulated world, ready to go look for that one stale leftover doughnut to have with his second cup of coffee. Then Annika threw him one last curveball.

"And now," she said, reaching her hands towards the camera, "I would like to acknowledge our budding little videographer." She was smiling. She got closer and closer to the screen. Kili14 was trying to get away from her. The camera was moving backwards now, the picture was shaking up and down. Annika started laughing.

"Mom!" Kili's voice was high and squeaky.

Annika took the camera away from him. She was laughing as she turned it around. "Time to take a bow, Kili!"

"Mom!"

John had to look away for a second because the camera was moving up and down so much it was making him feel queasy.

"Ta-dah!" said Annika de Groot then, triumphant. "Here she is: director, producer, and camera woman!"

Woman? John looked back at the screen. And found out that was true. Not only was Kili about fourteen years old, but she was a girl: a tall, skinny, red-headed girl.

#

The morning went by. John showered and shaved and put on his clothes. But the whole time he was thinking about Kili14 and her videos. He was thinking about her mother. Which was crazy, he knew, because all that stuff Kili had caught on film had happened on the other side of the world. It wasn't his business. He ought to be thinking about what was going on here, what had happened out at the Fairgrounds. Could there be any connection between those two things? He wanted to believe there wasn't, wanted to just forget about those men without souls and everything else that might be going on in Tanzania, but he couldn't seem to shake it. For one thing there was that tattoo of a black grasshopper on the arm of the one Nzige, that one who was raping the girl in Kili's video. And there was the dog tag with the black grasshopper on it that he'd yanked off the neck of that vigilante who'd killed Leti Tulafono. That couldn't be just a coincidence.

"Morning, Pops!" said Ham, tromping down the stairs.

"Morning, Sunshine!" John was sure glad to see him, even if he wasn't all that excited about being called "Pops." He hoped that wouldn't turn into a habit.

Ham went straight for the coffeepot. "You been up for a while?"

"Yeah," said John, "Had a bad dream."

"I hate when that happens. What about?"

"You don't want to know."

"Probably not," agreed Ham, grinning.

John went into the kitchen for more coffee while Ham headed for the den. He turned on the TV set and parked his butt on the sofa. The morning news was on. John dug through the pantry looking for that last day-old doughnut.

"Hey Dad, you seen this?"

"Seen what?" John gave up on the doughnut and took his mug of black coffee into the den.

"This."

Channel 4 was talking about what had gone down at the Fairgrounds. He watched the report for a minute. "Yeah, I've seen it."

"Hey, there you are!"

"Yeah, there I am." The reporters were trying to get a quote out of Detective John Briggs, but they were having a real hard time of it. The guy wasn't cooperating. At all.

"How come you didn't tell me about any of this?"

John was wondering how Ham could have missed it, being plugged in all the time like he was. "It was strictly need-to-know," he said with a smile.

Ham watched while the reporter blabbered on. "What really happened out there?"

John shrugged. "For once, it was pretty much the way they're telling it. Crazy drug addict was shooting people; couple of us cops tried to intervene. Before we could do anything, these three vigilantes took the law into their own hands."

"But were they really drinking the guy's blood?"

John nodded. "Sure looked that way." He gave Ham a serious look over the top of his coffee cup. "Don't go thinking they were vampires, though. Those don't exist."

"I know that!" said Ham, sounding insulted. "Still . . ."

"If you want proof," said John, "I killed one myself, and I don't have any silver bullets. And if he'd come back from the dead, Bill the Coroner would have let me know." He had fun for a minute, though, imagining that sick clown Scotty trying to feel up another corpse, only to have that corpse rise up out of the drawer on him.

"Silver bullets are for werewolves," Ham corrected him. "And I never said I thought the guy was a vampire. I'm just asking what's going on? It's not everyday somebody out there drinks somebody else's blood." He stared at the screen for a minute. "And I don't buy this bullshit they're spouting about it maybe being a gang initiation!"

"I don't either," said John.

"Then why do you think they were doing it?"

"I wish I knew." He and Jill at least had a theory, though, didn't they? Was that something he ought to tell Ham about? He looked over at his son. Almost sixteen. How much of what was going on in the world should he still be trying to protect him from? John decided he'd already

272

been exposed to the worst of it, to the killings and the vigilantes lapping up blood; the rest was pretty tame by comparison. "We do know the perp was high on Must," John said finally, "Jill thinks maybe that's what those vigilantes were after."

Ham puzzled over that for a minute. "You mean she thinks they were drinking his blood to stoke themselves up?"

"Maybe. It's a theory, anyway." Channel 4 had moved on to other stories now—didn't want to tax anybody's attention span—but John could tell that Ham was still thinking about the Fairgrounds.

"If that's true," he finally said, "how do you think they knew to go after him? How'd they know this guy had Must in his blood?"

"Good question. Maybe they could smell it."

"That's creepy," said Ham.

No argument there, thought John.

Chapter 37

"So, you've had a crazy week," said Jill, once they'd been seated at the new Seaside restaurant called the *Thai Phoon*. It was pretty busy because it was Saturday night and the place had only been open a month.

"Crazier than you know." She was sure looking good. John liked those silver earrings she was wearing, even though by the candlelight at the table he couldn't tell what was dangling at the end of them.

"You mean it's gotten worse since I saw you at the Treetops?"

"In a way, yeah." Had it, though? Truth was, nothing had changed except that now he knew about all this other shit going on over in Africa. It was like he was looking at the same scene, just from a bit higher up. The little waitress came by and took their orders. Her English wasn't all that good; John was hoping she got everything right. Seems like she especially had trouble understanding what "extra spicy" meant. At least she didn't mess up on the cold bottle of beer! John poured it into his glass while Jill took a sip of white wine.

"What else happened?"

John thought about how to answer that. Nothing. Nothing else *happened*, now that he thought about it; he'd just watched a couple of videos. Yet he felt like the world had changed. "I'm not even sure where to start."

"Just say whatever pops into mind."

"Zombies," said John, before he'd had the chance to think about how that sounded.

"Zombies?"

"Maybe that's the wrong word." He was wishing now he could take it back. "Maybe I'd better start over." Then he told her what he'd seen on the Internet.

Afterwards she just sat there, not saying much of anything. She wasn't even drinking her wine. She looked out the window once at the sun going down over the Gulf. "What do you think it all means?"

"Wish I knew."

"You really believe there's a connection between what's happening in Tanzania and what's been going on over here?"

"I keep wanting to say no, but everything keeps pushing me back the other way."

She ran a finger up and down through the sweat that had formed on her glass of ice water. "I tried to call Roger last night to ask him about the Nzige but I didn't get any answer. He must be leading one of his photo safaris, out in the bush."

John sat there with a half-frozen smile on his face. He took a long drink of beer. He'd known she was going to talk to the Bwana; she'd said yesterday she intended to. For some reason, though, he hadn't expected her to pick up the phone that fast! "I probably wouldn't care, if they weren't showing up over here. And I feel a little guilty about that. You see things going on on the other side of the world, awful things, and then you go right back to living your life like you still don't know about them, like they're not really happening . . ." John stopped, and shook his head. Where had *that* come from? It wasn't anything he'd planned to say. It was what he was feeling, though, wasn't it? It just slipped out.

Jill reached across the table and touched his hand, and in that instant everything in the world felt right again. "You can't save everyone, John," she said. "I've had to come to accept that. I understand what you're feeling, though, having lived over there. You drive through Nairobi on your way out of town and you see such poverty everywhere, such violence, and you know you can't do anything about it. You can't even stop and take a closer look or it will consume you."

She took her hand back. John was wishing she hadn't. He watched as she took another sip of white wine. "I wish I could let it go," he said, "but sometimes you get this feeling about the way things are fitting together."

She smiled. "I think that's called being a detective."

The waitress brought their food then, two steaming plates: spicy basil chicken for John and something called Pad See Ew for Jill. "What the heck *is* that, anyway?" he asked.

Jill laughed. "Rice noodles and vegetables. How's your chicken?"

John took a bite. He made a face. "Damn! Guess our waitress did understand what 'extra spicy' meant, after all. Maybe I shouldn't have told her that three times."

"You think?"

They sat and ate for a while. And John drank a lot of beer. "So," he said after a while, "Tell me what *you* think is going on."

"Well, I don't believe in zombies, John."

"Did I say I do? But that's what those men in Kili's video looked like. Go online when you get home and look up 'men without souls' on YouTube. You'll see what I mean."

"Maybe I'll wait until morning. I don't want to have nightmares."

"No, you don't," agreed John, remembering his. It still seemed so real that he shuddered. "I'm not saying they're really zombies, you know that don't you? Just that something is making them act that way. I guess what's really worrying me is I've seen a few people over here acting the same way."

They focused on their food for a while. John was thinking it was time he changed the subject anyway, when he finally figured out what those little silver things hanging from the ends of her earrings were. "Are those elephants?"

She looked up and smiled. "These?" She tapped one of them with her finger, set it swinging back and forth in the dim light at the table. "Yes. I got these in Kenya, last time I was there. Do you like them?"

"Yeah, I do."

She slipped one of them off and gave it to him so he could take a closer look. It was pretty realistic: had tusks and a trunk and everything. John handed it back to her. "Nice. You know, I don't think you ever did tell me what it is that you and Cynthia do over there. At least not exactly."

"Well, we've worked together on a great many projects, over the years." She tilted her head to one side and slipped the earring back on. "Most recently, elephant infrasound."

John gave her a blank look. "Come again?"

"Infrasound. Only recently we discovered that elephants communicate with each other using sound frequencies below those that human ears can detect."

"Sort of like dog whistles?"

"Same idea, yes. Though what dog whistles produce is ultrasound,

276

sound waves that are higher than those we can hear. Infrasound is on the other end of the spectrum, sound waves that are lower than those we can hear."

John tried to imagine that for a second. The woofers on the speakers of his sound system, turned all the way up. Tweeters turned all the way down. Sound so low you felt more than heard it. "What kinds of things do you think they say to each other?"

John could tell she really liked that question. "That's something I would dearly love to know." She'd gone someplace else for a minute. Maybe she was over there right now, out on the African savannah? "One interesting thing Cyn and I discovered recently is how far elephants can use infrasound to communicate. They seem to be able to recognize one another's voices from hundreds of miles away."

"Hundreds of *miles*?" Sometimes he couldn't get Ham's attention from across the damn room!

"I know, it's hard to believe. But apparently the sound waves travel not through the air but through the ground. It's fascinating."

They went on talking along those lines for a while. The evening went by. John managed to finish about half his chicken before it felt like it had completely burned his tongue off; Jill got most of the way through her plate of veggie intestines. It wasn't until the waitress had cleared their plates away, until they'd had yet another round of drinks, that the conversation turned personal. Jill started it. She was playing with the silver bracelet around her wrist, looking at it instead of at him. Then out of the blue she asked him: "Whatever became of Ham's mother, John?"

He could tell that was something she'd been wanting to ask for a while, but maybe never would have if she hadn't been on her second glass of wine. He thought about the best way to answer. There was only one thing that was true, but a lot of different ways to say it. "She passed away, about six years ago."

"Yes, I remember you saying that. I'm sorry."

She looked like she wanted to know something more. How much was he willing to tell her, though, tell anyone? "Yeah, me too." Sorry for a lot of reasons he wasn't sure he wanted to go into, sorry for a lot of things he didn't think Jill would understand.

"Does Ham remember her?"

"Oh, yeah," said John, though sometimes he wondered if most of what Ham remembered about her were the stories he'd told him. "He was almost nine when it happened, so . . ." *What DID happen, anyway?* That's what she wanted to ask him, wasn't it? He kind of wanted to tell her, to talk about it, but at the same time he didn't. It was still an open wound.

Jill was running one finger around the rim of her wine glass. It made a singing sound. "So, it's just been you two men since then?" she said, a little more upbeat, giving him a chance to steer away from the topic if he wanted to.

He wanted to. At least for right now. John knew what she was really asking with that last question and that was one he didn't mind answering. *No, there hasn't been anybody else since then.* "Yep. We take pretty good care of each other."

"So I've noticed," she said, smiling. She didn't ask him anything more about it after that, and he was just as glad. She was still looking at him pretty intently, though. What was she thinking? Was she wondering just how much of a hold Jenny still had on him, even after six years? Maybe she was trying to decide whether or not any of that mattered, when it came to the two of them. John hoped it didn't. One thing was for sure: he wasn't about to try and make his life look any better or different than it was. One of the good things about not being a kid anymore was feeling comfortable inside your own skin.

Just then, his cell phone went off. Regular old ringtone, so it couldn't be Ham. John pulled it out of his pocket and looked at the number. It wasn't one he recognized. Might be the Chief or Tom or God knows who, what with dark locust men running loose around town. "I'm sorry," he said, "I'd better see who this is."

She nodded and sipped some more wine.

"Briggs here."

"Hey, Boss, so you *are* there! I was starting to think you wouldn't pick up."

John wished now he hadn't. "Evening, Hotwire. You all healed up?" From then on out it was like he was having two conversations at the same time: one with Leroy Miller, on the phone, the other one with Jill's blue eyes.

"I can see again, if that's what you fucken mean."

"Yeah, that and the nasty cut on your head." Jill was looking at him like she was seeing a different side of him, and John guessed maybe she was.

"Not so sure about the head thing, Boss. Maybe that's not all the way better yet. Maybe that's why I'm fucken talking to you when I ought to be running the other way. But I might have something for you. Information," he said.

John perked up. *Maybe this is the break I've been hoping for.* "Oh yeah? Well, I sure could use a dose of that right now. You want to meet somewhere?"

"I do and I don't, man. You're getting too damned much attention these days. I even saw your ass on TV at the Best Buy. I don't know if I fucken ought to be seen with you."

"Tough luck, Hotwire, you're stuck with me. Nobody else on the Force is going to cut you any goddamned deals." Crap, he'd promised himself he would watch his language. But it seemed like Leroy always brought out the worst in him. Jill didn't look shocked, though; more like intrigued. Stand-up people usually were, when they got a peek at the city's ugly underbelly. John guessed that was why cop shows always got such good ratings. "You called me," he reminded Leroy, "You want to get together or not?"

"Well shit, all right, man. But when we meet could you at least wear a fucken disguise? Maybe clothes that look like you bought 'em this century?"

"You sound like my kid."

"That's a laugh, man."

Finally, something they could agree on. "So where'll it be? Kim's?"

"Let's branch out a little," said Leroy, throwing him a knuckleball, "How about we meet on the Capitol steps this time?"

"Capitol steps? What, are you moving uptown?"

Leroy laughed. "That's right, Boss! I'm king of the world now, man!"

King of the world. Leroy probably hadn't meant anything by that, but it hit John the wrong way. Maybe because that was how Tad Wellington had acted while he was gunning people down on the Division Street Mall. The way Leti Tulafono had acted, while he was killing everybody in sight at the Fairgrounds. "All right," John said finally, "When?"

"How about tomorrow at three?"

Sunday? The weasel must be desperate for cash. John looked at his watch like it was today they were talking about. "Yeah, sure. Look for me. I'll be the one wearing the Boba Fett costume."

After John got off the phone, Jill's blue eyes were asking him questions. Then she asked one out loud. "Was that one of your two-bit informants?"

Two-bit informants? Now John was sure she'd been watching too many cop shows! "Yeah, he's a real . . ." John was about to say "asshole," but at the last second changed it to "pain in the butt."

"You certainly meet some interesting people in your line of work."

"I don't know as 'interesting' is the right word for it, but yeah." They sat looking at each other across the table. The waitress came by and John paid the bill. "You got time to take a walk on the beach?"

"Sure, I'm not the one who has to meet a two-bit informant in the morning."

"Stool pigeon, please. Informant is too fancy a word for Hotwire. And actually, I'm not meeting him until afternoon. So I'm good."

They stepped outside the restaurant into the warm night air. It felt great out there with a breeze coming off the Gulf, with the smell of salt water, with lights from the hotels and restaurants reflecting off ripples in the dark water. "Let's head east," John suggested, "I don't want to go anywhere near the Fairgrounds."

"I don't blame you."

From what John had seen on the news, they'd closed the place down anyway. Probably wanted to give people a few days to try and forget what had happened there. John sure couldn't. He kept thinking about that one vigilante, the one who had come at him with blood on his mouth.

He and Jill crossed The Ribbon and walked out into the sand on the other side. There was a pier poking out into the Gulf about a half mile away. They headed in that direction. There were a lot of other folks out there walking, too, but in the dark and the breeze the beach felt sort of private. The moon was getting close to full, but kept moving in and out of the clouds. Waves were breaking on their right, little ones that were more like ripples. Then John remembered something.

"I'm sorry," he said, taking his cell out again, "but I promised Ham I'd check in with him. If I don't, he'll start wondering what happened to me."

"No, that's all right. Go ahead, please."

They kept on walking while John hit speed dial. The pier was just up ahead. It took a lot of rings before Ham finally picked up. He sounded out of breath.

"Hey, Dad, what's up?"

"Just checking in with you. What's going on?"

"Umm, nothing, really, just watching a movie."

"Oh yeah, which one?"

"*Night of the Living Dead.* That's always good for a few laughs."

"Didn't know it was a comedy."

"Neither did they when they made it."

John thought he could hear somebody in the background. Maybe just the TV set but it didn't sound like it. "Is Mick there?" He could see Jill looking at him out of the corners of her eyes. She had a funny little smile on her face.

"Uh, yeah," Ham said, after a long pause, "Is that all right?"

John thought for a minute. It wasn't, but he really didn't want to get into an argument right now, not with Jill listening in. "You should have told me ahead of time."

"You're right, Dad, I should have. I'm sorry about that. It just came up. She called right after you left."

"You still should have told me."

"You're right."

"Well, I'll be home pretty soon. Keep it clean, all right?" What the hell was he talking about? That made it sound like he wanted Ham to be sure and not mess up the kitchen! He hung up the phone, shaking his head.

Jill was still giving him that funny little smile. "Trouble?"

John sighed. "I don't know, probably not. He's got Mick there with him." John couldn't believe what he was thinking right then, that he was standing there worrying about the two of them having sex, when it was just a few weeks ago that he'd been afraid Ham might not even be interested in girls. Back then, he'd have been celebrating something like this!

"Do you trust him?"

"Well, yeah," he admitted, "actually I do."

"Then there's nothing to worry about, is there?"

"There's *always* something to worry about," John said with a laugh.

They walked along for a while and the pier got closer. Then Jill said: "Have you had the talk with him yet?"

"The talk?"

"Yeah, you know. *The Talk.*"

"Oh, right, that one. Well, yeah, I guess so. Sort of, anyway."

She laughed. "What do you mean, sort of?"

"Well . . . we *did* talk, but I think what I had to say to him on the subject was only about seven words."

Jill stopped walking. She was laughing again. "Seven words? What on earth were they, John?"

He stopped walking, too. "Never mind."

"No, really. I'm curious now. What were they?"

John remembered exactly what they were; he just wasn't sure he wanted to tell her. "All right," he finally said, "if you really want to know."

"Yes, actually I do. I'm curious as to what a man like you would say to his son. In that situation."

They were standing on the beach, close together. He was looking right into those blue eyes of hers. The wind kept blowing her hair across the front of her face. John could hear waves breaking behind him. He wasn't sure if he wanted anybody to know that much about him, if he wanted anybody—even Jill—to have that much of a peek at what went on inside of him. If he wasn't going to let her in, though, would he ever let anybody? "All right," he said. "All I told him was this: that sex without love isn't worth a damned thing."

Jill was quiet for what seemed like a long time. She stood there looking at him. She brushed the hair out of her face. "That's more like eight words, Detective." And that's when she kissed him, for the first time.

Chapter 38

Late Sunday morning John drove out to the Center to pick up Grandma, and took her to brunch like he always did. It was hard to think about much else besides Jill, though, and last night, and how they'd kissed on the beach with the sea breeze blowing her hair around, with the nearly full moon ducking in and out of the clouds. Grandma picked up on that.

"You're thinking about that girlfriend of yours aren't you, Honey?" she teased him on the way to Trudy's diner.

"Yeah," he admitted, "I am." Other things kept butting in, too, things to do with the case, but for the most part that was the truth. It was like one minute he'd just been going out with her and then, all the sudden, it turned serious. Hadn't it been serious all along, though? Yeah, in a way, but . . . But then he'd kissed her again outside her front door when he'd dropped her off at her townhome. And he'd asked her to come to Ham's birthday party, on Tuesday, at his house—she'd never been to his house before—and for some reason that felt like as big a step as anything else. What he'd wanted to do was go inside her place with her, spend the night, and he was pretty sure that was what she wanted, too, but then he'd remembered that Ham was home alone with Mick. Then he'd remembered telling Ham over the phone to "keep it clean." How would that have looked if he'd come dragging in the next morning?

Sex without love isn't worth a damned thing. That really was what he'd told Ham, a while back. And for the most part he believed it. Before Jenny there'd been a few times when . . . it just made you feel dirty, or what was worse, empty. If he'd gone on into Jill's place last night, wouldn't that have been the same as saying he loved her? Did he?

"You know, I still haven't met the woman yet," Grandma reminded him. "What did you say her name was?"

"Jill."

"Jill. That's a nice name. What does she do, anyway? I don't think you ever did tell me, did you?"

"No, ma'am, I don't believe I ever did. She works at the Zoo."

"At the *Zoo*? What on earth does she do there, John?"

"She works with the elephants."

"With the *elephants*? Lord have mercy! Baby ones?"

"No, ma'am. Full grown."

"*Elephants?*" She just couldn't seem to get her mind around that. "Well, what on earth does she *do* with them?"

"She takes care of them." That was a real short answer, but anything more than that would've probably been too much for Grandma anyway.

She was still shaking her head. "Girls working with elephants. Who'd have ever thought such a thing! It sure is a different world these days, especially for women. You think the two of you will ever have kids?"

John had a hard time not spluttering. "Ah, it's a bit early to be thinking about that, Grandma! I haven't known her all that long yet."

"Well now, that may be true, Honey, but at your age you don't have time to sit on your front porch swing, swatting at flies. You'd better get on with it if you're going to!"

John never was so glad in all his life to see that sign for Trudy's up ahead!

#

At three o'clock, after he'd finished having brunch with Grandma, John drove downtown to the Capitol. It was getting hot already, like it usually did this time of year if you weren't right on the ocean. Bright sunshine, big puffy white clouds. It was hard to believe that wasn't enough for some people, hard to believe they felt like they had to take drugs to get by. John pulled into the visitors' lot. He walked up the white steps towards the dome, looking for Leroy Miller. Lots of pigeons were there but no stool pigeons yet. There were people coming and going, even though it was Sunday, even though the place wasn't open for bribes or business.

"Afternoon, Boss." The weasel had walked up behind him. John almost didn't recognize Leroy. There was something different about him. Not his clothes: he was still wearing one of those black Metallica t-shirts. It was his eyes. They were so hard they glittered. Maybe he was still pissed off about getting hit in the face with pepper spray? That was bound to put a strain on any relationship!

"Listen, I'm sorry about what happened the other day, out at your shack. I'm sorry about your shack."

"Yeah." Leroy's eyes looked like a snake's.

"At least I saved your life." John felt like he had to point that out. That ought to count for something!

"There's that," Leroy admitted, "but you wouldna had to if you hadna led that fat bad ass out to my shack."

"I'm sorry," John said again, and meant it.

"In fact, I don't know if I really oughta be here talking to you now. For all I know that fat bad ass is in one of those buildings over there, lining us up in his scope!"

"Not unless the NRA has managed to legalize concealed carry for ghosts."

Leroy gave him a blank look.

"He's dead," explained John.

"Oh, well, that's all right then I guess. Saves me the fucken trouble."

Christ. John rolled his eyes. Like Leroy was man enough to take out Leti Tulafono! "Let's get on with it, Hotwire. You called this meeting, remember?"

"All right, Boss," said the weasel, "Let's get down to business. You want to turn the spigot all the way off on this Must shit, right? Well, I can take you to the man who can do that for you. It's gonna cost you something, though."

Was this really Leroy Miller standing in front of him? The same punk who was so scared he'd almost wet his pants, back on that night when they'd met at the Ferris Wheel to talk about Must for the first time? "I think we're getting a handle on it all by ourselves," said John. That was kind of a lie, but he didn't want the weasel to think he had any leverage.

"Think so? Found Mr. Big yet?"

John frowned.

"Figured out yet how he's bringing this shit over from Africa?"

John frowned again. Where was Leroy getting his information? That wasn't exactly common knowledge. "Who told you it was coming from Africa?"

"Same cat that can help you out, Boss. That is, if I put you in touch with him."

It felt like Leroy was making this up as he went along. "Oh yeah? Who is this guy anyway? Is he Mr. Big?"

Leroy laughed. "More like Mr. Little. It's not much of an operation, if you ask me. Sure has caused you a lot of trouble, though, huh? He can help you out, man. You can help him."

Big or Little, John couldn't figure out how a lovesick weasel like Leroy would know somebody like that, a Drug Lord And here he was pretending he was practically his agent! "Pretending" was probably the operative word. But John decided to play along. He didn't have anything better to do. "All right, so how do I go about meeting up with this Mr. Little?"

"That's easy, man," said Hotwire, "You pay me three thousand bucks and I take you right to him."

"Three thousand . . . !" That pissed John off for a second but then he couldn't help himself. He started laughing. "Are you out of your mind? I wouldn't pay you three thousand bucks to harvest your damned organs!"

"Take it or leave it, man," sniffed Hotwire.

"Well, shit, that was easy. I'll see you later, Leroy!" John started to turn away but as he did so the weasel reached out and grabbed him by the necktie. That's when John felt *his* T levels go up. Way up. "Don't ever do that again, man," he said, turning back around. "I'll beat the living shit out of you if you do."

There was a second there when John thought he might have to, but then Leroy let go. He lifted his hands in the air like he was giving up. "Sorry, Boss. I just don't want you to blow this opportunity, man."

What damned opportunity, thought John. He wasn't sure Hotwire knew anybody or anything. Still . . . if Leroy *could* lead him to the kingpin of this operation John might learn how Must had gotten over here in the first place. He might learn why the Nzige were showing up in his town. "Then give me a reason to believe you're not just bullshitting me!" John straightened his tie.

Leroy grinned. "I've got connections, man," he said, like he really thought he might be somebody.

"Right." *Jesus*, thought John.

"You can do a Ripley's if you want, Boss. You can believe it or not. You can either keep poking around trying to shut this shit off, or you can jump to the head of the line."

There really *was* something different about him, thought John. Could he afford not to take a chance? "That's a lot of money," he said, stalling for time.

"It'd be fucken worth it, though, wouldn't it man, if you could take this shit all the way off the street? Bust the pipeline?"

John wanted real bad to tell him to piss off but couldn't quite bring himself to do it. What if Leroy was telling the truth? What if the weasel really did have an in with whoever was distributing this shit? Could John afford not to take a chance? It was only money; the Department's money. Money John was sure the Chief would authorize, if he asked him to. Three thousand bucks was just a drop in the bucket, in the scheme of things. It would be money well spent if it meant they could shut Must off for good. And it might help Jill figure out what was happening to elephants over in Africa, might give her some information she could pass along to her friend, Cynthia Jones. He wondered if Hotwire's Mr. Little really could deliver on all of that. "Who is this guy you'd be taking me to?"

The weasel laughed. "If I told you that, you wouldn't need to pay me now would you, Boss?" For a second he seemed to lose his train of thought, as a couple of girls in short skirts walked past on the steps near by. "Tell you what, I'll throw you a bone. You remember when I worked that little sting for you a while back, when I was wearing a wire for you at McAdams?"

"Yeah, I remember. What about it?"

"Well the guy who was inside that warehouse, the one that dealt me the Must, he's the cat I'd be taking you to, if you can come up with the money."

"James Earl Jones?"

"That's what you called him, yeah!" Leroy was grinning like he'd just proved something. "That's not his real name, though. Be hard for you to find him without that. And you never even saw what he looked like."

John didn't think Leroy had seen him either, at least not on the night of the sting. "So, he's our Mr. Big?"

Leroy shrugged. "Or Little. Like I told you, man, it's not much of an operation."

John still didn't know whether or not to believe the weasel. But at least he could see a way now that Leroy might have met up with the guy. Maybe James Earl had seen Leroy talking to him outside the warehouse that night, and had figured out that John was a cop? How big of a Mr. Big could James Earl Jones really be, though, if he was out on the street himself, personally selling bags of Must to punks like Leroy Miller? Maybe it really was like the weasel said, though; maybe it wasn't much of an operation.

Why did James Earl want to make contact with him, with the police? Maybe he was running scared. Somebody—the Nzige, John figured—had just wasted Leti Tulafono and lapped up his blood. And at least two of those locusts were still out there. Could they be looking for James Earl Jones? If that was true, John figured he might be in a pretty good bargaining position whenever he met up with the guy.

"That's a lot of money," he said again, "You must know I don't have that much on me."

Leroy grinned. "I'll take whatever you've got for now, Boss!"

John took out his wallet. He actually did have a fair amount of cash on him because he and Mona had been prepared to buy information down on Tejon, before the Tulafono thing hit the fan. He took out five hundred-dollar bills and paid the weasel under the table right there, out in the open. He figured anybody who saw them would just think he was another lobbyist. They might have a hard time believing that Leroy Miller was a congressman, though.

"Not bad for a down payment!" said Congressman Weasel.

"All right, so when do I get to meet James Earl?"

"His real name's Yusuph," said Hotwire, smirking.

"Yusuph?"

"That's what I said, yeah. Muslim name, maybe, you think?"

"So when do I get to meet him?"

"Friday night."

That didn't sit so well with John. "Friday? Why Friday?"

"Because that's what he wants, man. That's when he can do it. And that gives you a few days to come up with the rest of the cash."

John thought about that for a minute. He didn't much like the idea of waiting another five days to try and get to the bottom of this, not with everything that had been going on in the city. But before Hotwire had called him he hadn't been on any timetable at all; this was at least better than nothing. And it didn't seem like he had a whole lot of options. "All right. Where do you want to meet?"

"In the parken lot at the Mercer Street Piggly Wiggly," said Hotwire, "Seven o'clock."

John nodded. He was impressed that the weasel had thought that far ahead, that he actually had a plan. "Just so you know, I'll be bringing somebody with me." John wasn't about to head into this all by himself. He wanted Tom Etheridge riding shotgun. And he'd feel even better if Tom actually *brought* his shotgun.

"I don't give a shit who you bring, man, or how many" said Leroy, "As long as twenty-five of them are named Benjamin."

Chapter 39

"Hey, Jill, come on in," John said when he met her down at the front door at 5:30, on Tuesday. She was carrying a little party bag with pictures of cartoon characters on it, and balloons of all different colors. She was wearing a bright blue top that showed off her eyes and made it look like she was part of the whole birthday package. He led her up the stairs to the main level.

"Pretty good climb you've got here," she said.

"Yeah, sorry about that. The elevator's broken."

She laughed. "That's OK, I need the exercise." They came out in the den. "This is nice," Jill said, looking it over.

"Thanks." It wasn't a bad little place, really, once you fixed it up! The table in the kitchen had a fresh white cloth on it, and Mick had set out the silverware; in the den the carpet was vacuumed and for once the sofa and chairs didn't have anything piled on them. The white curtains along the front windows were pulled back, and you could see the sun going down, off to the right

"Looks like you're facing south. Can you see the Gulf from here?" she asked.

"With a pair of binoculars."

"Ever get the sea breeze?"

"During hurricane season."

She laughed. Mick and Ham came tromping down the stairs then, full of energy. "Hey there, you two. Wow, Hamilton, don't you look nice!"

John looked up and saw that he was wearing some of his old black pants but along with that a white button-up shirt and a khaki vest. "Nice threads! Where'd you get the vest?"

"It was an early birthday present from Mick," he said with a grin, giving her a squeeze.

She must have changed up in Ham's room, too; she had on a crisp white top and a bright red skirt. You'd never know, thought John, that just a few weeks ago the two of them had been Visigoths! He found himself looking at Ham with different eyes then; his son seemed practically grown up all the sudden.

"So," he said, with what felt like a bit of a lump in his throat, "who's ready for dinner?"

#

"Mmm, John, you *do* make a mean plate of spaghetti!" said Jill.

"Told you." He was trying to think of the last time he'd had dinner sitting around the table. Must've been years ago. He and Ham still sat there for breakfast sometimes, but in the evening they always went into the den to watch TV. It had been different when Jenny was there, but that was so long ago he barely remembered.

"So, Mick," said Jill, making small talk, "What's your favorite subject in school?"

Mick blinked. "Well . . . it's not exactly a subject, but . . . Drama Club."

"Really? You like acting, then. Is that what you want to do some day?"

"Maybe." She laughed.

"Mick's really good at Math, too," interjected Ham, "She helps me out all the time."

"Well, my parents *are* accountants!" she said, a little sheepishly.

Like she had to apologize for that, thought John. From there they went on to talk about Ham's learner's permit and how hot the weather had been lately, until finally it seemed like everybody had finished their dinner.

"Anyone up for cake?" asked Jill.

"Does a zombie need a face lift?" said Ham.

Jill reached into the bag she'd brought with her and pulled out a round layer cake as white as a magician's rabbit, and put it in the middle of the table.

"Hey, that looks like coconut!" said Ham, getting all excited, "How'd you know that was my favorite?"

"I got some good advice," said Jill, winking at Mick.

Mick smiled, pleased with herself.

Jill had candles in her bag, too, shaped like the numbers one and six. Mick pretended to stick them into the cake backwards. "Sixty-one?" said John, playing along, "You don't look a day over fifty-nine, Hambone!"

"Very funny, Dad." But you could tell he was enjoying all the attention.

Jill lit the candles and turned off the lights in the kitchen and made everyone sing "Happy Birthday"—even John, who tried to warn her that he was tone-deaf. Afterwards, Ham blew them out with a puff so mighty it stripped some of the coconut flakes off the top of the cake.

"Hey, look, it's snowing!" cried Mick.

John sat there watching the white smoke from the candles rise up into the dark and it seemed like the years had gone by just that fast; it seemed like only yesterday that Ham was six and now here he was sixteen, practically a man. This was one of those things the two of them had been missing, John realized, ever since they'd been without Jenny: somebody who would make them stop and celebrate some of these mile markers along the way, whether they wanted to or not. If you didn't do that every now and then the time just got away from you; things just got smaller and smaller in the rearview mirror.

Jill turned the lights back on. "Who besides Ham wants a slice?" She cut about a quarter of the cake off for him and smaller pieces for the rest of them; even so Ham was the first one done and got back in line for seconds.

"This is a great cake," he said, "Did you make it from scratch?"

Jill laughed like that was the best joke she'd heard in ten years. "Let's just say somebody down at the Piggly Wiggly must have slaved all day over a hot oven!"

The Piggly Wiggly. That sobered John up. It reminded him that he was meeting Hotwire there on Friday so the weasel could take him out to see James Earl Jones. Or whatever his real name was. He wondered if that would close the book on Must for good. Maybe. Maybe it would over here, anyway. And that was all he cared about, wasn't it? If Must would go away, move back to Africa, he'd be more than willing to let go of it wouldn't he? He knew it was true and yet felt a little guilty for thinking that. Why? Because he'd seen Kili's videos now, seen Kili and her mother, Annika de Groot. Because he'd seen that little girl in the BBC documentary, talking about how evil men had slaughtered her sister. He'd seen those albino kids who were missing their hands. He wished now he hadn't. It was one thing to know that atrocities were being committed in faraway places like Malalongo; it was something else again to see the actual faces of the people who were on the wrong end of that.

"Maybe we should give Ham his presents now before he eats himself sick?" suggested Jill.

"Don't tell me you got me something else?" Ham asked her, "The cake was plenty!"

"Well, just a little something," she said. She lifted up the bag she'd brought with her and put it on the table.

"Oh, wow!" said Ham, looking at the cartoon pictures drawn on it, "Banjo and Kazooie! I remember these guys! I used to play that game all the time when I was a kid!"

Now *that* was funny, hearing Ham talk about how he used to do something when he was a kid! John remembered that game now, too, though. He remembered Ham playing it, over and over, after Jenny died. Maybe that, more than anything else, had helped him get through those hard days.

"Well, the bag itself wasn't supposed to be the gift," said Jill, "It was the only one they had left at the supermarket. You're certainly more than welcome to keep it, though!"

"You mean there's something inside?"

She laughed. "Yes, have a look."

Ham reached in and pulled out a carved wooden elephant. "Whoa! This is *cool!*"

"I actually know this elephant," said Jill, "His name is Ajax. A friend of mine carved it from some sketches and photographs I made while I was out in the field."

Ham passed it over to Mick and she held the elephant up, looking at it face-on. "How do you tell them apart?"

"Oh, they have nametags," Jill deadpanned, then laughed. "They do all look alike at first. But then you start noticing things like ear notches, or twists in the tusks, or the way they act in certain situations. Take Ajax here for instance: you can see that his left tusk splays out a little, and that he has a rather large notch on one of his ears. He's one of the biggest males, too, which helps in identifying him. And you can't see it from the sculpture, of course, but he's got a nasty streak." She laughed, maybe remembering something that had happened over in Africa. John imagined her running for her life through tall grass, with an elephant charging after her . . . Then it seemed as though she sobered up a little. He wondered if she was thinking about what was going on over there now, if she was worrying again about poachers.

"Thanks, Jill," said Ham, "this is really amazing."

John wasn't sure if he was talking about the elephant carving or the Banjo-Kazooie bag or maybe even the cake, which he was still working on every now and then, with gusto. "You ready for the next present?" John asked, pulling out his, the one he figured Ham already knew about. It was wrapped up in white tissue paper, with a red ribbon around it.

"Is this what I think it is?" asked Ham, excited. There was only one thing he'd been asking for for the past half-a-year!

"One way to find out."

Ham tore into it. "I knew it!" he yelled, holding it up over his head like it was some kind of trophy, "A smart phone!"

Mick said: "Let me see!"

"Thanks, Dad!" He was wearing a grin about as wide as his face. And then the two of them ran off to the den together, Mick telling him what apps he ought to download right this minute, Ham trying to figure out how to turn the thing on.

John and Jill smiled at each other across the kitchen table.

#

"It's getting a little stuffy in here," said Jill, after a while, "When I drove up, it looked like you might have a balcony. Or did I just imagine that?"

"You didn't," said John, "It's on the top floor. Would you like to have a look?"

"Let's do. I think Ham and Mick can keep themselves occupied for a while, don't you?"

John led her up the stairs. The balcony was off his bedroom, which made him a little nervous, because while they were cutting through he couldn't stop thinking—as much as he tried not to—about being in there with her. Somehow, though, he managed to get to the double doors on the other side. He opened them up. The sun had gone all the way down by then, and there was a nice breeze coming from the direction of the Gulf, cooling things off.

"And it's not even hurricane season!" quipped Jill, "This feels wonderful!" She leaned on the railing and let the wind blow her hair around.

John stood beside her, looking out over Palmer. The view wasn't all that great most of the time, but he had to admit it was better at night, what with the dark smoothing out all those hard edges. There were lots of stars up above now, too, like faraway reflections of the lights scattered across the city. There was supposed to be a moon, close to a full one, but right now it was hidden somewhere off to the east, behind a bank of clouds that was hugging the horizon.

"Do you think Ham is enjoying his birthday?" asked Jill.

"You know he is." John was scanning the street down below. It wasn't like he was expecting to see anything, really; it was just something he couldn't help doing. When you've been a cop for twenty years . . .

He hadn't been looking for anything, really, but all of the sudden he *did* see something—there was a dark shape moving around over at that construction site across the street. Rat, probably. If that was true, though, it had to be the biggest damn rat in the world! John watched for a while but it didn't seem like it was moving anymore. It had disappeared into the shadows.

"Sixteen years old!" Jill was saying, laughing to herself. "It's hard to even remember what that felt like!"

"I hear you." The rat at the construction site was gone now. John felt a shiver run down his spine just the same. What the hell was out there? He found himself thinking about Must addicts and dark locusts and men without souls.

There was a scream then, from somewhere out there in the dark, a scream that sounded kind of human but at the same time not quite— something in between a person and an animal, maybe, a scream that curdled his blood. A scream he felt like he might have heard before, in Kili's video from Malalongo.

"What the hell was *that?*" said Jill, standing all the way up and grabbing him by the arm.

"I don't know," John said softly, his eyes sweeping the street down below. There was something moving over there, at the corner . . . No, now it looked like nothing. He kept waiting for the scream to come again, but it didn't; everything was quiet now. Even quieter than it had been before. It was like everything out there that had been making noise had suddenly gone silent. It was like everything was lying low now, keeping out of the screamer's way.

John felt Jill shiver. Her hand was still on his arm. He turned and kissed her on her forehead, and then held her close, until she whispered in his ear: "Maybe we should go back inside?"

"Yeah, I think that's a good idea," he said. But it wasn't all that easy, letting go of her.

Chapter 40

On Wednesday, when John went to pick Ham up from school, he got there a few minutes early and sat parked along the curb in the traffic circle. These suspensions were making him think he never wanted to retire—what the hell did people *do* all day when they didn't have to go to work anymore? You could only take so many dish soap commercials! Ham came out of the building, still wearing the vest Mick had given him for his birthday. John smiled and shook his head. Kid had gone from being a Visigoth to a Yuppie, overnight! That felt like a bit of an improvement, anyway. Then Ham opened the car door and climbed into the front seat, surprising the hell out of him.

"Hey, Dad, how goes it?"

"I'm doing all right." Ham wasn't putting his headphones on, either. What had gotten into him? "Good day at school?"

"Not bad. Hey, Dad, I was thinking that maybe as long as you're picking me up, and you don't have to get back to work, maybe we could stop by and see Great Grandma?"

That sound was John's jaw hitting the floorboard. What was going on here? He was either sucking up or growing up! "She'd be mighty happy to see you. She asks about you every time I go out to the Center."

"Well, I guess today's the day!"

John felt like pinching himself. "She'll be over the moon," he predicted.

\#

"Now, once we get in there," John said to Ham as he pulled into the parking lot, "I want you to watch out for this old dude named Lester Covington. Real tall, bald head, hearing aid. Nice dresser, like you." John smiled. "But you don't want to get stuck in a conversation with him. He thinks I can talk to God on my cell phone."

"Can you?"

John laughed. "Wish I could. I'd ask Him a thing or two."

"Like what?"

That brought John up short. Sure, Ham looked sharp, and he was sitting in the front seat like he was all grown up, but was John really ready to have a serious conversation with him? "I don't know. Maybe how your mom is doing? What's eternity like? Softball questions like that."

Ham didn't say anything for a minute. "What was she like?" he finally asked.

John took a deep breath. Now *he* was the one getting questions that weren't really softball at all! "You don't remember her much, do you?"

"No, not much. It seems like I must have forgotten a lot. And I feel bad about that."

John felt his heart twisting around a little, inside his chest. "She was a sweet person," he said, "Just got started down the wrong road and never could find her way back." He said it again: "Sweet person."

Ham was quiet for a minute. "Am I like her?"

"Some. Both of you are smart and blonde and know how to get along with all kinds of people. You've got that rebel streak of hers, too, or you wouldn't be in trouble all the time with Mr. Sleeper."

"Asshole."

John laughed. "That's what she would have said, too." He opened the car door. "Tell you what: you help me out with Mr. Covington while we're in there, and I'll bail you out if Grandma comes on too strong about Mick. All right?"

"Deal," agreed Ham.

#

"Lord have mercy, can that be Hamilton Briggs?"

"Yeah, it's me, Great Grandma."

This just might make her century, thought John. She hugged him. She talked about how tall he was, how good-looking, how he was such a nice dresser. She hugged him again. The one thing Grandma didn't say was how much he looked like his mother. Jenny was there, in the room, but John was the only one who could see her. It was just like old times. But he'd forgiven Grandma for that, for the way she'd treated Jenny, a long time ago. There wasn't any sense in dredging that up now. John just tried to enjoy the moment for what it was. The woman who raised him and the son he was raising: it felt good to be there, in between the two of them. It made him feel like there was something firm on either side of him, like his life was held in place, a good place.

"I hear you've got yourself a girlfriend."

"Yes, ma'am. Her name is Mick. She goes to my school."

"Mick? Now is that short for anything?"

"Michelle."

"Well, that sure is a pretty name. Am I going to get to meet her someday?"

"Yes, ma'am, I expect you will."

John had promised to rescue Ham, but it looked like he was holding his own.

"How about your father here? You know, I haven't met his girlfriend yet either."

Ham shrugged. "Can't help you there, Great Grandma. She's nice, though. Mick and I both like her."

Grandma gave John a look. "So, Hamilton here has met her. His girlfriend Michelle has met her. When do I get to join the club, John?"

"I'm sorry about that, Grandma, really I am. We just haven't been able to work it into her schedule just yet. She keeps pretty busy out at the Zoo."

"The Zoo? Lord, yes, that's right. You told me about that. Now what is it she does out there?"

"She works with the elephants."

"Lord, yes, I remember now!" she said, "Isn't *that* something!"

John was wondering how he was going to steer her away from that topic when out of the blue his cell phone started vibrating in his pocket. He pulled it out and looked at the number that had flashed up on the dial. "Here she is now," he announced, "I'd better take this."

"Yes, I suppose you had better!" said Grandma.

Out of the corner of his eye, John could see Mr. Covington on the other side of the room. He was starting to move this way. Just like a damned bug attracted to a porch light! John nudged Ham and nodded in that direction, to warn him. Then he stepped away from everybody, over towards the edge of the common room.

"Hey, Jill," he said softly, thinking about how different things seemed now, how close he was starting to feel to her after these past few days. But her voice, when it came back at him, was frantic.

"John, sin's disappeared!"

He stood there stymied for a second, not knowing what she was talking about. Sin hadn't disappeared. Christ, you could find it everywhere you looked, all over the damned city! "What's that?"

"John, I got a call from Kenya this morning. Roger went out to Tsavo to take Cynthia some supplies, and when he arrived there he found that our research station had been burned to the ground!"

Oh, Cyn! She was talking about her friend Cynthia, the one she worked with when she was over in Africa. "Hold on a minute, Jill, slow down! What's all this again?"

She repeated most of it. Cynthia Jones had disappeared and the research station at Tsavo had been burned to the ground. "I'm afraid she may have been kidnapped!"

Jill didn't mention the Bwana this time, didn't say again that he was the one who had called her, but John was still thinking about it. Why did Roger Sutherland even have her phone number? Did he call her on a regular basis? John tried to shake it off. That wasn't the main point here. "What, are you thinking it might be poachers?" From that letter Cynthia had sent Jill a while back, you could tell she was hot on the trail of whoever had started killing elephants again. And people like that didn't take too kindly to anybody who tried to interfere with their business.

"Or worse."

John felt a chill run down his spine. He'd been thinking the same thing, but hadn't wanted to say it out loud. He'd been thinking that whoever took Cynthia Jones might be involved in something more than just your run-of-the-mill elephant poaching, that they might be mixed up in the drug-trade, in Must-trade. That they might belong to the Nzige. He let out a long breath. He saw that Grandma was watching him from across the room. She might be eighty-five years old, but she was no dummy. She knew something was up.

"I have to over there," Jill said suddenly.

"What are you talking about?"

"I have to go over there. I've got to try and rescue her."

"Are you out of your mind?" John said, a little frantically. He was shaking his head "no," though of course Jill couldn't see him on the other end of the line. "What do you think you would be able to do? Let the local police handle it!"

"The local police are no doubt involved," said Jill, like she knew that from personal experience.

"All the more reason for you to stay the hell away from there!"

Grandma raised her eyebrows when she heard him raise his voice, but John couldn't seem to help either what he was saying or how he was saying it. He didn't want Jill going over there. Period. He was afraid that if she did, he'd never see her again.

"I can't just stay here and do nothing, John! Look, I'm scheduled to fly over there and work on a research project with her anyway, later this summer."

"Yeah, but that's not until August!" He'd known about that for a while but hadn't started worrying about it just yet. It was like a storm cloud off in the distance, something to keep his eye on. "I'm not sure what you think you can do, even if you do go over there," he said again, almost pleading.

"Well, Roger and I could . . ."

Christ, there was the damned Bwana again! "Look, Jill, I don't know what you think you and some clown in a safari hat can hope to get done over there. These are some very dangerous people we're talking about!" Crap, that clown part just sort of slipped out. That wasn't going to help anything!

"Roger Sutherland is not just some clown," she said, getting her back up, "He's very well connected in both Kenya and Tanzania. If anyone can help with this, he can!"

John could tell this wasn't going to get him anywhere. Why was he trying to pick a fight with her anyway? "I'm just worried about you, Jill, is all," he cut in, "I really don't want you going over there. I don't see that there's much you can do to help Cynthia. I think you'd just be putting yourself in danger. You're a grown woman, though. You've got to do whatever you think you've got to do." Then a crazy idea popped into his head. "What if I went over there with you?"

She didn't say anything for a long moment. "I appreciate that, John, I really do. You're sweet. But I'm not sure what you could do, really, not knowing your way around the country. And how would Ham get along, while you were away?"

I don't know, thought John, *maybe I'd take him with me.* He'd be out of school in a few weeks anyway. John could practically see the look on Vice Principal Sleeper's face, though, if he was to tell him he was pulling his kid out early, so he could take him to Africa! John figured he could put a good spin on it, call it "an invaluable educational opportunity," and that would be true as far as it went . . . but what kind of father would take his son to a foreign country to chase after poachers and drug dealers?

"Well, when do you think you might be going?" he finally asked her. A little bit of a chill was creeping into his voice and he tried to hold it off, tried to fight it.

She took a deep breath. "Friday. That's the soonest I could get a flight out."

"Friday?!" That was only two days from now! And she'd already booked her damned flight? That meant she must have made up her mind even before she'd called him. And here he was thinking he had at least a little bit of a say in this! Why the hell had she even bothered to tell him? "Well at least let me take you to the airport then," said John, in a voice that was suddenly as stony as Chief Horsebreaker's face.

#

When John got off the phone, he could see that Grandma was still watching him from across the room. She left Ham with Lester Covington and came walking over.

"Trouble?" she asked, with a worried look on her face.

Trouble wasn't a good enough word to slap onto what was happening! John didn't know what word would be. "It's nothing, Grandma," he said, "Don't you worry about it."

"Well now, I will if I want to! What did your Jill say to get you so upset with her?"

John frowned. He felt like a little kid again, trying to hide something from her. He never had had too much luck with that! "She feels like she's got to go away for a while," he said.

"And you don't want her to."

"Well yeah, I'd rather she didn't." He looked across the Common

Room and there was Ham, still talking to Mr. Covington. He wished Grandma would just let this go, but he knew her well enough to know that she wouldn't.

"Why don't you just tell her you don't want her to go!"

Like it was that simple! John shook his head. Grandma came from a time when people belonged to each other more than they did these days. "I can't do that, Grandma. She's a grown woman. She can make up her own mind about what she wants to do. And it's not like we're married or anything."

"Maybe you should ask her before she leaves? Maybe if you ask her, she *won't* leave."

Ask her before Friday? All John could do was shake his head and laugh. "You never give up, do you? I don't think I'm ready for that just yet. And I know she isn't."

"Well, how do you know if you haven't asked her?" She was staring at him through the tops of her bifocals and now John knew how suspects down at the station felt when they were getting the third degree.

"I just don't think now's the right time," he said, squirming, "Maybe when she gets back. Maybe when all this is over with." All of what, though? Must? Africa? And what was he saying, anyway, that he *did* want to ask her to marry him? When did he make up his mind about *that*? It was all Grandma, wasn't it, trying to make up his mind for him? John wasn't ready. He liked Jill. He liked spending time with her, a lot. He sure as hell didn't want to lose her. But ask her to marry him, right now? She'd think he was out of his mind. And she'd be right to think that.

So John knew he didn't have any business telling Jill not to go, but that didn't mean he could make himself stop worrying about her. If poachers—or worse, the Nzige—had kidnapped or killed her friend Cynthia, they'd do the same to her without thinking twice about it. She'd have Roger Sutherland with her, but John didn't have much faith in the guy. From what he'd seen about him on his website, he wasn't anything but a big bag of hot air.

OK, so now I'm getting jealous on top of everything else. That wasn't good.

But it wasn't really Big Bwana Roger he was worried about. He was thinking more along the lines of Kili's video and drug smugglers and crazy witch doctor people who stole body parts from albino kids. He was thinking about poachers who would go out and kill an animal as magnificent as an elephant, just to cut off its tusks. He was thinking about the Nzige. And that's what Jill was planning on getting herself mixed up in?

Chapter 41

On Thursday, after John dropped Ham off at school, he decided he couldn't take all this uncertainty anymore. He called Chief Horsebreaker to ask him how many more days his suspension was going to last. "Much longer and I'm going to have to start looking for another job," he complained.

"I was just about to call you," said the Chief, "I think I've got you clear to start back tomorrow morning."

"About damned time!" After he hung up, though, he remembered that tomorrow was when Jill was flying off to Africa. And he'd told her he would drive her to the airport. Did that mean he was going to have to take some time off almost as soon as he got back on the job? When did her flight leave, anyway? He'd been so busy arguing with her about whether she ought to be going at all that he hadn't remembered to ask her. Now he guessed he was either going to have to call her back or drive out to the zoo. He decided he really wanted to see her in person.

It was late morning by the time he pulled into the parking lot. He went straight to the Admin Building. Marcy was sitting behind the desk, looking perky in a dark green blouse that set off her red hair.

"Well, well, look who's here!" she said, "I haven't seen you in a while!"

"Is she in, Marcy?"

"She has been. Give me a minute, I'll track her down."

"Thanks." John went around the room looking at all the same pictures again: crocs and zebras and Wild African dogs. And elephants. He stopped in front of one of those and stared at it for a minute. There really was something about them that was different from other animals. There were souls inside of those eyes. When you looked at a photo like this one you found yourself thinking not just about elephants in general, but about this one elephant in particular. Where was he headed when they took this shot of him? What did he have on his mind? Where was he now? John hoped to God he wasn't lying in a heap out on the savannah somewhere, with his tusks sawed off.

"John? She's over at the giraffe exhibit. She's wondering if you could meet her there?"

"Sure. Thanks, Marcy. I really appreciate it."

John was headed out the door when Marcy stopped him. "Do you think you can talk her out of it?" she asked.

John shook his head. "I seriously doubt it."

"But you'll try?"

"Yeah," he promised, "I'll try."

#

"Hello, John!" she called out as he came walking up, "It's good to see you."

"Good to see you, too." But then they both stood there like maybe they didn't even know each other all that well anymore. "I didn't know you worked with these fellas, too," John finally said, looking up at the giraffes. Damn, they were tall!

"I don't, really. I just like to watch them. They're interesting creatures. Not nearly as interesting as elephants, mind you, but interesting."

They were just beating around the bush here, weren't they? John decided to get to the point. "Before I came over here, Marcy asked me if I was going to try to talk you out of it."

"Well, are you?" she said with a smile.

"I'd like to, sure, but it seems like your mind is already made up."

"It is."

"Uh-huh."

"Look, John," she said, turning towards him, "What would you do? My best friend, someone I've worked with for nearly fifteen years, is missing. I can't just sit here and do nothing!"

"I understand that."

"Then you think I'm doing the right thing?"

"I didn't say that. But I understand why you're doing it."

They just stood there for a minute like they were looking at the giraffes, but John didn't think either one of them was. Not really. He

306

wondered if he should tell her that he'd been seriously thinking of getting a passport and following her over there?

"I wish you could go with me," she said then, almost like she was reading his mind, "but I know you've got Ham and your grandmother to take care of."

John lifted an eyebrow. She was right about Ham and Grandma. Well, he wasn't too worried about Grandma. She'd miss seeing him on Sundays if he was gone for very long, but they'd take good care of her down at the Center. Hambone was a different story. John would be a bad parent if he left him behind and a worse one if he was to take him over there with him. "I wish I could too, Jill. I think Ham and Grandma would be OK," he added, trying to be upbeat, "but I'm not so sure about the Chief."

She managed a little smile. "You're his right hand man, huh?"

"You know it. Of course, he's left-handed."

She laughed. "Did you come all the way out here to cheer me up, or have you been thinking about those black bean burgers we serve here?"

"Both," said John. And then they went and had lunch together.

#

They didn't talk much about her leaving once they got to the Treetops; maybe they'd both decided that it had to be, and that they'd get through it one way or another. For John's part he was hoping she'd get over there and figure out that there wasn't much she could do, then turn around and come back. Jill seemed as though she was trying not to think about it at all.

"How's the Must investigation coming along?" she asked, turning the spotlight back on him. That was one of *his* favorite tricks, damn it! But he decided he'd let her get away with it.

"It's coming." John wondered how much he ought to be telling her. He decided it probably didn't matter. She was leaving the country tomorrow and by the time she got back things should have settled out one way or another. So he went ahead and told her about the upcoming meeting with James Earl Jones, who they thought might be Must's Mr. Big, who had told Hotwire that someone from Africa was out to get him— maybe even the Nzige.

"And now Cyn has been kidnapped from the research station," she said in a faraway voice. "Probably by the Nzige, as well. I'm finding it hard to believe that this is all just a coincidence." She poked at her salad. "Maybe it's a good thing that I'll be over there and you'll be here, John. Maybe between the two of us we can figure this out?"

"Maybe."

"Maybe while I'm over there I can even find this Kili person and see if all those things she's been filming are tied in with this somehow? In that one link you sent me it looked like her mother ran a hospital somewhere. I think she even gave the name of the village, didn't she?"

"Malalongo," said John, a little reluctantly.

"That's it! Shouldn't be too hard to find."

Jesus, thought John; this was going from bad to worse! Bad enough that she was heading over there to try and rescue Cynthia from the African mob; now she was talking about going out into the bush, looking for men without souls! "Let me ask you something, Jill."

"Sure, anything."

"This guy Roger; he owns a gun, right?"

She looked puzzled. "Lots of them, yes."

"And he knows how to shoot one, right?"

"Of course! He's hunted Cape Buffalo before."

She seemed like she was getting her back up again. He couldn't blame her. He nodded. He'd heard enough from Mr. Sportsman, Tom Etheridge, to know that supposedly a Cape Buffalo was the most dangerous animal there was. More power to the Bwana. "Well, here's hoping he's just as good with drug dealers and zombies."

Christ, now she was looking like she might be pissed off at him! The last time John had been with her, at Ham's birthday party on Tuesday, he'd kissed her out there on the balcony and he'd felt like they might be going somewhere. Now, though, with this Africa thing in between them, it seemed as though they'd backslid a little. It was like neither one of them knew what to do now, or even what to say to each other. This was all a lot harder than John remembered. It seemed like he and Jenny fell in love without having to work at it; it just sort of happened and they did what came natural. The hard part didn't come until later. But this all felt like something he and Jill were having to navigate, or negotiate, or something. It felt like they were walking along the edge of a river, each of them waiting to see if the other one would be willing to stick a toe in. Maybe they were both afraid the water would turn out to be the wrong temperature? Or flowing too fast.

"Listen, Jill, I . . ."

She was looking at him. It seemed like she might be waiting for something, but he felt like there was a little bit of a wall in between them now, one he'd have to climb over if he wanted to get back to her. What had he been meaning to say? He'd been thinking a lot about what Grandma had suggested, that he ought to ask Jill to marry him. He knew that was crazy talk, yet he had half a mind to go ahead and do it.

"Listen, Jill, before you go . . ." *Before you go.* Damn, that was hard to accept, hard to say!

"What is it, John?"

He couldn't decide what was in her eyes and voice right now, whether it was just worry or something else? He took a deep breath, but in the end all he managed to ask her was this: "What time does your flight leave tomorrow?"

Chapter 42

It could've been a perfect May morning if John wasn't telling Jill Relson goodbye. The sky was pink and blue and chock full of big white summer clouds as he drove across town in the light 5 A.M. traffic. It was hard to believe she was really flying out today, hard to believe how crazy that was. But he tried not to think too much about it because that wasn't helping any. John pulled up at the Remington. He knocked at her door. In a few seconds it opened and there she was, looking like she didn't much want to do this either.

"Good morning!" he said brightly. No sense in sounding all down in the mouth about it now that it was a done deal.

"Thank you for taking me to the airport, John."

He picked up her bag. It wasn't all that heavy; maybe that meant this would be a quick trip? He was sure hoping. "Happy to do it." She was dressed to be comfortable for the long flight ahead, in blue jeans and a red-striped pullover shirt. She looked good as hell.

Then it was like neither one of them knew what else to say. John drove for a while, with the sun coming up. There was nothing but crap on the radio.

"I wish I didn't have to go," Jill said, after a while.

"Yeah, me too. Do you?"

"I suppose I feel that I do."

"Yeah, well, I guess you must, then." He hadn't meant for that to have any edge to it, but once it was out there he could hear that it did.

"It's just that Cyn and I . . ."

"Yeah, I know. You go way back. Look, I don't blame you for going, really. If it was me, I'd probably be doing the same thing." John thought about that for a minute, then changed his mind. "No, if it was me

I *would* be doing the same thing. I'm just worried about you, Jill, is all."
Yellow taxis were blowing past them on the freeway, weaving in and out of
traffic. John had turned due east now and that early morning sun was
shining right in his eyes.

"I know, I'm a little worried about me, too."

"Then don't go already!" Christ, he'd told himself this morning he
wasn't going to say anything like that. He'd told himself he wasn't going to
make this any harder for her than it already was.

"I feel like I have to."

Well, that sort of summed it up, didn't it? There wasn't much else to
say. He kept on driving. The sun was in his eyes.

\#

When they got to the airport, John went in with her, not knowing
whether she wanted him to or not. He didn't ask. After she checked in,
they walked around to the security gates and just stood there watching while
people with loose change and big belt buckles and nunchucks set off the
alarms.

"I got you a little something," she finally said.

Oh, shit. She was the one leaving; he should have been the one to do
that! And he didn't have a thing with him but the clothes on his back.
"You didn't need to do that, Jill," he said, feeling crappy.

"Just a little something." She handed it over. It was a hard plastic
case about the size of a billfold. She laughed. "You don't know how hard
it was, though, to find this in a cassette. You really should think about
joining the twenty-first century, John, and getting a CD player—maybe
even an MP3 player—for your car!"

"What I probably need is a whole new car." John looked at what
she'd given him. The Marshall Tucker Band, *A New Life*. "Hey, thanks. I
love this album. You know, I don't think I've ever even used that cassette
player."

"Let's hope it actually works then!"

John looked at the cover of the tape. There was the same picture he
remembered from the days when he'd owned the album on vinyl: a man on
a horse at the edge of a cliff was holding a fiddle, and he was looking out
over a canyon and river. "How'd you know?"

"Well, I *do* I listen to what you have to say, at least every now and
then!"

That made John feel even worse. He wondered if he'd ever really been listening to her. Even if he had thought to get her a going-away present, would he have known what to buy? "I'm sorry I didn't get you anything, Jill, I . . ."

"That's all right," she said, cutting him off, "I know you've been busy lately. "

Somehow, that didn't make him feel any better. He wanted to at least say the right thing to her now, but that wasn't working out so well, either. What was getting in the way? Just being a man, maybe, the damned testosterone? It seemed like that, sometimes. There were things you wanted to say to people but you just never could seem to get them out. "Jill . . ." He knew she really ought to be going through Security now and she knew it, too. She looked like she was starting to get a little antsy. But she hung on for another minute, waiting. "Promise me you'll be careful, all right?"

"I promise." She stood there a little longer, then said: "Well, I suppose I had best be going. They'll be boarding my flight soon and it's a walk to the gate." She still hadn't moved, though. "Tell Ham I said goodbye. I enjoyed his birthday party the other night."

"Yeah, that *was* fun, wasn't it?" He leaned in close then and kissed her. That was the easy part. Why couldn't he say what he wanted to say, why couldn't he tell her that . . . what? He couldn't even say it to himself, damn it! After a few seconds, she pulled back a little. "I have to go," she whispered.

"Call and let me know that you got there, will you?"

She touched his cheek with the tips of her fingers. "Don't worry, I will, Detective."

And just like that, she was gone.

#

In the car, on the way home, John popped in the cassette. *I've done my time, and a new life is gonna be mine.* Why hadn't he bought himself some tapes like this a long time ago? Too damned busy to even think about it, he guessed.

Once he got to the house he found that Ham was still in the shower. John looked at his watch and frowned. Kid was running a little late but at least he'd been able to get up and going all by himself. John fixed another cup of coffee and sat down on the sofa, wondering what to do now. It wasn't like he saw Jill every minute of every day, but just knowing she wasn't there had already left a big hole. At least he wasn't suspended anymore. There'd be plenty to do once he got to the office. And then he was meeting Hotwire tonight at the Piggly Wiggly. He picked up his laptop and checked his email, just to see how many advertisements he'd got overnight for products that would enlarge his penis. There was a message in the inbox from Jill. How the hell could that be? He'd just dropped her off at the airport a half-hour ago!

There it was, though, right in front of him, with the subject line *I miss you already*. He opened it and saw that she'd sent it this morning, before he'd even picked her up at her apartment.

I'm sorry I have to do this, John, I'm sorry I have to go away for a while. I think you understand, though. With any luck I won't be over there very long. And then I hope we can pick up where we left off. I miss you already. Love, Jill.

John sat there on the couch just looking at the screen, thinking about her on her way to Miami. She was supposed to change planes there and then she'd be out over the Atlantic, fifteen hours, she said, to Nairobi. Jesus H. Christ. Might as well be the other side of the world. It *was* the other side of the world, damn it! He looked at her message again. He hit *reply*.

"I miss you too, Jill," he said out loud. Even if he did write that, how long would it be before she got it? Did they even have access to the Internet over there? Had to, otherwise Kili would never have been able to post her videos. John just didn't know if there was Internet where Jill was headed, out in the back country. Tsavo. That was where she'd be headed first, he predicted; she'd be headed for Cynthia's research station. That's what he would do, anyway, to see if he could pick up her trail.

Christ, he wished he could be there with her! She could use a detective. She could use somebody who would kick the ass of anybody who tried to mess with her. Not some tourist-safari Bwana who would just as soon sell her to the natives for her body parts! He had to stop then and laugh at himself. He was too old to be acting this way, and too old to be believing in shit like witchcraft! It wasn't that *he* believed in it, though; it was that *they* did. Those people over there. Some of them, anyway. It said so on Wikipedia. And because *they* believed in it, that made them dangerous. Not dangerous like drug smugglers or elephant poachers could be—those were the guys John was *really* worried about—but they could still be trouble. Big trouble. John tried to shake it off. If he kept on thinking this way, he'd be a basket case by tomorrow morning!

"I miss you too, Jill," he said out loud again. And it turns out that, after a while, testosterone would actually let him type that out. After a while longer, it actually let him click *send*.

#

He hadn't been back at work for more than an hour when there was a knock at his office door. "Come in!"

It was Chief Horsebreaker. John looked up from his desk in disbelief. He couldn't remember the last time the Chief had actually knocked instead of just barging in.

"I wanted to see how you're holding up," he explained.

John tilted back in his chair. "I'm hanging in there. Been one hell of a long week, though."

Horsebreaker nodded. "I'll bet." He put John's badge and gun on the desk in front of him. "Did you see Jill off?"

"Yeah. She's probably in Miami by now." He still wasn't feeling any better about her leaving. Maybe now was the time to . . . "I was thinking about going over there after her. Do you think I can get some time off?"

If Horsebreaker was surprised by that, you couldn't tell just by looking at him. He had his stony face on. "I kind of need you here right now, John."

"I'm not talking today, Chief. I couldn't leave for a little while anyway. It'd take me a couple of weeks to even get a passport."

"You're getting a passport?"

Hearing Horsebreaker say that did make it sound a little crazy. "Maybe. Hell, I don't know." The Chief was standing there staring at him. "Something bad is going on over there, in Africa. I don't know exactly what it is yet, but my gut's telling me it has a lot to do with the trouble we've had over here." John couldn't figure out what was going on behind Horsebreaker's dark eyes, and that was making him nervous.

The Chief grunted. "Well," he finally said, "Things do seem to be slowing down a bit. Maybe in a couple of weeks . . ."

What was he saying? Did that mean it would be OK for John to take some time off later? Before he could decide whether or not he should ask the Chief to commit to that, there was another knock at the door. *What now?* "Come on in!"

Tom Etheridge poked his head through. "Oh, sorry, didn't know you weren't alone. Morning, Chief," he said to Horsebreaker.

"Come on in, Tom, I was just leaving."

"You don't need to. I was just stopping by to welcome John back and ask him when he was going to pick me up tonight. I'm looking forward to finally meeting your main man, Hotwire!"

"He's not my main man," growled John.

"So it takes two of you to handle him now?" quipped the Chief.

John thought Horsebreaker might be pulling their chains, but the Chief delivered his lines so flat it was hard to tell sometimes. "Tom's just coming along to make sure I don't kill the little son-of-a-bitch."

Horsebreaker grunted. "Good plan."

Chapter 43

Once John got Ham home and fed him dinner, he drove out to Tom's place. It was almost seven by the time he got there, but there was still plenty of light left. Etheridge came out of the front door of his two-story Cape Cod, looking like a walking advertisement for *Suits Big & Tall*.

"Where are we headed, anyway?" he asked as he eased his frame into the front seat beside John.

"Piggly Wiggly."

Tom laughed. "Good a place as any, I guess, to meet a squealer!"

John drove. "How are the kids?"

"Good," he said, "good."

They went to Palmer High, too, but Ham never mentioned them. They ran with a different crowd. Jocks and Barbies, Ham called them. "Carol?"

"She's doing all right. How's Hambone?"

"Turned sixteen this past week."

"No kidding? How the hell did that happen? Time sure goes by, man. Jill?"

It seemed as though Tom had tiptoed his way up to that one. "Still up in the air, I guess." John didn't realize until after he'd said it that you could take that a couple of different ways.

They shot the breeze some more until they got to the Mercer Street Piggly Wiggly. John pulled into the parking lot and started looking for Hotwire. "Where *is* that little shithead?" he wondered.

John drove past the entrance, trying hard not to run any shoppers down. Things were pretty busy—probably folks getting last minute things on their way home for the weekend. Finally, he did see the weasel, standing next to a stack of propane tanks. Smoking a cigarette, maybe even a blunt.

How the hell had he lived this long? John shook his head and pulled right up to the curb. Leroy waved and came walking towards them, grinning.

"Don't get in here until you've put that thing out," John barked as he opened the door.

"Huh? Oh yeah, sure." Leroy flicked the sparking butt off in the direction of all that propane. His eyes were bloodshot.

Jesus Christ, thought John, *he's stoned!*

"You all right, Boss? You look like somebody shot your dog."

"I don't own a damned dog."

Hotwire slid into the backseat and John could see him grinning in the rearview mirror. "No? Then somebody musta closed down your favorite doughnut shop, man."

As usual, John was getting pissed off. He had more important things to do right now, though, than beat the shit out of a weasel. "This is Tom Etheridge. Old friend of mine. He's coming with us."

"The more the fucken merrier," said Hotwire, "You a cop, too, man?"

"Off duty. That way I can kick your ass as a private citizen, if you keep shooting off your damned mouth."

Good, thought John; Tom was taking a shine to him.

Leroy just laughed. "Listen, man, everybody in the fucken free world knows about that good cop/bad cop routine. You guys oughta get yourselves some fucken new material."

"Actually, we just do bad cop here," said Tom. "Briggs'll kick your ass, too, if you give him half a reason."

Quarter, even. But this wasn't getting them anywhere. "Come on," said John, "Let's get this show on the road. Where are we headed, Hotwire?"

"Tristy City."

La Ciudad de la Tristeza, they called it, the City of Sadness. Swell. That place was bad news. Made Palmer look like Society Hill. John drove out that way. They were moving into what might have been a nice evening, some other time. The sun was working its way down; there was maybe a half-hour of daylight left. They were headed due west so John was driving right into it. He thought about this morning when he'd been squinting into it going the other way, driving east to take Jill to the airport. Where was she right now? Out over the Atlantic still, probably. She wasn't supposed to land in Nairobi until tomorrow morning, local time. Middle of the night here, she'd told him. John wondered if Big Bwana Roger was going to meet her at the airport? She hadn't said and he'd been afraid to ask.

They reached the causeway that split Tristy off from Palmer and Mayfair. It was a long pontoon bridge that humped up out of the swamp like the back of a giant water snake. They climbed it. From the top, for just a minute, John got a bird's eye view. Things down below seemed quiet enough.

"Take the first exit," said Leroy.

Orange light was reflecting off the lakes and swamps. John took the off-ramp from the highway and veered into Tristy. He kept on driving until they got to Valdez, the main street that went through downtown. For a Friday night, the place sure looked deserted.

"Town has gone to hell since the last time I was here," muttered Tom.

"It always was Hell," said Leroy, that great urban analyst.

"Where to now?" John asked him.

"Keep on driving until you hit Calderón. Then take a right."

John did. It was quiet everywhere they went. Too damned quiet. "Now what?"

"Keep going, man, we're almost there." They were driving through the last of the daylight. Shadows were building armies on either side of the street. John felt the hackles on the back of his neck start to rise. "Just up ahead," said Hotwire, "House on the right. That brick piece of shit with the chain link fence around it."

John saw it. He pulled up to the curb right in front. One level. Part red brick, part white-painted aluminum siding. Waist-high chain-link fence running around the yard. There was some dog on the other side of it. Looked like a Collie. *In this part of town,* thought John, *I'd want a pit bull.* There weren't any lights on inside the house.

"You sure he knows we're coming?" asked Tom.

"Oh, yeah," said the weasel, "I just don't think he wants anybody else knowing he's home."

They got out of the Nova. John could hear sirens somewhere in the distance. Must not be completely dead out there. "Come on, let's get inside." He didn't like just standing on the sidewalk with it getting dark. Somebody might be watching them.

Leroy opened the gate. The Collie came at them, barking. Hotwire pulled a gun on him. "Shut the fuck up, Asshole, or I'll blow your fucken hairy head off!"

"Don't be mean to the dog," growled Tom. He had a couple of greyhounds at home.

"That's his fucken name, man, don't blame me. Blame his fucken owner."

Tom was looking at him like he didn't believe a word. The Collie was still barking. Hotwire pumped a couple of bullets into the ground right in front of him. "Hush the fuck up, puppy," he said.

Asshole, or whatever his name really was, whimpered and slunk off into the bushes. Since when did Leroy Miller pack heat, wondered John? That made him nervous. Hotwire led them up to the front door and knocked. The sun had gone all the way down. They stood there on the stoop, in the dark, waiting. There weren't any lights on inside the house. The door opened a crack. The barrel of a rifle came poking out.

"Who is it?"

John recognized that deep voice at once. It was James Earl Jones.

"It's me," said Hotwire, like that ought to mean something.

Apparently, it did. "Ah, yes. I have been waiting for you, Le Roy. It is good that you have finally come." John couldn't focus on James Earl all that well in the dark. He was blacker than anybody John had seen in a while. "Come in quickly," he said, in that African accent of his, "Please, everyone, enter."

John was all for that. His eyes were adjusting to the lack of light. They were in what looked like a living room. There was a couch and a coffee table and a wall-sized TV. There were white curtains closing off the plate-glass front window. They worked their way back through the dark hallway. They came out in the kitchen. There was one dim light on there, over the countertop. The floor was black-and-white checkered linoleum; it looked like it had been laid down in the Sixties. There was a sliding glass door that let out to the back. John could see a little of the yard through the slits in the vertical blinds: patches of dirt, clumps of grass, and every now and then the long snout of the Collie, Asshole, as he whimpered and begged to be let inside.

The four of them sat down at a round wooden table. John could see James Earl better now. He could see that the man had a neat black beard and mustache, that he was wearing gold-colored wire-rimmed glasses. That his eyes were as black as black olives. Those eyes kept shifting back and forth, like they were trying to watch out for everything, everywhere, at the same time. James Earl had an assault rifle propped in his lap. John was no weapons expert but because he busted drug dealers for a living, he came across all kinds of bad shit in his line of work. He'd seen this type of gun before. Russian piece called a Kalashnikov. Serious hardware.

Nobody said anything for a while. James Earl lit a cigarette and the click of his lighter sounded like a gunshot going off inside the room. A stream of white smoke flooded up through the dark.

"My friend Le Roy tells me that you may be able to offer me protection, perhaps even a new life," said James Earl, eventually.

Le Roy? What kind of bullshit was that? Made it sound like the weasel had class! And what kind of crap had Hotwire been feeding James Earl anyway? "Is that right?" said John, giving Hotwire a nasty look, "Well, maybe we can. But tell me this first: why the hell should we? It's not like you've been doing us any favors!"

James Earl sat there in his chair and smoked for a minute. His eyes got narrow. "I can provide you with information which may be of use to you."

"It would have to be some damned good information," said John. What *would* it take, really? The names and addresses of anyone who was still dealing Must along the Gulf Coast? The name and address of Mr. Big, if there was one? Assuming John wasn't talking to him right now.

"I told Yusuph you would want to know where Must was coming from," said 'Le Roy,' helpfully.

Who the hell was this Yusuph anyway? Then John remembered: that was supposedly James Earl's African name. His real name. He noticed that Hotwire still had his gun out. "Might be a good place to start," said John, without promising anything. That wouldn't be enough to make him to want to stick his neck out for Yusuph—for one thing, he thought he knew where Must was coming from already—but he did want to hear what the guy had to say. Maybe he could tell them something more specific than just "Africa;" maybe he could tell John something that would give him a better idea as to exactly what Jill was getting herself into.

James Earl—Yusuph—took his time getting started. He looked nervous, skittish. His finger kept moving on and off of the Kalashnikov's trigger. He looked over at Hotwire. He looked out through the cracks in the blinds that were covering up the sliding glass doors. John could hear Asshole whimpering out there in the yard.

I don't blame you, Boy, he thought, *I wouldn't want to be out there tonight, either!*

"It is a bit of a complicated tale," said Yusuph Earl Jones.

"We're not doing anything else right at the moment," said Tom, leaning back in his chair and folding his arms.

Yusuph took a deep breath. His eyes shifted back and forth in the light coming off the countertop. He said: "Very well."

Chapter 44

John heard other dogs in the distance now, howling. James Earl Jones started his story.

"At one time we belonged to a rebel organization, my brother Adeen and I. This was in Tanzania. The professed aim of that organization was to overthrow the government, or at least make governing difficult for those who were in power. That is what we told ourselves, in any event." He laughed. "In truth, we were not particularly idealistic. Or even political. Well, perhaps some of us were. But my brother and I—and I suspect many others—had no real interest in such things. It was more that we wished to live lives without moral constraints."

James Earl paused to take a drag on his cigarette. "In truth, we were nothing more than drug smugglers," he confessed, "Young men who manufactured reasons to live lawless lives. We took whatever we wished and labeled our actions as rebellion against an oppressive and corrupt regime."

Was he regretting that now? John couldn't tell. Even if he *was* feeling bad about whatever he'd done over in Africa, selling drugs on this side of the Atlantic seemed like a strange way to try and make up for it!

"Then one day, *he* came. Colonel Muka. That is when everything changed. At first it appeared that he, too, was interested only in smuggling drugs, though on a much larger scale. He and his men took control of our operations. We wanted to resist him, but were afraid to do so. He was not someone to be trifled with. Under his direction we began bringing a new drug into our country, from across the border in Kenya. We did not know what it was. It was some time, however, before any of us began to question his motives, and authority. This drug was not being directed to the usual markets in Dar es Salaam, or even to other large cities beyond our borders. Instead it was routed to the interior, to regions where there is no one other than native tribesmen. Why would such people wish to indulge in civilization's vices? How would they even pay for them? My brother and I had no interest in trinkets and goats. It was a business arrangement which made no sense to us. One day we decided to follow this path that Colonel Muka had forged, to see for ourselves just what was afoot in the hinterlands."

Dogs were still barking and yapping out there in the dark. Every now and then Asshole's snout would bump up against the other side of the glass. John wondered if Yusuph's group of lawless young men were the Nzige? Or had those lawless young men been absorbed by Colonel Muka's Nzige, once he came on the scene? Yusuph took another drag on his cigarette.

"This is the path the drug took. Someone—we never knew precisely who—would bring drums filled with liquid to the port of Mombasa, in Kenya. There, my brother and I and others would load those drums onto our ship. Then we would sail south along the coastline and deliver them to the docks at Dar es Salaam. Until the day we grew curious, that is where we believed the path came to an end. Up until then we had assumed that the liquid we were delivering was itself Colonel Muka's drug. Once we decided to investigate, however, we discovered that the drums were processed further, that in a laboratory in Dar es Salaam a man named Doctor Leemo would transform the contents of those drums chemically into blue crystals, those same crystals with which you are no doubt familiar."

Must, thought John.

Yusuph Earl Jones seemed very far away at that moment, as though telling his story had taken him all the way back there, to Tanzania. A cloud passed over his face. He didn't seem to be enjoying the trip much.

"From there the final product was transported to the Interior. To our surprise we discovered that Muka was simply giving that product away. Apparently, he wished to observe its effects. Apparently, this was some sort of strange experiment. The man is quite mad, actually. From what Adeen and I observed, the drug made the men in that region extremely aggressive, and seemed to be highly addictive. We were never quite clear as to what Colonel Muka's intentions were, however. We speculated that perhaps he hoped to administer the drug to an army under his control, thereby enhancing its effectiveness and brutality, with the aim of making it into some sort of elite fighting force. If indeed that was his aim, however, then his experiment seemed a dismal failure. For from what my brother and I observed, the aggression of those men could not be controlled. They turned on one another as often as they fought with any designated enemy. They could not be directed. That, however, was not our concern. Our concern was that Colonel Muka's goals were not in line with our own, that he actually did have political and revolutionary aspirations whereas we, we finally realized, did not. From that moment forward, we began making plans for how we might escape from his influence, strike out on our own."

Asshole kept on whimpering outside the sliding glass doors. Dogs all over the neighborhood kept on raising a ruckus. With one more drag James Earl finished his cigarette, and stubbed the butt out in a white plastic ashtray in the middle of the table.

"I wish that is all we had done, that we had simply vanished one day. But circumstances conspired to present us with an opportunity, a temptation which neither I nor Adeen was quite able to resist. There was a storm at sea, in between Mombasa and Dar es Salaam. Our ship was driven off course. Eventually we made landfall but far away from Tanzania, on the island of Comoros. Our ship was heavily damaged. For several weeks we were forced to remain there, making repairs. At some point during that time we came to the realization that no one had come looking for us, that perhaps no one would ever come looking for us. That perhaps Colonel Muka believed we had been lost at sea.

"Thus, once our ship was seaworthy again we had a decision to make: should we return to Dar es Salaam or strike out on our own? Our ship was filled with the drums from Mombasa. We had only to find out how to transform what was in those drums into Colonel Muka's drug, we felt, in order to make a great deal of money. We still had connections within Muka's operation, of course; we had only to make discreet inquiries. Doctor Leemo himself was so corrupt as to be incorruptible, but we felt we might be able to entice one of his technicians to join us. There was always a risk inherent in such a plan, of course: while luring one of Leemo's technicians away we might alert Colonel Muka to our presence, we might arouse in him the suspicion that we were still alive. And indeed, that is what transpired. Not at first, however. At first, things seemed to go well. The technician joined us on Comoros. With his help we were able to transform the drums from Mombasa into Colonel Muka's drug."

John held up a hand to stop him. "And what exactly was in those drums, Yusuph? You never did say."

"Did I not?" He frowned. "I felt certain I had." He paused. He seemed to be recalibrating the line of his story. "For a long time, Adeen and I did not know. We simply accepted without question the drums that were delivered to us in Mombasa, and carried them to Dar es Salaam. But once we made the decision to follow Colonel Muka's line of supply from beginning to end, it became important for us to know not only the drug's destination but its origin. And so we investigated the Kenyan side of his operation as well."

In the background Asshole the Collie was no longer whimpering. He was making a low, threatening growl that set John's nerves on edge. Had Asshole seen a squirrel or was somebody out there? James Earl was looking through the glass doors, too. "What was being supplied to us," he finally said, solemnly, "was the blood of elephants."

#

It took John a moment to process those words. Even then they didn't quite make sense. But they should have. Because they tied in with everything that Jill's friend Cynthia had told them in her letter, about the uptick in poaching at Tsavo. He and Jill had even talked about it before, that poachers might be taking elephant blood, but it had never occurred to him that it might be on a scale such as this, that somebody might be taking drums of their blood, shiploads of it. Somehow that seemed even grislier than simply killing the animals for their tusks. John wanted to know more about that end of the operation, because that was where it seemed like the danger might lie for Jill. But before he could ask any questions, James Earl Jones had pushed on, telling them the rest of his story.

"What we most feared indeed came to pass. Muka somehow became aware of our presence. Comoros was no longer safe for us. We needed to go much farther away. Thus, we set sail, our ship filled with Must now, for South Africa. By the time we arrived there, however, we had become much more nervous; even Johannesburg seemed to us to be too close to the Colonel. Knowing how ruthless he was, remembering the brutality he had sown in the interior of Tanzania, we did not wish even to be on the same continent with him. Where might we best sell his drug, then? We thought at once of America, of course, as your country has an almost endless appetite for such things. As fate would have it, my brother Adeen actually knew someone who lives here, an old friend from his days at the University. It would be a long way to travel but would also mean that there would be an ocean between us and Colonel Muka.

"Many months went by. My brother communicated with his friend and made the arrangements. We sold our ship and purchased passage on a larger one, for the two of us and Leemo's technician and our precious cargo. We set sail. It was a journey of several weeks but that too would help in concealing our whereabouts. Eventually we arrived here and with the help of Adeen's friend were able to enter your country. Port officials everywhere are the same, apparently," he added with a smile. "They can be bought rather easily.

"Everything was going according to plan until one day, quite recently, Muka's agents appeared. How did they find us? I still do not know. Though I suspect some of the news reports about the killings here, and the strange behaviors of the killers, may have reached an international audience, that perhaps those reports found their way to Africa. I suppose that is unimportant now. All that matters is that Muka's men did in fact find us." He paused, fingering the trigger of his assault rifle again.

"They killed my brother's friend. They killed Adeen. I do not know the present whereabouts of Dr. Leemo's technician."

Yusuph looked off into the darker shadows at the far side of the room. "And now they are hunting me. Since I became aware of their presence I have moved, several times, trying to remain one step ahead of them. I would like very much to leave, to how do you say—'make a run for it'—but I dare not. I fear they are watching every way out of the city. And that is why I need your help, Detective Briggs, your protection. I need safe passage out of your city."

John sat there looking at him and his Kalashnikov in disbelief. You had to hand it to the guy; he had balls. But John supposed any guy who would steal drugs from somebody like Colonel Muka would have to. "I'm a little confused here, Yusuph. Like I said before, it's not like you've done us any favors. We've got crazy sons-of-bitches out there trying to burn down the city, and you're the one who lit their torches for them. So I find myself sitting here wondering why the hell I should want to help you save your own hide."

He smiled. "A fair question, my friend."

"Then answer it!"

"There is still a supply of Must left," he said. "I am prepared to offer it to you in exchange for safe passage. Le Roy tells me you have a program known as 'witness protection,' that you may be able to relocate me to another part of your country."

"Le Roy has been watching too much TV," said John, glaring at the weasel.

"Think about it, man," Hotwire said with a grin, "Every last blue rock of Must off the street, just like that. And then you've got it, if you need it, to walk any junkies back down."

John wondered where Yusuph's supply was stashed, how much was left of it. He wondered how many of Muka's men were over here, trying to track Yusuph down. Just those three vigilantes, or were there others? Maybe because John was taking so long to answer, Yusuph jumped in and offered to sweeten the deal.

"You may wish to help me, also, Detective Briggs, because Le Roy has informed me that a very close friend of yours is on her way to Africa at this very moment. He tells me she intends to follow a path which must inevitably lead her to Colonel Muka."

John shot a glance across the table at Hotwire. Leroy wouldn't look him in the eye. How the hell did that chickenshit weasel know anything about Jill? Had he been spying on the two of them? There'd be time to beat that out of him later, when Yusuph wasn't there and Leroy wasn't holding a gun. *What should I do right now, though*, wondered John. He didn't want to admit to James Earl that Jill was even over there. But at the same time he felt like he needed to hear whatever Yusuph had to say. If Jill was in even worse danger than he thought—and he thought she was in plenty— and if James Earl could tell him something that might help her get out of it, then John felt like he had to hear it.

"Even if what you're saying is true," he said carefully, "I don't see how anything you could tell me could possibly be of any help to her."

"I have information which may be crucial to her survival."

John glanced over at Tom. He looked about as skeptical as John was. "What kind of information?"

"Names," said Yusuph, "The names of those within the Kenyan government whom she should avoid. Muka would not be able to smuggle elephant blood out of the national parks, much less out of the country, if he did not have influential connections."

John mulled that over. What James Earl was telling him was probably true. Even Jill had said the whole system over there was corrupt.

She was jumping head first into a snake pit. Was there any way of pulling her out? Would helping this drug-dealing bastard really buy her anything? While John was trying to sort all that out, Asshole the Collie started barking in the backyard. And kept on barking. That got everyone's attention, real fast. John tried to look out through the gaps in the vertical blinds, but couldn't see anything from where he was sitting.

Yusuph held up a hand, calling for quiet. Very slowly, he reached back over his shoulder and killed the one light above the countertop. The room went almost completely dark. There was still light coming in from outside, though, from a full moon that had been cut up into slivers by the vertical blinds.

Leroy got out of his chair. Crouching down, he crept towards the sliding glass doors, being careful to stay out of the moonlight. Asshole was still barking. Leroy got to the edge of the door. He stood up and put his chest flat against the wall right beside it. He leaned his head out a few inches and peeked through the gaps in the blinds. "There's somebody out there," he whispered.

Yusuph had lifted the Kalashnikov up out of his lap and now he was pointing it towards the sliding glass doors. "Colonel Muka's agents," he announced, grimly, "They have found me."

"It's a whole lot worse than that, man," said Leroy, "It looks like a bunch of fucken zombies."

Chapter 45

"We must prepare ourselves," said Yusuph. He was up and out of his chair. He was moving through the slivers of moonlight coming in through the blinds. He was pulling open the pantry door. He dragged a wicker basket about the size of a laundry hamper out into the middle of the kitchen floor. It was chock full of guns.

"Holy shit," said Leroy, "It's like fucken Christmas Day!"

Outside, in the yard, Asshole was still barking. "You had best arm yourselves," advised Yusuph.

John reached into the basket and pulled out an assault rifle. It made what he had in his shoulder holster look like a pea shooter.

"He's even got fucken hand grenades!" shouted Hotwire, happily.

Jesus, thought John. Talk about somebody who was expecting company! Leroy was stuffing a couple of grenades into his jeans. John was hoping he wouldn't accidentally pull one of the pins. He didn't much care if Hotwire blew his own balls off; he just didn't want to lose his. He sort of had this dream he might still need them someday.

There was a spray of gunfire out in the yard. "Get down!" shouted Yusuph.

John had hit the deck already. He heard a loud yelp from Asshole the Collie and then Asshole didn't bark anymore. John looked through the sliding glass doors, trying to see what was out there, and that's when he noticed drops of blood on the other side of the glass, trickling down through the moonlight.

"They may be coming through the front as well," said Yusuph Earl Jones, "Detective Briggs, will you guard the hallway?"

Who put the goddamned drug dealer in charge? He had a point, though, thought John. Somebody needed to cover their backs. John crept over to the open doorway that connected up to the hall and stationed himself there, behind the end of the kitchen counter. That would keep him out of the line of fire that was bound to come, sooner or later, from the backyard. Straight ahead the dark hallway led up to the front, but there was a dog leg to the right at the end that kept him from actually being able to see anything in the living room. Along the way there was a spur off to the left, too, one that John was guessing led to any bedrooms out on that wing. They'd be coming from that direction, too; they'd be climbing in through the windows.

Who would be coming? Muka's men. Muka's hit squad. Men without souls. He checked out the lay of the land again. Whoever was coming, they'd have to march down the chute that was the hallway right in front of him. Whoever was coming, he could mow them down. Then he had this sudden feeling he'd seen all this before. Déjà vu: wasn't that what they called it? It wasn't quite that, though. He'd seen something like this before, all right, but it was in that game Ham and Mick liked to play, that one with all the zombies in San Francisco.

The sliding glass doors blew out behind him. John heard the chat-chat-chat of assault rifle fire. The kitchen was full of bullets and shards of glass.

"Sonofafuckenbitch!" shouted Hotwire.

Yusuph had tipped the kitchen table over onto its side. He and Tom Etheridge were crouched down behind, using it as a shield. From where John was squatting he couldn't see Leroy. Had the weasel been hit? Yusuph and Tom were shooting back now. The flashes from their guns looked like strobe lights inside the dark kitchen. The white strips of the vertical blinds were flowing into the house towards them like streamers, pushed by a strong breeze that was blowing in from outside. John still couldn't see Leroy.

Looking past Tom and Yusuph and the overturned kitchen table, John could see dark shapes out there now, in the yard. Those men without souls, or whatever they were, were coming. Then he heard something behind him. He swiveled around. There was a scratching sound coming from the front of the house. He tried to blot out the firefight that was heating up behind him and stared down the dark hallway. Nothing there yet. *Something* was coming, though; John could feel it. He thought again about all those video games he'd seen Ham and Mick play, how it seemed like they were always stuck in some situation like this. Usually, they got out of it. But fucking *how?* John wished he'd paid closer attention. Not that that would have helped much, probably. Ham and Mick always had plenty of extra lives saved up, that was part of their strategy. John didn't have that luxury. At least he had almost unlimited weaponry, thanks to Yusuph Earl Jones's basket of fun.

They were kicking down the front door now. John tried to look left down the dark spur in the hall, but couldn't see anything yet. He pointed his gun straight ahead towards the dog leg that led to the living room. When they came, they'd be coming around that corner. Behind him, in the kitchen, there was a steady stream of gunfire.

"Take that, zombie motherfuckers!"

John was surprised at how glad he was to hear Hotwire's voice, to know that nobody had killed the chickenshit weasel yet. *If anybody's going to kill him,* thought John, *it ought to be me.*

WHOOM!

Leroy must have thrown one of his hand grenades. John looked back over his shoulder just in time to see zombies pushing their way in through the vertical blinds. They were just men but they were something else, too; there was something not quite right about them. It was the way they moved in the dark. It was the way they kept coming at you. Tom and Yusuph were mowing them down. Bodies were piling up in the threshold. And in those flashes of lightning that were coming from the ends of Tom and Yusuph's gun barrels, John thought he saw red eyes. Guys who were Black or White or Hispanic, but all of them with red eyes.

Men without souls, John thought again, and it was like he'd fallen into that video that Kili had made in Malalongo; it was like he and Tom and Yusuph and Hotwire were all in that village in Tanzania, the one he had watched get swarmed under.

Then John heard something behind him again and swiveled his head back around. Somebody was there, at the end of the hallway. John trained his gun on him. What the hell was he waiting for? There wasn't much chance it was one of the neighbors, stopping by for a cup of sugar! The shape made a sound. It was high and screeching. A flash lit up the hall as Hotwire threw another grenade, and John got a quick look at the man in front of him. He was only five-foot-seven or so, Hispanic, dressed like he might work for a lawn service. Twenty years old, maybe. That's what John would have put down if he'd been writing up a report. Just a guy. But at the same time, he was something more than that. Or less. His eyes flashed red for a second when the light from the hand grenade hit them. He was making a huffing sound. Then he screeched again and came at John, swinging what looked like a hatchet. John put him out his misery.

Another one came around the corner, into the hall. John had to blow him away, too. Was somebody like Muka controlling them, had he sent them here to murder Yusuph Earl Jones? Or were all of them just desperate for more Must and this seemed like a good place to get it? John wondered if the stash Yusuph had talked about was here in the house somewhere. Surely the guy wasn't that stupid, surely he wouldn't have kept it here? At the moment, that didn't matter. What mattered was that in spite of what Yusuph Earl Jones had told them, it looked like this Colonel Muka might have figured out a way of molding Must addicts into an army. Or at least a force that could be unleashed. John had to kill another one. Their bodies were filling up the hallway. And still they came, climbing over the dead ones in front of them, wave after wave of dark locusts. When John got a second he looked over his shoulder and saw that the guys in the kitchen were still at it, too; there were enough bodies stacked in front of those double doors now to build a fucking levee.

He couldn't afford to look in that direction for long, though. More Must zombies were coming down the hall. He opened fire at them. Zombies were spilling out of the spur to the left now, too; they had to be climbing in through the bedroom windows. The assault rifle finally ran out of ammo. John pulled his pistol out of his shoulder holster and emptied that at them, too. They were still coming. John wished now he had one of Hotwire's grenades. He looked back towards the pantry. The wicker basket was only about ten steps away. He could make it, easy, but that would mean giving the hallway up to those men without souls. He'd never get there and back in time to stop them from taking it. Not at the rate at which they were coming. But it wasn't like he had much choice unless he wanted to try and hold them off with his bare hands. Had everybody in Tristy City turned into a goddamned zombie? It sure seemed that way. It looked like there might be hundreds of them. John made a low run across the back of the kitchen, sprinting for the basket in front of the pantry.

"Watch your backs," he cried out as he went, "I can't hold them off!"

"Want me to hit the hall with a grenade, Boss?" asked Leroy, hopefully.

"Do it!"

He did. Pulled the pin with his teeth like he'd been doing it his whole life. There was a big grin on his face. He crouched down for what seemed like forever, counting, holding the grenade like a pitcher holding onto the baseball, waiting to see if the guy at first was going to try and steal second.

Throw it, you shithead, thought John, *Throw it!*

Finally, he did. And it blew up just perfect, right inside the mouth of the hallway. There were screams and then bits of what used to be people sprayed into the back of the kitchen.

Christ. Turns out maybe Leroy wasn't such a bad guy to have on your side in a firefight, after all! John grabbed a couple of Glocks out of the basket, one for each hand. More zombies were coming out of the hallway now, pushing through the smoke and human rubble. John gave them both barrels. It wasn't doing much good, though. They were giving up ground by the minute.

Blam, blam, blam! He let loose with another volley. And it was right about then that his cell phone went off, in his pocket.

Son-of-a-bitch! Talk about your bad timing. It was just his basic ringtone, so he couldn't tell right up front who it was. He was just glad he wasn't hearing "Free Bird,", because that would have meant it was Ham, because that might have meant he was in trouble. It couldn't be Hotwire; he was otherwise engaged. Grandma Briggs? She never called this late. The Center? John hoped not. He wanted to look at the phone to see what number was showing up there, but before he could get the chance it stopped ringing.

Shit! John shot off a few rounds. The more he thought about it, the more he thought it had to be the folks at the Center, calling to tell him that something had happened to Grandma. He couldn't check that right now, though—not unless he wanted to take a bullet for it.

Shit! He was so pissed that he emptied both Glocks into the stream of zombies that was still coming around the corner, out of the hall. He tossed the empties aside. He turned around to get something else out of Yusuph's basket, thinking to himself that this wasn't going to cut it. There were just too many fucking men without souls and only four of the good guys. They were getting overwhelmed. And that's when he got an idea. A crazy idea, maybe, but what they were doing now wasn't getting them anywhere.

"Hotwire!"

"Yeah, Boss?"

"Get over here!"

"Sure, man, sure."

He was coming this way. John kept getting glimpses of him and then total blackout as around them gunfire lit up the dark. When he was close enough, John grabbed him by the arm. Just then his phone spit out an alert sound. Whoever had tried to call him must have left a message. Who the hell would be leaving him a message? The Center. Had to be the Center. But there wasn't time to think about that now; he had to save all their hides. And he thought he knew how to do it.

"What the fuck are we doing here, Boss?"

"Just stand right there," said John.

"What for?"

While Leroy was whining, John had been feeling along the wall with his other hand.

"Let go of me, man, I still got one grenade!"

"Hang on just a second, this is better," said John. He found it. The switch for the overhead kitchen lights. He flicked it and suddenly everything in the room leaped up at him. There was a rock pile of broken bodies. There were still plenty of zombies coming at them from both sides, but as soon as the light flicked on they fell back, screaming and covering their eyes. John saw then that there were puddles of blood on the linoleum floor. There was blood on the walls. Christ, there was even blood on the ceiling! The kitchen was a slaughterhouse. The zombies were adjusting to the light now, lifting their red eyes up to look at them. And that's when they saw Leroy. Just like John had planned.

The zombies started screeching. They started backing up through the shattered double doors. They started backing up into the hallway, stepping over their dead.

"What the fuck are you doing, Boss?" cried Hotwire

John just kept on holding him there, in the light, kept holding him out there for those men without souls to see. They broke and ran.

"What the fuck is up with them, Boss?" said Leroy.

In a matter of moments, the kitchen was theirs again. Nobody else was coming through the hole in the wall that had once been a set of sliding glass doors. Nobody was coming down the hallway from the front of the house. There wasn't anything in the kitchen now but them, and a pile of dead bodies, and a wispy trail of white smoke. John glanced over at Hotwire, at his albino-white skin, at his pink stoner's eyes. The weasel was grinning.

"Why'd they take off running, Boss? What spooked 'em?"

"You did," said John. "Your face was too damned ugly to behold."

Tom Etheridge stood up from behind the tipped-over kitchen table. "Zombie season over?" he said. He looked around the room and whistled. "I'd say we about bagged our limit."

"Where's Yusuph?" asked John.

"He was just here."

He didn't seem to be there now. John looked around the room, wondering if he'd been shot, or if maybe he'd slipped out on them in the midst of the fighting. It was hard to tell with so many bodies lying around, with so much smoke in the room. Then John heard something, a rattling sound.

"Le Roy!" Yusuph's deep voice. It sounded shaky. It was coming from somewhere down below. "Le Roy!"

There was a low whistling sound that went along with it. Yusuph was lying on the floor, on the other side of the tipped-over table. He was bleeding. Bad. Hotwire and Tom and John all crouched down beside him, to see if there was anything they could do. One good look told John there wasn't. He thought about getting his phone out and dialing 9-1-1, then decided Yusuph wouldn't live to the end of the call.

"Le Roy?"

"I'm right here, man."

Yusuph's gold, wire-rimmed glasses were still on his face, but they'd been bent sideways and had fallen off his nose. John reached down and straightened them out so he could see through them again. "Thank you," he wheezed. Yusuph looked up at John. He knew who he was. "Detective Briggs," came whistling out of what was left of his lungs.

"I'll call an ambulance," said John, though he knew there was no point.

Yusuph was shaking his head like he was trying to say "don't bother." He grabbed John by the arm. "Your friend," he said, and his voice was a slow leak of air, "Your lady friend, the one Le Roy says has gone to Africa."

Jill? John still couldn't figure out how Hotwire knew about her, how he knew so damned much about his personal life. And he sure as hell didn't appreciate the fact that the weasel had relayed that information to a stranger, to a drug lord no less! But John figured he'd deal with that later. "What about her?" he said.

"You must . . ." Yusuph stopped. He'd run out of breath. His mouth kept on moving but for a moment there wasn't any sound coming out of it. "You must . . . you must tell her to avoid Colonel Muka, at all costs. As well as his friends."

Yeah, thought John, *I got that. Colonel Muka is bad news.* But at least he was in Tanzania, and Jill was headed to Kenya. If she would stay put, she might be all right. Not that he really thought she *would* stay put. She'd be off following Cynthia's trail, wherever it led. What was Yusuph saying about Muka's friends, though? That was supposed to be one of his bargaining chips, wasn't it, one of those things he was going to trade John for safe passage out of the city? Well, he was about to pass out of the city now! "Who are Muka's friends?" John asked Yusuph, while he still could.

Yusuph Earl Jones whistled something. John couldn't understand a word. His eyes rolled back in his head. For a second, John thought he'd lost him, but then the drug dealer managed to claw his way back to this world. "Odumbe," he muttered, "Suji. Adongo."

None of that meant a damned thing to John. It sounded like gibberish. The guy was delirious. He was speaking African. Or whatever you called the language they spoke over there.

"Smith. Ongondo." Yusuph was breathing hard.

On Donder, on Blitzen? That's almost what it sounded like to John. Then he finally realized that what Yusuph Earl Jones was giving him was a list of names. The names of Muka's "friends." And he hadn't really been listening. At least not close enough that he could actually remember any of the ones that had already been said. John wondered if there was some way he could get Yusuph to repeat them. That seemed a bit much to ask, what with the guy dying and all.

"Sutherland."

John froze. What was that last one again? It was a name he recognized. "Sutherland?" But that was . . . that was the Bwana, wasn't it? Unless there was somebody else over there with that name! "Sutherland?"

Nothing but whistling was coming out of Yusuph's mouth now.

"Sutherland?"

Nothing. Yusuph didn't even nod his head. Then the little bit of light that was left in his eyes went out altogether.

Chapter 46

John stood up. He was angry. Who was he angry at, though? Jill, for running off to Africa alone when she knew it was dangerous as hell? Yusuph, for having brought Must into his city in the first place? Hotwire, for being such a little chickenshit weasel? Well, Jill was half a world away and Yusuph had just checked out, but Hotwire was conveniently standing right there. John grabbed him by the front of his black Metallica t-shirt and slammed him up against the nearest bloody wall. "How do you know so much about Jill?" John hissed through clenched teeth.

Hotwire threw his hands up in the air. "I got fucken eyes and ears, don't I? I'm a snitch! That's my fucken job! Look, man, you're better off knowing all this shit, aren't you? Now you can warn her!"

John wasn't so sure that he was better off knowing. Maybe he wished he didn't. He stood there for a few seconds more, holding Leroy pinned against the kitchen wall.

"Let him go, John," said Tom softly, behind him.

"You heard the man," said Leroy, "let go of me."

John did. The little shithead wasn't worth an assault charge. "Sorry, Hotwire," he said, stepping back. He threw the prick a bone. "I've got to hand it to you. You kicked some zombie ass just now."

Leroy was grinning from ear to ear. "I did all right, didn't I, Boss? Say, who the hell was calling you anyway, right there in the middle of our fucken little war?"

Who was calling? John had completely forgotten about that. Did it matter anymore? Nothing seemed to matter right then except that Jill was walking into a trap. She was on her way to Kenya to meet Roger Sutherland, not knowing that he was mixed up in all this.

"Let's find out." John pulled out his cell and scanned through his list of missed calls. The number didn't look familiar. At all. It wasn't like any phone number he'd ever seen. John stared at it. "That's weird." Then he remembered that whoever had called him had also left a message.

It felt strange to be doing something so normal as checking his voice mail while he was standing in the middle of a pile of bodies. He noticed that his hands were shaking as he punched the buttons on his phone.

You have one new message, said the recording. The voice sounded like some woman on valium. *First message.*

"Hello, John, it's me, Jill. I'm sorry I missed you. I realize it must be quite late there. I'm guessing you may have gone off to bed already." She paused and while she did John glanced at the clock on the kitchen wall. It was spattered with blood. Late, but not all *that* late. It was only ten-thirty.

"I just wanted to let you know I've arrived safely in Nairobi. It's already morning here and I slept on the plane, so in a little while Roger and I will be heading out into the back country. I'll try to call you again, though, before we get into the dead zone. I hope you and Ham are doing well. I miss both of you already." She paused again. "Well, I guess that's all for now. Take care, John."

"Shit!" So, she was over there with the Bwana. John wanted to call her back right now and warn her; he wanted to let her know what Yusuph Earl Jones had said. But whose phone was she calling from? Obviously, it wasn't her cell. Why wasn't she using her cell? Maybe she didn't have coverage over there. Maybe it was out of charge. But whose phone was she using, then, the Bwana's? Maybe it was a pay phone at the airport? She'd said she would try again, though, before she got to the dead zone (Jesus, that sounded ominous!), which made him think maybe she was on the Bwana's cell. Which meant he couldn't really call her back. Could he?

Tom came over and stood beside him. "Who was it?"

"Jill."

"She all right?"

"I don't know." John was standing there with his cell phone in his hand, not sure what to do next.

A thousand things were running through his mind. Where would she be headed now? Out to the research station at Tsavo, probably. Unless the Bwana decided to take her straight to Muka. John tried to shake that off, tried not to make things worse by imagining the worst. OK. Say the Bwana *was* mixed up with this Colonel Muka somehow. That didn't mean he'd take Jill to him. Based on the pictures John had seen of them together, Sutherland cared about her. If that was true then wouldn't he try to keep her away from Muka? But would he be able to, once she got on Cynthia's trail? John thought he knew where that trail would lead. And Jill, being Jill, would want to follow it.

"We'd better get out of here," said Tom, "This place is giving me the creeps and for all we know those zombies might come back."

Must zombies. Men without souls. Dark locusts. The Nzige. John stood there looking at all those dead bodies, wondering how many more of them were out there. Wondering how many of them there were over in Africa. Tom was right. They shouldn't just be hanging around. "I hear you."

They made their way through the hall to the front of the house, guns out, stepping over bodies along the way. Once they got through the door and were out on the front porch, they could see that fires were burning now, all over the city. They could see people running back and forth through the streets, looting. At least nobody had stolen or torched John's car. *Probably because it's a piece of crap*, he thought to himself.

While they were making a run for the Nova John made up his mind: he punched the button for that last missed call so his cell phone would dial it back for him. It kicked straight to voice mail. *Shit.* The Bwana must have turned his cell off. Either that or he was talking to somebody else. John hung up. Once they were inside the car, though, he found himself wishing he hadn't. Maybe he should have left Jill a message? After he'd started up the Nova and had pulled out into the street, he decided to try the number again. This time he heard the phone ringing on the other end. He dodged some kids that ran across the road right in front of him. The ringing ended and his call tripped into voice mail again. Why wasn't anyone answering?

Please leave a message at the tone. That voice couldn't be the Bwana's; it was another one of those generic women used by the phone companies. This one sounded British.

"Jill," he said into his phone, "It's me. John Briggs!" He was feeling a little self-conscious, knowing that Tom and Hotwire were listening in. Knowing that Roger Sutherland would probably get to hear whatever he said. "I'm glad you made it over there safe. Listen, though, this is important. You've got to stay in Kenya. Whatever you do, don't cross over into Tanzania. Understand? Stay at the research station in Tsavo. I'm coming for you, OK? I'm coming for you."

Maybe that was stupid, he thought as he hung up the phone. Maybe he shouldn't have left that message. Because it meant he was letting the Bwana know what his plans were. Would it matter to him that John was coming? Did he even know who John was? If he didn't, he'd probably be asking Jill. But maybe it wasn't such a bad thing to let him know he had competition. That there was somebody else out there who cared for her, who was willing to cross the damn ocean to try and look out for her.

Jesus. Was that what he was thinking about doing? It had to be. That was what he'd just said, wasn't it? *I'm coming for you.*

"Are you really going over there, Boss, to fucken Africa?" It was Hotwire, in the back seat, eavesdropping. Hard not to at such close range. "You must have it bad for her, man!"

John gritted his teeth. He kept driving. The streets were filling up with lawless little chickenshit weasels like Leroy, weasels that in some ways might be worse than a few goddamned Must zombies. There were more of them, anyway.

Yeah, I've got it bad for her, he thought then, answering Leroy in his mind: *I think I might even be in love with her.*

He wasn't sure how all this was going to play out, though. He wasn't sure how he was going to pull it off. He didn't have a damned passport yet. He sure as hell didn't have any extra money sitting around, just waiting to pay for an airline ticket to Africa! Two tickets, he reminded himself, if he decided to take Hambone with him. He didn't know how the hell he was going to do any of this; he just knew that he was. He just knew that he had to, somehow.

The End

The adventure continues! Look for John, Jill, Ham, and Hotwire to return soon as their story moves to Africa in **Black and White***, volume two of the* **Must Trilogy***.*

ABOUT THE AUTHOR

Brice Austin was born in Nashville, Tennessee, and holds an undergraduate degree in English Literature and Portuguese from Vanderbilt University. He is a graduate of the Creative Writing M.A. program at the University of Colorado, Boulder, where he won a Henfield/Transatlantic Review award for fiction. He has since published short stories in a number of literary quarterlies, as well as one collection of stories, *The Afterlife Road* (Owl Canyon Press, 2012). He lives in Broomfield, Colorado, with his wife and three children.